D1324916

M: ... nce
novels and novellas that round... bestseller
lists and have won ... ...
National Reader's Choice Award. A seven-time nominee
for the prestigous RITA® award from Romance Writers
of America, one of her books was made into a CBS-TV
movie called THE SOUL COLLECTER. Maureen
recently moved from California to the mountains of
Utah and is trying to get used to snow.

A.C. Arthur was born and raised in Baltimore,
Maryland where she currently resides with her husband
and three children. Determined to bring a new edge to
romance, she continues to develop intriguing plots,
sensual love scenes, racy characters and fresh dialogue;
thus keeping the readers on their toes! Artist loves to
hear from her readers and can be reached through her
contact form or via email at acarthur22@yahoo.com

USA Today bestselling author **Joanne Rock** credits her
decision to write romance to a book she picked up
during a flight delay that engrossed her so thoroughly,
she didn't mind at all when her flight was delayed two
more times. Giving her readers the chance to escape
into another world has motivated her to write over
ninety books for a variety of Mills & Boon series.

Island Escapes

Island Escapes:
Caribbean
Kisses

MAUREEN CHILD

A.C. ARTHUR

JOANNE ROCK

MILLS & BOON

His Accidental Heir © 2017 Joanne Rock

ISBN: **978-0-263-30042-0**

MIX
Paper from
responsible sources
FSC® C007454

Printed and bound in Spain
by CPI, Barcelona

HER RETURN TO
KING'S BED

MAUREEN CHILD

To my husband, the man who is always there when I need him and who still makes me laugh every day. I love you.

One

"A jewel thief?" Rico King demanded of his chief of security. "Here in the hotel?"

Franklin Hicks scowled. The man was late thirties, stood six foot five and boasted a shaved head and sharp blue eyes. "Only explanation. The guest in bungalow six—Serenity James—reported that some of her diamonds are missing. I've already interviewed the maid and room service."

Bungalow six. Rico could have pulled up the map of the hotel on his computer, but there was no need. He knew every inch of his place. He knew that the bungalows were set apart from the main hotel—for privacy, since a lot of his clientele insisted on seclusion. People like Serenity James, an up-and-coming Hollywood darling who, in spite of her name, lived life on the edge.

The actress might claim to want to avoid photogra-

phers and nosy guests, but according to security, there
were men streaming in and out of her bungalow at all
hours. Any one of them could have made off with the
diamonds. He hoped it would be that easy.

"What about Ms. James's 'guests'?" Rico looked up at
the other man. "Did you talk to them, as well?"

Snorting, Franklin admitted, "We're still running
them all to ground, but I don't think it was one of them,
boss. If those diamonds were taken by one of her 'guests,'
they'd have helped themselves to more than just the one
necklace. Whoever took the diamonds was picky about it.
Took the stones that would be easiest to pry out of their
settings and sell. Smells like a professional job to me. Besides, you have to remember we've had two more reports
of stolen property in the last few days. Gotta be a pro."

"Not good news," Rico mused.

His hotel, the Tesoro Castle, had only been open for
a little more than six months. It was new, fresh and exclusive and had quickly become the hot spot for celebrities and the überwealthy who were looking for a private
getaway spot. Tesoro Island sat in the middle of the
Caribbean, but it was privately owned. No one landed
here—private yacht or cruise ship—without permission
of the owner, Walter Stanford.

Which meant that those seeking privacy had nothing
to fear from paparazzi, except for the occasional over-
achiever who used telephoto lenses from a boat anchored
far offshore.

Tesoro was lush and secluded, and the Castle was like
Disneyland for adults: there were infinity pools, the best
spas in the world and sweeping ocean views from every
room. The hotel had deliberately been built small, to
keep it a select destination. There were only a hundred

and fifty rooms, not counting the private bungalows scattered across the grounds. The interiors were opulent, service was impeccable and the island itself carried an air of dreamy seduction. For those who could afford it, Tesoro promised a world of languid pleasures for all of the senses.

And damned if Rico was going to allow his hotel's reputation to be stained. If there was a professional thief operating in his place, then that thief would be found.

"Security cameras?" Rico demanded.

"Nothing." Franklin scowled as if the word tasted bitter. "Another reason to go with the professional thief theory. Whoever it was, they knew how to bypass the cameras."

Perfect.

"Set up a meeting with your men. I want eyes and ears everywhere. If you need to hire more security," Rico said, "call my cousin Griffin. King Security can have more men here tomorrow if we need them."

Franklin bristled. He'd once worked for Griffin King and his twin, Garrett, and had decided to leave in favor of being chief of security here on the island. He clearly didn't care for the suggestion that there might be something he couldn't handle. "I won't need more men. The team I've got is the best in the world. Now that I know we're looking for a pro, we'll find him."

Rico nodded. He understood pride and he knew that Franklin's had been pricked. He was in charge and having a professional thief on the grounds was a direct slap in the face. But pride notwithstanding, if Rico decided they needed more help, Franklin would get extra men whether he liked it or not.

This hotel had been Rico's dream. Built to his exact

specifications by King Construction, the Tesoro Castle was the epitome of luxury hotels. He'd been working toward this project for all of his adult life. He owned several hotels and each in its own way was spectacular. But this place on Tesoro was his crowning achievement. He'd do whatever he had to do to protect his name and his investment.

Shaking his head in irritation, Rico turned and stared out his office window at the view spread out below him. The island of Tesoro, Spanish for "treasure," was aptly named.

Miles of unspoiled beaches, aquamarine ocean, thick jungles with amazing waterfalls hidden away in the stands of trees. Sunshine every damn day and unlike most of the Caribbean, the trade winds blew across Tesoro almost constantly, keeping the heat—and flying insects—at bay.

Rico had spent months with Walter Stanford, negotiating for his own slice of the old man's paradise. Hell, he'd even had some of his cousins come in and talk to the older man for him. Of course, Rico mused, that had worked out for Sean King, since he'd married Walter's granddaughter Melinda.

After the negotiations, the months spent building this place and the time and expense of furnishing and staffing this hotel to get it just right…irritation blossomed into quietly restrained fury. No one was going to ruin this place.

His guests came to Tesoro looking for beauty, privacy and security and he would see that they got it.

Just the thought of jewel thieves on the island had him gritting his teeth and flexing his hands into fists that had no one to punch. He supposed it was only natural that thieves would find their way here to Tesoro, where the rich flocked in droves. Just as it was natural that when he found whoever was behind this, he'd see them locked away for decades.

But a professional thief risked a lot to make a play on Tesoro. The island was too small. Too difficult to get to and to leave from. And since no ships had left the harbor in days, whoever the thief was, he was still on the island and he still had the stolen property on him.

Jewel thieves.

Suddenly, those two words began to echo over and over again in his mind as warning bells started clanging inside his head. Even then, though, Rico assured himself that the little voice inside his head had to be wrong.

No way would she risk that.

Not even *she* would have the nerve to chance facing him again.

But what if she had?

"Boss?"

"What?" Rico glanced over his shoulder at Franklin.

"You want me to contact Interpol about this?"

The international police force with hundreds of member countries didn't make arrests or have its own jail, but it could and did provide much-needed data on suspected thieves, killers and just about any crime imaginable.

"No," he said, ignoring the look of surprise on his head of security's face. Instead, he turned back to look out the window over the playground he'd built for the rich and famous. Rico's brain was racing with possibilities and his adrenaline surged at the idea that he just might be at the threshold of the revenge he'd waited five years to take.

No chance in hell he'd bring Interpol into this before he knew whether or not his gut instinct was right or not.

"We'll handle it on island," he said, never taking his gaze from the horizon, where the sunlight glinted off the water in bright shards. "Once we've got the thief, we'll decide what to do then."

"Your call," Franklin said, then he left, closing the office door behind him.

"Yeah, it is," Rico told himself aloud. And if this jewel thief turned out to be the woman who'd stolen from him once before...Interpol would be lucky if there was anything left of her to hand over.

"Papa, please. Leave now before it's too late." Teresa Coretti glanced from her father to the closed door of his suite and back again.

She was so anxious just being here on Tesoro, even her nerves had nerves. But she'd had to come. The moment she'd realized where her father and brother had gone on their supposed vacation, Teresa had had no choice.

"How can I leave?" her father asked with an exaggerated shrug and a smile. "I've not finished my holiday."

Holiday.

If only.

If Nick Coretti was really taking a sabbatical from his avocation, no one at the Tesoro Castle would have lost any of their possessions. No, her father could call this a holiday if he wanted to, but the truth was he was working. As he always was.

Dominick was a shorter, older, Italian version of George Clooney. His tan was permanent, and his sharp brown eyes missed nothing. His black hair was gray-streaked, but that only seemed to give him an air of distinction. He was polished and always a gentleman. He had been a faithful husband until Teresa's mother's death ten years ago.

Since then, he had used his considerable charm to smooth his way into high society, where, he said, "the pickings are always worth the effort." He loved women; women loved him. And he was the best jewel thief in the world—not counting Teresa's brothers, Gianni and Paulo.

Her father was always on the lookout for his next job. She should have known that he would never have been able to resist the allure of Tesoro. For him, it was the mother lode.

The problem was, this fabulous hotel belonged to Rico King and that was really not a good thing.

It had been five years since she'd seen Rico and just thinking his name sent a ripple of heat along her spine. Like it was yesterday, she could see those blue eyes of his as he stared down at her. She could almost taste his mouth on hers and hardly a night went by that she didn't dream of his hands sliding across her skin.

She'd spent so much time trying to get Rico out of her mind as well as her life—and here she was. On *his* turf.

Warily, she turned her head for a quick look outside to the terrace, as if half expecting to see Rico standing there. Glaring at her.

But the elegantly furnished deck was empty save for the glass-topped table, the chairs and matching chaise and a silver bucket holding her father's favorite brand of champagne. Which, she thought, brought her right back to the problem at hand.

"Papa," she started, "I asked you to stay away from Rico King, remember?"

Nick flicked an imaginary piece of lint from the elegantly tailored suit jacket he wore, then smoothed one hand along the side of his perfectly styled hair. "Of course I remember, my angel. And as promised," he continued, wagging a finger at her, "I have refused all temptation to relieve Mr. King of his valuables."

Teresa sighed. "That's not what I meant, Papa. Tesoro is Rico's. Being here, stealing from his guests, you might as well be lifting *his* wallet. You're tempting fate, Papa. Rico is not exactly an understanding man."

"Ah, Teresa," Nick said, carrying his crystal flute to the terrace where he refilled his glass and took a sip before continuing. "You were always too nervous. Too…" He paused, tipped his head back and tried to come up with the right word. Finally, he added sadly, *"Honest."*

A wry smile curved Teresa's mouth. Where else but in her family would honesty be considered a fatal flaw? She'd lived on the fringes of the law since she was a child. Before she was five, she could identify a plainclothes police officer as well as a possible mark with alacrity. While other children played with dolls, Teresa learned to pick locks. When her girlfriends were taking driver's education, Teresa studied with her uncle Antonio, the master safecracker.

She loved her family, but she'd never been comfortable with stealing for a living. At eighteen, she had broken it to her father that she had gone on her last job. Instead, she became the first Coretti in memory to go to school and be legally, gainfully employed.

Her father still considered it a tragic waste of her talents.

While her mind raced, she watched her father settle on the chaise and stare off at the resort spread below.

Rico had built something amazing here, she thought, but that didn't surprise her. He was a man who never settled for less than the best, no matter the circumstances. She'd learned that when she first met him so long ago in Cancún.

At his hotel, Castello de King—King's Castle—Teresa had been one of the innumerable chefs in the immense hotel kitchens. In her first real job after culinary school, she was excited simply to be a part of the hustle that took place in that amazing kitchen. Teresa had believed that working in that hotel was the best thing that had ever happened to her—until she met Rico himself.

She'd worked late one night and before heading to her apartment, Teresa had treated herself to a little relaxation. She'd carried a glass of wine out to one of the beach lounge chairs and sat to enjoy the night, the moon on the water and the lovely sensation of being absolutely *alone*.

Then *he* had appeared, walking along the water's edge, moonlight shining on his dark hair and making the white shirt he wore seem to glow. He'd worn tan slacks and his bare feet had kicked through the water with every step. She couldn't seem to look away from him. He was tall and dark and as he came closer, she realized he was *gorgeous*. He was also her employer. Rico King, playboy, gazillionaire, hotelier and at the moment, as alone as she.

In an instant, her mind replayed that scene.

He glanced up as if sensing her gaze on him and when he saw her, he smiled and headed for her. "I thought I was alone on the beach."

"So did I," she managed to say.

"Shall we be alone together?"

Teresa still remembered that faintest hint of an accent coloring his words. His eyes were a piercing blue, his hair as black as the night and his smile was temptation personified. She couldn't have said no to him even if she had tried—which she hadn't. Rico had sat on the sand beside her and they'd shared her glass of wine and spent the next couple of hours talking.

Teresa came out of the memory and mentally warned herself to stop reliving the past. To stop indulging in thoughts of him and what might have been. She was here on Tesoro—in Rico's hotel—for one reason only: to get her family out of there before Rico discovered them. If only her father had listened to her. But Nick Coretti was a force of nature and when the prize was rich, no risk was too much.

Rico *would* find them. Teresa knew that man too well to think that he would allow jewel thieves to operate freely in his place. It was only a matter of time. Which meant that she had to get the Coretti family off Tesoro. Fast.

Teresa followed her father to the terrace. The sunlight was bright, the sky a brilliant blue and a soft breeze carried the scent of tropical flowers as it lifted her hair off her neck.

"Papa, you don't know Rico like I do. He *will* catch you."

Her father snorted, then shook his head and chuckled. "*Bellissima,* no Coretti has *ever* been caught. We are too good at what we do."

True, she thought, but the Corettis had never come up against an adversary like Rico before, either. Yes, various police forces from several countries had tried and failed to pin a crime on the Corettis. But their interest in the family of thieves had been purely professional.

For Rico, this would be personal.

"Papa, you have to trust me on this." She laid one hand on his arm. "Please, let's get off the island while we still can."

He clucked his tongue at her. "You have made far too much of this man you once cared for. Always you believe he is searching for you. Searching for *us*."

"He did search for me, remember?"

Nick waved that away. "You pricked his pride when you left him, my darling. It is understandable. No man would care for losing such a lovely woman from his life. But it's now five years. I believe it's time you stop worrying about this man."

Five years or five minutes. Rico was the kind of man who *never* left a woman's thoughts.

Besides, her father didn't know everything that had happened between her and Rico. Some things she hadn't been able to share, not even with her family.

Watching her father now, looking like the lord of the manor as he stared out over the luxurious view spread below him, she thought that under any other circumstances, he and Rico might have been friends. They were two of the most stubborn, willful men she had ever known.

And realizing that meant she had to admit she was fighting a losing battle. Dominick Coretti would never leave a job half-finished. And now that he had begun to infiltrate the guests at the Castle, he wouldn't leave until he was good and ready.

Which made him a sitting duck for Rico. Every hotelier in the world knew the Corettis. They weren't invisible. They were simply so good at what they did, there was never any evidence against them. They were high profile, wealthy and they didn't hide in out-of-the-way spots. Nick Coretti, like all of those who came before him, believed in living his life to the fullest. The fact that he did it with other people's money didn't change anything.

Ordinarily Teresa might have worried that coming here herself would give up the game because Rico would notice her. But her family was here. In plain sight. And now diamonds were missing. Rico would put the two together.

Her father stood, poured more champagne and stepped to the wrought-iron lace of the balcony railing. He might have been enjoying the view, but Teresa knew him well enough to know that he was looking not at the resort, but at its guests. He would be scoping them out, looking for his next target—assuming he hadn't already chosen one.

For all his charm, Dominick wasn't a man to be crossed. As head of the Coretti family, he might as well have been a general ordering his troops around. When he made a plan, that was it. The rest of the family fell in line.

Except for Teresa. As a kid, she'd been intrigued by the Coretti family legacy. As a teenager, she'd begun wishing that they could stay put in their house outside Naples. That she could *belong,* instead of traipsing all over Europe. They never stayed in one place more than a month and only came back to their home base occasionally, so it was impossible to make friends. Teresa and her brothers had been homeschooled and along with the usual—history, math and such—had taken classes on lock picking, safecracking and forgery. By the time the Coretti children were adults, they were each prepared to carry on the family dynasty.

That was when Teresa had taken her stand. Her father had raged and argued, her mother had wept and her brothers hadn't really believed she would do it. But in the end, Teresa had become the one Coretti in generations who *hadn't* joined the family business. Which made her a puzzle to her brothers and an irritation to her father.

"You're making too much of this, Teresa," he chided now with a sad shake of his head. "This is no different from any other job, and when we have finished, we will be gone. With no one the wiser."

"You're wrong, Papa," she argued again. "You don't know Rico as I do. He's a dangerous man."

Dangerous to *her,* anyway.

That got Nick's attention. "Did this man harm you in some way? If he did—"

"No." She interrupted him quickly. The problem, she thought, was that the Coretti family had a history with Rico that her father knew nothing about. And now wasn't the time to tell the story. "He didn't hurt me. But Papa, he won't allow thieves to operate in his place. He'll find you and when he does…"

"What can he do?" Nick laughed a little and sipped at his champagne. "He will have no proof of anything. You should know better, Teresa. The Coretti family is not so easy to catch."

"Obviously it is not as difficult as you might wish." A deep, familiar voice spoke up from directly behind her.

Teresa went absolutely still.

She would know that voice anywhere.

With a weird mixture of dread and anticipation, she slowly turned and looked into the eyes of Rico King.

Two

"What's the meaning of this?" the older man in the room demanded, striding in from the terrace to face Rico. "Who are you? What are you doing in my suite?"

"Papa," Teresa said, rising from her chair, "this is Rico King."

"Ah," Nick mused with a half smile. "Our host. Still, this doesn't give you the right to intrude uninvited."

Rico steamed silently and hated the fact that he had to *force* his gaze away from Teresa's to meet her father's. The glint in the other man's eyes told Rico the older Coretti had known exactly who Rico was. This was all part of the game. "The fact that you're a thief on my property gives me all of the rights I need."

"Thief?" The older man bristled and puffed up until his chest was so full of air, Rico wouldn't have been surprised to see him lift off the floor and float about the room.

"Papa, please." Teresa stepped in between the two men like a referee interrupting a prizefight. Facing Rico, she said, "We'll leave. Right away."

"You're not going anywhere," he told her and felt that bubble of righteous anger fuel him again.

Five years, he told himself. Five long years wondering where the hell she was. If she was dead or injured. If she was laughing at him from some other man's bed. No. She wasn't leaving. Not until he was good and ready for her to be gone. And at the moment, he didn't know just when that might be.

She went pale and her brown eyes shone with too many banked emotions to identify. If he had cared to try. Which he didn't, he assured himself. Instead, Rico dismissed her and focused his gaze on the other man in the room.

Dominick Coretti was stylish, confident and even now Rico could see the gleam of exhilaration in his eyes. He was already trying to think of a way out. A way to salvage a situation that had turned on him unexpectedly. Well, there was no way out for him—unless he did exactly as Rico wanted.

"I am insulted that you would think me a thief," Nick began, clearly sticking to his routine of outraged guest. "And I will not stay where I am clearly unwelcome. My family and I will book passage off the island by this evening."

"Your family will not be allowed to leave until the jewelry you've taken has been returned."

"I beg your pardon—"

"There is no pardon here," Rico told him flatly. Oh, he had to hand it to the man. He was pulling off the insulted-guest routine so well that if Rico hadn't been sure of his facts, he might have believed him. Problem was, there was no doubt in Rico's mind just who the Coretti family really was.

"Once the jewelry is returned," he said with a knowing smile, "you and your son can leave. My *wife* will remain with me."

"Wife?" Nick echoed.

"Wife?" Teresa yelped.

Finally, Rico looked to her again and was pleased to see stunned shock on her beautiful features. Her eyes were wide, her mouth open and color had rushed in to fill her pale, honey-toned cheeks.

"That's crazy."

"It's true."

"You said nothing to me of marrying this man," her father accused.

"It wasn't important," she argued without even glancing at the other man.

Those three words slapped at Rico and only served to fan the flames of his anger. *Not important.* Their marriage. Her running out on him. Her family stealing what was his. *Not important.* Anger was rife inside him and he struggled to keep his tone and his expression from revealing his feelings. "That's not what you said at the time."

"How is it I was not told of this marriage?" The accusatory tone in her father's voice singed the air.

"Papa—"

Rico didn't believe the other man's outrage for a second. He knew all about the Corettis. He'd done his research over the last several years. And though the private investigators he'd hired hadn't been able to locate Teresa, they'd come up with quite a bit of very interesting information. Enough to see the whole damn family locked away, if he wished.

So, no, he didn't believe Nick's performance. He knew that thieving had been a way of life for the family for generations. Lying was their stock in trade.

"I'm not playing this game," he said simply, quietly.

"Game?"

He glanced at the older man, then shifted his gaze back to the woman who haunted him. "As I said, return the jewelry you stole and you and your son can leave the island. Teresa will stay here. With *me,* until you bring me the gold dagger that was taken from me five years ago."

"You cannot hold my daughter here against her will," Nick said, the steel in his voice telling Rico this was a man accustomed to being obeyed.

"It's that," Rico said, staring at the other man now, "or I go to Interpol."

Nick waved that threat away with a negligent, well-manicured hand. "Interpol doesn't worry me."

"Once I hand over the information I have gathered on your family over the years, I think you'll feel differently."

Dark brown eyes narrowed. "What information?"

"Enough to end you," Rico promised, ignoring Teresa's soft gasp.

"Impossible," Nick blustered, but concern glinted in his eyes. "There has never been evidence found against my family."

"Until now." Rico gave him a smile. "Private investigators can go where the police can't. And if the law should receive this information from an anonymous source…"

Nick Coretti—or Candello, as he was registered here—looked as if he'd been cornered. And he had.

Now the years of hiring the best private investigators in the world and collecting data and evidence were finally paying off—just as he'd known it would one day. Rico had been methodical as only a King could be when faced with an enemy. Add to that heritage the Latin blood that swam in his veins and revenge tasted sweeter than he had even imagined.

"Your sons are not always as careful as their father," he said, watching suspicion and then a cautious wariness shine in Dominick Coretti's eyes.

"You're bluffing."

Rico smiled slightly and, without taking his gaze from Nick's, said, "Teresa, tell your father I don't bluff."

"He doesn't, Papa," she whispered and the sound seemed to echo in the plush suite. "If he says he has evidence, he does."

A frown crossed Nick's face then and Rico knew he had the man's attention.

"What is it you want?"

"I've already told you. I want what your family stole from me five years ago."

Nick shot a look at his daughter. "I think you stole something from me, as well."

He hadn't *stolen* Teresa, Rico thought. He'd let his heart rule his head for the first and last time in his life. And just look where that had gotten him.

"Fine, then," he said. "Call it an exchange. You return my property and I will return yours."

He knew he was being insulting and he just didn't give a royal damn.

"Property?" Teresa hissed the word as her back went poker straight and her shoulders squared as if for battle.

She lifted her chin and looked up at Rico. "I'm no one's property. Least of all *yours*."

He inclined his head in a nod. "Don't bother being offended. I'm not interested in keeping you."

She reacted as if she'd been slapped.

Rico ignored her. "You can go as soon as I have the Aztec dagger back in my possession."

Not only had Teresa used him and then vanished, she'd done her disappearing act right after the centuries-old dagger had gone missing from Rico's collection. He knew, thanks to information his P.I.s had gathered, that Teresa's brother had stolen it from him. And he wanted that dagger. It was a ceremonial dagger, used in the Aztecs' religious sacrifices, that Rico's great-great-however-many-greats-grandfather had found in an archaeological dig more than two hundred years ago. Not only was it ancient and a piece of history—it had been handed down in his father's family for longer than anyone could remember—and Rico would have it returned.

Once he had that—and his personal revenge on Teresa—he could be done with her and the past.

As if Nick wasn't in the room with them, Teresa took a single step closer to him before stopping herself. Staring up into his eyes, she said, "I got a divorce five years ago. I hired an attorney in Cancún and he filed the papers. He sent me the final decree."

"It was a fake," he said sharply.

Rage escalated as he remembered her attorney, a good friend of Rico's, coming to him, telling him about Teresa's divorce plans. Because that attorney had owed Rico, he'd given his allegiance to him rather than his client. Together, they'd faked a divorce decree and let her believe the marriage had been dissolved. Of course, he had tried to use the address she gave the lawyer to find her. But she had disappeared again, losing herself somewhere in Europe.

There had been a few times over the last five years that Rico had regretted his decision. But at the time, he'd been too tormented by the way she'd left. Too furious at the way she'd used him only to vanish, to let her go. And still too…enamored of her to allow that disappearance to be final.

Now he was glad he'd done it. For the satisfaction of seeing her shock, if for nothing else. She had thought herself in charge. Assumed that she had left him behind in her tangle of lies.

Even now, he knew she was wondering how he'd found her here. How he'd managed to pluck her from the hundreds of guests currently staying at the Castle.

It hadn't been hard.

As owner of the hotel, he had access to the guest registry and finding Teresa had been surprisingly easy. She'd signed in under the name Teresa Cucinare—Italian for "cook." Once he suspected her of the thievery, he had zeroed in on her, then confirmed his suspicions with a quick talk with the front desk.

When his employee had described Teresa Cucinare as drop-dead gorgeous with wide brown eyes and a dimple in her right cheek, Rico knew he had her.

Five years, three months and ten days.

Not that Rico was counting or anything. But he knew down to the damn minute when this woman—*his* woman—had disappeared.

He'd spent a lot of time thinking about what he would say to her. What he would do when he finally found her. And now here she was and all he could do was stare at her.

He finally allowed himself the time to simply drink her in. From the top of her head down her incredibly lush and curvy body to the tips of her red-painted toes, displayed so nicely in her high-heeled sandals.

Hunger roared to life inside him and smothered even the rage and frustration that had been Rico's constant companions these last five years. She'd married him. Used him. And then left him looking like a damn fool. There was no forgiveness for that, Rico told himself.

But damn, she looked even better now than she had when they were together. Clearly, the last five years hadn't been difficult ones for Teresa Coretti.

Coretti.

When he'd married her, he'd had no idea that her last name was infamous throughout Europe. He'd discovered that much later, after she had gone. He'd been able to follow her trail as far as Italy, but after that, it was as if she'd gone up in a puff of smoke. She was as adept at protecting herself as the rest of her family was. The police had never been able to pin a crime on the Corettis and Rico hadn't been able to find her, no matter how many P.I.s he'd hired in so many different countries he'd lost count.

But all of that was over now. He had her. Here. At his place. And damned if she'd get away from him again.

"Rico—"

Her voice was low, breathless, sexy enough to jolt through him like a bolt of lightning. Damn, Rico hated to admit—even to himself—that he was still affected by her. Five years and he still wanted her more than his next breath.

But this time that want, that need, would be assuaged on *his* terms.

"Been a long time," he finally said, keeping his gaze fixed with hers.

"I know—"

"What amazes me—" he spoke quickly, interrupting whatever she might have said "—is that you had the guts to show up here."

"If you'll let me explain…"

"Why? So you can spout whatever lies you've rehearsed for this occasion?" He shook his head. "I don't think so."

"Now, I think we can all discuss this in a civilized manner."

Rico's gaze darted to Teresa's father. Dominick Coretti. Head of a family of thieves and no doubt the man who had taught his daughter her precarious sense of honor. Studying him, Rico had to give the man credit. Caught red-handed, Nick Coretti looked unflappable. As if nothing more important had happened than his champagne had gone flat. This despite the fact that everyone in the room *knew* that he'd been outmaneuvered.

"Civilized?" Rico repeated. "Is it civilized to steal from others? Is it civilized to use your daughter to keep a man busy so that you can steal from him?"

Nick's eyes narrowed. "I don't use my children."

"Just train them, do you?" Rico sneered.

"That's enough." Teresa took a breath and then, deliberately turning her back on Rico, she faced her father. "Papa, will you excuse us?"

The older man looked from his daughter to Rico and back again. "Are you certain, Teresa?"

"I'll be fine," she assured him. "Please."

"Very well." Nick tugged at the lapels of his suit, lifted his chin and met Rico's gaze. "I will not be far."

"That would be best," Rico told him. "And I would advise that you not consider trying to leave the island."

Nick stiffened, clearly insulted. "I would not slink away like a coward, leaving my daughter behind."

Rico wasn't so sure, but since he was anxious to get the man out of the room, he didn't say so aloud. Instead, he waited until Nick had left the suite before saying to Teresa, "The harbor's closed. He won't get out."

"He wouldn't leave me," she said stiffly.

"Honor among thieves, you mean?" Rico snorted a laugh. "Hard to believe coming from the woman who used me just long enough for her family to steal what was mine."

"I didn't—" She stopped, shook her head and muttered something he couldn't catch before she looked up at him. "What did you mean when you said we're not divorced?"

"Just that. The decree your lawyer sent you was a forgery."

She huffed out a breath and folded her arms across her chest. "A forgery." Swinging her long fall of hair back behind her shoulder, she fired a glare at him. "And I'm guessing that was your idea."

"It was."

She sucked in a gulp of air. "You've got a lot of nerve calling my family cheats and liars. You're no better."

"That's where you're wrong," he told her, moving in closer, pleased when she scurried back a step or two. "I never stole from you. I never lied to you. I didn't *use* you."

"Maybe not," she countered, "but you tricked me. You let me believe we were finished. And why? So you could find me and what, keep me locked in a dungeon here on the island?"

He gave her a small smile. "Sadly, I have no dungeon here at the hotel. But I'm sure I can come up with something appropriate."

"You can't be serious." Teresa gave a quick look to either side of her, as if expecting help to come riding to her rescue. But there was nothing. They were still alone in the luxury suite and the tension simmering between them grew thicker by the moment.

"I've never been more serious." He leaned in close to her ear and whispered, "You're still my wife."

He'd waited for this moment. To have her in front of him, telling him to his face that their marriage had been nothing but a lie. That it had been a ruse to allow her family access so they could steal from him.

And now that the moment was here? It was every bit as sweet as he'd dreamed it would be.

She turned her head slightly and glared at him. "You know as well as I that you can't keep me prisoner, Rico."

He shrugged and tucked his hands into the pockets of his black jeans. As his gaze locked with hers, he said, "I won't have to. You'll stay with me of your own accord."

"Why would I do that?"

"I've already told you and your father that I have enough evidence to put the Coretti family in jail for centuries."

"You would do that just to get even with me?"

"Don't doubt it for a moment," he said tightly. "You would be surprised what I might do to someone who deliberately used me. Cheated me."

"I didn't cheat you," she started. "When I found out my brother had—"

"I'm not interested in your explanations," Rico spoke up, cutting her off as he moved in close enough to lay both hands on her shoulders. The feel of her again after all this time was almost too much for him. He steeled himself against his body's instinctive reaction to being with her and focused instead on that still-hot ball of rage in the pit of his stomach. "The time to explain was five years ago, Teresa."

She flinched and he knew his words had been a direct hit. Oddly, that knowledge didn't give him as much pleasure as it should have. "All I want from your family now is what's rightfully mine."

Her eyes widened and as if he could read her thoughts, he shook his head. "No, Teresa. I'm not talking about you. I'm talking about the Aztec dagger your brother took from me. I want it back. And until I get it, you're not going anywhere."

Three

Teresa could have sworn she actually *felt* a lock tumble on the box Rico had trapped her in. He was right. No matter what he wanted or asked or demanded of her, she'd give it, because she couldn't risk her family going to prison.

She felt more vulnerable with Rico now than she had on the night she'd first met the staggeringly sexy man on a deserted Mexican beach. And back then, one look at Rico and her knees had gone weak. Now, though, she couldn't risk showing any weakness at all. The man in front of her might still be her husband—but he was a stranger.

She'd tried to keep up with him, of course. She hadn't been able to rid her mind or heart of his memory, so she'd fed the need to see him by reading tabloids and looking him up on Google. And though it had chewed at her heart to see him squiring some beautiful model or actress around, it had also met the need she had to see his face. He hadn't exactly lived the life of a monk since the last time she'd been with him. But she couldn't hold that against him, could she, since they were divorced.

Or so she'd thought.

"I can't believe we're still married."

His mouth curved into a brief, sardonic smile. "Believe it, Teresa."

She shook her head. "But I paid the attorney. He sent me the final decree."

"Esteban came to me when you hired him," Rico told her. "He owed me a debt."

"And you used me as his payment?"

"You can actually accuse *me* of using *you?*" There was no smile now, only fire flashing in his blue eyes as if the anger churning inside was manifesting into actual flames. "I think we both know the real truth."

She couldn't blame him for believing what he did, but it just wasn't accurate. "I didn't use you, Rico. I wouldn't."

"I would find that easier to believe if you hadn't vanished—along with a valuable antique."

She pushed one hand through her hair, fingers tangling in the thick, black mass. Even now, she could kick her brother Gianni. Five years ago, she'd specifically asked her family to leave Rico alone, but Gianni hadn't been able to help himself. Instead, he'd taken the gold Aztec dagger that Rico prized above everything else. And in doing that, Teresa's brother had made Teresa's decision for her.

"I didn't know the dagger had been stolen until you told me that last morning."

"And I should believe you?"

She sighed. "Believe me or don't."

"Your family took it."

"One of my brothers, yes." God, she was shaking. Seeing him again was so hard. Harder than she would have thought. Seeing him look at her with an angry distance in his eyes was even more difficult.

There had been a time when his eyes shone with passion and something more. Five years ago, she had been swept into a romance so wildly unexpected it had almost been a fairy tale.

And it had all ended with a shattering crash. Much like Cinderella finding herself facing midnight—unwilling to see the magic end.

"I can't believe we're still married. Or that you would go to so much trouble just to punish me."

"You should have known that I wouldn't let you go," he told her.

"I suppose I should have." Teresa looked into his eyes again, hoping to see…what? Love? Passion? Once, she'd seen everything she had ever dreamed of in his eyes. But those days were gone and she had no one to blame but herself. She never should have allowed herself to fall in love with him. And when she did, she never should have kept her identity a secret. Never should have run without at least *trying* to explain. But rewriting the past was a futile mental exercise. Nothing would change what had happened. Nothing would bring back the magic she had once found in Rico's eyes. Because all she read in those blue depths now was a cool detachment that tore at her even as it forced her to adopt a defensive posture.

"What was the point of holding on, Rico? I would

have thought you'd be happy to let me go after the way things ended."

"You took what was mine," he said simply, his features as stony and aloof as an exquisitely carved statue.

For one heart-stopping second, Teresa thought he might have been talking about *her*. That he had considered her important enough to him that he'd purposely kept them legally tied together. Then, as she continued to stare into blue eyes that refused to warm, she admitted the truth to herself. His holding on to her had nothing to do with *her*—it was all about the dagger that Gianni had stolen.

She closed her eyes briefly and wished herself anywhere but here. When she opened her eyes again, though, she was still looking at Rico, still feeling his icy stare dig right through her.

"I didn't know my brother was going to steal the dagger."

He laughed. "You think I believe you?"

"Probably not," she admitted. "But I wanted you to know that."

"Five years later, you decide to try honesty." He shrugged her statement off. "You and your family. Very versatile. You'll even make a wild attempt at the truth if you think it will serve better than a lie."

"This isn't about my family," she argued. "This is about me. And I'm trying to tell you the truth of what happened."

"*Thank you,*" he said, sarcasm dripping from the words. "Now I know. It changes nothing." Rico moved past her, walking to the terrace that overlooked the hotel he'd built and the surrounding grounds.

When she followed him, he didn't even look at her

when she spoke. "How long do you plan on keeping me here?"

"Until your thieving family returns my property."

She flushed and was grateful he hadn't seen it. Hard to argue with the truth, no matter how much she'd like to. "This is only about the dagger then?"

"Oh," he said, turning to face her. "It is about much more than that."

The warm, soft trade winds blew across the terrace, ruffling Rico's collar-length black hair. His eyes were shuttered, emotion carefully hidden beneath a veneer of contempt.

She shivered a little at the ice in his gaze and remembered a time when his eyes had held nothing but heat when he looked at her. A time when the two of them hadn't been able to keep their hands off each other. A time when passion had sizzled in the air and hunger was never sated. But the past was as ephemeral as the trade winds, blowing through her heart and mind and passing all too quickly.

"What exactly is it that you want from me, Rico?"

"I want *you*," he said flatly.

The ice inside her melted in a flash, dwarfed by a rush of heat that boiled her blood and fried her bones. "You what?"

"I want you here," he said, leaning casually against the railing. Feet crossed at the ankles, arms folded across his chest, he added plainly, "In my bed."

"You do?" Had she read him completely wrong? Had he really kept their marriage alive because he still felt something for her? Was this his way of telling her that he wanted them to be together again?

"For one month," he qualified, splintering whatever

rainbow-and-unicorn thoughts that were still revolving through her mind.

"What?"

"You heard me," he said. "And you're lucky I'm not demanding the *five years* that you were gone."

She blinked.

"You will stay here for one month. You will share my bed like a good wife."

"You are *not* going to blackmail me into sex."

"Of course not. But we will sleep in the same bed. And when we *do* have sex again, Teresa, it will be your idea," he said, giving her a knowing smile. "You remember how good it was between us…"

Oh, she really did.

"So blackmail won't be necessary."

He was probably right, God help her.

"As I was saying," Rico continued, "at the end of that month, your brother returns my property and I let you go—with a *real* divorce this time. More," he added when she opened her mouth to speak, "I'll give you the evidence I hold against the Coretti family. You can destroy it yourself."

Wow. Her brain had a lot to sift through: everything he'd said, the cold way he'd said it and the right way to react. Her thoughts tumbled over each other in a crash of confusion until she was finally able to concentrate on the single word that stood out from the rest.

"Destroy?" she asked. "You'd turn it all over to me?"

"I will," he assured her, then lifted one shoulder in a casual shrug. "And I don't lie."

She frowned at the little slap, but instead of arguing the point, she turned her mind to what he'd promised. If she could destroy any evidence on her family, the Corettis would be safe again. But as her father had said, no one before Rico had ever managed to catch them in the act. How could she be sure that Rico had what he said he did?

"How do I know you have anything for us to worry about?"

"As you told your father not long ago, I don't bluff." He pushed away from the railing. "I have enough on them to make any law enforcement agency do a dance of joy as they close a cell door on your father and brothers."

A knot tightened in the pit of her stomach. Rico was a man who said what he meant and always meant what he said. If he promised retribution, then it would be delivered with a vengeance. If he said he could lock her family away, the cell door was as good as shut.

Her heart felt as if it were being squeezed by a cold fist. Looking into his eyes only made the chill she felt go deeper. Though he stood no more than three feet from her, the distance separating them could just as easily have been measured in light-years. "This is about revenge, then?"

"Absolutely." He smiled, but it was an empty echo of the smile she remembered. The smile that still haunted her dreams. "Did you expect me to declare my love? To have spent the last five years pining away for the woman who stole from me and vanished?"

"Pining away?" she repeated with a short laugh. "Please. I've seen the pictures of you in the magazines. Actresses. Models. Socialites. You didn't look like you were crying on their shoulders, either."

One corner of his mouth quirked. "Jealous?"

Desperately. "Hardly."

His gaze narrowed on her. "A thief from a family of thieves. Why should I believe you?"

"I didn't steal from you," she argued, beginning to feel a flutter of outrage building inside.

"Your family did, which makes you as guilty as they."

Okay, she had to give him that. She was a Coretti, after all, despite the fact that she'd never taken part in one of their jobs. "So it's revenge on my entire family that you're after?"

"No, Teresa," he said, moving closer, lifting one hand to cup her cheek. The tender touch was muted by the hard glint in his eyes. "From your family, I want only my property. From you…I want only the pleasure we'll find together during the next month."

Everything inside her rippled and pulsed. Just those few words were enough to build a fire in her blood. How was it fair that he had been with countless women over the last five years while she had lived like a nun? How was it fair that he could whisper the word *pleasure* and have her ready to fall into bed with him?

"And if I'm not interested in sex with you?" she asked, with a mental *hah!* "Would you force me?"

His blue eyes flashed a warning. "You think I would—*could* do that?"

"No," she murmured, shaking her head for emphasis. "I don't."

He nodded. "Good."

"But," she said quickly, "apparently you're not above blackmailing me into your bed."

"You're my *wife*. You belong in bed with me. And as I've told you, I don't have to blackmail you into sex. Soon, you'll be *begging* me to take you," Rico told her with a smile. "And I will be happy to acquiesce. Think of it. You spend the month with me and I don't see your family locked away."

"I don't remember you being so hard…" Her words trailed off as she shook her head sadly.

"A lot has changed in the last five years," he told her.

Her eyes were golden-brown and dreamy, just as he remembered them. Her scent was the same, too, faintly floral with a hint of summer nights. His hands itched to hold her and he told himself he was just eager to get started on the revenge for which he'd waited so long.

But it was more than that and he knew it.

The memory of this one woman had tormented him enough that no other woman had ever come close to erasing Teresa from his mind. It was time now to exorcise that memory so he could move the hell on.

"Do you agree to my terms?" He asked the question because he wanted to hear her say yes. He wasn't the kind of man to take a woman against her will—and it pissed him off that she could even suggest it to him. But he wasn't above making sure the woman he desired didn't have much choice, either. At least in Teresa's case.

She was the only woman who had stayed with him, thoughts of her eating away at him day and night. And it wasn't just her betrayal that made her so unforgettable. No, it was more than that, though the fact that she'd lied to him and used him gnawed at Rico constantly.

She was the woman who had made him *feel* more than he ever had. Hell, he'd *married* her when he had been sure that he'd never want to be with one woman for the rest of his life. With Teresa, though, he hadn't second-guessed anything. He'd listened to his heart and thought her a gift. He'd married her because he hadn't been able to imagine his life without her. He'd let down his guard around her and had ended up paying for that.

After she had vanished, he'd figured out that she hadn't been a gift, but a curse. Now he was going to get past the old anger and sense of betrayal. He was going to use her to pave his way to the future.

A future *without* Teresa Coretti.

"So?" he asked, a casualness he didn't feel coloring his tone. "What is it going to be, Teresa? Do you stay with me for a month or do you wave goodbye to your family as the jail doors slam shut?"

She lifted her chin, fixed her gaze on his and whispered, "I'll stay."

Teresa was surprised Rico had let her out of his sight.

Although, she told herself an hour later, maybe she shouldn't have been. He knew all too well that she wouldn't do anything to endanger her family. So of course she would agree to his terms. And of course she wouldn't make a break for freedom. And of course she would end up having sex with him. How could she not? Teresa had been dreaming about Rico for five years. Sleeping beside him wouldn't be enough and she knew it as well as he did.

She walked along the dock, headed for the boat launch where her father and brother waited. Rico had made arrangements for her family to be taken from the island to St. Thomas. From there, they could take a plane back to Italy and hopefully retrieve Rico's dagger from Gianni's collection. Thankfully, her brother hadn't sold the dagger, as he did most things the Coretti family liberated from their owners. Gianni had a small, priceless collection of his own and she knew that dagger was a part of it.

In one month, her family would be back to return the antiquity and free Teresa.

A soft breeze caressed her and tossed a long lock of her hair across her eyes. She plucked it free, plastered a fake smile on her face and studied her family as she approached them.

Her father was cool and calm—nothing shattered the reserve Dominick wore as elegantly as the three-piece suits he preferred. But Paulo looked agitated. He paced back and forth in front of their father, gesticulating wildly and arguing. Though his words were caught by the wind and carried away from her, Teresa had no problem guessing what he was saying. He was furious and she knew that her brother in a temper was someone to avoid. Though there was no chance of that now. She had to face them both, give them Rico's ultimatum and then watch them go.

"*Cara,*" her father murmured as she came closer. "You're leaving with us after all?"

"No, Papa," she said and withstood the urge to throw herself into her father's arms for a hug she badly needed. "I'm staying here."

"For how long?" Paulo demanded.

"A month."

"Hell with that!"

She looked up at her older brother and winced when she saw just how angry he was. He was tall and dark and right now his brown eyes were flashing with fury. "Paulo, you being mad isn't helping me."

"I'm supposed to just accept this?" he asked. "Just leave you here with that man for a month?"

"Yeah. We all have to accept it." Reaching out, she gave Paulo a brief hug and felt better when he squeezed her back. Paulo and Gianni had always looked out for her. Since she was the baby of the family *and* a girl, it was to be expected, she supposed. So naturally Paulo would have a hard time seeing her caught in a web he couldn't get her out of.

"Like it or not," she said, looking from her brother to her father, "Rico is still my husband."

"Yeah, and I want to know how *that* happened," Paulo muttered.

"Me, as well," her father said.

"I'll tell you everything when I leave here, okay?" Teresa took a deep breath and blew it out in a rush. "Look, the important thing to remember is that Rico won't hurt me."

"No, just trap you."

"Paulo…"

"Color this any way you choose, Teresa," her brother said, "but the hard truth is, he's using *us* to get you back into his bed."

She winced and tried not to look at her father. Maybe Paulo was right—but what her brother didn't know was that Teresa was torn about her own reaction to the situation. Yes, Rico wanted his dagger back, but was it also possible that he wanted *her,* too, even if he couldn't admit it to himself?

"Surely not," Dominick muttered.

"Why else would he keep her here for a month?" Paulo threw his hands high in disgust. "He knows we could get hold of Gianni and have that damned dagger back here by tomorrow. He's doing this deliberately. To keep Teresa where he wants her."

"This is not acceptable," her father said shortly.

"Papa, we're *married.*"

"This does not give him the right to—"

Thankfully, he didn't finish the sentence. There was

only so much more Teresa could take today. Besides, she knew Rico well enough to know that nothing would change his mind. Firing a glare at her big brother, she said, "One month. Then you can return the dagger Gianni stole and Rico will let me leave. *With* the evidence he's gathered about us."

Paulo pushed one hand through his hair. "I still don't like it."

"I don't either," she admitted, "but we don't have a choice."

"I won't leave you here with him," her father said softly. "I won't use my child to bargain for my own safety."

"What Papa said," Paulo muttered. "If your ex wants to throw us in jail, let him."

She loved them both for wanting to make the sacrifice, but she couldn't allow it. "You'd all go to prison for years."

"But you didn't do anything wrong," Paulo argued. "Not right that you should be the one to pay this price."

Teresa fought down a tide of guilt that seemed to swell up from the bottom of her heart. If that were true, she thought, she wouldn't be in this mess in the first place. She had been wrong. She'd lied to Rico from the beginning and then she'd run away rather than tell him the truth.

"Gianni stole the dagger, that's true," she said, with a glance over her shoulder at the Tesoro Castle up on the hill behind her. "But I'm not entirely innocent in this either."

"This doesn't feel right, Teresa," Paulo told her, "leaving you here. With *him*."

Shaking her head, she looked back at her brother. "He's still my husband, remember?"

Her father gave her a long look. "Not for much longer."

"One month, Papa. I'll tell you everything at the end of the month."

One of the island's launch boats fired up its engine, shattering the quiet and bringing home the fact that soon Teresa would be alone with a man who'd waited five years for revenge. Sadly, she was both concerned about that…and aroused.

Talking to her family again, she said, "Don't worry. I'm not in any danger. Rico's angry, but he would never hurt me."

"He's keeping you here against your will," her father reminded her.

"I'm staying because I choose to stay, Papa," she said.

He frowned, glanced at the launch boat that would take them to St. Thomas, then turned back to her. "We've already tried to call Gianni. He's not answering his phone. We'll find him, though, and get the dagger your *husband* requires."

Briefly, she wondered where her oldest brother had vanished to this time. Gianni hadn't been around much in the last couple of years and when he did spend time with the family, he was even more secretive than usual.

"Wait a month before returning, Papa. Rico means what he says."

"I will wait," Nick answered with a hard look at Paulo, who was grumbling under his breath. "If you're sure you want to do this."

Want was a strong word, she thought. Oh, she *wanted* Rico, there was no denying that. But if she had any real choice, would she choose to stay with a man who could barely stand to look at her? Probably not. But the truth was, they were all out of options.

"I'm sure," she said and hoped her voice sounded stronger than she felt at the moment.

"I still don't like it," Paulo muttered.

"Neither do I," their father agreed, then stepped close enough to draw his daughter into the circle of his arms. He held her tightly for a long moment and Teresa snuggled in, taking the comfort he offered before he leaned back to look at her. "You are the one who decided to not be a part of the family business, Teresa. It is not right that you are the one to pay for your legacy."

She forced a smile she didn't feel. "It's only a month, Papa. Then I'll really be free. And so will my family. That's all that matters."

He huffed out an exasperated breath then snapped, "Take the bags to the boat."

With a last look at his sister, Paulo scooped up their luggage and headed down the dock.

"You're certain you'll be safe here?"

"I will," she lied. Of course, she wasn't worried about Rico actually *hurting* her. Not physically, anyway. But every time he looked at her through eyes that spat fury, a new emotional wound opened up inside her.

Nodding, Nick looked up to the white hotel on the crest of the hill behind them, as if he could see straight into Rico's eyes. When he turned back to his daughter, he sighed. "I should have listened to you, *cara,* about staying away from this man. I swear to you now, when this month is over, Rico King will be nothing but a bad memory. For all of us."

He had never been a *bad* memory to Teresa, though. And she knew that after another month with him, most likely spent in his bed, she would never again be able to pry him out of her mind. But her father didn't need to know that her heart was still uncertain when it came to the man who was now pulling their strings like a master puppeteer.

"It'll be fine, Papa."

Still frowning, he nodded. Then he kissed her forehead and stepped back. "One month, Teresa. We will come back for you in one month."

She nodded too, though her heart was breaking. Her family was leaving and any minute now she would be alone with the one man who could shatter her heart and soul. "I'll see you then."

She watched them board the small craft and stood on the dock, gaze locked on the boat until it was no more than a smudge on the horizon. Then she turned and stared up at Rico's castle—wondering what kind of dungeon he had in store for her.

Four

A half hour later, her family had left the island and Teresa was exactly where Rico wanted her. In the bedroom of the home he'd had built for himself on the island. Just beyond the hotel, there was a rise of land that overlooked the ocean on one side and the forest on another. Rico had known the moment he'd seen it that this was where he would build his house.

And though he had furnished it and staffed it and lived in it for almost a year now—it had felt empty to him until today. Now *she* was here and the palatial home felt…crowded.

He watched her walk around the room, stepping tentatively, as if she expected land mines to be lying beneath the gleaming bamboo floor. White linen curtains rippled and danced in the island breeze that wafted through the open windows. Birds in the trees beyond sang in harmonies that lent a peaceful air to this confrontation that was *anything* but peaceful.

In her red silk shirt and dark blue slacks, she looked like a jewel dropped from the sky against the background of his room's white walls and furnishings. He waited for her to speak. To say *something* about what had happened five years before. Hell, to beg him to release her. But she gave him nothing, and a part of him wasn't surprised.

Narrowing his gaze on her, he blurted out, "Was it all a lie? Right from the beginning?"

She turned so quickly her dark hair swung out around her in a curtain of silky movement. "What do you want me to say?"

Tricky question.

"I want the truth, but somehow I doubt I'll get it," Rico said, never taking his gaze off the woman across the room from him.

"Then why should I say anything?" she countered. "You wouldn't believe whatever I told you."

How the hell could he? He kept his distance purposely. He didn't quite trust himself when he was too close to her. The need in him roared for satisfaction and the anger was just as raw.

Oh, he'd never hurt her. He didn't hurt women. But damn it, he didn't want to blackmail her into staying with him, either. Damn her for bringing him to this. And damn her for putting him here, in this position. Soon enough, though, he would have her panting to have him making love to her once again. Then he would remind her just what she'd given up by disappearing so long ago.

No other person in the world had managed to twist Rico up like she had. She'd dug so deeply inside him, there was no room for anyone else. He had his family, of course. The Kings were loyal down to the bone.

But there hadn't been another woman in his life since Teresa and his body was clamoring for what he'd denied it for too damn long.

Sure, he'd gone out with women. Had even brought a few of them back to his rooms at the hotel. But he'd never brought one to his home before. Never taken one into his bed. Not since Teresa.

He knew what it looked like to the world at large, but the world saw what it wanted to see. A billionaire playboy. The man with a succession of gorgeous women on his arm. But those women never touched him. Never shared his bed. And none of them would admit to it, because none of them could stand letting the public know that *they* hadn't been able to coax a King into their beds.

So as Teresa had lied to him, Rico had lived a lie for five long years and now that the end was in sight, he wanted her so badly he was hard as stone. So yeah, better he keep his distance.

"Try me. Tell me why. Why any of it?"

"Telling you why won't change anything, Rico. Why go there?"

"We never *left* there."

She shrugged and walked to the French doors opposite his bed that led to the terrace. She stared out and he knew the view she was looking at. The white sand beach. The aquamarine ocean beyond. The banyan trees and the double-wide hammock strung between them. There was a stone patio out there, surrounded by so many different varieties of flowers it took the breath away even as it urged you to breathe deeply, to savor the scents and tastes on the wind. There was a boat at his private dock, a yacht that Rico took out when he needed complete privacy and time to think. And when it was still and quiet enough, you could hear the waterfall in the nearby forest that splashed over rocks worn smooth by time and the relentless rush of the river.

He'd built his treasure, his paradise on Tesoro. And now that she was here—it felt complete.

"There's nothing I can say to you, Rico."

"There's plenty you could have said five years ago," he countered.

She blew out a breath and shook her head. "If I give you a reason, will it make this better for you?"

Nothing would. Nothing could. "Give it a shot."

"Fine," she said, crossing her arms over her chest in a classic self-defensive posture. "I slept with you because you were gorgeous. Famous. Rich. What girl wouldn't go to bed with you?"

A fresh spurt of anger shot through him even as he identified the lie in her words. She was too dismissive. Too careless to be telling him any kind of truth. But this lie would serve him as no truth could.

"Good. Then the next month will be easy for you," he said, at last crossing the room in long, slow strides that had her automatically backing away. "I'm still famous. Still rich. So being with me again won't be a hardship for you."

He saw her pale slightly. Then she stiffened her spine and squared her shoulders.

"I'm ready to pay my debt." She glanced at the bed, then to him. "Now?"

God, yes.

"No." He enjoyed the flicker of surprise he caught in her eyes. "I've already told you, I don't bargain for sex,

Teresa. When we come together again, it will be because you *need* me. Not because you are paying a bill owed by your family." She flushed and the color was lovely on her skin.

By the time he was finished with her, she'd be pleading with him to take her. "Your things have been brought here from your suite at the hotel."

"Here? To your house?"

"Here. To my *room*," he corrected. "Our room—for the next month, anyway."

She stiffened her spine but flattened her lips together to keep from saying whatever was stuck in her throat. Didn't matter, he told himself. Nothing mattered now. Nothing but finally getting the revenge he'd promised himself so long ago. And still, he had to ask. "One more question."

"Only one?"

"Were you planning your family's theft from the beginning?"

"Would it matter if I said no?"

He thought about that for a second or two. "No, because how could I believe a thief?"

She winced and he almost felt guilty—almost.

"Get dressed. We're going to dinner."

She frowned and couldn't stop herself from asking, "Dinner?"

Her surprise told him he had caught her off guard. Good. Now all he had to do was keep her there. "Be ready in an hour."

After he left Teresa in his room, Rico stalked down the long hallway leading to the front of the house. He didn't notice the throw rugs in bright tropical colors or the sunlight glancing in through the front windows to lie on the gleaming tile floor. His mind was too busy, his emotions choking him too completely to be interested in the mundane. Right now all he could think about was the fact that Teresa was back with him. And what that was going to mean.

In long strides, he marched down the long, elegant hallway directly to the library. Once there, he sealed himself inside, walked to his desk and sat down behind it. Snatching up the phone, he hit the speed dial and waited for the connection to be made.

"Hello?"

His cousin Sean's voice sounded clipped and a little harassed. Rico smiled. "Catch you at a bad time, Sean?"

A huff of resignation came before Sean King said, "No. Just recovering from my latest heart attack. Mel had another false alarm."

In spite of everything going on, Rico had to grin. Sean King had, since marrying Melinda Stanford, become a changed man. Wasn't so long ago that Sean himself would have laughed at the image of himself as devoted husband and father-to-be. Now, though, he was the prototypical family man. And since Melinda's due date was only a week or two away, he never let his wife out of his sight. Every sigh she made sent Sean into a tailspin, and watching his anxiety escalate over the last several months had been *very* entertaining. While Melinda was sailing through her pregnancy, it was about to kill Sean.

"I swear," Sean said under his breath, "sometimes I think Mel's doing it on purpose. I'm sitting here watching the game and she lets out this little whimper-slash-groan. I jumped up so fast I knocked my beer over and dumped a whole bowl of popcorn on the floor. The dog loves me."

Rico laughed. "If it's this bad before she goes into labor, how will you survive the real thing?"

"Once it actually *happens* I'll be fine," Sean argued. "It's this waiting and waiting that's making me nuts. And between you and me, I think Mel's doing this stuff just to watch me jump."

She probably was. Melinda was great, but she did love keeping her husband on his toes. "I'm sure she's as nervous as you are."

"Who's nervous?" Sean replied. "I'm not nervous. I'm just hyperprepared." He grumbled something under his breath then added, "Right now, she's eating ice cream and laughing at me."

In the background, Rico could hear Melinda's laughter and the excited barking of their dog, Herman. Soon they would have their child and be even happier than they were already. Hard not to be jealous of that.

"You're a lucky man," Rico told him.

"Yeah, and she never lets me forget it," Sean said, laughing. "So what's going on?"

Secrets were impossible to keep inside the King family. So naturally Rico's brothers and cousins all knew about his marriage to Teresa—and the fact that the divorce had never gone through. Hell, with a lot of the Kings now living across Europe, Rico had had unpaid "detectives" keeping their eyes open looking for Teresa so that Rico could finally end what was still lying between them.

The King family was tight. And since Sean had led the King Construction project to build this hotel and Rico's home—then stayed on Tesoro when he married Melinda—the two cousins had grown even closer. They'd spent many nights having a drink together, talking about work and family and what Rico would do if he ever caught up to Teresa Coretti King.

Now that he finally had, Rico had to talk to his cousin about this. He took a breath and said simply, "She's back."

"She?"

"Teresa."

There was a long pause and Rico knew his cousin was as dumbstruck as he'd been just a couple of hours ago. Idly, he picked up a pen off the desktop and flipped it between his fingers.

"Are you kidding me?" Sean's voice ratcheted up a notch or two before he stopped and talked to Melinda. "Rico's wife showed up. Yeah, I'm finding out." When he came back, he asked, "She just showed up at the hotel?"

"Not alone. She was with her father and brother—who were doing what they do best."

"Oh, crap. They were pulling jobs on your guests?"

"Yeah. Serenity James lost a necklace and there were a few others hit, as well." Just thinking about it infuriated Rico all over again. Of course he'd made sure the Corettis turned over the stolen property before they left the island, but the fact that thefts had occurred at all seriously pissed him off. "They returned the jewels before they left."

"Before you tossed 'em off the island, you mean."

"That's about it."

"And you didn't alert the police because…"

"Because I made a deal with Teresa."

"Oh, man, do I want to know what it is?"

Rico tossed the pen to the desktop and watched it roll off the far edge. Leaning back in his chair, he outlined his plan for revenge and waited for Sean's reaction. It didn't take long.

"So basically you took her prisoner?" A yelp from Melinda in the background caused Sean to say, "I know, Mel. I'm finding out." Then he asked, "Okay, so where's Teresa now?"

"In my bedroom."

"Oh, for God's sake, Rico—"

"She's still my wife, Sean." He prepared for a battle. He'd talked to his cousin many times about the frustration he'd felt over the years. Now that his revenge was at hand, though, Rico almost felt…guilty about wielding it. So he'd called his cousin for some backup. Which, it appeared, he wasn't going to get.

"She's your wife but you haven't seen her in five years."

"You don't have to remind me," Rico said, flipping the pen between his fingers.

"So what're you planning to do? Lock her up?" Sean asked. "Chain her to the bed?"

"I hadn't considered it, but…" Now that erotic image seared itself on his brain as he considered it.

Fine. He was kidding. Probably. Although the thought of Teresa chained to his bed awakened a mental image that suddenly made him completely uncomfortable. Pushing out of his chair, Rico paced the perimeter of the room. Even the air of home seemed different now, with Teresa here. She was just up the stairs and it was taking everything he had to keep from storming up there. He knew she would see his hunger for her, but it would only mirror what she was feeling and push her closer to coming to him.

Sean sighed. "What's the plan?"

"Just what I said." Rico stopped at the wide front window overlooking the meticulously landscaped front yard.

"She stays with me for one month. Then her family returns the dagger and I divorce her."

"Uh-huh." Sean blew out a breath. "Until that happens, what're you gonna do with her?"

He knew what he *wanted* to do with her. His body was rock hard and just knowing Teresa was upstairs, in a room with a wide, comfortable bed, made even breathing difficult. But he had time. His wife would be here, with him, for a solid month and in that time he would find a way to finally and completely get Teresa out of his mind for good.

But for now, "We're going to dinner at the hotel."

Sean snorted. "Sure. When your missing wife reappears after five years of running from you, you want to put off revenge long enough to have a dinner date."

"It's not a date." Even the word had Rico scowling.

"Then what is it?"

"It's dinner." Rico slapped one hand to the wall beside the window and glared out at his yard. "I'm not romancing her. I'm not courting her. We both have to eat and I don't want her out of my sight. Don't make more of this than there is, Sean."

"Sure, sure. Not a date. Just revenge foreplay. Got it all planned out, huh?" There was a distinctive smile in Sean's voice that irritated Rico beyond measure.

"Is there something wrong with a plan?"

"Nope," Sean said. "Just be prepared, cousin."

"For what?"

"For when your plan blows up in your face."

Teresa's stomach was in knots. Just being with Rico was tearing her up. And waiting for whatever was going to happen next was making her a little crazy. Who knew what he would do? She never would have expected to be held hostage and since he'd surprised her once, she had to wonder what else was ticking through his mind.

Oh, she had known the minute she slipped from their suite at the Castello de King five years ago that she had made him her enemy. It had broken her heart at the time, but over the last five years, she had tried to heal. Tried to forget the fact that she had run away from a man who had loved her. And though her inner wounds had healed over, the scar tissue was still tender. Being here with him now, Teresa knew that even more pain was headed her way. There was no chance to avoid it. When this month with him was over, that was it. All dreams would be dead. All hope gone.

So should she treat this month as the punishment Rico considered it—or should she embrace it and pack in as many memories as she could? Enough to last her a lifetime?

"If I turn this around," she whispered into the quiet room, "and look at this month as a gift from the fates…" What? She wouldn't be in pain later? She'd get the happy ending to her fairy tale?

"No," she told herself, refusing to even begin to blow a bubble of hope that was doomed to burst. "But at least this time with him will be easier. For both of us."

She almost laughed. Nothing about this was going to be easy, no matter how she colored it. The man she had loved so desperately wanted her—but only for the revenge she could provide. There was no happily ever after in her future. But she still had the choice to either accept this coming month as he'd described it—a punishment—or to look at it as one last thing she could share with Rico.

The door to the bedroom opened on a hush of sound

and she turned to look at the man standing in the doorway. He took her breath away. In this palace of tropical pastel colors and varying shades of white, he stood apart. Dressed entirely in black—slacks, long-sleeved shirt, shoes—he looked…dangerous. And she knew he was. At least, to her own sensibility. His black hair was too long, curling around the collar of his shirt. His blue eyes shone against his tan. His mouth was a grim slash. He tucked his hands into the pockets of his slacks, leaned one shoulder against the doorjamb and fixed his gaze on her.

She felt that look as surely as she would have a touch. Heat washed through her and her breath came in short, sharp gasps. Oh, she was in very deep trouble here. And she couldn't even really regret that he had ensured she stay with him. How could she? She'd missed him for five years. Now that she was with him again, how could she *not* enjoy it?

"You're ready. Good. We're leaving." He straightened up, turned and walked out of the room, clearly expecting her to follow.

She glanced into the mirror and gave herself a quick look. She was wearing a lemon-yellow dress, with narrow straps over her shoulders, a deeply cut back and a full skirt that ended just above her knees. Her long black hair was drawn back into a tumble of curls that fell down between her shoulder blades and the gold hoops at her ears winked in the light. She looked good and she knew it.

Yet Rico had almost looked *through* her. As if he hadn't seen her at all. As if she was no more important to him than any of the other furnishings in his lovely home.

She was nothing to him now.

And so the pain began.

* * *

Once they were at his hotel, Rico stalked across the main dining room. He kept one hand at Teresa's back as if to assure himself she wouldn't bolt. But the feel of her bare skin beneath his palm was a fire that wouldn't be denied. Heat spilled up his arm and through his chest to spread lower until simply walking was an agony. The low back of her dress showcased the pale honey tone of her smooth skin and made a man's gaze dip lower, to the curve of her behind. Then Rico's mind took over, just to drive him completely around the bend.

Nice job, he told himself silently. *You're supposed to be punishing her and instead, you're torturing yourself.* Yeah. This month was going to be a piece of cake.

While the maître d' hustled to escort them to his private table, Rico's gaze slipped around the room. Black tablecloths, candles on every table, the flames flickering in the soft wind drifting in through the opened windows that allowed the scent of flowers to wash over the room. Muted conversations, the clink of crystal and classical music being pumped through the stereo system all came together to make King's Castle on Tesoro's dining room the elegant sanctuary it was. Waiters moved swiftly, silently through the maze of tables. Champagne corks popped, wine was poured and the finest food in the world was served. He had built this, following the vision he'd had to create a lush, sensual retreat. A place where reality took a backseat and dreams came to life. Where sensual pleasures were enhanced and fantasies sprang to life.

Now he himself was caught up in one of those fantasies.

He noticed the furtive glances of other men as they

passed and he knew they were admiring Teresa. Well, hell, who could blame them? She was beautiful, but more, there was an inherent pride in the way she held herself. The tilt of her chin, the flash in her eyes. He knew they saw all of that, because he had seen the same the first time he met her—when he had known he had to have her.

That need was as fresh tonight as it had been so long ago.

The booth at the back of the restaurant had a view of the entire room, yet remained set apart. Private. *His.* He felt her shiver as they stepped into the shadows and he hid a smile. He liked knowing that she was off balance. Rico had the power here and he wasn't going to give it up. Sensing Teresa's nerves smoothed the jagged surfaces of the simmering anger and raw need clawing at Rico's insides.

She gave the maître d' a smile and then slid across the burgundy leather seat. Rico's heartbeat skittered wildly, but he buried the reaction to her smile and told the tuxedoed man beside him, "Champagne."

"Right away." He scurried off and Rico slid into the booth beside Teresa.

"Champagne?" she asked.

"We're celebrating, aren't we?" He leaned back and laid one arm across the back of the bench seat. "After all, it's been five years. A reunion deserves champagne, don't you think?"

"Reunion." She laughed a little under her breath, but the sound didn't mask her anxiety. "Is that what this is?"

"You have been in the wind for five years, Teresa," he said, his voice low enough that only she could possibly hear him. "I think we both deserve to mark this... *occasion.*"

In seconds, a waiter appeared tableside and uncorked the champagne. After pouring some for Rico and getting a nod of approval, he poured two glasses and then disappeared, leaving them alone again.

Teresa took a long sip, then sat back, closed her eyes and sighed.

That soft, breathy sound shot through Rico like a bullet. His body was hard as stone and his mind was struggling to keep the memory of her betrayal sharp and clear so that his body and heart couldn't surrender again. He'd already lived through that once. He wouldn't do it again.

"I'm surprised your father agreed to the deal I offered him."

Her eyes opened and brown eyes met blue. "Did you think he wouldn't?"

He shrugged. "I have no idea how a thief thinks."

She sucked in a breath. "Are you going to be throwing that word around for the whole month?"

"It's appropriate, don't you think?" He paused for a sip of his champagne and let the bubbles slide down his throat. In the flickering candlelight, her golden-brown eyes glittered. "If not for your family's occupation, we wouldn't be here."

Her eyes never left his face. "And you'll never let me forget it."

"Why would I?" He set the crystal flute down and stared at her, meeting her accusing glare with one of his own. He was the one who had been cheated, lied to, stolen from. How she had the nerve to act like the injured party was beyond him. But he wasn't going to let her get away with it. "You don't like the word *thief*? Which would you prefer? Criminal? Burglar? Or perhaps *cat burglar* would be more specific."

Her fingers swept up and down the slender stem of her champagne flute. His gaze caught the motion and fixated on it. He imagined that small, dainty hand sliding across his body and it took everything he had not to reach out and grab her. Drag her to him across the bench seat and haul her across his lap where she could *feel* what she was doing to his body. He wanted his hands on her again. He needed to feel the flash and heat of her body against his.

This month was either going to satisfy his need for payback—or kill him.

"The Coretti family has been doing what they do for generations."

Just like that, it was as if ice water had been poured in his lap.

"And that makes it all right?"

"I didn't say that."

"You used me for your family's sake and then left when the job was finished."

Her eyes went soft and then hard again in a blink. As if she'd deliberately shut out whatever it was that had caused that momentary weakness. "I've told you. I didn't know they were going to take the dagger until the job was done."

"Very convenient."

"Nothing convenient about it," she muttered, then lifted her chin and met his gaze squarely. "If you think it was easy for me to leave you, you're crazy."

"Easy or not, you did it," he said and as memory and anger roared into life inside him, his accent became more pronounced. He heard it in his whispered words, but couldn't seem to tame it. "I have never been used before or since. That makes you *special,* Teresa. And I won't rest until you've returned my property and paid for what you did."

"I have paid," she told him and her voice sounded unbelievably weary. "For five years, I've paid for what I did, Rico. But it doesn't matter what I say, does it? You won't believe me."

"No," he agreed. "I won't. That's the downside of being a liar. Even when you claim to be telling the truth, no one will listen."

How the hell could he? She'd ripped him in two when she disappeared. Never before or since had he allowed a woman to slip into his life as Teresa Coretti had. She'd crept past his defensive shields and burrowed her way into his heart. His soul. In the short time they were together, she'd given him more than he had ever hoped to find.

Then she'd been gone.

And the cold that had filled him once he'd learned that she and her family had used him had never really ebbed. Being beside her now, he felt sexual heat, but even that wasn't enough to burn off the stinging chill of the memory of her betrayal.

All around them, couples leaned across tables, laughing and talking in soft murmurs that added to the romance of the room. But here at his table, there was a distance between him and Teresa that might as well have been a brick wall.

"Then why are we here?" she asked after several long moments of silence. "If you don't want to talk to me or hear my side of things, why didn't you just lock me in your bedroom?"

Good question. But the answer wasn't one he was ready to give her. How could he admit to her that having her standing there in his room had pushed every one of his buttons? She'd been too close, the situation too intimate. He'd needed time. Time to think about exactly how he wanted this to go. Time to get his own raging need under control. Because he wouldn't be led around by his sexual desire. This time, where Teresa was concerned, he wouldn't allow his brain to be clouded by desire.

"Have to eat." His tone was dismissive and the sentence short and sharp. He wanted her to know that it didn't matter to him that she was sitting beside him smelling like hot summer nights.

"Fine. We'll eat." She took another long drink of her champagne, then sighed heavily. "Then maybe you can tell me exactly what you expect of me for the next month."

His body stirred. Oh, he expected plenty. "I think you already know."

She closed her eyes briefly. "I suppose I do. Not getting enough action from the models and actresses you squire around?"

One eyebrow arched. "Been keeping track of me? Flattering."

"Not really," she said with a sniff. "It's hard not to know what you're up to when you're splashed across magazines and newspapers—complete with pictures of you and the bimbo of the week."

"My life is none of your business." He scowled at her and left it at that. He didn't care for the disapproval in her voice. She was the one who had walked out. Who was she to pass judgment on anything he did? Let her think what she would. Her opinion of him meant less than nothing, didn't it?

"You're right. It's not my business. But answer one question for me. Why didn't you just let me go five years ago? Why stop the divorce and go to the trouble of sending me a forged decree?"

His fingers clenched around the delicate crystal stem and Rico had to force his grip to relax before the glass simply shattered in his hand. When he finally spoke, his voice was low and even, despite the anger churning within.

"You ran. From *me*." His gaze caught hers and he noticed the flicker of...was it shame shining in her light brown eyes? If so, he was glad to see it. "I'm a King, Teresa. We don't lose. Ever."

She pulled in a long, shuddering breath. "So this is a game? A competition? I can leave but only when *you* say so?"

"If this is a game, it is one you devised," he reminded her. "But it is one I will win."

"You're wrong," Teresa said softly, with a slow shake of her head. "No one's going to win."

His heart fisted in his chest and that tight knot of pain told him she was probably right. By the time they were through, there would be no winners.

Only survivors.

"Are we interrupting?"

He knew that voice. Scowling, Rico turned to the man standing beside his table. He slanted a hard look at his cousin Sean, then smiled at the lovely, *very* pregnant woman by his side.

"Would it matter if I said yes?" Rico asked his cousin.

"No," Sean said.

"Yes." Melinda spoke up at the same time. She gave her husband's arm a light swat, then shrugged and looked at Teresa. "We are interrupting, but honestly, I just had to get out of the house."

Sean wore slacks and a long-sleeved white shirt. Melinda's long black hair was pulled back into a ponytail gathered at the base of her neck. Her blue eyes looked tired and she was dressed in a long skirt and a clingy top that emphasized her pregnancy.

"You mentioned you were going to dinner," Sean put in, already helping Melinda slide across the leather seat. "And we thought that sounded like a great idea."

He settled at the end of the booth, directly opposite Rico, and gave him a grin. Rico blew out a sigh, but short of tossing his cousin out, there was no way to get rid of him. Besides, Melinda was much too nice to be treated badly because of her idiot husband.

"Hey, champagne!" Sean spotted the bottle nestled in a silver ice bucket and signaled to a waiter for another glass. Remembering his wife, he also ordered a bottle of sparkling water.

While they waited, Rico looked at Teresa. "This is my cousin Sean King and his beautiful wife, Melinda Stanford King."

"Stanford?" Teresa asked. "Any relation to Walter Stanford? The man who owns this island?"

"He's my grandfather."

Rico watched Teresa curiously as the two women fell into an easy conversation. She had known about Walter Stanford. So she'd done some research on Tesoro before arriving on the island. To help her family? Or to find out more about Rico and where he was living now?

She laughed at something Melinda said and the delicious sound settled over him like a warm blanket. Seeing her now, he wasn't looking at his betrayer, but simply a woman so lovely it took his breath away. And he realized that the tightness in his chest was easing.

Maybe it was a good thing Sean had horned in on dinner. Having the other couple here was definitely easing the tension at the table. Though it would no doubt return when the evening was over and they were back at Rico's house.

"So," Sean asked with a smile as the waiter arrived and poured Melinda a glass of the sparkling water. "What's new?"

Rico glared at him. Sean's sense of humor could be irritating at the best of times. Tonight was not the best of times.

"I should ask that of you," Rico said. "When we spoke earlier, you were watching a game. What made you decide to come here instead?"

"This promised more action than what was happening in that game. Dead boring." He took a sip of champagne, then leaned his head toward his wife. "Besides, Mel's getting a little twitchy. Waiting for the baby to make a move can make you restless. Thought she'd have a good time getting out of the house."

"Please," Melinda said with a laugh. "It wasn't just *me* trying to get out for the evening. You were going stir-crazy."

"Maybe a little," Sean allowed and draped one arm around her shoulders.

Shaking her head at her husband, Melinda turned to Teresa. "Sean tells me you've been living in Europe the last few years. What do you do for a living?"

Rico slanted a look at her and waited for her answer. He, too, was interested in how she'd spent her time the last five years. When he'd known her, she'd been one of the chefs at his Cancún hotel. Had she kept her love for cooking, or had that been part of the ruse she'd used to get close to him? How could she be so familiar to him and yet feel like such a stranger?

Teresa glanced at him briefly, as if she'd guessed what he was thinking. Then she turned her full attention to Melinda. "I'm a chef. I've been working at different restaurants in Europe for the last few years."

Melinda frowned a bit. "No home base?"

"No," Teresa said with another glance at Rico. "I move around a lot."

To avoid being found, no doubt, he thought, even though he wondered why. It wasn't as if she had known he was looking for her. So why hadn't she gone back to her family? The ones who had been important enough to her to betray her husband?

"That sounds great," Melinda said. "I love living on the island. Couldn't imagine being anywhere else." She reached out and caught Sean's hand in hers. "I do love to travel, though, so I envy you that. But I really can't empathize with the chef thing. I'm a terrible cook."

"True," Sean put in. "She made tacos last week and even the dog wouldn't eat them. And he'll eat anything."

"Thank you," Melinda said wryly.

Her husband gave her a hard, fast kiss. "Didn't marry you for your cooking abilities," he said with a grin. "We can hire cooks."

"Thank goodness. Or we'd starve," Melinda put in. "Though right now, I'm looking too well fed to be starving."

"You look gorgeous," Teresa said.

"That's what I've been telling her." Rico smiled gently at his cousin's wife. "A pregnant woman is nothing but beautiful."

"And big," Melinda put in. "Don't forget big."

"When're you due?" Teresa asked.

"Officially? A week." The woman winced and shifted position uncomfortably. "But it feels like any minute to me."

Sean shivered dramatically. "Don't say that. At least wait until we get home again."

Melinda patted his hand. "Sean's practiced making the hospital drive from our house five times."

"Smart," Teresa said.

Rico snorted.

Sean sneered at him.

"The hospital is only ten minutes away," Melinda said with an indulgent smile for her husband.

"There could be traffic," he said, defending himself.

"On Tesoro?" Rico laughed and shook his head at his cousin. "The landmass is so small, if you were on the other side of the island it would still only take you twenty minutes to reach the hospital."

"Fine, fine." Sean poured his wife another glass of sparkling water, then topped off his own champagne. "Just wait until *your* wife is pregnant. Then we'll see how funny you think this is."

Silence dropped over the table with a thud of awkwardness. Teresa winced. Melinda slapped her husband's arm again. Rico frowned and Sean took a deep drink of his champagne. "Going to be a long night."

Five

Going to be a long night.

Sean King's words echoed over and over again in Teresa's mind as she waited in Rico's bedroom hours later. He'd already promised that they would sleep in the same bed. But there was no way she could relax until he was here.

She figured she now knew how a sacrificial virgin must have felt just before being tied to an altar stone. Of course, she was no virgin—that ship had sailed long ago. But the nerves were there. The anxiety about what she should do. He'd said nothing would happen between them unless she initiated it. So. *Should* she?

In spite of the anxiousness holding her in its grip, Teresa was…aroused. And she'd thought that over the years she had managed to bury what she'd felt for Rico. She had never met another man who could stir up her insides with a single look. She had thought that Rico was her one chance at happiness and when she'd left him, she had accepted that she would never have him again.

Now she was here, and Teresa was forced to admit, at least to herself, that the thought of going to bed with Rico again had her body burning in anticipation.

It had been so long since he'd touched her. So long since she'd felt the intimate slide of his body into hers. The mental images crashing through her mind made her legs tremble so badly that she was forced to drop into the closest chair. Teresa took a deep breath and let it out slowly, hoping for calm. Calm, though, was impossible to find.

She looked around his bedroom, noting that the space was done in shades of soothing white, from cream to ivory and every shade in between. There were splashes of color in the paintings on the walls and the jewel-toned pillows stacked on the bed wide enough to qualify as a soccer field. The bamboo floor gleamed like old honey in the soft lighting. The chair she sat in was one of two drawn up before a now cold fireplace of river stone. A table between the chairs held a carafe of lemon water, left there by one of Rico's efficient yet nearly invisible staff.

She poured herself a glass of water and drank half of it down, hoping to ease her dry throat. But there was no help there, either. She wasn't thirsty, she was *needy*.

Oh, she hated to even let that thought race through her mind. Hated knowing that her body and heart were still vulnerable to Rico even after five years.

When she'd first met him, he had been open, warm. He'd drawn her in so easily, sweeping her into an affair and a romance and into marriage before she'd even had time to notice how quickly things were moving between them. Even if she had noticed, she wouldn't have cared. It had all felt so right. As if they'd somehow been fated to find each other. She had *loved* completely, for the first time in her life, and she had hoped it was forever.

Now his warmth was gone, covered by a veneer of ice that put a hard glint in his pale blue eyes, and Teresa knew that she was to blame for the change in him. She set her water glass aside and scrubbed her hands up and down her arms, as if she could chase away the chills dancing along her skin. Despite the sexual heat simmering inside her, the cold sensation of impending disaster just wouldn't dissipate.

"Where is he?" she muttered aloud, more to hear a sound in the stillness than for anything else. "What's he waiting for?"

Why wasn't he storming into the bedroom and finding a way to make her beg for him?

Another rush of heat swamped her and she pushed up from the chair. Her knees were weak, but her will was strong. Whatever game Rico was playing, she wasn't going to cooperate. She refused to sit still and worry herself into what her mother used to call a state. Rico expected her to just sit here in this lush *cell* and await his arrival. No doubt he knew exactly what she was going through and was enjoying it.

"But what choice do you have?" she murmured. "Where could you go, even if you were willing to run away again? You're on an *island,* for heaven's sake."

Even if she could, she wouldn't have run. Not again. Everyone made mistakes, she assured herself, but only really foolish people made the *same* ones over and over again.

Muttering, grumbling and trying to get a grip on her

own skittering hormones, Teresa stepped out of the bedroom onto the flagstone terrace.

Instantly, the flower-scented breeze wrapped itself around her as it rattled the leaves on the surrounding trees, sounding like hushed whispers in the dark. At the edge of Rico's property, the ocean sighed into shore, moonlight shimmering on the surface of the water. It was perfect. Dreamlike. She only wished she wasn't too tense to enjoy it.

"Planning to run again?" Rico asked from behind her.

As she whirled around to face him, he continued, "There's nowhere to go this time, Teresa. You can't get off the island until I *let* you go."

He was backlit by the room behind him and in his black clothes, with his black hair and his face in darkness…he looked like a shadow of doom. He wasn't, though. Because ghosts or shades or whatever you wanted to call them didn't give off heat as Rico did. Even from across the patio, she was dazzled by it.

"I wasn't running," she managed to say. "I was waiting."

"For?" He stepped out of the bedroom and walked across the patio toward her. Moonlight shone in his eyes, but his luscious mouth was a grim line and his body language was anything but relaxed.

"I was waiting for you, Rico, and you know it," she said. "I've been here. Alone. For two hours. Is making me wait part of the thrill for you?"

"Thrill?" He moved in so close, she instinctively took a step back. But the metal railing around the patio stopped her retreat and dug into the small of her back. "You think I'm enjoying this?"

"I think you're loving it," she told him as nerves gave

way to the Italian temper her parents had gifted her with. "You had to wait five years, but you're finally getting back at me."

"Did you expect anything less?"

Had she? On those rare occasions when she'd allowed herself to imagine meeting Rico again, she'd never wondered what he'd say to her. What she could possibly say to him. Her imaginings had been more rich fantasies of desire and the passion that still haunted her. In her dreams, she and Rico hadn't wasted a lot of time *talking*. But she was rapidly discovering that reality was much harder to live with than fantasies.

Teresa stared up into his eyes and knew she was in no position to be angry at him. Though temper still simmered inside her, it was slowly draining away. After all, this was her fault. She was the one who'd lied to him so long ago and those lies had eventually brought them here. To this moment.

"No," she said. "I suppose not."

"Why did you come to Tesoro, Teresa?"

She pushed her hair back from her face with one hand, then let it fall to her side again. "When I realized my father and Paulo had come here, I tried to get them away before you found them. That's all."

"I don't think so." He moved in closer and she leaned back because she couldn't move with the railing pressing against her spine. He slapped both hands down on the iron on either side of her, effectively caging her between his arms, and then bent his head until his eyes were boring into hers. She looked into those so familiar and yet so different eyes and saw nothing soft or tender or loving. All that shone back at her was temper and ice.

"I think you came because you *wanted* me to catch you at last. Because you couldn't stay away."

"You're wrong." She shook her head, determined to deny his words. If he was right, then she was a monumental fool.

"Am I?" His voice dropped to a husky whisper that hinted at intimacy. "You could have phoned your father. Warned your brother to leave. Instead, you came here, to my place."

All right, yes. She could have phoned. Could have tried to talk to her family long-distance from the safety of her apartment in Naples. Oh, she'd told herself that they wouldn't listen to her if she called. That she would have to convince them in person. But what if Rico was right? What if her hunger to be near him again had sent her right into his revenge plan?

Oh, God, she hoped not. Because that would mean her feelings for him were still too rich, too deep for her own good.

"Think about it, Teresa," Rico urged, his mouth just a breath away from hers. "You came to me. And now that I have you…"

Her insides swirled and heat rushed through her in a blink. Her throat went dry and her breath locked in her chest. Funny, but his idea of revenge—keeping her in his bed for a month until she surrendered to the want clamoring inside her—was just what she'd been dreaming about ever since she'd left him. The punishment for her would be when the month was over and he gave her the divorce she had thought she'd gotten years ago.

He brushed his lips across hers. Once. Twice. Just the barest touch of his mouth to hers and fireworks exploded inside her. She shivered and watched as he pulled away, then straightened, taking a step back from her.

"Now that I have you," he repeated, "we do this *my* way."

"What is your way, Rico?"

"That you'll find out soon enough." He turned toward the bedroom. "Come. It's late and I'm tired."

Tired?

She was still struggling for breath as she watched him go. Her knees were rubbery and her head was spinning. Her heart was racing and at the core of her, she felt hot and achy. A barely there kiss had reduced her to this— and hadn't seemed to affect Rico at all.

She was tangled up in knots and he was *tired.*

Teresa pulled in a deep breath and let it out slowly as she followed Rico. Whatever he had planned for her, it looked as though it wasn't going to happen tonight. So it seemed she was just going to have to learn to live with the jittering nerve endings and the screaming hormones. Because she wasn't about to let him know just how much his kiss had awakened in her.

He already had the power here. No point in crowning him a true King.

For the next few days, Rico was like a man holding on to a live electrical wire. His body was in a constant state of burning. He was touchy. Jumpy. And so damned horny he wondered if a man could die from *want*.

The plan had been to keep Teresa with him at all times, taking every chance to touch her. To kiss her. To make her so crazy she'd beg him to take her. Joke was on him though, as he was the one suffering.

He walked into the tropical bar, glancing around at the

crowd gathered beneath rainbow-colored umbrellas. Not far away, waves rushed to shore, leaving frothy footprints in their wake. Surfers rode the waves and tanned beauties lay stretched out under the sun on royal-blue chaises that looked like sapphires on the white sand. And here in the bar, conversations were loud, laughter was bright and liquor flowed as freely as the sea.

He scanned the faces gathered there and finally found the one he sought. Teresa was behind the bar, helping Teddy, the bartender, serve drinks. Rico wasn't sure why it irritated him to find her there, helping. But it did. Hell, she was supposed to be miserable. Instead her eyes were shining, her smile wide and welcoming, and when she laughed at something a customer said to her, everything inside Rico tightened into a fist.

Before he could go to her, though, a hand came down on his arm and he looked to his left. Serenity James, Hollywood's latest darling and Rico's current annoyance, smiled up at him.

She tossed her caramel-colored hair back from her shoulders to make sure her no doubt surgically enhanced breasts in her impossibly small bikini were displayed to their best advantage.

"Rico, I've been hoping to see you," she said, her voice a breathy promise of sex in silk sheets. "I wanted to thank you for finding my diamonds."

The diamonds she was wearing right now. Apparently in the young actress's eyes, beachwear also demanded accessories clearly worth more than half a million dollars. The stones glittered against her tanned skin and she ran one fingertip over the diamonds, as if to reassure herself they were still where they belonged.

"It was my pleasure," he said politely, though it cost

him. He flicked a glance at Teresa, still laughing with her customer. She was supposed to be suffering, he told himself. Instead, she was making herself at home on Tesoro. He'd noticed over the last few days just how often she lent a hand to one of the staff. The bar today, yesterday it had been some crisis in the kitchen and before that, he'd caught her helping one of the maids whose service cart had been upended by a drunken guest.

Teresa was ingratiating herself with everyone on the island. Including Sean and Melinda King. He knew that Melinda and Teresa had spent some time together since their shared dinner that first night. According to Sean, Teresa was wonderful, being good company and keeping Melinda from worrying about the unknown terrors of her impending labor.

She was winning hearts and minds everywhere. And she was making him just a little insane. His plan was going nowhere fast and time was slipping by. Meanwhile, he was trapped with the empty-headed actress smiling up at him as if she wanted to take a bite out of him. Perhaps at some point in his past he would have been tempted to allow her to do just that. But since meeting Teresa, no other woman interested him in the slightest.

So he gritted his teeth and focused on getting rid of Serenity James as quickly and discreetly as possible.

"As a guest at Castello Tesoro," he said, "you are my priority, Serenity. We want you to be happy and enjoy your time on the island."

"Well, that's the nicest thing anyone's said to me all day." She threaded her arm through his and steered him off to her table. "Join me for a drink so I can thank you again."

Annoyance scratched at the base of his spine, but he

kept his professional smile firmly in place. There was no way out of this and Rico knew it. He was used to playing host to the wealthy and the spoiled. And sometimes that meant temporarily burying his own wants and needs to keep the guests happy. Besides, Teresa wasn't going anywhere.

He took a seat beside the actress at her table. While Serenity told him all about her latest movie and asked him where she could find some real "action" on the island, Rico's mind wandered to the brunette behind the bar.

For three days and nights, they'd shared his home. His bedroom. His *bed*. Every night he lay beside her in the dark and called on every reserve of willpower he possessed to keep from touching her and taking what he still thought of as *his*. His mind filled with images, memories, of burying his body deep within hers. Tension coiled so hard and fast inside him it was a wonder he slept at all. But he would finally fall asleep, only to wake up with Teresa curled up against him, her arm flung across his chest, her head nestled on his shoulder. The scent of her filled his lungs and made waking both pleasure and agony.

Though she went to sleep clinging to the edge of the bed like the last leaf on a tree in autumn, by morning, Teresa was all over him.

She wasn't being tortured by his plan.

He was.

Serenity dragged the tips of her bloodred nails across the back of his hand. But rather than the seductive sensation she no doubt hoped it was, all Rico felt was irritation. He drew his hand back and gave her a smile. "If there's anything we can do to ensure your stay is a pleasant one, you must tell me."

Instantly her grass-green eyes flashed with interest and more. No, that wasn't what he'd meant, but women like Serenity saw only what they wished.

"Now that you mention it," she said on a throaty purr, "why don't you and I go to my cottage right now and have a private party? We could get to know each other better and—"

Before he could speak, he heard Teresa's voice come from directly behind him.

"A private party?" she repeated, coming around to sit on the arm of Rico's chair. She laid one arm around his shoulders and he felt her breast press against him as she leaned in.

Curious as to what she was up to, he didn't say a word to stop her.

"Shouldn't you be behind the bar mixing drinks?" Serenity asked coolly, her gaze moving up and down Teresa's outfit of cotton-candy-pink T-shirt, white shorts and flip-flops with dismissal.

"Oh," Teresa cooed, "I'm much more than a bartender, Ms. James."

Rico was enjoying himself. Teresa's hand slid back and forth across his shoulder, then moved up to the nape of his neck, where her fingers threaded through his hair with slow strokes. His skin was sizzling and every drop of blood in his body suddenly rushed south.

"Now, if you don't mind," Teresa said, giving the other woman a sweet smile, "my *husband* and I have other plans."

"Husband?" Serenity looked from Rico to Teresa and back again. "You're *married?*"

Rico bit back an oath as the actress's voice hitched high enough to be heard at the surrounding tables. His marriage had never been public knowledge. His and Teresa's time together had been so short that not even the media had caught on to it before she had disappeared from his life. Now, though, that looked as if it was about to change.

"Well, damn it," Serenity said on a full-bottom-lip pout, "you could have *mentioned* it." When she stood up in a huff, she punched her breasts out to make sure he could appreciate what he'd be missing, then turned and sashayed—the only word to describe the swing of her hips and the long stride of golden legs—out of the bar.

When she was gone, Teresa made a move to get up, but Rico caught her around the waist and dragged her down onto his lap. Her sexy, curvy behind nestled on top of him and Rico knew a whole new world of discomfort. He groaned, but held her in place. Yes, there was pain, but there was also need and want and a hunger like he hadn't known in five years. She wiggled, trying to get up, but her movements only fanned the flames licking at him.

"Let me up," she said in a whisper. "People are watching."

"You made sure of that when you walked up and rubbed yourself against me," he told her, enjoying the memory almost as much as the feel of her sitting on him.

"I didn't—" She broke off. "Fine. I did."

"Question is," he asked, "why?"

She looked down into his eyes and seemed to consider whether she would answer or not. After a long minute or two, she tore her gaze from his and muttered, "You looked like you wanted to be rescued."

"Ah." He hid a satisfied smile. He hadn't needed saving. Teresa had chased off the actress for her own reasons. Maybe his plan of seduction was actually working better than he had thought. "That's another lie. You're very good at it, by the way, but not good enough."

"Well, if I read you wrong and you *didn't* want to be saved from a conversation with that vacuous twit, I'm so very sorry."

A smile ticked up the corner of his mouth. "Twit? Have you met Ms. James before, then?"

"I don't need to talk to her to recognize the type," Teresa said, studying her fingernails now as if the secrets of the universe were scribed there.

"Which is?"

She shrugged and that little movement had her shifting on his lap again. Rico had to hiss in a breath to keep from groaning aloud. It was the sweetest kind of pain he'd ever known and he was in no hurry to ease it.

"She's pretty and has great boobs, which she probably paid a fortune for, and that's about it."

Rico smirked at her. "You can tell this with a glance?"

"Absolutely," she said. "But if you want to chase Ms. Boobs, just say so."

He shook his head. "I'm not interested in Serenity."

"Not how it looked from the bar." And she was back to studying her nails.

"You were jealous."

She stiffened in outrage and glared at him for good measure. "I don't know what you're talking about."

"Yes, you do." He dropped one hand to her thigh and relished the feel of her sun-warmed skin, bared by her white shorts.

She shivered and tried to scoot to one side, but his other arm wrapped around her waist held her exactly where he wanted her. He continued to stroke her thigh and felt the tremble shaking her slide under his own skin, as well.

Surrounded by guests enjoying the beach, Rico felt as if he and Teresa were alone. Only the two of them in this moment. And hell, it would have been much easier on him if they *had* been alone. Then he could just stretch her out on the sand, strip her clothes off and give in.

"You are lying again. To me. To yourself."

She huffed out a breath and squirmed on his lap, which only served to make him harder and her more aware of it. Instantly, she stilled. "What do you want to hear, Rico?"

"The truth," he said, in a direct challenge. "That you didn't like seeing that woman with me."

She laughed, but the sound lacked her usual musical quality and came off as strained instead. "If I were the jealous type, the last five years of seeing your picture in magazines and newspapers, always with a different woman, would have drummed that right out of me."

"So you tell yourself. And yet…"

Teresa took a breath, slanted her eyes to his and murmured, "Fine. I didn't like the way she was pawing at you. Heck, she was practically drooling. Happy now?"

Short answer was yes. A longer answer would take more time. At least a couple of hours. In his bed. Even his taste for revenge was muted by the fire inside him. All he wanted, all he could think about, was getting her naked and—if he didn't stop thinking about it he'd never be able to walk out of the bar.

Reluctantly, he relaxed his hold on her and she quickly got to her feet. She looked down at him and her eyes were bright, her mouth parted as her breath came fast and hard. He caught one of her hands in his and rubbed his thumb across her knuckles. She pulled her hand free a moment later and he allowed it.

"I'll see you back at the house," he said quietly. "One hour."

She swallowed hard and suddenly looked just a little... anxious. "Rico—"

"One hour, Teresa. Then we settle this between us."

She gave him a brief nod, then moved back to the bar. Alone, Rico stared out at the sea, trying to empty his mind of every wicked thought and desire that raced through it. What he needed was a cold shower, but what he wanted was more heat. Teresa's heat. The fire he had only ever experienced with her.

And soon he would have it.

Six

Teresa was standing on his bedroom terrace when he arrived. The tropical breeze smelled of saltwater and flowers. The sound of the ocean was like a heartbeat in the distance and the dappled shade from the surrounding trees danced and shifted with the wind that lifted her hair from her shoulders in soft waves.

Her heart was pounding. Every nerve in her body was standing straight up and buzzing. She felt electrified from the inside out. She couldn't sit still. Couldn't stand without moving, pacing. Could hardly breathe through the knot of anticipation lodged in her throat.

Back at the beach bar, when she'd been sitting on Rico's lap, she'd felt the hard proof of his desire for her. And even there, surrounded by strangers, she'd wanted nothing more than to turn in the chair, straddle him and—
Oh boy, she was in very serious trouble.

Feeling this way for your husband was one thing. Wanting the man who only wanted to use you then discard you was simply a road map to misery. God, she remembered so clearly what it was like to be loved by Rico King. To be the reason his eyes warmed when she walked into a room. To know that he was right there if she stretched out her hand. To have his arms come around her in the middle of the night, making her feel safe and treasured.

And she knew what it was like to lose all of it.

Now she would have to lose it *again,* and Teresa didn't know if she'd be able to bear it this time. Because she'd already lived through years of emptiness without him, so this time when she left, she knew exactly the kind of cold, dark place that would be waiting for her. She'd do anything to avoid that wide chasm of utter loneliness again. But there was just no way out.

Her careening thoughts skidded to a halt when she actually *felt* Rico's presence. Slowly she turned to see him standing in the open doorway, watching her. The wind caught his hair and tossed it across his forehead. His blue eyes were fixed on her and his mouth was tight, as if he wished he were anywhere but here. And yet…there was heat and tension spiraling between them, binding them together with invisible tendrils of desire and need.

Whatever else also lay between them—lies, betrayal, anger—this was just as real. This living, breathing passion that was so strong it was pushing her to take the first steps toward him even now. It didn't matter why he wanted her. Only that he did. She couldn't take another moment without feeling his hands on her. She'd wanted for so long and now she could *have.*

He held his ground, half in the bedroom, half out, and

waited for her to come closer. Every step was a test in courage. Every breath a victory. She couldn't look away from his eyes and when she saw a flash of heat dazzling there, she crossed the last of the space separating them in a dash.

Teresa threw herself at him and he caught her, encircling her in his arms, holding her tightly to him so that she could feel every ridge and plane of his body. She felt the thick hardness of him pressed against her middle and instantly she went hot and wet.

Here, her mind whispered. *Here* was where she belonged. Where she always wanted to be.

What sounded like a growl erupted from his throat as he threaded his fingers through her hair, tipped her head back and held her for his kiss. She met him eagerly, hungrily. Their mouths fused, tongues twisting and dancing in a frenzy of need. Breathing was short and labored. Hands slid up and down burning bodies and when he suddenly turned and walked her backward toward the bed, she kept pace.

Teresa fell back onto the mattress and kept her arms around Rico's neck, as if a part of her was afraid that he would stop now. Take that one step away and return to that careful, cold distance between them just to torture her. But she wouldn't let him. Not this time.

Every night she slept beside him and every morning she woke up entangled with him, feeling the heat of his body pouring into hers just before he bolted from the bed and left her there. Alone.

She was done.

Let the revenge begin.

She didn't care *why* she was there anymore. Or even

why he wanted her there. It was enough that Rico was with her again, laying his body atop hers.

Finally he tore his mouth from hers, looked down into her eyes and whispered, "You're wearing too many clothes."

"You, too."

Nodding, he rolled to one side of her and got up just long enough to yank his clothes off and toss everything to the floor. Teresa did the same. Her T-shirt, shorts and sandals were on the floor in seconds and her bra and panties quickly followed. Then she was naked, standing in front of him as the sunlight streaming through the terrace doors caressed their already-heated bodies in a golden warmth that seemed to soak deep into their bones. That light was reflected in his eyes as he looked at her and Teresa shivered in response.

He was beautiful. Just as she remembered him. His body was tanned and every muscle was sharply defined. He was also hard and ready and glancing at his erection made Teresa quiver deep inside. Right where she wanted him.

As if reading her thoughts, Rico reached for her, then tumbled her back onto the mattress. Heated skin met the cool silk of the duvet beneath her and seemed to heighten every one of her senses to overload.

Rico's hands skimmed over her body. Her breasts, her nipples, her abdomen and finally lower, where he cupped her heat and rubbed the heel of his hand against her until she was writhing beneath him.

Her gaze still locked on his, she watched as her responses to him fed the flames dancing in those pale blue depths. She chewed at her bottom lip and a soft moan slipped from her mouth as he dipped first one finger and then two into her heat.

Teresa sighed at the blissful sensation of his touch on her body again. Everything was so familiar and yet so new. Almost as if this was their first time together. Her hands moved over his shoulders and down his arms, stroking, loving the feel of his skin beneath her hands. He was so hard and strong and so warm to the touch.

He bent his head to her breast and as she watched, he took one of her already-peaked nipples into his mouth. She gasped at the first touch of his lips and tongue. She moaned as his teeth scraped across the sensitive tip and then she arched into him as he suckled her.

His hand stroked her core while his mouth drove her even closer to the edge. Again and again, he drew on her breast, as if he could taste all she was. She felt that drawing sensation down to her bones and all she could think was, *yes. This is all just as it should be.*

This was what had tormented her dreams for so long. The memories of his touch, his caresses, his mouth, his hot breath dusting across her skin. All she needed now to feel complete was his body pushing into hers, locking them together as they were meant to be.

He lifted his head as if he'd heard or sensed her thoughts. Staring into her eyes, he whispered, "You feel so good, Teresa. As I remembered and more."

"Rico..." That single word came out strangled as knots of need lodged in her throat and breathing was more and more difficult.

Her hips lifted into his hand and his thumb brushed across one particular spot of sensation that had her reaching blindly for him. He kissed her again and again, mouths meeting and parting, breath mingling, their heavy sighs coming in tandem.

Teresa struggled to find her breath as Rico drove her toward a climax she didn't want to experience without him inside her. "Be with me, Rico. Be *in* me."

He hissed in a breath, dropped his forehead to hers for a moment and then eased up enough to look into her eyes. "No, Teresa. When I have you, it will be *my* way."

Her heart broke a little even as her body was clamoring for more. "Don't," she urged, framing his face in her hands. "Don't use what's between us for payback."

His hand on her core stilled and her body ached.

"If I wanted to torture you," he said softly, kissing her mouth, her nose, her eyes, "I would step away now and leave you hungering for me as I hungered for you so long ago."

Guilt rushed in and chewed at her heart. She had walked out on the man she loved without explanation. Without apologies. Just disappeared one day and as far as he knew, never looked back. But it hadn't been easy for her. She'd left a piece of her soul behind when she'd slipped away from his life. A piece she could never reclaim.

"Rico, I hungered, too," she whispered and felt the sting of tears in her eyes. "I didn't want to leave you. I had to—"

Sunlight shone in the black of his hair and glittered across his blue eyes. Outside the terrace doors, the surrounding trees were filled with birds screeching and singing. Inside, silence was as heavy as stone.

He shook his head. "No more. The past is gone. What we have is now. This month and no longer."

There it was. He couldn't have been clearer. From

the first time he'd proposed this blackmailed month to this very moment, Rico had laid down his expectations. One month. No longer. Her insides twisted and her heart wept, but her body was more interested in the *now*. In the completion of the orgasm that had been promised.

"This month, then," she said softly and thought that she saw, however briefly, a flicker of regret in his eyes. But in the next moment, it was gone anyway.

She smoothed one hand across his face as he touched her again, sliding his fingers deep inside her. He stroked her inside and out, increasing the rhythm of his caresses until all thought but one was chased from her mind. She needed.

All she could see was his eyes. Those blue depths that were filled with so many colliding emotions she couldn't identify them. All she felt was the tightening coil inside her, threatening to explode.

"Rico, please. Now. Be with me." She bucked against him and tossed her head from side to side. Her heartbeat clamored in her chest and it felt as though every muscle in her body was clenched. Feet planted on the mattress beneath her, she moved into his hand, seeking more, needing more.

When he stopped touching her and pulled away, she groaned tightly. "Don't stop. Please. Don't stop."

"I'm not," he said through gritted teeth. "I couldn't even if I wanted to."

She heard a drawer open and close, then the distinct sound of a foil wrapper being ripped open. She opened her eyes, looked at him in time to see him sheathe himself and her mouth went dry again. He was the most beautiful man she had ever seen. How had she ever had the courage to leave him and what she'd found with him? How would she ever survive without him again?

But those thoughts and the millions of others that would no doubt torment her for years to come had no place here now. Here there was only she and Rico. And the passion rising in the room.

Teresa lifted her arms to him and parted her legs in welcome. His body covered hers and in the next breath he entered her, sliding into her heat in one long, smooth stroke. She sighed in soul-deep pleasure at the feel of him within her once more. So long. It had been so very long.

Teresa's head tipped back on the mattress and she lifted her legs higher, wrapping them around Rico's waist, holding him to her, taking him as deeply as she could. She wanted to savor the moment. Imprint the feel of him inside her on her brain so that the sensation became a part of her. So that she would never truly feel alone again.

"Look at me," he whispered and Teresa opened her eyes to stare into his. Her own desire was reflected back at her and matched by what was shining in his gaze.

He set a rhythm that she eagerly met and as they looked into each other's eyes, they raced toward completion together. Teresa shouted his name as pleasure, raw and wild, crashed over her and as her arms locked around him, she heard him groan, felt him stiffen as his own release claimed him.

And locked together, they tumbled over the edge and willingly fell into oblivion.

A half hour later, Teresa was feeling wonderful. Sprawled across a bed, her lover—her husband—lay beside her. Every inch of her body felt well used. Her heart was full and in that moment, her mind raced with possibilities.

Maybe this month wouldn't be the end after all, she thought, refusing for now to remember Rico's words, *This month and no longer.* Maybe it could still be different. Maybe this time with him would be a beginning. A fresh start. A time for them to meet as equals and realize that what they had found together was too precious to throw away. Maybe there could still be a happily ever after.

But not, she knew, until the past had finally been put to rest.

"Rico," she said, voice soft in the quiet room, "I want you to know that when I left five years ago—"

"Stop." He cut her off with one sharp word. Turning his head to meet her eyes, he said, "I'm not interested in remembering old lies—or hearing new ones."

His cold tone was like a verbal slap. "I wasn't going to—"

"Teresa," he said on a sigh, "this changes nothing between us, so don't look at me with stars in your eyes."

God, she had been. And she should have known better. But how was she supposed to protect her heart against hope?

"I need a shower." Rico pushed off the bed, gave her a quick look and said, "That was good, thanks."

"Thanks?" Stunned, she looked up at him. "That's it? Just *thanks?*"

He shrugged. "Were you expecting outpourings of love and devotion?" He smiled briefly and shook his head. "All we share now is sex and this hotel, Teresa. And that only for the next month."

Hurt crowded around her heart and squeezed painfully. Just a short while ago, he had been a part of her, sharing something *amazing,* and now he'd draped that icy demeanor over himself like a damn cloak. There was distance in his voice and a careless attitude that tore at the last remaining shreds of five-year-old dreams.

"That wasn't just *sex,* Rico." There was more between them than that. Wasn't there?

He met her gaze thoughtfully for a long second or two. Then he said simply, "Yes, it was."

Turning his back on her, he stalked toward the spa-like bathroom and tossed over his shoulder, "You should get cleaned up. We're expected for dinner at Sean and Melinda's."

Then he closed the bathroom door behind him and left her, suddenly cold and very much alone, in the middle of the bed.

Dinner was an eternity.

Pretending as if nothing was wrong only built the tension inside Rico until he felt as though he would *snap.* He'd finally escaped to the patio of Sean's home, where he stood alone in the starry darkness. Solar lights made circles of gold on the neatly tended lawn. Mature trees surrounded the house and yard and a stone walkway led down to the ocean.

He listened now, letting the soothing charge and retreat of the surf sink into him, hoping to relax some before rejoining the others inside. It wasn't easy to act as though all was well. It went against his nature to be less than honest. He was uncomfortable with pretense. Lies were tangled webs, snaring everyone who came close. And the lies Teresa had told so long ago were still strangling him.

Rico had never been one to accept lies. When he was a boy, his mother had concocted stories with impunity to get whatever she wanted. He'd never been able to believe a word she said because lying had become second nature to her. When Rico was eleven, she had at last given him up to be raised by his father, Mike King. He remembered his father coming to him several months later, asking him if he missed his mother. The sad truth was, he hadn't missed her at all, because he'd never really known her.

Her lies and impossible-to-believe stories had ensured that she was a mystery, even to her son. When she died ten years ago, she had still been a nebulous figure to Rico. He had no idea who she had been. What she'd believed. If she'd loved him at all. The lies had clouded everything.

Truth was much cleaner. Much more…efficient.

But lies kept entangling him.

For example, the lie he'd told himself: that having Teresa back in his bed would rid him of the remains of his desire for her. Instead he wanted her now more than ever.

And that shook him.

Then there was the lie he had told Teresa: that it had been simply sex that they'd shared. It cost Rico to admit it, but he couldn't hide the truth from himself. What he'd just experienced with Teresa was something else again. His whole damn body felt as if it were burning up from the inside. The tension that had been clawing at him since he'd first seen Teresa here on the island was as raw and fresh as ever. He felt as tightly wound as he ever had and he knew that his revenge plan had suddenly turned on him.

He turned away from the garden view and looked at the well-lit house behind him. Through the wide bay window in the huge kitchen, he could see Teresa with Melinda, and the two women seemed to be having a good time. No one would guess that only a couple of hours ago, Teresa had been wild in his arms. Or that he'd seen hurt in her eyes when he'd dismissed what they'd shared.

But he knew, and the memories were choking him.

"Plan not going so well?"

Rico glanced at Sean as his cousin walked out to join him on the patio. "What makes you say that?"

"For starters, you're strangling that poor, innocent beer bottle."

Rico cursed under his breath and carefully eased his grip on the bottle neck. "I've a lot on my mind."

"Yeah." Sean looked over his shoulder at the two women standing in the home King Construction had built for his family. "It's pretty clear just what's on your mind."

"Stay out of this, Sean." Even Rico heard his accent thicken as his voice dropped to a dangerous tone. He'd spent most of his early youth in Mexico with his mother. Much later he had gone to California to live with his father's family. And still, at emotional or stressful times, the music of an accent appeared in his speech.

Sean lifted both hands in false surrender. "Hey, I'm out. What you do to screw up your world is your business."

Annoyance flared and Rico scowled at the other man. He loved his family—all of them. But he knew their flaws and the worst one was that in the King family, even when they were "butting out," they had their say. You never had to wonder what your brothers or cousins were thinking, because there hadn't been a King born yet who could keep his opinion to himself. Every last one of them was sure he was right and didn't care who knew it. Made for some interesting family get-togethers and some very loud discussions.

Scowling, Rico took a sip of beer that he didn't want

and willed the icy brew to cool off the fires within. It didn't help any. "How's Melinda feeling?"

"Oh, nice change of subject. Very subtle." Sean snorted and leaned one hip on the patio railing. His gaze still focused on his wife through the wide bay window, he sighed. "She's nesting. I swear, Rico, the more nervous I get, the more *serene* she gets."

"Probably in self-defense," Rico mused. "Watching you go crazy with worry, she can either go with you or…"

"Yeah." Sean scraped one hand over his face. "Okay, yeah, I am going a little nuts. But damn, Rico. I'm about to be a *father*. That's just scary as hell."

"It must be." For one incredibly brief instant, Rico's mind dredged up an image of Teresa, pregnant with his child. Then that image shattered and he mentally swept up the shards and disposed of them.

"I mean," Sean was saying, "what the hell do I know about being a father? What if I mess it up?"

"You won't."

"Yeah? My dad wasn't the best role model in the world."

True. Sean's father, Ben King, had many sons and had never married any of their mothers. He had done his best by his children, but he hadn't always been around for them. Rico could understand Sean's doubts even as he knew that Sean would never let down his children or his wife.

"You're better than that."

"I'd like to think so," Sean admitted, then he gave a shaky laugh. "But the God's truth is, this is…huge. My kids will be looking to *me* for answers, about life and the world and—" He shook his head and took a long pull of his beer. "Okay, freaking out a little, I guess."

"It's understandable." Rico slapped his cousin on the back. "But some of your brothers are fathers. Surely they can give you some tips."

Sean laughed a little and shook his head. "Yeah, if you listen to Lucas, his Danny is ready for college and the kid's just about to turn three. And as for Rafe, his and Katie's daughter, Becca, is only a few months old. He's still as confused as I feel."

Chuckling in spite of everything, Rico reminded him, "In the last few years, how many of our brothers and cousins have begun multiplying? Think about it, Sean. If they can handle being fathers, so can you."

"How do I know *they're* doing it right?" Sighing, he admitted, "Nope, there's no hope for this kid. I'm all he's got and I don't know what the hell I'm doing."

All joking aside, Sean really did look as though he was worried about this, so Rico took pity on his cousin.

"You will love your son, Sean. That's all he really needs from you."

"Well, that much I can do for sure," Sean said with a nervous grin. Shaking his head again, he admitted, "You know, nothing in my life has ever made me so happy and at the same time scared me boneless as the idea of my son being born."

"I think," Rico told him, "that is how it is supposed to be." He used his beer to point at the kitchen window. "Besides, look at your lovely wife. Does she look worried? No. Because she has you. And because she knows that the two of you are making a family."

Sean blew out a breath. "When did you get so damn smart?"

Rico laughed at the idea. *Smart.* If he was smart, he wouldn't have wedged himself into his current situation with Teresa. "It's not being smart," he said. "It is knowing my family. And you will be a good father, Sean."

"Hope you're right." He grinned. "No backing out now. Hey, did I tell you Melinda and I are taking the baby to California for Christmas? Get a chance to let everyone meet our new son and I can show her around Long Beach…"

Rico was only half listening now. His focus was Teresa. She was wearing a short-sleeved green silk blouse and a pair of white slacks and she looked…edible. His insides twisted anew as fresh desire pulsed in his bloodstream. She smiled and tossed her hair back from her face. The line of her throat was elegant. The shine in her eyes was magnetic. Her lush body was everything a man dreamed of.

"Oh, yeah," Sean said on a laugh, catching Rico's attention. "Your plan's working real well. Damn, dude. You can help me, but you can't dig yourself out of your own mess."

Rico straightened up. He ignored Sean's teasing and snapped out, "Melinda."

Behind the glass, Sean's wife had doubled over, one arm wrapped around her belly. Teresa was hovering over her and throwing a frantic look to Rico.

"Holy—" Sean broke off and ran. "It's time. Get the car."

Seven

In fifteen minutes, the four of them were at the hospital and Melinda and Sean were taken away to the mysteries of the maternity ward.

Then time started ticking past so slowly that Teresa almost thought they'd stepped into some vortex where time had actually stopped.

The waiting room was long and narrow. It had mint-green paint, beige linoleum floors and the most uncomfortable chairs she had ever experienced. And why, she asked herself, did all hospitals smell the same? In America, Italy, even here on this beautiful tropical island, hospitals stank of antibacterial cleansers and fear. She wrapped her arms around herself, stood up and walked out to the light-filled hallway. Across from her was a nurses' station, manned by one very tired-looking woman. Teresa didn't bother to ask any questions, mainly because Rico had been plaguing the poor woman for hours now and Teresa just didn't have the heart to bother her more.

During the long night, anxious husbands and excited grandparents had come and gone from this waiting room, and still she and Rico waited. Teresa took a seat in the narrow, nearly empty lobby, ignored the small television on the wall playing an old movie she had no interest in and stared instead at Rico, who hadn't stopped pacing since they arrived. She could understand that.

She'd realized from the moment she met him that as a King, he didn't accept inactivity easily. He was a man who took charge. Who stepped in to do what needed doing. It was part of his nature. His heritage. And now he was in the position of being able to do *nothing*.

Helplessness was not something he was even remotely familiar with.

"You might as well sit down," she finally said. "This could take a long time."

"It has already been *hours*." Frowning, he glanced at her, then fired a hard look at a passing nurse. "How much longer? And how can we know if no one will tell us anything?"

Teresa took a chance and threaded her arm through his. When he didn't shrug her off, she called it a win and smiled to herself. "Let's take a walk."

"What?" He looked down at her. "Where? I don't want to go far—what if…?"

"We won't be far," Teresa said, touched that he cared for his family this much. It was these few moments, when he was unguarded, that allowed her a glimpse of the man she'd met so long ago. This man was the Rico she remembered. The stranger was the man who had jumped out of bed as if it were on fire.

"Didn't you tell Sean that nowhere on this island was far from anything?"

"Good point." He blew out a breath and scraped one hand through his hair. "All right, then. I could use some fresh air."

"And I think the nurses could use a break, too." Teresa patted his arm as they walked past the nurses' station. She paused there only long enough to say, "We're going outside for a few minutes. If Sean comes out looking for us, tell him we'll be right back."

"I will." Her gaze fixed on Rico, she said, "You take your time."

Teresa laughed, but Rico's expression didn't change in the slightest. He still wore a frown that would send most people scrambling for a place to hide. Shaking her head, Teresa led him to the elevator, then punched the button for the main floor. The two-story building wasn't large, but it spread out over quite an area. It was the only medical facility for the islanders. Without it, people who needed serious medical help would have had to board a boat for St. Thomas.

She'd learned a lot in the last few days. Rico's employees were eager to talk about him and the island paradise where they lived. They had told her all about what the Kings had done for Tesoro since moving here. For example, they had donated enough money to see to it that the small hospital now boasted top-of-the-line, state-of-the-art equipment. They'd hired more doctors and nurses and made it possible for most emergencies to be handled on island.

They'd rebuilt the dock and improved the harbor, making it easier for charter ships, as well as local fishermen, to pull into port. In town they'd arranged for more of the islanders to sell their wares to the tourists who now flocked to Tesoro. The Kings had done good things on the island and everyone here seemed to appreciate it. But Teresa knew that if she commented on any of this to Rico, he would shrug off her admiration and call it simply good business. He was a complicated man and maybe that was one reason she was so drawn to him. Because at the heart of it, very few men were complicated.

At the ground floor, Rico practically lunged off the elevator and Teresa had to hurry to keep up with him. Outside the night was quiet, the wind was soft and the sound of the ocean rumbled in the distance. It felt good to get out of the claustrophobic waiting room. It felt even better to have Rico beside her.

Teresa took a long, deep breath and blew it out again. "Nice to get out of the hospital for a while."

"Yes." Rico looked back over his shoulder at the brightly lit entrance. "But not for too long. I want to be nearby when—"

"We will be." Teresa took his hand and was pleased when he didn't pull away. Small victories. She led him across the side yard, their steps muffled by the thick grass. "But waiting for hours can be hard. You have to get out now and then."

He snorted, but the tension in him eased a bit as the trade winds continued to rush past them, carrying the scents of flowers and the sea with them. "And how do you know so much about women in childbirth?"

Teresa smiled and squeezed his hand. Whatever else was between them, for the moment they were on the same side, allies against the unknown.

"I grew up all over the world," she said finally, tipping

her head back to look up at the night sky, dazzled with stars. "Our home was in Italy, but we were rarely there."

"I wondered why I have more of an accent than you do."

She shrugged as if it didn't matter, when the truth was all of her life she had longed for a place to call home. Even her own apartment in Naples wasn't home. Just another temporary refuge.

"Hard to adopt a particular accent when you're never in one place long enough to pick up the rhythms of the local speech."

"Hmm…"

His noncommittal answer told her that he was thinking about the Coretti family and their tradition of thievery keeping them on the move. But she wasn't going to talk about her family now and ruin this momentary truce.

"Anyway, we were living in New York and my mother's sister was having a baby. I was about sixteen, I guess."

"And you waited as we are now?"

"We waited. For hours." She sighed and shifted her gaze from the skies to him. "It seemed to take forever."

"And did your father fill his time by stealing from the patients and doctors?"

She stopped dead and turned to face him. Her gaze met his and she was sorry to see the stony glint in his eyes again. "Can you never let it go, Rico? Not even for a while?"

"Why should I?" he demanded.

"Because I'm not my father." Her voice was quiet but strong. Her gaze never left his as she added, "I've never stolen anything in my life. I'm not a thief."

A muscle twitched in his jaw as if he were fighting an

internal battle over what to say and what to hold back. Then he blurted, "So just a liar, then?"

The verbal slap hit home and she winced. It seemed that their momentary truce had ended and her sorrow was quickly swallowed by impatience. He was determined to see her only as treacherous and Teresa had no idea how to change his mind.

"And you've never lied? Are you that perfect, Rico?"

"Not perfect," he countered. "But I don't lie to the people who matter to me."

"Ah," she said, crossing her arms over her chest and giving him a sharp nod. "So you're a picky liar. Only a select few. I'm guessing women?"

"Mostly," he admitted and didn't look bothered by the admission at all.

"And that's okay?"

"I didn't say that."

"You didn't have to." She shook her head and asked, "What about me? Did you tell me pretty lies when we met?"

His jaw clenched and it looked as though he were grinding his teeth into powder. "You're the one who lied to me, remember?"

"So you were honest with me, but not with other women." She laughed shortly. "Well, hell, Rico. You're wasting your time being a hotelier when you should be a saint."

Furious now, she let her temper reign because that was so much easier than dealing with the disappointment and regret threatening to choke her. Teresa spun around and took two steps away from him before he caught her with one strong hand and whipped her back around to face him.

"I never claimed to be a saint," he muttered, his accent suddenly flaring into life and coloring his words with a seductive tang he probably didn't intend at the moment. "But I never lied to *you*."

"What about the phony divorce papers?"

He frowned, gritted his teeth and kept quiet, silently admitting he had no answer for that.

Taking a deep breath, she looked up into his eyes and searched for the man she loved behind that wall of ice he'd built between them. "I didn't want to lie to you, Rico. I didn't want to leave you, either. But there was nothing else I could do. Can't you understand lying to protect someone?"

"I can't understand a family who demands that kind of loyalty."

"Really?" She tipped her head to one side and met him, glare for glare. "Because the King family isn't loyal?"

"We don't cheat for each other," he snapped. "We don't lie to protect each other."

"But you would if you had to."

His mouth flattened into a grim slash and his eyes narrowed. She could see that he was thinking about it, considering…and not really enjoying the answer he was coming up with.

She took a long breath. "Rico, I'm not asking you to forget what happened five years ago. But maybe you could try to see it from my side."

"Your side? All I know of your side is one thing." He released his hold on her, shoved his hands into his pockets and stared over her head at the surrounding trees. "You chose them over me."

"They're my family."

His gaze shot to hers. "And I'm your *husband*."

"Do you really think it was easy for me?"

"All I know is that you did it," he ground out. "Easy or difficult, you made your choice and we were both forced to live with it."

Pain squeezed her heart and radiated out to every square inch of her body. There was nothing she could say to that. No excuse. No plea for understanding. Rico would never see what she had done as anything less than betrayal.

Their gazes locked, unspoken tension practically humming between them in the soft island air. The ocean was a murmur of sound and somewhere in the distance an animal's screech sounded out.

There was so much to say and so little all at the same time. Teresa had hoped that they might find a way to reach each other again, but for every step forward she took, Rico moved that much farther away. He was slipping away from her even as she stood beside him. Missing the feel of his touch, Teresa scrubbed her palms up and down her arms in a futile attempt to ease the chill of the cold that was deep inside her.

"Teresa," he asked quietly a moment later, "what happened?"

"What?" She shook her head and looked at him in confusion.

"With your aunt," he said, reminding her of the story she had been telling. "What happened?"

It took her a second, but a smile curved her mouth as she looked at him. Nothing had been solved. They were still on opposite sides of the same battle. But his question told Teresa that Rico, too, missed their all-too-brief truce. So she willingly played along and dipped back into her memories.

"After what seemed like forever, she had a baby boy. I saw him when he was just a few minutes old." Her smile brightened. "Luca was so tiny. And he looked just furious at the indignity of being born."

Rico smiled with her and for one long moment, it was almost as if they were…united. And it was so good Teresa didn't want that moment to end, though she knew it would. For whatever reason, Rico had decided to put their argument aside and go back to their earlier, almost friendly position. She was more than willing.

"Then I will try to be patient as we wait for the newest King to make his arrival."

"They know it's a boy?"

"They do," he said, nodding. "Just last month I helped Sean paint the baby's room."

"Melinda showed me the nursery. You guys did a nice job. I love the blue and chocolate-brown." She stopped and laughed a little. "Wow. I just realized it was only a few hours ago that we were at Melinda's house and it feels like days."

He nodded, looked past her at the hospital entrance and said, "The waiting takes a toll."

"It does." She followed his gaze and said, "We should really get back."

"Yes. We should." He looked as reluctant to end this alone time as she felt and Teresa told herself not to make more of it than there was. Still, a tiny nugget of hope settled into a corner of her heart and wouldn't be budged.

He took her hand in his and the warmth of his skin washed through her. She held that feeling to her and told herself to remember. To etch that sensation into her heart and mind so that one day soon, when he was far out of reach, she'd be able to take out this memory and relive the feel of her hand in his.

When he led her back to the hospital, they were silent, even their footsteps muffled on the grass.

By dawn, their wait was over.

Sean strutted down the long hallway to the waiting room and greeted them both with a wide grin stretched across his face.

"Melinda's great and so is our son." He slapped his hands together and scrubbed his palms before shoving both hands through his hair. "It was—Melinda was—*amazing*."

Rico bolted out of his chair, crossed the room and gave his cousin a brief, hard hug before stepping back and slapping Sean on the shoulder. "Congratulations! You're a father!"

"Terrifying, man," Sean told him with a shudder. "I won't lie."

Teresa winced a little at that word, half expecting a knowing glare from Rico. She was surprised, and pleased, when it didn't come. She walked to Sean and gave him a hug. "Do we get to see him?"

"Absolutely." Sean grinned at both of them again. "I came to get you so you can admire and stare with awe at the newest King."

Rico took Teresa's hand again as they followed Sean along the corridor and she had the feeling he hadn't even noticed doing it. The move had just come naturally. As if he'd needed to be linked with her for the occasion. That nugget of hope grew just a bit in spite of the fact that she tried hard to prevent it.

The hospital was small, so it didn't take long to get to the nursery. There were only three newborns nestled into clear bassinets. And only one of those three was a boy. While Sean stared at his son with the bemused expression of someone who had survived a battle when he hadn't expected to, Teresa just looked at the baby. He was perfect. Tiny and pink-cheeked and so beautiful she felt a knot of envy lodge in her throat.

"He's a good-looking baby, Sean," Rico said softly and his hand tightened imperceptibly on Teresa's.

"Yeah." Sean rocked on his heels and finally tore his gaze from his son. "He really is. You want to go see Melinda?"

They did and once in the private hospital room, Teresa and Rico stood on either side of the new mother's bed.

"He's beautiful," Teresa said.

"I know!" Melinda smiled and sighed, then unnecessarily smoothed the blanket and sheet covering her. "I can't believe he's finally here."

"What's his name?" Teresa asked, looking from one new parent to the other.

"Stryker," Sean announced with a secretive smile for his wife.

"It was my father's name," Melinda added, beaming at Sean. "My grandfather was really pleased when we told him what we were going to name the baby. And it means a lot to me, too."

"It's a big name for such a little guy," Sean mused.

"I think he will grow into it," Rico told him, with another slap on the shoulder. "Stryker King. It sounds strong."

"Yeah." Sean had a silly grin on his face. "It does."

Teresa watched Rico and his family and wished that she really belonged in that circle of familiarity. But she was a temporary blip on the King family radar. She wouldn't be here to watch Stryker grow up. She wouldn't be here to build on the friendship she and Melinda had begun. In less than a month, she would be gone and the island would go on without her. As would Rico.

She took a breath and held it. To distract herself, she glanced around. The private room was a pale yellow and a single bedside light glowed, throwing soft shadows across Melinda's features. She looked tired, but more happy than Teresa could have imagined.

Melinda grinned up at them and reached for Rico's hand. "I'm so glad you guys stayed. But you must be exhausted."

"You're the one who did all the work," Teresa pointed out.

"Hey, I was here too, you know," Sean chimed in.

His wife gave him a smile usually reserved for heroes. "You were, sweetie, and you were great." Then she sighed and leaned back into her pillow. "I am tired, but I'm so wired right now there's no way I could sleep, you know?"

"Well, if you are not tired, I'm willing to bet that you are at least hungry," Rico said.

"Oh, God." Melinda laughed. "I'm so hungry if I had any chocolate syrup to drown them in, I'd eat the sheets right off the bed."

Teresa laughed.

"But the nurse tells me that breakfast isn't served for another couple of hours…" She glanced at her husband. "I'm going to get Sean to go home and bring me a nutrition bar. Or a bag of cookies. Or both."

"I think we can do better than that." Rico leaned over the metal bed rail and kissed Melinda's forehead. Then he straightened and looked at Sean. "I will have our chef prepare something and it will be here within a half an hour."

"Oh, boy! You are a god among men, Rico," Melinda said on a sigh of gratitude.

"That has been said," he allowed.

"That's breakfast for *two,* right?" Sean put in hopefully.

"Of course."

"Feel better already." Sean grinned. "Of course, making himself the hero here, there'll be no living with him now. Good luck to you, Teresa."

A strained silence erupted suddenly as everyone in the room remembered at once that Teresa was on Tesoro only temporarily. Taking a breath, she swallowed hard and said, "Congratulations again, Melinda. Your baby is gorgeous."

"Thanks." She took Teresa's hand and held it for a second or two, offering silent support. "Once I get out of here, come to the house. I'll tell you all of my horror stories."

"Can't wait." Teresa smiled, then walked around the end of the bed to join Rico.

"We will see you soon." Rico lifted one hand to Sean and slipped out the door, drawing Teresa with him.

As they walked down the hall and passed the nurses' station for the last time, Teresa said, "That was nice of you. Sending them breakfast, I mean."

"It is a small enough thing to do." He tried to shrug it off and hit the elevator button for the ground floor. In moments the doors had opened again and they were striding out of the hospital into the cool of early morning.

"You really don't like being told you're nice, do you?" She studied his profile.

"Only because I'm not. And you would have said the same yesterday."

Her steps faltered a bit, but she caught herself and hurried on. True, after he'd climbed out of bed the day before and looked at her with ice in his eyes, she wouldn't have called him nice. But he had a heart, she knew he did. She'd just seen evidence of it. And five years ago he had offered that heart to her.

Was she solely to blame for the changes in Rico? And if so, how could she undo it?

Once they were in his car and buckled up, she asked, "How will Sean get home? We brought him here."

"I'll have someone bring his car to the hospital for him."

Teresa smiled. "Nice again."

He blew out a breath and glanced at her. "Expedient."

"You can't convince me, Rico." She shook her head and relaxed back against her seat, giving in to the fatigue that had suddenly begun to drag at her. "You're a nice guy and that's not a bad thing."

"Don't make me what I'm not, Teresa," he warned and fired up the engine. "It won't serve either of us."

Sunrise streaked the sky with soft colors that grew bolder nearer the horizon. The ever-present wind sighed through the opened car windows.

She understood what Rico was trying to tell her. But in the soft light of the breaking dawn, she looked at him and saw him for *exactly* what he was.

The love of her life.

Eight

A week later, Rico stood in his office at the hotel, staring out the window at the sprawling view beyond the glass. From here he could see most of the village, the harbor and all the way to the horizon. He wasn't noticing the inherent beauty of the view at the moment though. Instead, he was trying to focus on the myriad problems facing him.

Running a luxury resort such as Castello Tesoro meant that there were small crises in the making at all times. Usually he accepted them as simply a part of his world. But with Teresa back in his life, he was less focused and so, less prepared to handle it all.

In the last few days, he had already dealt with a small fire caused by a candle left burning in one of the bungalows. No injuries, thank God, but a chaise and several throw pillows were toast. Then there was the tourist who broke an ankle jumping from the top of a waterfall on the property. He was in pain but he was lucky he hadn't broken his neck instead. Naturally, the hotel would pay for his hospital bills and Rico was arranging for private transport back to the States.

There were the small, everyday problems, as well: sunburns, jellyfish stings, drunks and the occasional brawls between guests. It was the sort of thing you expected to deal with as a hotelier. What you *didn't* normally come up against was an executive chef with appendicitis.

Rico turned his back on the window and faced his general manager, standing on the opposite side of his desk. "How long will Louis be out of commission?"

"According to the doctor, at least a week." Janine Julien, a woman of about sixty with the organizational skills of a general, tapped her computer tablet. Janine had been with him since Cancún. She'd chosen to leave her home in Mexico for the island of Tesoro and Rico had been pleased by the decision. The woman kept her finger on the pulse of the hotel and was often able to anticipate and prevent problems before they happened.

"Louis will be fine," she added. "But with him out of commission for a while, I'm more concerned about what's going to happen here. As you know, the hotel is booked solid for the foreseeable future. There's a wedding scheduled this weekend and I can't stress enough how much time Louis spent with the bride's mother going over the selected menu. She is *not* going to be happy."

"We have other chefs." Rico shrugged. "They are more than capable."

"Sure they are," Janine agreed. "But Louis keeps the kitchen running. He's more than a chef. He's the one voice amid the chaos that people listen to. We've got a problem, Rico."

He had more than one, he told himself grimly. But at the moment, straightening out the mess in the hotel kitchen took precedence over Teresa.

"And I think I've found the solution."

"What?" Rico came around his desk and perched on the front edge. Folding his arms over his chest, he asked, "A solution already?"

The woman met his gaze and said, "Your wife."

Since she had been here on the island, Teresa had become known to everyone. If they'd been surprised to discover he was married, no one had mentioned it. Rico only hoped they were as discreet when the marriage was over and Teresa was gone from the island and his life.

That thought made him frown, so he pushed it aside and turned his focus back to the older woman.

"What about Teresa?"

"She was in the kitchen helping the staff prepare when Louis collapsed." Shaking her head, Janine said, "I happened to be there, too, to discuss the individual cakes for the upcoming wedding. I saw how she took charge." Shaking her head, she continued, "I was flustered, I'll admit it. But Teresa? She checked on Louis, had someone call the hotel doctor, then had another chef drive him to the hospital. And while all of this was going on, she got the kitchen moving again."

Janine shook her head, still clearly impressed with what she'd witnessed. "Everyone was shaken, but Teresa just stepped up and took charge. No one questioned her. They got back to work, and in spite of what had happened to Louis, the staff never missed a step. She's still down there now, running things. I thought you should know."

Rico didn't know whether to be grateful or furious. Once again Teresa had proven herself to him and to his staff. She wasn't cowering in his room, as a proper hostage should be. Instead, she was making herself a part of the fabric of Castello Tesoro. He knew, too, that the fabric would unravel once she was gone.

And she would be gone.

He couldn't risk believing in her again. Couldn't take the chance of keeping her here with him, knowing that her thieving family might show up at any time. But that wasn't the truth at all. He didn't give a damn about Teresa's family and knew he could handle them if they ever showed up on Tesoro again.

This was about *her*. The woman he'd once married. The woman he had trusted. Believed in. Only to be betrayed.

Well, if she was trying to ingratiate herself with him now, it wouldn't work. Of course he'd allow her to help; he wasn't an idiot and a talented chef didn't fall out of the sky when needed. But her help was all he was interested in.

Pushing up from the desk, he barked out orders. "Contact the hospital. Take care of Louis's bill and get him whatever he wants. I'll go see him later."

"Right." Her gaze tracked him as he stalked across the room toward the office door. "Where are you going?"

"To the kitchen." He glanced over his shoulder at her. "I'll see for myself if Teresa is working out as head chef or not."

A few minutes later Rico stood in a doorway, watching the choreographed confusion in the gigantic kitchen and couldn't help but be impressed. The first thing he noticed was that the classical music Louis insisted on piping through the room had been replaced by rock, with a beat that kept the entire staff moving from station to station at a busy pace. The pastry chefs worked at a mound of dough, the salads were being prepared at a long marble counter and the prep chefs were busily preparing tonight's soup selections, as well as setting up the ingredients for the rest of the menu.

And in the middle of the chaos stood Teresa. Her black hair was pulled back and tucked up under a chef's hat. She wore a white coat over her street clothes and directed traffic in the big room like a traffic cop at a particularly busy corner.

She paused to take a sip of a sauce, then directed the chef to add something else. She inspected the pastry chefs' work and grinned at them in approval. Someone shouted a question and before they'd finished speaking, she was there, lending a hand.

Rico shook his head as he watched her. Sunlight poured in from the skylights in the roof and that golden light seemed to follow Teresa wherever she went. She shone, plain and simple. He was impressed. He didn't want to be, but there it was. Teresa had stepped in when she was most needed and was taking charge of what could have been a disastrous situation.

Everyone knew that the chefs in any big kitchen had rivalries and jealousies driving them. Without Teresa, there would have been a power play with several of the chefs making a bid to step into Louis's position. With her, the kitchen was running as well as or better than it had before.

Frowning to himself, he had to admit that there was much more to this woman than he had long believed. She wasn't here of her own free will. He had practically kidnapped her, blackmailed her, holding the freedom of her family over her head. Yet instead of standing by and watching disaster strike his hotel, she had jumped in, unasked, to save the day. Why? He had to wonder.

Unnoticed, he watched her and as he did, something within him stirred. Not the heat of desire that was a continuous, overwhelming pulse tearing through him. This was something else. There was warmth beneath the heat and a rush of feelings that he'd been denying for five long years.

As soon as he sensed that warmth settling around his heart, he bit off an oath and walked away.

It had been great to be back in a big kitchen.

Teresa had told Melinda that she'd spent the last five years working in a series of different restaurants around the world. And it was true. But they were small places—mom-and-pop diners, coffee shops and bakeries. She'd worked in a patisserie in Paris, a bakery in Gstaad and a pretzel shop in Berlin. She'd spent time in Italian restaurants in Florence and tea shops in London.

But not since she left Rico in Mexico had she worked for a five-star restaurant. Truthfully, when she had first disappeared from his hotel in Mexico, Teresa had worried that he would track her down and find her, so she'd hidden away in small eateries that most people overlooked. But after some time, she had simply gravitated to those places as if she were punishing herself by refusing the opportunity to do what she did best—run a big kitchen.

But today that had changed. She felt terrible that Louis had taken ill, but she also had to admit that she had loved the challenge of stepping into his shoes, however temporarily. She'd worked tirelessly for hours and when the guests had all been served and the ovens shut down, she'd stayed late to supervise the massive cleanup required.

By the time she was ready to go back to Rico's house and her gilded cage, Teresa was exhausted. And felt better than she had in far too long. She let herself in through the front door and quietly shut it behind her. A smile was still on her face as she headed down the long, slate-tiled hallway toward Rico's bedroom. As she passed the shadow-filled living room, his voice stopped her.

"Why did you do it?"

"Rico?" The room was dark, save for the pale, watery light spilling in from the night beyond the wide windows. "Why are you sitting down here in the dark?"

She heard a click and instantly, a fire blossomed to life in the gas hearth. Multicolored slate tiles in shades of blues and grays made up the fireplace insert. Leaping flames and fiery light jumped around the room, highlighting the man who stood before it. "I want to know why you helped out in the kitchen, Teresa. You didn't have to. It wasn't up to you to prevent a disaster."

She walked into the room, hardly noticing the brightly patterned throw rugs scattered over the floor. She paid no attention to the oversize brown leather couches and chairs or to the gleaming oak tables between them. She barely glanced through the wide window providing a spectacular view of his yard that swept down to an ocean that frothed with phosphorescent light.

"I wanted to help."

"I know that. What I don't know," he repeated, "what I need to know, is *why?*"

"Is it really so hard to understand, Rico?" she asked, walking close enough to him to stare up into eyes that were shadowed in the low light, yet danced with the reflections of the flames.

"Yes," he whispered, gaze locked on her, moving over her features as if he'd never seen her before. "You had no reason to. I forced you to stay here on the island when you had no wish to. I've threatened your family with imprisonment and have made you a hostage. So yes, it is hard for me to understand why you would step in during a crisis at my hotel."

Teresa shook her head sadly. He couldn't see how much she loved him. Or if he did, he chose to not recognize it. So how could she explain that for her, there hadn't been a choice at all? "I wanted to help *you*, Rico. Louis got sick and I was right there, so I helped."

"What are you trying to do to me?" His voice was low, deep and rough. As if every word had to scratch its way past his throat.

"Do to you?" She huffed an impatient breath. "Nothing, Rico. I'm here for a month. Would it be easier on you if I sat in a corner and cried over being trapped here by a man who clearly can't stand to be around me unless I'm in his bed?"

"Maybe," he muttered thickly as he shoved one hand through his hair. "I don't know anymore."

Teresa didn't even know what she was feeling now. Impatience, irritation, a swell of love that was so rich and deep it filled her entire body and throbbed in her heart.

"Rico, would you rather I just sit on your bed naked, awaiting your pleasure? Would that be hostage-like enough for you?"

"Yes. No. *Yes*," he ground out, then continued in a ragged voice, "if you behaved as if you were frightened or worried, that would make more sense to me. Instead you make yourself a part of things here, even knowing you won't be staying."

"If it would help, I could whimper for a while."

He snorted. "You wouldn't know the first thing about whimpering."

A small smile curved her mouth. "At least you know me that well."

All trace of amusement drained from his features and his eyes flashed in the firelight. "Once I thought I knew you better than anyone I have ever known."

Her heart ached at the wistful tone in his voice. How much she had destroyed when she'd left. How much she'd given up, never to find again. How much they had both missed in the last five years because of a twist of fate. If Gianni hadn't stolen that dagger... If she had told Rico the truth about her family when she first met him...

But *if*s were nebulous creatures and changed nothing.

"You did know me, Rico."

"No." He shook his head and reached for her, dropping his hands onto her shoulders and pulling her up close. "I thought I did, but you weren't real. You weren't mine."

"I was, though," she argued, *willing* him to believe it.

"Not then," he answered. "Your heart was torn, your loyalties tested too deeply for you to have been mine alone. But tonight, you *are* mine."

He was right. In spite of her love for him, she *had* been torn between Rico and her family. Maybe she'd been too young to appreciate what she had found with him. She only knew that if faced with the same decision today, she would do it all differently. She would tell Rico everything and trust him to do the right thing.

God, she'd been an idiot.

She was in love with her husband and that was the one thing she could never tell him.

Rico had been waiting for her for hours. Convinced that she had an ulterior motive for offering her help when it was most needed, he'd worked it over and over again in his mind and still was no closer to discovering what her plan might be. She had to know that he hadn't changed his mind. That no matter how much she integrated herself into life on the island, he would still watch her leave at the end of the month.

She'd become friends with his cousin and his wife. The hotel staff was in love with her and he couldn't even walk into his own damned home without catching her scent. The memory of her laugh. The hush of her sighs.

When she left, it would tear a gaping hole in his life, but she *would* leave. That was their bargain and he would hold up his end. He would give her the divorce she had paid for five years ago and he would never again trust his heart to a woman.

Because even now she was keeping something from him. He didn't know what, but it was easy to read in her golden-brown eyes that she was deliberately *not* telling him everything. What her secret might be this time, he had no idea. And it bothered him more than he wanted to admit that she was *still* hiding things from him.

But through the frustration and the irritation, one thing continuously rang true. He hungered for her. He wanted her now more than ever. And the whole time he'd been here, in the dark, waiting for her, his mind had devised all manner of things he wanted to do with her when she returned. Now that she was here, in front of him, smelling so good, he drew in breath after breath just to taste her scent…Rico didn't want to wait even the length of time it would take to get to the bedroom.

"You're driving me insane, Teresa." His hand cupped her cheek, then slid around to the back of her head.

"You're not alone in that," she told him and went up on her toes.

He kissed her, hard, taking her mouth in a rush of desire and all-encompassing need. She tangled her tongue with his, leaning into him for support and wrapping one leg around his hips, pulling him closer. He ground his body against hers, letting her feel the hard, hot, demanding part of him, and she groaned into his mouth, feeding the frenzy.

The staff was gone for the night. The house was theirs. And in the dancing, firelit shadows, he shoved the hem of her T-shirt up so that he could cup her breasts. Through the fragile lace of her bra, he stroked his thumbs across her nipples, eliciting a moan of pleasure from Teresa's throat.

That soft sound stoked the fires inside him into a blaze that quickly engulfed him. Rico could hardly breathe for the need crouched in his chest. He flicked her bra open and cupped both of her breasts in his palms.

She held on to him, fingers grasping at his shoulders as she pushed herself into his touch. "Rico, more. I want more."

So did he. But he wanted her naked.

"Clothes," he murmured, letting her go briefly. "Off. Now."

"Oh, yes." Nodding, she pulled her T-shirt up and over her head, then tossed it aside. He watched her step out of her shorts, displaying the lacy, pale pink thong she wore beneath them.

His mouth went dry and his pulse skyrocketed. He kept his gaze locked with hers as he quickly tore off his own clothing and threw it to the floor. When he was naked, her gaze dropped to his erection and she sighed in anticipation.

She reached out one hand to curl her fingers around him and he hissed in a breath at the first touch of her hand. She smiled up into his eyes and stroked, rubbed and caressed him until his eyes were rolling back in his head and he had to fight for every breath.

Body taut, tension coiled, he was so close to exploding he couldn't risk her fingers on him another minute. He caught her hand in his and shook his head. "Enough."

"No," she said breathlessly with a shake of her head. "It's not nearly enough."

He had to smile. His Teresa was a passionate one and he loved that about her. No simpering, coy females for him. Rico appreciated that his woman wanted as hungrily as he did.

His woman.

That thought echoed in his mind until he deliberately shut it down.

He pulled her up against him, enjoying the feel of her lush, curvy body pressed to his. Again, she hooked her leg around his waist and he felt the heat of her core against his hard length. He groaned tightly and backed her up until she bumped into the arm of the leather couch. When she went to fall back onto it, he caught her, turned her in his arms and eased her down until she was bent over, her luscious, beautiful behind displayed to him.

She propped herself up on her elbows and looked back at him over her shoulder. She wiggled her hips suggestively, licked her lips, took a breath and said, "Touch me, Rico."

Her welcome, her *passion* undid him. He reached down and tugged that thong from her and rubbed her tender flesh with strong strokes. She moaned again and pushed her hips up, bracing her feet apart on the floor, giving him easy access to drive them both over the edge.

His brain splintered, thoughts dissolving under an onslaught of pure sensation that tore through him. Rico had never lost control of himself this way. Never allowed a woman to reach past his well-built defenses to glimpse the man he was beneath the sophisticated veneer. But Teresa did it without even trying.

Rico's finely honed control simply snapped. He couldn't wait another minute. Couldn't be denied the ecstasy of being surrounded by her wet heat. He bent over her, letting her feel how badly he wanted her. She turned her face to him and their tongues met in a fast, delving exploration, then he straightened and positioned himself behind her.

Her breath came fast and hard. She threw her hair out of her face and turned her head to watch him. Her eyes gleamed and she licked her bottom lip with a long, slow swipe of her tongue.

He ran his hands up and down her back, following the line of her spine and the curve of her behind until she was groaning with need and twisting beneath his grip.

His thumbs swiped down into the heat of her and spread her inner core to his gaze. She was hot and damp and as he stroked her she moaned, "Rico, please. Touch me. Touch me."

He did, stroking her inside and out as his own body screamed for him to enter her. To claim her as his.

Heart racing, his blood thrummed in his veins and urged him on. Teresa looked back at him again, her breath coming harder, faster, and she whispered, "Hurry."

He grinned at her eagerness. His Teresa had never been shy about lovemaking. When they were first together, they had christened every room in his suite over the Cancún hotel and what they had done on his terrace one memorable morning still woke him up at night, wanting to do it all again.

"Please," she muttered, bracing herself on the leather cushions and wiggling her hips in invitation. "Now, Rico. Do it now."

"Now," he agreed and pushed himself into her depths.

She cried out his name at his entry and everything in him fisted painfully. She was so hot, so tight and felt so right. He rocked in and out of her body, hating every retreat and welcoming every surge as the blessing it was.

Again and again, he pushed them both higher and higher, the rhythm they set breathtaking. The only sounds in the room were their heavy breathing and the hiss and snap of the fire.

He leaned over her, cupped her breasts in his hands and tweaked her nipples as his body continued to plunge into hers. She groaned and rocked back into him, doing all she could to match his movements.

She humbled him, aroused him and left him shaken to the heart of him. Desire pumped like a wildfire through his body even while his mind stood apart and realized how precious she was. How special to him. How his life would be even emptier once she was gone from it.

But Rico didn't want to think now. Didn't want to recognize future or past. All that existed was the present. This moment snatched out of time where he and Teresa could be who they were destined to be. Two halves of a whole.

That thought staggered him, so he pushed it aside. He gave himself over to the sensations cresting inside him. Rico looked down at her and saw her bite down on her bottom lip as she fought to claim the release that was so close to each of them.

He felt her internal muscles clench and strain around him and knew her climax was only moments away. He gave her everything he had and when she shrieked his name, he buried himself as deeply as he could inside her and then joined her on that steep slide into completion.

Nine

When he could think again, when he could *move*, Rico gently disentangled their bodies, then helped her shift position onto his lap as he took a seat on the couch. Wrapping his arms around her, he held her carefully, as if she was fragile and likely to break.

Which, he realized, was ironic, considering what the two of them had just done. But Teresa had always brought out his protective tendencies. It seemed that had not changed. Right now she was warm and trembling in his arms, still reacting to the explosive climax that had shattered them both. And though his body was sated, Rico already wanted her again.

"That was," she said on a sigh, "*incredible.*"

"Yes, it was." He let his head drop to the back of the couch. His eyes closed and a groan lodged in his throat as he realized what had just happened. What he'd done without even thinking about it. But then, that was the problem, wasn't it? He *hadn't* been thinking at all. "It was also incredibly stupid."

"What?" She looked up at him, her hair a wild tangle around her face, her mouth puffy from his kisses and her eyes still shining with satisfaction. "What do you mean? How was any of that stupid?"

He blew out a breath and met her gaze. "I lost control."

"I know," she said, giving him a slow, sexy, very tempting smile. "I liked it."

"So did I," he admitted. He lifted his head, stared into her eyes and added, "But I didn't stop for a condom."

"Oh. *Oh.*" She bit her lip, took a breath and said, "All right, that was stupid. But this wasn't only your fault, Rico. I wasn't thinking either."

"Small consolation." Rico had never lost control like that. But then, only Teresa had ever touched him so deeply that his brain shut off and let his body take over.

"If it helps any, I'm healthy." She laid one hand on his chest. "I haven't been with anyone since you."

Those words rattled around in his mind and then slipped down to center around his heart. He shouldn't have cared, but he did. Shouldn't have been pleased, but he was. For five years he had imagined his *wife,* thinking herself divorced, being with other men. Letting them kiss her, taste her. Giving to them what had been only his. To know that none of those torturous imaginings had been real was a gift he hadn't expected.

He dropped one hand to the curve of her breast and slowly stroked his fingertips across one hard, dusky nipple. She sighed in reaction and he felt his groin leap to life again. So did she and she smiled knowingly. That small smile touched something inside him that he didn't want to explore too closely.

It was enough that she was here. With him. For right now. He hadn't looked to the future since the night she'd disappeared from the hotel in Mexico. Instead, his thoughts had always gone back to when she had been there beside him. Smiling, laughing, giving him a secretive look that told him she wanted him as badly as he wanted her.

Rico had never planned on giving her a confession about their time apart, but since she had been so open with him, he could do no less and still retain any sense of honor in his own mind. If he was honest with himself, he would have to say that he'd enjoyed having her think that he had moved on to other women. But now, especially with what had just happened between them and with her admission, he couldn't let her go on believing his lie of omission.

Lie. He was only now seeing that as much as he hated being lied to himself, he was as guilty as anyone when it came to convenient untruths.

"I have not been with anyone since you, either." He watched surprise flash in her eyes and pleasure quickly followed.

"But—" She shook her head. "All of the pictures of you with models and actresses…"

"Things are not always what they seem." He ran one hand up and down her bare back in long, slow strokes, loving the feel of her skin beneath his palm.

"All right, then answer me this." She took a breath, blew it out, and asked, "Why haven't you been with any of those women?"

He laughed shortly. "Because unlike you, I *knew* I was still married."

She flushed and the soft color filling her cheeks made her look even lovelier, though he wouldn't have thought that possible.

"And you?" he countered. "What kept you from other men?"

She was silent for several long, tense seconds before she said, "You're the only man I wanted."

Heat spilled through him instantly. He realized that he *wanted* to believe her. He wanted to think that she had missed him as desperately as he had missed her for the last five years. But if she felt so strongly about him, how could she disappear from his life? How could she have lied to him about who she was? And how could she have stayed away for so long?

She leaned her head against his chest and he knew she could hear his heartbeat slamming against his ribs. Since she'd arrived on Tesoro, Teresa had tried to explain her past actions to him and he hadn't been interested in listening. Now, though, he wanted to know. Needed to hear her explanation, whatever it was. And yet he had to wonder if he would be able to believe her.

His mind was a rushing torrent of contradictory thoughts. His blood burned in his veins. His body was hard and ready to take her again.

What this woman could do to him was dangerous.

What he had just done to her, he reminded himself, was unforgivable. Even if they were both healthy, he thought, no condom meant there was a chance at an unexpected pregnancy. And they had to talk about the possibilities.

"Teresa," he said softly, turning her face up to his. "I must know. Are you taking birth control?"

"No." She shook her head, then laid her hand over his, holding his hand to her breast. "I'm not. But don't worry, Rico. Everything will be fine. What are the odds I could be pregnant from one time?"

It depended on whether or not the gods had a sense of humor, he supposed. He remembered how not too long ago he'd actually imagined Teresa pregnant with his child. Now, through his own stupidity, there was a chance that would happen.

"I was never much of a gambler, because the odds are usually against you." He shook his head, still having a hard time believing that he had put them in this position. "I must apologize to you. For losing control of myself."

"Don't," she said, meeting his eyes. "Don't you dare apologize. I wanted this. I wanted you. I'm glad you lost control, Rico, and if I am pregnant…we'll deal with the situation if it presents itself."

Deal with it.

He didn't know exactly what she meant by that, but he knew very well what would happen if she was pregnant with his child. They would stay married. The divorce he'd promised her would never happen.

And that would mean he would have to find a way to live with the still-rich memories of her betrayal. His chest tightened as if iron bands were wrapped around his body, squeezing mercilessly.

How could he spend his life with a woman he couldn't trust? Would he ask himself every day if *today* was the day she would bolt?

Shaking his head, he wrapped his arms around his

wife and wondered if passion would be enough to save a marriage born in deception.

A few days later Teresa and Rico went into the village to shop for gifts for Melinda and her new son.

The day was warm, the wind was soft and two of the small launches used to transport guests from St. Thomas were docked at the harbor.

Tesoro village looked, Teresa thought, like a movie set. It was too perfect to be real. The street was narrow and lined on either side by brightly painted shops. From pastels to jewel tones, each building was as different as the wares it offered.

There was a bakery, and the scent of cinnamon wafted through its open door to tempt pedestrians. There were souvenir shops, a chocolatier that Teresa really wanted to visit, and every other kind of shop you could imagine, all catering to the wealthy tourists who came to the island to vacation. At the end of the winding street there was a small grocery store that mostly served the locals and there was a spectacular view of the ocean from every point on the tidy street. The shops huddled close to the freshly swept sidewalks. Windows gleamed, reflecting the bright light of the sun, and terra-cotta pots positioned outside the tidy stores held trailing bouquets of brightly colored flowers.

There was so much to see, Teresa swung her head from side to side in an attempt to miss nothing. "It's so pretty," she said, with a glance up at Rico, walking beside her. "Like a postcard."

"That's been said," he agreed. "In fact, Sean and I hired photographers to take photos of this street at different angles and at different times of the year. Then Walter picked the ones he liked and we had postcards made to be sold in all of the shops. Proceeds go directly to the island, and the citizens here vote on how the money's spent."

She just stared at him for a moment, letting the surprise she felt show on her features. "In Mexico you stayed out of local politics. Said you only wanted to run your hotel. You weren't interested in joining committees or getting involved with the other hoteliers or the tourist industry."

He shrugged and shifted his gaze to pass over the main street, now crowded with a few of the tourists staying at his hotel. "Everything changes."

She sighed, staring up at his profile. "Not everything," she murmured, knowing that her feelings for him would never change. Of course, she also knew that Rico wouldn't believe her even if she was foolish enough to admit to still loving him. So she kept that piece of information to herself.

"There were two boats in the harbor," she pointed out. "I mean, besides the local fishing boats."

He nodded, tucked her arm through his and started walking again. "Sometimes there are more hotel guests coming in from St. Thomas than usual."

"No cruise ships are allowed to stop here, right?"

He glanced at her. "How did you know that?"

Well, because when she found out that Rico had bought land on Tesoro with the intention of building a hotel, she'd spent a lot of time researching the island. She'd wanted at least to know what he was doing and where he would be living—even if she couldn't be with him. Which was how she had known that Melinda's grandfather owned the island outright. And that it was one of the bigger privately held islands in the Caribbean.

Walter liked keeping his island as private as possible, but he also was aware that the shopkeepers needed to make a living. So he'd compromised and allowed small ships to bring in tourists to stay in the hotel and give the islanders a steady income while at the same time protecting Tesoro from being overrun with too many people.

When she first read about him and his stubborn refusal to welcome cruise ships, she had thought the older man was shortsighted, not letting his island progress. But looking at the village now, she could appreciate his decision. She imagined these tidy streets jam-packed with crowds of people—snapping pictures, drinking too much, dropping trash on the pretty streets—and actually shuddered at the mental image. Walter had been smart to protect this place.

Now, to answer Rico's question, she hedged a little. "I read up on the island when I found out my father and brother had come here."

He scowled at her and she was sorry to see that bringing up her family had instantly soured his mood. But better that than letting him know she'd been keeping tabs on him for years.

"I admit, I was surprised that your family chose to come here for a 'job.'" Rico started walking again and Teresa kept pace. "It's a small island—thieves are spotted more easily, and, as it turns out, *caught* more easily, as well."

True, her father's ego would be bruised for years over Rico actually catching him. Police departments all around the world had been trying and failing to do it for years.

But Rico was different. As tenacious as he was, she had known that coming into contact with him again would bring disaster down on the Corettis. Which was exactly why she had warned her family off. Rico King was nobody's fool. His eyes were too sharp to miss anything and he wasn't one of those wealthy types who only occasionally stepped in to keep an eye on what belonged to him. Rico was hands-on. He would know everything happening with his properties.

Especially since he'd been robbed himself, he was on a higher alert than most people would have been.

Still, she hadn't been all that surprised when her father and brother had come to Tesoro.

"My father enjoys a challenge," she said, and couldn't help the small smile that curved her mouth. Whatever else Dominick Coretti was, he had always been a warm and loving father.

"He should try *not* stealing then," Rico told her flatly. "Give himself a real challenge."

"Don't think I haven't suggested it." Teresa lifted her face into the wind and sighed as the cool air slid past. "But…"

"Once a thief, always a thief?"

Teresa let that statement go because it was pointless to argue with him about the Coretti family business. He would never understand the centuries-old legacy that Dominick was so determined to keep alive. Teresa's worry was that her father wasn't getting any younger and perhaps his skills weren't as good as they had been once—though she would never suggest such a thing to him in person.

She didn't want to see her family in prison, though. And heaven knew the Corettis had more than enough money to retire. It wasn't, she thought, the actual stealing that her father loved so much as the adventure of having every day be a different one. Of finding a way into a heavily guarded estate. Of out-thinking security parameters and disabling electronic surveillance equipment. He *liked* pitting himself against an adversary, so thinking of a way to get her father to hang up his black gloves was going to be difficult.

That was a problem for the future, though. She only had a little more than two weeks left with Rico. She could spend that time arguing with him over the Coretti family business…or she could simply enjoy what she had while she had it.

"Oh, my." She stopped dead in front of a shop window, drawing Rico to a stop, as well. "How beautiful."

In the jewelry shop window, on a bed of black velvet, sat rings, bracelets, earrings and necklaces, all set with blue-green stones that Teresa had never seen before. They shone in the sunlight like pieces of the sea, trapped forever in settings of gold and silver. Pure avarice struck her and the Coretti legacy reared its ugly head as she curled her fingers into her palms to keep from trying to grab them all right through the glass. "They're beautiful."

"They are." Rico stood beside her, but in the reflection of the glass, she saw that he was looking at her, not the jewelry. "They're Tesoro topazes. The gemstone is found only on this island."

"So jewel prospecting is a pretty good job on this island, then?"

He laughed shortly and she suddenly found his eyes even more appealing than the glittering stones and precious metals spread out in front of her. "Occasionally a hotel guest will stumble on a find while out for a hike. But the islanders know where to look for the best stones."

"It would be fun," she mused as her gaze swung back to the shop window. "Like a treasure hunt."

"The jewelry you see here is Melinda's work," he said after Teresa spent another minute or two practically drooling on the glass.

"Melinda?" Teresa looked at him.

"She makes the jewelry and it's sold here."

"She's incredibly talented," Teresa murmured. "And I think I'm more than a little envious."

"On the other hand," Rico told her, capturing her hand in his again, "you are a chef and Melinda is a miserable cook. So for survival's sake, I would choose your gifts over hers."

A flush of pride and pleasure filled her and just for a second or two she allowed herself to fully enjoy the look in his eyes and the warmth of his hand in hers. But even as she watched, the gleam in his eyes faded slightly. So she spoke up and kept her tone light.

"Well, then," Teresa said with a half smile. "Guess it would be pointless to buy her that lovely bracelet as a new-mom present. I mean, since she made it."

"True." He pulled her hand through the crook of his arm and steered her along the street after she gave one last look at the shop window. "When Sean and Melinda became engaged, he bought her a ring and only later found out that she had made it herself."

Teresa laughed at the image and enjoyed the fact that just for now, they were smiling together. Taking a walk, enjoying the day, as if reality had taken the day off. It was almost as it had been five years ago. But, of course, it couldn't last.

When Rico's cell phone rang, she felt a quick flash

of annoyance. Just when things were going so well. She stopped and waited as he glanced at the screen.

"It is the hotel," he said, then answered it. "Yes?"

His gaze shot to hers and Teresa was disappointed to see his easy expression drain away to be replaced with the cold, cautious one she'd become so accustomed to.

"What is it?" Her voice was as resigned as she felt.

"A phone call," he said. "From your father. The hotel is forwarding it to my cell."

"My father?" She hadn't heard from her father since the day he left. Mainly because Rico had commandeered her cell phone—no doubt so she couldn't make escape plans. She took the phone from him and tried not to worry at what might have happened to make her father call. "Papa?"

"Bellissima, are you all right?" Nick's voice was hurried, anxious. "I have not heard from you and when I try to call your cell, I get only your answering machine."

"I, um, lost my phone," she said, with a quick look at Rico, who only seemed amused. Yes, she'd lied *again*. But she couldn't very well tell her father that Rico had commandeered her phone to ensure that she didn't call her family to plot an escape.

"Good, good. I am glad you are all right. This King person, he is treating you well?"

"I'm fine, Papa. Rico has been very…" She paused and caught his eyes. One black eyebrow lifted, as if he was waiting to see exactly what she would tell her father about their time together. "…*kind*."

He snorted.

Her father only muttered something in Italian that she thought it was better Rico hadn't heard. Then he spoke again.

"When this is all over, *cara,* you will tell me all about how you could marry this man without telling your papa."

"I will," she promised, though she knew that conversation wouldn't be a pleasant one. No man wanted to hear that his daughter had been so swept away by passion that marrying a man she hardly knew had seemed like the rational thing to do.

"But for now," her father continued, "there is a small *problema, mi cara.*"

"Problem?" she repeated for Rico's benefit, and his scowl deepened accordingly. "What's wrong?"

Her father huffed out a breath. "We cannot find Gianni," he admitted finally. "He, too, is not answering his phone—why do my children plague me with machines they do not bother to use?—and he has not been in touch with us. He is not here in Italy and no one has seen him in weeks."

Her brother could be anywhere in the world. If he didn't want to be found, no one would be able to locate him. But why wasn't he answering his phone? It wasn't like him to simply disappear without telling the family when he would be back.

There were only two weeks left in Rico's ultimatum, and if Gianni didn't return Rico's dagger at the end of the month...the Coretti family would end up in jail. As to what Rico would do with *her,* she couldn't even guess.

"Did you try reaching him at his apartment in London?" she asked, keeping her gaze now firmly away from Rico's.

"*Si, si.* Of course we tried. Paulo is traveling, trying to run Gianni to ground." He sounded completely disgusted with the whole situation. "Paulo is in Monaco right now. If he finds Gianni there, he will call me immediately. I am going to Gstaad. He had a woman there last year and perhaps…"

That was the trouble with having a wandering family. They all had connections all over the world. Gianni could be anywhere. But the fact that he wasn't answering his phone had Teresa more than a little worried. What if he had been arrested somewhere? What if he was right now sitting in a jail cell and *couldn't* call?

She chewed at her bottom lip as she considered the possibilities. Then she realized that if one of the Coretti family had been arrested, it would have made all of the news programs. So clearly Gianni wasn't in jail. So where, exactly, was he?

"Papa, if you can't find him in Switzerland," she said, "call Simone in Paris. She might know where he is."

"Ah, of course!" Her father sounded joyful at the suggestion. "Simone and Gianni…" And off he went again in fluent, musical Italian.

Teresa stole a glance at Rico and was sorry she had. He didn't look happy. His blue eyes were almost cobalt and a muscle in his tightly clenched jaw twitched with his effort to control his anger.

"You will be well, *bellissima*," her father said when he had wound down. "All will be taken care of. But we *might* need a little more time…"

Oh, no. "Hold on, Papa."

Taking a breath, she covered the phone with her hand and spoke to the man glowering beside her. "Paulo and my father are having a hard time finding Gianni," she explained.

"He's the one who took my dagger?"

"Yes," she said shortly. "And it seems he's disappeared, at least *temporarily.* They're looking for him, but Papa says they might need a little more time and—"

Shaking his head, he snatched his phone from her and said tightly, "Signore Coretti. You have no more time. There are two weeks left. If my dagger is not returned, the evidence I hold goes to Interpol."

She could hear her father's loud blustering and his shouted demand, "And what of Teresa? What happens to my little girl?"

She held her breath, waiting for the answer to that question. Rico's gaze met hers and she saw no softening in those cold blue depths. No warmth on his features when he said, "She will no longer be your concern. As she is my *wife,* I decide what will happen."

He shut off the phone and dropped it into his shirt pocket. Looking down at her, he repeated, "Two weeks, Teresa."

"And then?"

"We will see when the time comes." He took her hand in his, but it wasn't a comforting grip. More like a jailer's hold on a flight risk. "For now, let us go to the chocolatier for Melinda's gift."

She followed after him because she had no choice. But the truth was, she'd have followed him anyway.

There were only two weeks left. And whatever his plan for Teresa entailed, she knew it didn't include staying with him.

So while her family panicked and searched the globe for Gianni…Teresa was going to try to enjoy the moments she had left with the only man she'd ever love.

Ten

Two days later, Rico arrived home earlier than usual.

Ever since that phone call from Dominick, there'd been new tension between him and Teresa. It was as if they both realized that time was running out and neither of them knew quite how it would end.

Over the last couple of weeks so much had changed between them that Rico wasn't comfortable with his old plan of revenge and payback. Now he was more focused on Teresa herself and what they might have found together. Though the complication of the Corettis still stood between them.

He knew she was worried about her family. Anxious at the thought of her brothers and father going to prison. And yes, he knew that it was his threats that had brought them all to this point.

The difference was that now he hated to see her on

edge. Hated knowing that it was because of *him* that she had to fear for her family. And he really hated that he was falling under her spell again.

He couldn't trust her, but that didn't seem to matter. Old feelings were back and they were growing into something even bigger than they'd once been.

Scrubbing one hand across his face and then shoving that hand through his hair, he tried to find a way through this mess of his own design. But there was nothing. He had backed himself into a corner.

Moving quietly through his darkened house, he headed unerringly for the bedroom where Teresa would be waiting for him. A sharp tug of pleasure dragged at the edges of his heart at the knowledge. Oh, he was in deep trouble.

His steps faltered as he heard low-pitched voices—one of them a man's—coming from his bedroom. Rico went instantly still. Someone was in his bedroom, with Teresa. What the hell? She wasn't screaming for help, which only fed the flames of suspicion burning inside. On alert now, he eased closer to the partially closed door and peered inside.

Everything in him urged Rico to charge into that room and find out who the mystery bastard was. But this time his mind won over his instincts. He had to know what was going on and if he slammed in, the hurried conversation would end. So instead he moved closer and listened.

"Bastien, you have to *go*," Teresa said, her voice hurried, yet determined.

"Not without you." The man's voice was deep and adamant.

Rico's blood rushed to his head and he curled his fists at his sides. But before he could give in to the jealousy pouring through him as though from a tap turned on full blast, Rico peered into the room and saw an older man, dressed all in black. His gray mustache covered half his face and his bushy gray brows were wiry.

So, not a romantic encounter.

"Your father sent me to get you away," the man insisted, tossing a nervous glance over his shoulder at the open terrace doors. "He cannot find Gianni or the dagger."

Teresa sighed. "My brother wasn't in Paris, either?"

"No." The old man lowered his voice even further, but his insistence was sharp. "We are still looking, but your father does not wish you to stay with this man— your husband—any longer. He worries for your safety."

Rico scowled at the door. As if he was a danger to Teresa? Insult slammed into him but was buried deep as he waited for her reply.

"Tell my father I'm safe, Bastien. And I can't leave the island."

"*Si,* you can. I have a fishing boat waiting at the harbor." The older man reached out and took her hand. "From the mainland, we board the plane your father has waiting. It will take us to him."

Anger flared so bright and hot, Rico could hardly see. Teeth clenched, his jaw muscles felt tight enough to snap. He could already feel what would happen next. Teresa was going to do it again. She would run to save her family. She would break her word and disappear. Again.

He took a step forward, intending to stop her before she got one step outside his house, but he halted suddenly when Teresa spoke.

"You don't understand, Bastien," she said, words tumbling from her in a rush. "I *won't* leave. I gave my word to Rico and I won't break it. Not again. He's my husband

and I...*care* for him. I won't hurt him by disappearing one more time, Bastien. I agreed to stay here for a month and I'm going to."

Rico laid one hand on the doorjamb to steady himself. His world had just been rocked. Teresa had shocked him straight to the bone. She cared for him. *Love?* Did she still love him? While he stood there outside the room, something flickered to life in the center of his chest. Warmth filled him along with the territorial urge to go to her, hold her tightly to him and sweep her into bed, where he would damn well *keep* her for the rest of their time together.

He shifted position slightly so he could see Teresa better. Her long, thick hair was pulled back into a ponytail at the back of her neck. She was wearing the dark green nightgown he loved to strip from her, with a short white robe over it, loosely belted at her waist. Her long, tanned legs were bare and planted wide apart as if in a fighting stance. But it was the expression on her face that caught and held his attention. She looked...fierce. She was defying her father's attempt at a rescue. In favor of Rico.

This time she had chosen *him*.

"Your father will not be happy." The older man was speaking again.

"My father is the one who taught me that once your word is given, it is sacred," Teresa told him. "I won't cheat Rico. Tell my father to find Gianni. He still has two weeks to bring the dagger here."

Through the anger at Dominick's duplicity rose a new and unexpected feeling inside Rico. Trust. That warmth rushing through him was enveloping as he watched the woman who was his wife. And though he warned himself to be wary, he knew that something between them had shifted tonight.

Gathering together the threads of his anger, Rico pushed the door open and stepped into the room. Both Teresa and the older man whipped around to face him. She looked stunned and embarrassed. The man she'd called Bastien just looked worried. As he should.

"Get out," Rico said, voice tight with the effort of holding on to the anger churning in his gut.

The man didn't need to be told twice. He scuttled for the terrace doors and only stopped at the threshold when Rico spoke up again.

"Leave the island tonight," he advised. "If I see you here tomorrow I'll have you arrested for trespassing."

One bob of the man's head told Rico he was understood. In another second, the man was gone and he and Teresa were alone in the room.

"I can explain," she said quickly.

"You don't have to." Rico looked down at her and felt that rush of warmth again. She was beautiful. She was proud and defiant and she was his. For now, anyway. "I heard everything before I came in. Your father sent him."

She blew out a breath before lifting her chin high enough that she met his gaze. "Yes. Bastien is a family friend. Sort of an honorary uncle, I guess."

"Uh-huh." Despite everything, he felt a quick flash of irritation for Nick Coretti. Yet how could he blame the man for trying to save his daughter? Rico or any of the Kings would have done the same for one of their family. Though it burned that the older man had almost put one over on him. Would have, if Teresa hadn't chosen to stay.

"So your father arranged this *escape*."

"He's worried about me," Teresa told him with a heavy

sigh of frustration mingled with exasperation. "He can't find Gianni or the dagger."

"Are you certain that it is *you* he's worried about?" he asked. "Or is he more concerned with the idea that he and his sons are going to prison?"

She flushed and a spark of anger lit her eyes briefly. "Of course he's thinking about that, too. But sending Bastien was about *me*."

Scowling, Rico said, "Maybe. But it was a foolish thing to do."

He pulled his phone from his pocket, handed it to her and said, "Call him."

She took a deep breath and held it. Then she punched in her father's number and listened to it ring. "Papa?" She flicked a glance at Rico. "Yes, Bastien was here. I wouldn't go with him."

Rico heard the older man's shout and almost smiled. He, too, hated it when a plan fell apart. As his own plan concerning Teresa had, he thought grimly. But he'd consider that and the ramifications later. For now...

"Let me talk to him." He held out one hand and waited until Teresa slapped the phone onto his palm. Dominick was still shouting at his daughter when Rico interrupted him.

"Do not try something like that again," he warned, holding Teresa's gaze while he listened to Nick Coretti sputter.

"She is my daughter. I want her safe," Nick said finally.

"I understand that," Rico told him, and he meant it. He would do whatever he had to do to keep a member of *his* family safe. But that didn't mean he was going to let Nick off the hook. "Teresa is safe with me. But if you try to get her off the island again, I'll make sure you and your sons are locked up forever."

The man on the other end of the line was quiet for a long moment, then said, "Agreed."

"Good." Rico looked into Teresa's eyes and added for both her and her father's benefit, "I am a man of my word. At the end of the month, once I have my dagger, I'll hand over the evidence I hold."

"And," Nick said firmly, "you will release my daughter."

He should. It was part of the deal he'd made. Not to mention the fact that he had spent the last five years working to get his errant wife out of his mind and heart. But now, looking at Teresa, Rico knew that he couldn't let her go.

Yes, he'd given his word. But he couldn't, *wouldn't* let Teresa leave him and disappear again. She was a part of him. A part of his life here on the island and without her…no.

It was unthinkable. But he couldn't very well say that to her father. So instead he said only, "We made a deal. I will stick to it—as you should."

He ended the call and felt the world beneath his feet tilt precariously. All his life Rico had done his best to be a man of his word. To avoid lies and deception. And now the only way he could get out of a bargain he had struck was to break every one of his personal rules.

Which meant he had to find another way out of this.

"He's scared," Teresa said as explanation, dragging him out of his thoughts and back to the present.

"I know." He reached for her before he could stop himself, cupping her cheek in the palm of his hand. "Any father would be. What I want to hear is why you didn't go with Bastien."

She was silent for a few seconds, as if she was considering just how to say what she needed to say. Finally she said quietly, "Five years ago, I made the choice I thought I had to. But tonight I didn't want to repeat the same mistake."

He stiffened slightly, as he always did when reminded of that time five years past. He'd shut her down whenever she had tried to tell him about the night she had left. He hadn't wanted to hear this before, but now he needed to. Rico had to know why she'd left him. Why she'd run— so he could believe that she wouldn't do the same now.

The bedroom was cool and dimly lit from the moonlight pouring in through the open terrace doors and the twin bedside lamps casting golden light across the bed and floor.

"Tell me." His words were short and clipped, but they seemed to release her from a tension that had coiled inside her for too long.

When her eyes met his again, they were damp, looking like gold coins drenched in water. If her tears spilled over, it would tear at his heart, he knew. Rico steadied himself, then took her hand and led her to the bed. Sitting down, he drew her with him and repeated, "Tell me."

"I'm glad you're finally willing to listen."

"I wasn't ready before," he told her. "I am now."

Nodding, Teresa tried to smile, but gave that up quickly. "All right, but first you have to know that when I was eighteen, I told my father that I wasn't going to be a thief. That I wanted a different kind of life."

He hadn't expected to hear that and as he thought about it, he laughed shortly.

She glared at him.

"Sorry," he muttered. "I was just imagining how your father must have taken that decision."

A reluctant smile curved her mouth. "Not well. He was horrified. And disappointed. But in the end, though he didn't understand my decision, he respected it."

Rico silently gave Nick Coretti half a point of admiration for backing off and giving his daughter the room she needed to grow her own way. Not that he was willing to forgive the old thief or anything.

"I took that job at your hotel," she said, starting off slowly, her soft voice hesitant, as if she wasn't sure how to put it now that he'd given her the chance. "And I asked my family to stay away." She smiled wryly. "Usually they did as I asked, not wanting to bring down suspicion on me in a place where I happened to be working. But that was before I took a job with Rico King."

She shook her head and caught his eyes again. "The temptation was too much. The richness of your guests at the Castello de King was enough of a draw all on its own, but there was more. They knew about your dagger. There had been some piece written about it—"

Rico remembered that. Someone had done an interview with him for a national magazine article on the Cancún Castello and during the meeting the reporter had seen the Aztec dagger in a case on his desk. There had been questions and photos and apparently that had been enough to attract the attention of professional thieves.

He hadn't worried about it at the time, because his security at the hotel was top-of-the-line. But the Corettis, he was discovering, were very worthy adversaries. "I remember that article. Go on."

She nodded and threaded her fingers together in her

lap, restlessly tugging at them until he laid one hand on top of hers to hold her still.

"My oldest brother, Gianni, loves antiquities. He couldn't resist the lure of that dagger and where he went, so did my father and Paulo." She looked up at him again and held on to his hand tightly. "I swear I didn't know they were going to hit the hotel until after it was done."

Staring into those wide-open, pale brown eyes shining with misery and regret, he could only nod. Rico believed her. But then, if he hadn't been in such pain over losing her, he would have believed her long ago.

Satisfied, she kept talking. "When you discovered the dagger missing, I just…had a feeling. Then you contacted the police and were vowing to hunt down the thieves no matter what it took."

He remembered that, too. His fury at being robbed. The crushing need to retrieve something his father had passed on to him.

"While you were with the police, I searched through the guest register and found my family under one of their more familiar assumed names."

Familiar. Assumed. She had grown up quite differently than he had. Now he saw that lying, to Teresa, had been second nature. Just the way things were done. And he had to admire her for breaking away from the only life she had ever known. What kind of strength was that, to turn your back on your family? Your legacy?

"Gianni was already gone with the dagger," she was saying and Rico came out of his thoughts to listen to the rest of the story.

"My father and Paulo were packing." She winced. "They had already sent what they'd taken from your guests by overnight mail to our home in London."

And those, Rico told himself, were diamonds, rubies and emeralds that would never see the light of day again. *At least,* he told himself wryly, *not in their original settings.*

"I begged my father to call Gianni, to get him to return the dagger, but it was too late. My brother had boarded a plane right after—" She broke off.

"Right after stealing from me," Rico finished for her.

"Yes. There was no way to reach him and I'm not sure I would have been able to convince him to return the dagger even if I could have talked to him." She sighed and shook her head, pulling one hand from his to push a stray lock of hair behind her ear. "Maybe if I had confessed that we were married—" she mused. "But I just couldn't do it. You were furious, I knew I would have to leave you and there wasn't a point in telling my family and hurting my father over a marriage that would be ending anyway."

He gritted his teeth and she saw him fight for control. When he finally found it, he spoke again. "This explains the robbery," Rico said quietly. "And why you didn't tell your family about us. It does not tell me why you ran from me. Why you chose them over what we had together."

She pulled in one long, shuddering breath and slid off the bed to stand up. Facing him, she wrapped her arms around her middle, accidentally opening the fall of her robe, giving Rico a glimpse of luscious, tanned skin and the tops of her breasts beneath her nightgown. He had to force himself to focus on what she was saying.

"I left my father and Paulo packing and went back to our suite. Do you remember how you were? What you were saying?"

"No," he said. All he recalled clearly was the helpless

anger that had had him in a choke hold, strangling him with a sense of helplessness that no King could accept.

"I do," she said softly. "You told me that if it was the last thing you ever did, you would hunt down those thieves. You would see them in prison for a lifetime." She tightened her grip around her middle and held on as if clutching a lifeline in a choppy sea. "You said you would do whatever it took. That you and I would find them. Together. Then you asked if I had seen anything, heard anything unusual around the hotel."

"And you lied to me."

"Yes." She swallowed hard and nodded. "I lied. To protect my family."

"Why, Teresa?" he asked, though he already knew the answer. Her father. Her brothers. Her connection with them ran deep. Perhaps deeper than the link she had had with a new husband and the promise of a future too vague to be real.

"Because I couldn't help you track them down, Rico. I couldn't do what you needed me to do, but I couldn't stay and *not* help you, either. I would have been living a lie every day, praying that you wouldn't discover my secret." She shook her head so wildly her ponytail swung behind her head like a pendulum. "It was a disaster. Any choice I made, I hurt someone I loved. I didn't want to lie to you, but I thought that *one* lie was better than a lifetime of them."

"You should have told me," he said, pushing up from the bed to lay both hands on her shoulders. "You should have trusted me."

She laughed now and the sound wasn't musical at all. It was like shards of glass being ground under steel wheels.

"Trusted you? I should have told you that the thieves were my family and please don't prosecute?"

He frowned at her as her words resonated inside him.

"Would you have believed that I had nothing to do with the theft?" she demanded, all traces of tears gone from her eyes now, replaced by sparks of rising temper. "The first thing you said to me when you found me here was that you thought I had married you only to give my family access to your blasted dagger."

Now it was his turn to feel a rush of shame. Yes, he had convinced himself years ago that Teresa had only married him to help her family's thieving. But that had never made sense and he'd known it even while he'd allowed the thought to drive him insane. The Corettis were, if nothing else, *excellent* thieves. They didn't need to use Teresa. They'd gotten past his security and out of the country almost before he'd known he'd been hit.

No, blaming Teresa had been his pride talking. The wound she'd left when she disappeared had festered until that convenient lie he'd told himself had simply been a way of deflecting the truth.

That she'd chosen another over him.

"You're right," he said, his voice hardly more than a hush.

She blinked at him and shook her head. "Excuse me?"

One corner of his mouth lifted briefly. Of course she would be surprised. He hadn't given her any reason to think he would be on her side in *any* argument.

"I said, you are right. I would have accused you. I would have been wrong, though." He slid his hands up to hold her face between his palms. His gaze bored into hers as he willed her to believe him. "I know you weren't a part of it. And I can even understand a little now why you made the choice you did."

She huffed out a breath. "Thank you."

"But I need to know why you chose differently tonight, Teresa."

Leaning into him, she said solemnly, "Because I didn't want to hurt you again, Rico. Because this time *you* were more important. This time I had to trust you."

"Good answer," he murmured and bent down to kiss her. He'd meant only to plant a brief, hard kiss on her lips.

But at the moment of contact, Teresa wrapped her arms around him and held on. She opened her mouth and tangled her tongue with his and they were linked, as they were meant to be, always.

Rico groaned and held her tighter. Lifting her off her feet, he turned back to the bed, laid her down and then lay down beside her. Rising up on one elbow, he looked down into golden-brown eyes. Then he kissed her again and lost himself in the arms of the only woman in the world who held his heart.

Rico met Sean for lunch at a small restaurant near the harbor. It had been two days since Teresa had turned down a chance at escape. Two days since she had chosen *him* over her family. He liked knowing that she was on his side in this, but he had to wonder how long that would last if her family didn't return the dagger.

Because if that happened, he would go through with his threat. He would hand over all of the evidence he'd collected over the last several years to Interpol. And once he did that, he would lose Teresa. How could he expect her to stay with the man who had imprisoned her family? No, he knew damn well she would never forgive him for that.

And if they *did* deliver the dagger as promised, then he would have to hold up his end of the bargain and not only release Teresa, but divorce her, as well. He couldn't keep her here without going back on his word and couldn't let her go without losing a piece of his soul.

Time was ticking past. With every beat of his heart, that internal clock moved on, pushing them toward the end of the month. Toward the end of his time with Teresa.

He couldn't stand that thought.

This month had started out with him holding her against her will, yes. But that had changed, hadn't it? She didn't act like a hostage—with the run of the island, working in the hotel kitchen, coming to his bed eagerly. Whatever it was that was still humming between them, it was something that would die the moment he sent her family to prison.

"You look like hell." Sean sat back in his chair and sipped at a bottle of beer.

"Thank you. It is good to have family to turn to in times of trouble." Rico picked up his own beer and took a long swallow, hoping to ease the knot in his throat. It didn't work. "How are Melinda and Stryker?"

Sean's grin lit up his face. "Great. Seriously great." He shook his head. "The baby's keeping us both up all night, every night, but I don't even mind. Right now I'm like a zombie, but I've never had so much fun."

A pang of envy rippled through Rico, but he ignored it. No point in wishing for things that weren't going to happen. *Unless,* a voice in his mind whispered, *Teresa is already pregnant. Then your problems are over, aren't*

*they? You stay married. You keep her with you. And you
have the family you've always craved.*

He straightened in his chair as that nebulous idea took
root in his mind.

"So." Sean spoke up and Rico came out of his thoughts.
"You said you wanted to talk. What's going on?"

"That is a question with too many answers."

"Pick one."

"I am trying to decide what to do about Teresa."

"Ah," Sean said, smothering a laugh. "The brilliant
plan falling apart? Wow. Wish I'd seen that coming. Oh.
Wait. I *did*."

Rico sneered at his cousin. "Very helpful, thank you.
There is nothing better than an *I told you so* at just the
right moment."

"Happy to help." Sean reached for a nacho loaded with
beans and cheese, then popped it into his mouth, crunch-
ing with a grin on his face.

"Right." He should have known his cousin would love
this. A King liked nothing better than an entertaining "I
was right, you were wrong" chat. Shaking his head, he
leaned forward, bracing his arms on the glass-topped
table. The bright yellow table umbrella shaded them from
the noonday sun and all around them hotel guests were
either boarding day boats for fishing trips or sitting at
the bar having tropical drinks. "Her father hired a man
to help her escape. Seems he hasn't found her brother yet
and he wants more time."

"Escape? Okay, I'm guessing she didn't go anywhere,
yes?"

"She stayed." Rico took a sip of his beer. "She wouldn't
leave."

"Interesting." Sean smiled, then narrowed his eyes.

"Aside from the failed rescue, do you think her father's stalling deliberately?"

"It's possible," Rico admitted, thinking back to the sound of Dominick Coretti's outraged voice. "But I don't know that he would take this kind of risk with his family. So if I assume he really does need the extra time, what do I do about it?"

"What do you want to do?"

Rico sent his cousin an exasperated glare. "If I knew that, would I be asking for your opinion?"

Sean laughed. "Okay, no. I'm no fan of Teresa's family—they're thieves." He shrugged. "But you locking up her family isn't going to score you points with her, either."

"Yes, I know that, as well." Talking to his cousin was supposed to help him straighten out his thoughts.

"So go with your gut, Rico." Sean was still smiling. "You want Teresa. She wants her family safe. Do what you have to do to make everyone happy."

"Let the thieves go free?"

"It's family, man," Sean said, smile fading into a thoughtful frown. "Look at the Kings. What haven't we been willing to do to keep family safe?"

He was right, Rico knew. And the answer, it seemed, was simple after all. A King would risk anything for family. And Teresa—not to mention the child she might be carrying—was his family.

Eleven

Another week of her month was gone and Teresa felt as though she was listening to the inexorable tick of a countdown in her head. Every morning she woke up beside Rico and every evening the heat between them sizzled anew. And every day gone was one less that she had with him.

Sitting on a chaise on the beach below Rico's house, Teresa curled her feet up under her on the floral cushion. She swept her gaze across Rico's private slice of the Tesoro paradise and sighed. A yacht was docked at Rico's private pier and the brass fittings winked in the bright sunlight. "Oh, God, I don't want to leave."

She loved it here. Loved the easy, relaxed way of life on the island. She loved having the wild beauty surrounding her wherever she went. She loved working in the hotel and she'd already made some good friends here. The hotel staff, Sean and Melinda.

But mostly she loved being with Rico. For so long she'd yearned to be with him again and now it was as if she was living in a perfect dream world.

But the sad part about dreams was that eventually you woke up and the dream shattered.

A wind off the ocean buffeted her, waves crashed against the shore, sending spray into the air, and Rico's boat creaked noisily as it rose and fell with the surging sea. Out on the horizon, dark clouds gathered, promising a coming storm, and birds in the tree behind her chattered as if in warning.

The wind kicked up, sending grains of sand stinging into her skin like tiny bullets. She hardly noticed since the pain around her heart went so much deeper.

What was she going to do without Rico in her life?

"I was looking for you."

His deep voice coming from right behind her didn't surprise Teresa. It was as if she'd conjured Rico out of thin air just by thinking about him. She hoped it would work that well in the coming years, but somehow she doubted it.

"You weren't worried, were you?" She tipped her head back and shaded her eyes with one hand. "I thought I already proved to you that I'm not going to leave the island before the end of the month."

He sank into a crouch beside her and reached out one hand to tuck her hair behind her ear. That one slight touch sent shivers of anticipation rattling through her body. He gave her a half smile and shook his head.

"You did," he said with a nod. "You gave me your word. I wasn't worried. I just wanted to see if you'd like to take a ride around the island."

His hair blew in the ever-present wind, the white shirt

he wore was open at the throat and the sleeves were rolled up. His black jeans looked worn and comfortable. He was also barefoot and, for some reason, that only heightened his sex appeal. The man was a walking orgasm.

"With you?"

He gave her another half smile. "No. With Sean."

"Funny." She nodded, held out one hand to him and let him help her up from the chair.

For the last week, Rico had been attentive, seductive and *romantic* in a way she hadn't experienced since they were first together. Every day he had a new adventure for the two of them. They had spent one day out on his yacht, alternately swimming in the ocean and climbing aboard to dry off and make love. They'd had a romantic seaside dinner in the village and finished the evening off by dancing in the moonlight. One day he had even taken her treasure hunting for Tesoro topazes.

There had been picnics on the beach and lazy swings in the hammock. Long walks and sitting together at night in front of a fire built more for romance than warmth.

It had been a perfect week. Perfect in ways that made her miserable to think of losing Rico forever. But in all the time they had spent together, not once had he talked about the possibility of her staying. Not once had he hinted he *wanted* her to stay. And not once had he said that he didn't want the divorce he had promised her.

So though she was being romanced, she had finally figured out that Rico was simply saying goodbye to her. A long, drawn-out, incredibly sweet and romantic goodbye.

And that broke her heart.

Still, she wouldn't let him see that she knew what he was doing. Wouldn't let him know that her heart ached to be with him. That the thought of leaving made her feel as though she had been hollowed out and left an empty shell.

If he could make these last few days together special, then the least she could do was join him in the pretense. There would be plenty of time later for the tears that seemed to be constantly near the surface. So for now she smiled up at him and let him see only the pleasure she felt at being beside him. "Are we going in a car or on your boat?"

"For what I want to show you, we'll have to take the car."

"I'd love to."

She bent to pick up her sandals and then followed him from the beach and across the manicured lawn to the driveway in front of his home. A small red sports car sat in the shade of several trees, waiting for them.

Once they were in the car and buckled in, Rico fired up the engine and steered the car out of the driveway and down to the main road. But instead of heading toward the hotel and the village, he turned left and sped along the narrow, paved road.

"You've been here nearly three weeks," he said, his voice carrying over the growl of the engine. "And I thought you might like to see the rest of the island."

Before you go.

He didn't say it, but he didn't have to. She knew exactly what he meant. A bubble of pain opened up in the center of her chest, but Teresa fought it down. Being here with Rico was too nice to spoil with thoughts of what was going to happen all too soon.

"Thanks. I would."

She'd seen a lot of Tesoro from his boat and he had taken her to the foot of the hills to search for topaz. But there was still so much she hadn't seen. Still so much she hadn't done. Leaving tore at her and she turned away from him so he wouldn't see the sorrow in her eyes.

Instead, she looked at the landscape as they passed. As they got farther from the village and the hotel and Rico's house, the land changed, shifted. Stands of jungle were so thick the trees looked like a solid green wall. Even the sunlight barely made it through the leafy foliage. It was like driving through a green tunnel. Then they emerged into the light again and Teresa gasped at the beauty spreading out on either side of the car. Meadows with wildflowers dancing in the breeze. Patches of farmland, even a small vineyard. And at the edge of the island, a beach with sand so white it hurt the eyes to look at it and the ocean beyond.

"It's so gorgeous here." She leaned in to Rico to make sure he heard her.

He grinned, whipping his hair back from his face as he turned to smile at her. "It is. And what I'm going to show you now will take your breath away."

That happened just looking at him, Teresa thought. But she was so glad to see pleasure in his eyes, in the easy curve of his mouth, she only said, "I'm ready."

He laughed and stepped on the gas, sending the little red car hurtling along the road at a speed that brought a laugh from her throat.

The road wound on and Teresa hoped the ride would never end. She could spend eternity like this, she told herself. Beside Rico, off on an adventure together, with the wind in their hair and the sun on their faces. But eventually Rico pulled the car over and turned the engine off.

She looked around and saw a wall of rock spilling

down into a patch of trees that looked cool and shad-owed. "Where are we?"

"You'll see." He got out of the car, came around to her side and opened the door. "Just leave your sandals here. You won't need them."

Then, taking her hand, he led her into the cool shade of the stand of trees. Birds sang, the wind blew and under it all, she heard the steady roar of the ocean. But as Rico led her on, her bare feet making no sound on the sandy ground, that roar became louder and she noticed it didn't have the sighing rhythm that she'd become used to. "What is that?"

He looked at her and grinned. "One moment and you'll see for yourself."

Using a series of timeworn rocks as steps, he led her down a narrow path through the trees. The roaring sound was even louder now and Teresa thought she knew what to expect. She was only half-right.

Stepping out into a clearing, she saw the waterfall she'd guessed was their destination. But she hadn't been prepared for the sheer beauty of the place. It was de-serted. Private. Water spilled from a rock overhang into a pond below that then drained down into a river whose twists and turns were swallowed by the jungle surround-ing them.

Trees shielded the pond from most of the sunlight. Grass and vines clung to the rock face on either side of the waterfall itself, and the surface of the pond below frothed with the power of the surging water slamming into it.

He smiled at the expression on her face, then turned and led the way along the rocks until they reached the pond.

"This is so beautiful," she said, looking up at him. "Thank you for bringing me here."

His smile faded slowly as he looked at her. "I wanted to see it with you. It's too far out from the hotels and the village for many of the tourists to know about. And most of the locals don't come here." He turned his gaze on the waterfall and the surrounding beauty before looking back at her. "So it's where I come when I want to be alone with my thoughts."

And he'd brought her here. Shared this with her. Her heart was touched and broken all at once. Who would he share his secrets with when she was gone? How would she bear it, knowing that one day he'd leave her memory behind and move on for good with some other woman?

"Teresa?" His brow furrowed and he set both hands at her waist. "Are you all right?"

No. "Yes. I'm fine." She nodded, plastering a smile she didn't feel on her face. "I should have brought a bathing suit."

His eyes flashed and his lips curved in a wicked, completely tempting smile. "Here you won't need one."

A swirl of excitement fluttered to life in the pit of her belly and she went with it. As Rico undressed, so did she, and in a few short seconds, they were jumping into the pool at the base of the waterfall, swimming toward the curtain of water dropping from the overhang.

She hooked her arms around Rico's neck and pressed close to him, loving the feel of his skin against hers. The cold, clear water fell over and around them, sealing them into a bubble of privacy that seemed to lock the rest of the world away. Here it was only the two of them. And that was just as she wanted it.

When he kissed her, Teresa gave him everything she

had, everything she was. She poured her heart into the
kiss and hoped he could feel her love in her touch.

His hand dropped to her core and slowly rubbed her
center until she was writhing in his arms. The cold water
on her skin and the heat he engendered with his touch
combined to make Teresa feel as if she were about to
splinter. And when her climax hit, she clung to him, their
mouths fused, their breath sliding from one to the other
and just for that perfect moment, they were *one*.

Much later, after making love in a patch of sun-
warmed grass, the two of them lay sprawled together
beside the waterfall. The roar of the water was the only
sound and Teresa was torn between sheer happiness and
the grief of knowing that all too soon this time with her
husband would end.

"What will you do when the month is up?"

She tipped her head back to look up at him. "I don't
know. Go back to my apartment in Naples, I suppose."

Features grim, he nodded and said, "I've been thinking about this, as well, Teresa."

"Really?" Was he going to ask her to stay? Could he
put aside what had happened between them five years
ago and allow for a future? Hope, that treacherous little
beast, jumped up and down inside her.

"Yes." He went up on one elbow and looked down at
her. All trace of the romantic was gone from his expression. His features were drawn and tight and the hope inside her withered a bit in response.

This couldn't be good.

"I've been thinking that you should not leave the island."

And just like that, hope was back. She smiled up at

him and felt the strangling knots around her heart loosen a little for the first time in years.

"You want me to stay?" *Please say yes.*

"Yes," he said. "At least until we know if you are pregnant."

This was why she rarely allowed hope to inflate inside her like an oversize balloon. Because when the inevitable happened and that balloon popped, the fall back to reality was a crushing one.

Rico didn't want her. He wanted the child they might have made together. So much for fresh chances. For starting over. He couldn't let go of the past and she couldn't change it for him, so they were at a standstill.

"That's why you want me here," she said, for her own benefit more than his. She needed to hear herself say it. "Because I might be pregnant."

"You will admit, there is a good chance you are." He laid one hand against her flat abdomen as if already claiming the child that *might* be inside her. "And if you are, you will stay here. With me. No divorce."

She pushed away from him and scrambled to her feet. Looking down on the gorgeous man sprawled naked in the sunshine, she felt only disappointment. Regret. And a deep, bone-searing sorrow that would probably be with her for the rest of her life.

"But the only way you want me is if I'm pregnant." God, it cost her to say those words.

"I did not say that," he countered, coming to his feet in a slow, languid movement.

"You really didn't have to," she muttered, pushing her still-damp hair back from her face with both hands. "God, I'm an idiot."

"Teresa? Surely you see that we are good together. Staying married wouldn't be a hardship on either of us."

His tone was so reasonable. The look on his face so patient. Teresa wanted to scream.

Shaking her head, she reached for her clothes and tugged them on while she talked. "No, Rico. I won't be part of a marriage that's described as *not a hardship.*"

"You are deliberately misconstruing what I said."

"I don't think so," she countered, shooting him a quick glare while she hopped on one foot to pull on her shorts. "I think you said just what you meant."

He got dressed too, but with more casual, easy movements than she managed. "You are overreacting."

"Really?" She hooked her bra and then grabbed her shirt. Pulling it on, too, she asked, "Then what would your reaction be if I asked you to forget about prosecuting my family?"

He went still as stone, his pale blue eyes fixed on her, looking like chips of ice.

"Could you let them go?" She already knew the answer but she had to hear him say it.

Then he surprised her. Again.

"If I let them go," he said shortly, his voice as cool as the gleam in his eyes, "what do I get out of it?"

She threw her hair back out of her eyes. "I'll stay with you."

"For how long?"

This cost her. Humiliation flushed her cheeks as she realized she was blackmailing her husband into keeping their marriage alive. He wanted her. The passion between them was strong. And this last week she'd seen a side of him she hadn't seen since five years before. Maybe, she told herself, if she stayed and they were together long enough, love would eventually win the day.

"Forever," she said simply, surrendering her last ounce of pride. "Or for as long as you want me."

He took a long, deep breath and steadied himself. His eyes were shuttered, emotions sheathed to keep her from reading whatever he was thinking. It seemed to take forever before he finally said, "It's a deal. The Corettis go free and you stay here. With me."

She should have been happy. This was exactly what she had wanted so badly. To be able to remain with Rico here on the island. But getting it this way left her feeling as empty as she had during the previous five years. She could only nurture that small, now silent surge of hope and pray that eventually it would prove enough to conquer Rico's heart at last.

That hadn't gone at all as he'd planned.

Rico had spent the last week being the most attentive husband in the world in an attempt to get her to beg him to let her stay. That way he could keep his word to her family and hold on to his pride at the same time.

But she'd turned the tables on him.

Pacing the perimeter of his office two days after their sojourn at the waterfall, he felt caged. As if somehow he had wandered into a trap of his own making and now there was no way out.

"It was telling her that I wouldn't let her leave if she was pregnant," he muttered, scraping one hand across the back of his neck.

But he didn't know how he could have handled that any differently. Yes, he wanted her. Yes, he *loved* her still. But he couldn't tell her that without handing her all of the power in the negotiation that was sure to follow. So instead he got a wife who had once again become a hostage for her family.

She had traded her freedom for theirs and now he would never know if she would have chosen to stay simply because she loved him.

"Idiot." He kicked his desk for good measure as he made another pass around the room and the resulting pain was only what he deserved.

When his secretary buzzed through, he answered angrily, "I don't wish to be disturbed."

"I know, sir, but there's a man here to see you. He says it's urgent."

Scowling, Rico demanded, "Who is he?"

"He says his name is Gianni Coretti and that you're expecting him."

Twelve

Rico felt a surge of both anger and satisfaction. At last there was a target for the fury writhing inside him. "Send him in."

Gianni Coretti was tall, with short black hair, sharp brown eyes and the look of a man who didn't have much patience. Good, Rico thought. Then they were well matched. Gianni was wearing a well-cut suit and looked more like the head of a corporation than an infamous thief.

He crossed the room in several long strides and offered his hand. Rico merely looked from the outstretched hand and back up to the man's eyes. He gave nothing away, though mentally he was shouting, *Why are you early? I still have four days with Teresa!*

Which was ridiculous, of course. The whole point of this bargain he'd begun what felt like a lifetime ago was to have the Aztec dagger returned. That piece of family history that had been entrusted to him by his father. That's what he should be interested in. Instead all he could think was, if Gianni was here with the dagger, then Teresa would go.

But no, a voice in his mind whispered. She wouldn't. She'd bargained herself away for his assurance that he wouldn't see the Corettis jailed. Teresa was going to stay.

For all the wrong reasons.

Damn it.

"I've heard quite a bit about you from my father and brother," Gianni was saying as he let his hand drop to his side.

One eyebrow lifted. "Not flattering, I imagine."

"Not in the slightest," Gianni agreed with a grin. "But that's not important now, is it? I have what you asked for." He reached into his suit jacket and from the inner pocket pulled a cloth-wrapped item. "You can have it as soon as I have the evidence you gathered against my family."

Rico only crossed his arms over his chest and braced his feet wide apart. "Let me see the dagger first."

Gianni chuckled and shook his head. "This is what is wrong with the world today. No one trusts anymore."

Amused, Rico pointed out, "Says the thief."

"Touché, and yet it saddens me that the world has become such a cynical place."

He hadn't expected to almost like Teresa's brother, but damned if he didn't. "Makes stealing more difficult, does it?"

"There is that," Gianni acknowledged as he carefully unwrapped the ancient dagger he'd stolen five years before. "This...is magnificent." His gaze locked on the antiquity, he smiled as if watching a lover. "Intricate carvings, jewel-encrusted handle—but it's the *history* behind this piece that sings to me." He glanced at Rico. "And to you, I believe."

"Yes," Rico admitted, barely glancing at the once all important dagger. "It has been in my family for generations and we have all, at one time or another, felt the hum of history in that blade."

Gianni nodded, still studying the dagger. "When I took this from you, all I saw was its beauty. The jewels, the gold." He shrugged. "I am a mercenary man, trained to appreciate the finer things."

"That belong to others."

"As you say." Gianni shrugged that off and continued while Rico listened, oddly fascinated. This should have been a short meeting. An exchange and then a fast goodbye. Instead, Teresa's brother was acting as though they were old friends settling down for a visit.

"As I was saying," Gianni mused, looking down at the dagger in his hand, "when I first took the dagger, all I saw was its worth. But I couldn't bring myself to fence it. Couldn't sell it. It became a part of my collection and also, it became a sort of talisman."

"What do you mean?" Interested in spite of himself, Rico waited for an answer.

"As I held this dagger in my hands, for the first time in my life I felt the history of a piece." He turned it, studying it thoughtfully. "And I began to see that I had not been taking *things* from people. I had been stealing away pieces of their lives."

Surprised, Rico only stared at him. This was not the kind of thing he expected to hear from a professional thief.

"I, too, was shocked by this revelation," Gianni admitted with a wry smile. "It is not the sort of feeling a thief most appreciates."

"I don't think your father and brother share your philosophy."

"No." Gianni laughed and shook his head. "Not yet, anyway. But everything changes, does it not?"

He'd said that to Teresa not so long ago, Rico realized. And now all he could think was that *some* things would never change. He would always love her. And because he did, he realized what he had to do.

He had to let her go.

Rico had always thought that cloying cliché, "if you love something, set it free," was bull. He believed more in the "if you love something, hold on to it with both hands so you don't lose it" way of thinking. But now he understood that cliché. It tore at him to realize the hard truth, but there was no other choice for him.

Teresa had once again given up her own life for the sake of her family. She had once again made a sacrifice. The last time, he hadn't been a part of it. He had been left out of her choice altogether. Thinking back, he couldn't say what he might have done had she come to him with the truth. Would he have seen past his own anger at her lies? She'd kept so much from him back then. But had he been any more honest? They had fallen in love so quickly and their marriage was so new they hadn't had time to build the bridges of trust that would have seen them through bad times.

So. Would he have had her family arrested five years ago? He didn't know. He only knew what he should do *now*.

"Your ultimatum," Gianni said quietly, "had my family scrambling all over Europe to find me."

Rico laughed shortly and brought his mind back to the conversation at hand. "Your father thinks you should answer your phone."

Gianni grinned. "If I did that, he would call me more often."

"I feel the same about my own family at times." A shame they were meeting as enemies, since Rico had the feeling the two of them might have been friends.

"Well, then, we two have some business to conduct," Gianni said, holding the dagger so that the overhead light caught the blade and glinted like diamonds. "Here is your property. And now I would like to see this evidence my father claims you hold."

Rico nodded, walked to his desk and unlocked the top drawer. He took out a thick manila envelope and carried it to Gianni. Handing it over, he said, "That is everything I collected over five years." As a compliment of sorts, he added, "There wasn't much to be found."

Gianni grinned. "The Corettis are not easy to catch."

"I noticed," Rico said and took the dagger when it was offered.

The heavy gold weight felt solid, right, in his hands. He was relieved to finally have it back and yet...it felt like a hollow victory. He had set his sights on the return of his property and hadn't looked beyond that. Now he could see that retrieving his dagger could cost him the woman he loved.

Gianni opened the envelope and flipped through a few of the pages. He whistled low and long before looking up at Rico. "What you have here would have seen me and my family locked away for some time." He tucked the pages back inside and slapped the envelope against his palm. "Tell me, would you really have done it? Seen Teresa's family jailed?"

Setting the dagger down onto his desk, Rico pushed one hand through his hair and looked at the other man, standing quietly, watching him. It was past time for complete honesty, he thought. With himself as well as everyone else.

"Had you asked me that question two weeks ago," he said, "the answer would have been yes. Absolutely. Now…"

Gianni's eyes warmed as he smiled. "You *do* love her. My sister."

"I do."

"Which makes what I have to say next that much more uncomfortable. You have to release her from this bargain you and she struck."

"I know."

Gianni's eyebrows lifted high on his forehead. "You surprise me. I'd thought I would have to…convince you to uphold your end of the bargain."

"The bargain has nothing to do with this. Letting her go is the right thing to do," Rico said, a sharp stab of pain accompanying those words.

The thought of losing her broke his heart. But if he kept her here, he would never really *have* her. If she left… there might be a chance for them later.

"My father was right about you," Gianni said softly. "You are a dangerous man."

Before he could figure out what the other man meant by that, his office door flew open and Teresa stormed inside. She was wearing her white chef's uniform and as she slammed the door behind her, she snatched the hat from her head and tossed it aside.

"Teresa," her brother said warmly, "you look wonderful."

"Gianni, I'm not leaving," she said flatly.

"How did you know he was here?" Rico asked.

"Your assistant called to tell me when Gianni arrived. I had a soufflé in the oven and couldn't get away until just now."

Rico sighed and shook his head. She had friends all over the hotel and they were apparently willing to spy for her.

"Your brother was just leaving. As are you," Rico said. "The bargain is finished. Go back to your family."

She looked as though he'd slapped her and he winced. It wasn't his intention to bring her more pain.

"We talked about this, Rico," she reminded him, hands at her hips. "I'm staying."

"I've reconsidered." He ignored Gianni just as Teresa was. "We made a deal. The month is over."

"You can't mean this," she muttered. "What if I'm pregnant?"

"Pregnant?" Gianni scowled at Rico.

He waved the man's outburst away with one negligent hand and focused solely on Teresa. "Are you?"

Teresa chewed on her bottom lip, then grumbled, "No."

Disappointment welled inside him as his last hope at keeping her faded. But he had to do this for her. Damn it, he had blackmailed her into a monthlong affair. He would not blackmail her into being his wife. Since reason wasn't working with her, he released the anger churning inside him.

"You think I *want* you to be a sacrifice for your family? *Again?*" He shook his head. "No, Teresa. You'll go and you'll do whatever it is you want to do without worrying about trading your life for theirs."

"No one asked her to sacrifice—"

"Be quiet, Gianni," she snapped and took two furious steps closer to Rico.

He saw the fire in her golden eyes and loved her even more. She was magnificent in her fury as she was in every other aspect of her life. This woman was everything to him. And his only chance to prove that was to force her to go.

"I don't want you here," he blurted out.

She sucked in a gulp of air and fired another glare at him as she shook her head. "You're *lying,* Rico. You said you didn't lie to those you care about, but you're lying now."

"Teresa, I think we should—" Gianni said patiently.

"*Basta!* Enough!" She snapped the words out and held up her hand, palm out toward her brother. Gianni shrugged and leaned one hip against Rico's desk, settling in to watch the show.

"You're an idiot," she said, frowning at Rico.

Gianni laughed.

Rico scowled and murmured, "Thank you."

"I'm not *sacrificing* myself by staying here, Rico," she said, coming closer now, keeping her gaze fixed on his. "I'm staying because I *love* you."

A flare of heat swelled in his chest and Rico breathed easy for the first time since she had stormed into his office. Maybe there was light in his darkness after all. "I love you, too. I always have."

Tears swamped her eyes and a tremulous smile curved her mouth. Reaching up, she laid her hand on his cheek and sighed when he turned his head just far enough to plant a kiss in the center of her palm.

"What about before, Rico? The past. Will that always be there between us?"

That was one thing he was sure of. "I don't care about the past, Teresa. All that matters to me is the future. *Our* future."

"And my family?"

He slid a glance at Gianni, still watching them with a bemused expression on his face. "If I can handle the Kings, I think I can live with the Corettis." He pointed a finger at the other man. "As long as they stay out of my hotels."

"Agreed." Gianni nodded.

"But you were going to let me leave," Teresa complained, drawing his attention back to her. "Why?"

"Because you had to *want* to be here. With me. It had to be your choice," he whispered now, as if only the two of them existed. "But if you had left, I promise you I would have followed."

Her smile wobbled, then grew more bright. "Really?"

"I would have traipsed all over Europe and beyond, romancing you, seducing you, winning your heart until you chose to come home. With me."

"Home?"

"Our home. Here. On Tesoro."

"Our home, Rico, is anywhere we're together." She went up on her toes and kissed him lightly. "You are my family, Rico. And I will always choose you."

Gianni cleared his throat and stood up, interrupting. "I will tell Papa what happened here. He'll be disappointed that you're not coming home, but I think he'll understand."

Teresa went to her brother and hugged him tightly. "Thank you, Gianni."

He shrugged and kissed her forehead. "You should know," he said, talking to Rico now, "Papa will probably want another wedding for you two—since we weren't invited to the first one."

"Yes, about that," Teresa said.

"Doesn't matter now, little sister," he said, "as long as you're happy. And I can see that you are."

She grinned at him, then watched as he walked to the cold fireplace on the far wall. "Gas?" he asked.

"The switch on the wall," Rico told him, knowing just what the other man was going to do.

Gianni hit the switch, gas flames erupted and he went down on one knee in front of it. Carefully, he tossed the envelope of evidence onto the flames and watched as it burned. When it was nothing but curling paper and ash, he stood again to face his sister and Rico.

"Now that's done, I can go."

"Where, Gianni?"

"London, for now." He went to her and pulled her in close for another hug. Then, looking from her to Rico, he said, "You don't have to worry about me anymore. The reason Papa couldn't get me on the phone this month is that I've been in talks with Interpol."

"What?"

He smiled at Teresa's shock. "In exchange for immunity, I'm going to work with their people. Help them catch thieves for a change." He shrugged. "Could be fun. And I think I might be able to talk Paulo and Papa into doing the same."

"Good luck with that," Rico said on a laugh.

"It's worth a try," Teresa said and beamed at her brother. "I'm so proud of you, Gianni."

"Imagine. *Me*. Working for the police." Shaking his head, he walked to the door and paused only long enough to look back at Rico and say, "Treat her well, Rico. I'll be in touch."

When he was gone, Rico grabbed Teresa, pulled her against him and just held on. Burying his face in the curve of her neck, he inhaled her scent and dragged it so deep inside him he would never take another breath without tasting her on it.

"I love you, Teresa Coretti King."

"I'm going to want to hear that a lot," she said, leaning back to look up at him. "I love you so much, Rico. I always have. Living without you was so horrible—"

"Shh. That's done. It's gone. Neither of us will ever have to feel that misery again, that's all that matters."

"Being here. With you. On Tesoro. It's perfect." She leaned her head on his chest and whispered, "Take me home, Rico. To *our* home."

"First," he told her as he stepped away, "I have something for you."

"All I need is you, Rico."

He grinned at her. God, he felt freer than he had in years. Just hearing her say that filled him with the kind of joy he had never really expected to feel again. But this had to be done. "Trust me. This you need."

He walked to his desk, opened the top drawer and took out a small velvet box that he had looked at every day for the last five years. When he brought it to her, he opened it and Teresa gasped.

"It's your ring," he said unnecessarily. "The one you

left behind with your note, telling me only that you had to leave."

"Oh, God." She stared at the yellow diamond and clapped one hand over her mouth. "It almost killed me to take that ring off, Rico. It—you—meant everything to me." Shaking her head, she murmured, "You kept it. I can't believe you kept it all this time."

"Sometimes," he said, "I admit, I thought about selling it or even tossing it into the sea."

"Oh, God…"

"But something kept me from it," he admitted as he plucked the ring from the velvet and slid it onto her finger. He sealed it there with a kiss, then met her eyes, now drenched again in what he knew were tears of happiness. "I think a part of me knew that we would find our way to each other again.

"Because you are my one. My only. And now the ring—and you—are back where you belong."

"And this time," Teresa whispered as she lifted her face for his kiss, "my romantic, wonderful husband, it's forever."

"It is a deal," he said with a smile, then kissed her with all the love he held in his now healed heart.

* * * * *

TO MARRY A PRINCE

A.C. ARTHUR

To everyone who found their Prince Charming
and to those who may still be looking.
Dreams do come true!

Chapter 1

He took her breath away, and for Landry Norris, stylist to Hollywood's most glamorous women and debonair men, that was no small feat.

That thought caused the very smooth and elegant curtsy that she'd practiced just before boarding the plane to come off with a bit of hesitation. Still, she smiled brightly as she lifted her head and came to a standing position. He—the Crown Prince Kristian Rafferty DeSaunters—stood before her in all his regal and hot-as-hell glory.

There had been a flurry of activity in the last couple of days, all of which had culminated in this moment. Landry clasped her hands in front of her cream-colored peplum top and gray pencil skirt, hoping she had made the correct outfit selection. That was her thing, after all—finding the right outfit for the right occasion and pairing it perfectly with the person who would wear it. Very rarely was she that person. But Malayka Sampson, one of Landry's newer clients, had changed that.

In her briefcase, which she had left downstairs in the massive marble-and-gold-decorated foyer, was a signed contract between Landry Norris LLC and Malayka Sampson, the woman soon to be princess of Grand Serenity Island. That title and all that went with it had both surprised and impressed Landry when Malayka breezed into her Los Angeles office to share the news. On Malayka's finger was a huge emerald, while the woman's face sported a triumphant smile. Landry figured she'd be smiling too if she were wearing that rock.

Before that, Landry had only dressed Malayka for three functions—the Oscars, which Malayka attended with renowned producer Siegmond Elrey, the Met Gala and New York Fashion Week. Malayka was a cold call client, something Landry rarely accepted. One—she wanted to keep her personal stylist company small and intimate so that she could specially cater to her clients. And two—because most of the cold calls meant she had no idea who the potential client was or what type of funds they were working with.

She'd taken a gamble on Malayka Sampson and it seemed to have paid off, in spades.

"Have a seat, Ms. Norris," the prince said in a low, deep voice that made Landry think of hot baths and back rubs.

She moved carefully to one of the cherrywood upholstered armchairs and gingerly took a seat. Considering Landry was used to being around wealthy people, handling gowns worth more than her childhood home, visiting mansions and attending movie premiers, being a guest in the royal palace on a Caribbean island felt unfamiliar to her. It was new and exciting and just a little bit nerve-racking.

From what she'd seen so far of the palace—it was lavishly decorated and spoke of the wealth and prestige of the people who lived there. Take this office for example, she thought with a quick glance at the floor-to-ceiling windows and grand stately furniture, it was one hell of a space. Roughly the size of the top level of her condo back in LA, the room was meticulously decorated with gold-leaf-framed portraits, Aubusson rugs and a large glossed wood desk where the gorgeous crown prince sat.

"It is Miss? You're not married, are you?"

She could see his lips moving but had been too wrapped in the wonder of her surroundings to pay attention to what was being said.

"Excuse me?" she replied with a shake of her head, a silent admonishment to herself in hopes she would get it together.

He sat back in that dark leather chair, his honey-brown complexion combined with the pale gray color of his Italian-cut suit jacket providing a stark contrast. Behind him the white plantation shutters that covered each window were opened so that slices of sunlight slipped into the room.

"I asked if you were married."

He sounded annoyed but his facial expression remained the same.

Dark eyebrows draped dramatically over velvet brown eyes. His jaw, not exactly strong but precise, just like his nose and ears. It was almost as if he'd had his pick of physical attributes and he'd done an excellent job putting them together.

"No. I'm not married," she managed to finally reply.

A curt nod was the only telling sign that he'd even heard her answer as he immediately reached for a folder on his desk and opened it. He stared down at the papers that she presumed had something to do with her. The amount of paperwork she'd completed before coming there reminded her of when she'd purchased her condo. Grand Serenity Island had a tough security system. She presumed it was that way only for persons who would be staying in the palace, and not for every tourist who wanted to visit this Caribbean haven.

"You've been in business for two years. Landry Norris LLC is the name of your company. You're a personal stylist. So you select clothes for adults to wear?"

He was speaking as if he were reading from cue cards and didn't quite understand what the words meant. It irritated her. She'd grabbed the arms of the chair and squeezed as she restrained the urgency to speak her mind.

When he looked up, his thick, perfect brows raised in question.

Landry cleared her throat, realizing he was expecting an answer.

"I assist my clients with choices that will enhance the way they look and feel. I help them select clothing that will suit their natural features and lifestyle. When a person is looking their best it can be a confidence booster. My job is to not only dress clients, but to assist them in their personal growth."

She spoke succinctly and from the heart. Her job was her passion and while she knew others might not see it as an "important" career, it was hers and she was proud of it. By the time she'd finished speaking her hands were calmly in her lap, her head tilted just slightly as she waited for the prince's next comment.

"Malayka Sampson," he continued, as if her statement had been as interesting as reciting the alphabet. "How long have you known her?"

"Our first contact was via email in late November. She

needed a dress for the Oscars—that's an American award show," she informed him.

"I know what the Oscars are," he countered quickly.

He *would* know, she thought. The royal family of Grand Serenity had been the guests of the president of the United States on numerous occasions in the last eight years. When Landry was inclined to pay attention to the political arena, for reasons other than keeping up with the fashions worn by the First Family and the many dignitaries they entertained, she'd seen Prince Rafferty DeSaunters, the widower who ruled this island, and Princess Samantha DeSaunters a few times. She also remembered another royal sibling, a brother, one who was pictured in magazines and newspapers more often than she'd seen any of the others. But as for this one, the crown prince, the one who would rule the island following Prince Rafferty, she had not seen as much.

The prince continued, "How did she learn about you and what did she ask of you?"

"Another one of my clients had a party and Malayka was there. As I've heard from both of them, my name was brought up in their discussion, and Malayka sent me an email a few days later."

"Why didn't she call you? Did your other client not give her your number?"

"At that time of year I am extremely busy going over resketched gown proposals and backup wardrobe pieces. There are fittings and accessory meetings, as well as lunches with reps of designers I may consider for next year's awards season. My cell phone is always on and always with me, but there are times when I may not be able to answer. My clients know this and have been known to send a text or an email. Sometimes it's easier to give a quick response that way, when I'm unable to speak to them personally at the time."

If this were an interview, Landry might be failing. She was very aware of that fact.

Smile more. Be friendlier. Stop being so defensive.

Those were her mother's words as she warned Landry for the millionth time about finding the right guy.

First impressions are everything.

"How many clients do you have?" was his next question.

Landry resisted the urge to sigh. "Ten."

"So few. Do you plan on expanding?"

"I plan to run a small and personal business, one where I can really get to know my clients and thus provide them with the best service possible."

He looked somber. The expression had not changed since the moment she'd sat down. "And you like catering to people?" He paused. "Why?"

"There are only some people I like catering to, Your Highness. Malayka Sampson is my client and she's hired me to dress her for the events leading up to the wedding. That's the only reason I'm here on your island. And if we're finished, I really must meet with Malayka—we have a great deal to get done before the engagement party."

She'd stood then because sitting was no longer an option. Her hands were now shaking, her heart beating a tense rhythm as she fought to remain calm. When in actuality, she was extremely annoyed. She did not like being questioned as if she were considered disingenuous, or that her business was not up to his standards. Yes, he was the prince of a gorgeous island, but he was still a man and Landry wasn't used to cowtailing to any men, or women for that matter.

He'd surprised her by standing as well. It was a quick motion, one he either hadn't expected to make, or didn't appreciate having to make. As he came around that large desk, Landry remembered the book she'd read on the plane about royal protocol. Most men in America did not stand when a woman did. An attestation to the whole chivalry is dead mantra. Here, the men—correction, the royal men— were different. At least that's what the book said.

"Welcome to Grand Serenity Island," he stated and ex- tended his hand to her.

Landry hesitated momentarily, but then accepted his hand and looked him in the eye.

Did the earth shake? Was that thunder she heard? Who turned up the heat in here?

A wave of heat flowed steadily from her fingers to her wrist, up her arm and rested embarrassingly in her cheeks. He looked down at their hands about a second or so before she did. He was a few shades lighter than her mocha hue.

When she looked back, it was to see him staring at her. She could swear her thoughts were mirrored in his expres- sion. Prince Kristian DeSaunters was not blushing as she feared she probably was, but he did appear shaken. It was a faint change from the stern and serious look that had been in his eyes just moments before. His lips pressed together tightly until he almost seemed to grimace.

"Thank you," Landry replied but made no attempt to remove her hand from his grasp.

His fingers moved over hers as their gazes held.

"No rings," he spoke quietly.

"I'm not married," she answered. "I thought we already established that fact."

Neither was he, Landry thought. He was single and dashing and still holding her hand. It felt natural and odd at the same time. Welcome, yet a bit too familiar for their first meeting. And still, she did not pull away.

"I look forward to seeing more of you," the prince continued. "More of your work, that is."

Right, she reminded herself. She was here to work, not to ogle this man.

"Thank you, Your Highness. I plan to do my very best," she said in her most professional tone, just as there was a knock at the door.

He was still holding her hand when someone entered, already speaking.

"Hey Kris, we need to talk about tomorrow's meeting with the board of directors and then—" her voice trailed off as the stunningly beautiful Princess Samantha Raine DeSaunters came to a stop right beside them.

The prince dropped Landry's hand as if she'd had a palm full of hot coals.

Landry then finished with the roller coaster of emotions brought on by the introduction to Grand Serenity's royalty, bid a quick farewell before making a hasty retreat.

"Who was that and what did you do to run her away like that?"

Kristian stared at the door Landry had just passed through. He was asking himself an array of questions at the moment, none of which he wanted to share with his younger sister.

"That was Landry Norris. She's Malayka's stylist," he replied then moved to stand behind his desk once again.

He closed the file his assistant had compiled on Ms. Norris and her business venture. The picture that was included—the one that had captured him the moment he'd first seen it earlier this week—was tucked securely in the back. That's where he'd finally put it yesterday, when he couldn't rationalize why he kept staring at it.

"You're kidding, right?" Sam shook her head as she

continued to walk into the office, taking a seat in the chair that Landry had vacated. "Why does she need a personal stylist? She already has her hairdresser and makeup artist here."

Kris took his seat. "I was going to ask you that same question… Do you have someone who selects your clothes for you?"

It seemed like a silly question to ask, especially when posed to his sister, who lived in the same house with him. In his defense their *house* was unlike usual homes. It was a palace, after all. Wonderland, that's what Vivienne DeSaunters, their mother, used to call the family home. Located high on the cliffs of Grand Serenity, a Caribbean island just north of Colombia and Venezuela, the royal palace was a sprawling white structure with jutting towers capped in gold domes. It was roughly the size of twenty-five of the homes in the town below, and housed the rulers who had governed the island for the last sixty-five years.

His family resided in a large wing toward the center of the house with the majority of the rooms overlooking the cliffs that fell off into the glorious turquoise sea. Before Vivienne had come to live in the palace windows had been barred and locked, as one of the former rulers, Marco Vansig, had not been a particularly kind man, thus soliciting more enemies than he could eventually ward off. Under Vivienne's progressive and feminine hand the barred windows were removed and replaced with practical weather-resistant glass ones that sparkled and brought in every ounce of sunlight and the island's magnificent view.

Kris's father, Rafe, had the largest group of rooms in that wing of the house as the reigning prince of the island. Kris and each of his younger siblings, Sam and Roland, had their own rooms situated among the areas of the massive dwelling in a way that provided them all with the privacy they seemed to desire. It wasn't easy living under the titles they held, finding solace within the walls of their private rooms was sometimes all they could manage. At least it was that way for Kris.

As the crown prince, the one who would ultimately succeed his father in ruling their country, Kris carried a tremendous weight on his shoulders. One which was now causing a great deal of stress for him.

"I am not your average woman, I suspect," Sam replied to his question with a quirk of her lips. "I love beautiful clothes and accessories, but I like to have the final say in what I wear or purchase for that matter."

She always looked good, Kris thought, as he stared across his desk at his sister—younger than him by six years—looking vaguely amused by their conversation. Samantha Raine DeSaunters was a beautiful woman with her smooth milk-chocolate complexion, and thick coal-black hair. Her skin tone and assessing eyes came from their father, while her outgoing personality and the innate need to take care of everyone around her were undoubtedly traits obtained from their mother.

"I think it's safe to say that you are nothing like Malayka Sampson," was Kris's dry response.

Sam agreed with the nod of her head. "I don't know that there is anyone like her. Did you know that she has already begun planning the wedding?"

Kris sat back in his chair, folding his hands in his lap, a position in which he could easily be mistaken for his father. "The date is set for December first. The date has significance to her and she wants a grand celebration. Those were Dad's exact words."

"And he plans to give it to her?" Sam asked.

"He does."

She cursed.

It was soft and way too dainty to carry much weight, still Kris realized the severity of the situation at hand especially because it made his normally pleasant sister vent in such a way.

Malayka Sampson was engaged to their father. She was a thirty-seven-year-old American who would, in just seven months, become the princess of Grand Serenity Island. As such she would manage Wonderland...no, that was his mother's. It belonged only to her. It always would. Malayka would manage *the palace* and she would take over much of the community and public relations duties that Sam now held. She would become the new face and voice of the island, while his father continued to rule via business and policy the way his father had before him.

"I don't like her and neither does Roland," Sam told him.

Her words came as no surprise to Kris. Sam and Roland tended to agree on a number of things. Kris was the one who was usually treading on the outside of the sibling bond. That was part of his birthright as his father had taught him from the time he'd been old enough to speak. He was the future ruler, thus he had to lead, always.

"She makes Dad happy," Kris replied. "That is all that matters." For now, he thought, wisely keeping that last part to himself.

"She makes me want to do bodily harm and you know that is not my character," Sam added with a slight chuckle.

"I know. But there are more pressing matters at hand. The Children's Hospital brunch is coming up later this week and the Ambassador's Ball is later this month. Is everything in order?"

Sam nodded, looking down at the notepad she'd brought with her into his office. "Just a few final details for each event and they're all set. As I mentioned when I came in,

I have meetings with the board of directors at the hospital tomorrow and after that, I'll be spending the rest of the afternoon at the Bella Club."

Kris nodded as he reached for a pen to make note of his sister's whereabouts the following day. He also had access to her business calendar on the private network the monarch shared. Roland's and Rafe's business calendars were also available to him. However, Sam had a number of personal ventures that meant a lot to her. Kris respected that and envied his sister's passion in helping wherever she could. The Bella Club was an organization Sam had started to offer refuge, counseling and rehabilitation to troubled young adults between the ages of thirteen and eighteen.

"That sounds good," he said as a thought entered his mind. "Would you mind taking Landry Norris with you tomorrow?"

"Who? Oh, the personal stylist?" she asked with a lift of her precisely arched brows. "Why would I do that? She's Malayka's employee, not mine."

"She is a guest in the palace and a tourist. You are on the board of tourism."

"So are you," she countered.

Kris didn't bother to frown, even though he completely recognized the never-ending sibling game that often had each of the royal children pointing out the other's duties to see who had the most on their plate. Kris always won, hands down. Which was why, this time, he was delegating the responsibility.

"I'm meeting with the finance board at nine. That will take up at least three hours of my day. Dad and I then have a late lunch scheduled with Quirio Denton, the real estate mogul who wants to build his next resort here on the island. I won't be available again until dinner," he stated matter-of-factly. "And as you know, because you've been doing this since you were sixteen, it is our practice to provide a detailed tour of the island to visitors of the palace within twenty-four hours of their arrival."

She gave a slight nod. "That's when we know they are arriving and when we've invited them. Malayka hired this woman without consulting any of us. I say let her conduct the tour," Sam rebutted. "It would give her practice since it will soon be one of her duties as *princess*."

That title, above Sam's other words, echoed throughout the room.

"She's not the princess yet," Kris remarked, in a tone that was much stronger than he'd anticipated.

Sam tapped her fingers on her notepad. "Fine. I will take the stylist with me. It'll give me the chance to find out more about Malayka and why she really wants to marry our father."

"I don't know if you'll get much by way of gossip from this Landry Norris. She strikes me as a professional."

"Oh really?" Sam asked, this time leaning forward tossing him a knowing grin. "What else about her strikes you, big brother?"

Kris looked away. He concentrated on the notes he was jotting down, instead of his sister's question, which made him uncomfortable.

"I performed a cursory interview of her. I have a copy of her contract with Malayka and I checked the references she provided. This is how I came to the conclusion that she is a professional."

"Right, because you're very thorough when it comes to investigating who enters these walls. I get that. But what I'm really asking is, what was going on between you and the stylist when I came in? You know, when you two were standing close enough to have kissed."

Kris looked up quickly then, staring at his sister in

shock. Composure came immediately afterward because even with his siblings, Kris had to remain in control. A leader always set an example.

"As Malayka's stylist she's now palace staff. Personal dalliances with the staff are inappropriate."

"Hmm." Sam made a sound and stood with her notepad tucked under one arm. "Tell that to your brother. He's had more dalliances with staff, visitors and whoever else he could find, than the both of us."

Kris made a similar sound as he stood, undoubtedly agreeing with his sister. Roland was another matter entirely.

Sam was almost out the door when she looked back at him and said, "Still, I have to admit the two of you looked awfully cozy and mighty cute together."

She was gone before he could think of another statement of denial where he and Landry Norris were concerned. When he sat back in his chair, he struggled to dismiss any thoughts he'd had when Landry had stood so close to him. When he'd definitely wanted to—against all his training and upbringing—kiss her.

Chapter 2

Classy and elegant, that's the look Landry was going for tonight. After all, it would be the first time Malayka was presented to the entire royal family. Butterflies danced in Landry's stomach as she pushed wayward strands of hair from her face and zipped the back of Malayka's dress.

"There," Landry said, looking over Malayka's shoulder into the floor-length mirror.

It was one of four mirrors which had been sealed together in an arch shape situated at the back of the walk-in closet. Who was she kidding? This was not a closet. The room was at least the size of two bedrooms outfitted with racks for hanging clothes, shelves for shoes, medium-sized drawers for purses and smaller ones for scarves and jewelry. Even with all the items that Landry had brought with her and the ones she'd shipped a week before, there was still a good deal of space before Malayka would come close to filling this room. The dresses tried on tonight were specially ordered designs, four of which Landry would have to ship back to the designers first thing tomorrow morning.

"You look stunning," Landry continued.

Malayka turned to the side. She looked at her plump bottom and rubbed a hand over her flat stomach. Turning again so that she could see herself from another angle, Malayka smoothed her hands over the bodice of the dress. The neckline was cut higher than Malayka was used to but she still seemed pleased. The woman loved to display the cleavage from her size D breasts, something Landry figured Prince Rafferty also appreciated.

"This will be the first time since we've announced our engagement that I've been in a room with all of Rafe's children," Malayka said in that smoky voice that reminded Landry of the time she'd met Grace Jones.

"They'll certainly have to agree that you are more than ready to dress the part of being princess of this beautiful island," Landry told her as she moved away from the mirror and began packing up the other gowns that Malayka had tried on.

She'd been in there for the last two hours trying to figure out which dress Malayka would wear. Luckily, the hair stylist and makeup artist had already been there by the time Landry arrived, so that part of getting ready for tonight's dinner was complete.

From behind her she could hear Malayka making a sound and mumbling something. Landry kept moving. Whatever Malayka had said was apparently not meant for her to hear.

One of the first things Landry learned about working in an industry with wealthy and famous people was to mind her own business. This lesson had come just months after she'd graduated with honors, receiving a bachelor's degree in Apparel Merchandising and Management from

California State Polytechnic University in Ponoma. She'd been ecstatic the day she found out she'd landed one of the coveted internships with *Harper's Bazaar* in New York. There, she had assisted with sample trafficking, creating shoot boards and supporting market editors with office duties. It was just a few weeks after she'd been in New York that Landry met Peta Romanti, the A-list actress who was, at that time, launching her own fashion line. *Bazaar* was doing a full spread and in-depth interview with Peta in the weeks leading up to her launch.

Landry had recognized the woman immediately and used every method of control she could think of to resist acting like a complete groupie. Throughout the day Peta barked orders, sending interns and even editors scrambling to do her bidding. Landry had been busy with other assignments all that morning, but in the afternoon she'd offered to help out during a photo shoot. Happy to have someone else go into the lion's den, Landry's supervisor had given her an armful of dresses and instructions to take into the dressing room and see which one Peta wanted to wear. The actress-turned-designer had decided to capitalize on this interview by modeling clothes from her own line for the spread in the magazine. As she'd walked up to the dressing room door Landry could hear the argument. Something about Peta's boyfriend being arrested for public nudity as he'd stood on a sidewalk arguing with the hooker he'd hired, who he was then accusing of stealing his wallet. Landry stood at the door, not sure whether she should knock and go in, or come back later—even though there wasn't really a "later" since they had already been behind with the shoot.

The decision was made for her as the door abruptly swung open and Peta yelled in her face, "What are you doing there? Are you listening to my conversation? You'd better not speak one word of it!"

All Landry could manage to say was, "I have your dresses if you're ready to try them on."

The afternoon had proceeded with Peta—once she'd asked Landry her name—calling her every five seconds to do any- and everything for her. That day led to Landry being invited to Peta's Paris fashion show three weeks after that and later to receiving personal invitations and previewings to Peta's collection from the moment Landry opened her doors for business. Keeping her mouth shut had been an invaluable lesson and Landry reminded herself of that constantly.

Now well versed in the ins and outs of the personal stylist business, Landry admitted, there wasn't much to be said about Malayka Sampson. She'd been in LA for just about a year when Landry had first met her. When she'd queried her services, Landry had discreetly asked around about the woman, who was neither an actor nor singer, or notable figure. All that could be said was that Malayka had been at all the right parties and premiers. She had dinner with the governor and lunch with a senator. There were pictures of her with record producers and none other than Peta Romanti, which had been the deciding factor in Landry choosing to work with her.

Landry figured that was enough of a platform to style Malayka for the months leading up to her wedding. Add that to the gorgeous scenery that Landry was already aching to see more of, and this was a good opportunity for her career. Her family, however, would say otherwise.

"The men are never a problem," Malayka was saying, loudly this time. "It's the females who are always jealous."

Landry had been closing the box filled with jewelry

she'd brought into the room with her. The sound echoed throughout the high-ceilinged room. She cleared her throat.

"I'll see you in the dining room in a bit," she said as she quickly clasped the lock on the box and picked it up.

The dresses to be returned were all bagged and hung on a rolling rack she'd pushed down the long marble-floored hallway to get to Malayka's private rooms. In her estimate, the palace was roughly the size of at least two Beverly Hills hotels, and that was only a hunch. Earlier that day Landry had been met outside of Prince Kristian's door by a pinch-faced older woman with a heavy accent who escorted her to a room that seemed a couple city blocks away. She figured her approximation was almost accurate.

"You're going to dinner?"

Apparently that surprised Malayka, whose dramatically arched brows were raised as she touched the diamonds glittering at her neck. The woman was just a shade or so lighter in complexion than Landry. They probably maxed out at the same height when neither were wearing heels—five feet six inches tall. She was older than Landry who had just turned twenty-six last week. A marvelous plastic surgeon and a good regimen of weight loss supplements were most likely responsible for Malayka's slim, but stacked, size six frame. Her hair, or rather the expensive wigs she wore, were of the highest quality and were always on point. As was her makeup, courtesy of the other two stylists she'd brought to the island with her. She was perfect to look at, but not the friendliest person in the world.

"Yes. I was told to be ready at six," Landry said as she lifted her arm and looked down to her watch. "I've got twenty minutes to make it or the stern warden lady that gave me the directive might pop a button in that crisp uniform she wears." Landry made sure to chuckle after her words. She wouldn't have the future princess thinking she had no respect for the staff.

Malayka only blinked, the long fake eyelashes fanning dramatically over her smooth skin. "I thought it would be a private dinner tonight. Family only."

Landry nodded and headed out of the closet. "See you in a little bit," she yelled over her shoulder without turning back.

She moved through the sitting area of Malayka's room. It was the size of the entire front end of Landry's studio in LA, plush cream-colored carpet and gorgeous antique furnishings, complete with stunning oil paintings of what she suspected might be the landscape of the island draping the walls. The knobs on the double doors were crystal and reminded Landry of the old doorknobs in her grandparents' house. She was certain these were real, as opposed to the ones Nana used to joke about selling and becoming rich.

When the rack and the other two bags she'd left on the couch in the sitting room were through the doors, Landry turned back and closed them with a quiet click. Then she sighed. The last couple of hours had been taxing but worth it, she supposed. Malayka did look good and that was her sole purpose for being there, so she whispered a *job well done* to herself and headed back in the direction she'd remembered traveling to get there.

These were the glossiest and prettiest floors she'd ever seen and Landry had been to a lot of sophisticated venues. Nothing compared to this palace. The word *palace* alone meant this place was classier than anything she could ever imagine. It was certainly living up to its hype, and she was only in the hallway.

Columns jutted from the floor to the ceiling, some wide, some slim, all giving an air of royalty as she moved through. What seemed like secret alcoves encased sculptures of pirates and ships. Closer to her rooms there were busts of people she was sure she had never heard of, but who nevertheless looked extremely important. The color scheme here was the barest hint of peach flanked in beige-and-gold textured wallpaper, highlighted again by the swirling marble floors. There were large floral arrangements on small round tables; the tropical plants added bursts of colors and scents as she moved through the area. Every few feet or so, the walls would break to an opening that displayed a gorgeous mermaid sculpture and fountain in its center. This one showcased a courtyard that had access to the outside so sun and sea-salted air filled the atmosphere.

It was just around the corner from that courtyard that Landry's rooms were located. Yes, she had a sitting room, also a private bathroom, bedroom and balcony. The space was elegantly decorated. She probably could have comfortably stayed here during the times she was not taking care of Malayka. The stern-faced lady had told her that she could simply pick up the phone on her nightstand and dial zero for assistance, which included having meals brought to her room. Free room service in a royal palace; for a second, Landry thought she could get used to living like royalty.

That thought had her chuckling as she entered her suite, pushing the clothes rack to the much smaller walk-in closet she was using for some of the items she'd preselected for Malayka. There was a coat closet and another enclosure, which she figured was supposed to be a linen closet. But Landry had decided to store her own clothes here.

She rushed into the bathroom to shower and slip into the dress she'd already chosen for herself. Being a college student and working two jobs, added to the two years she'd spent in New York when her internship had been extended, had taught Landry how to dress in a hurry. She lined her eyes, stroked on mascara and added a bit of color on her eyelids. The quick makeup routine stalled momentarily when she discovered she was getting low on her favorite lip gloss. It only took another second or so for her to browse through her makeup case and settle on a nude gloss instead. Swiping that on quickly, she found her earrings—silver buttons that matched the bangle she pulled onto her arm. Slipping into five-inch-heel sandals was next before standing again and grabbing a random bottle of perfume and spritzing herself generously. Her hair was already up in a messy bun and once she looked into the mirror, Landry decided it was the perfect accent to the otherwise neat and almost demure dress she wore.

It was navy blue, with a layer of lace over the tight bodice and full asymmetrical skirt. There was also a slip to the dress, crinoline, the most despised fabric in Landry's opinion. Still this dress needed that extra poof to the skirt. As she stood looking in the mirror, moving from side to side the way she'd seen Malayka doing, Landry thought she looked like the twenty-first-century Audrey Hepburn. She smiled because she liked it.

Moments later she was leaving her room, only to come face-to-face with a man who looked nothing like the dour staff worker who had promised to escort her to the dining room. No, this was no older person. He was young and built and wore the white dinner jacket and black pants like a seasoned model. His face was breathtakingly handsome and when he smiled, Landry almost swooned.

"Ms. Norris. I would be honored to escort you down to dinner," he said with an extravagant bow.

When he was once again upright, Landry touched the sides of her dress and curtsied—because something told her this guy was royal. He had to be. He was too beautiful to be just a mere human.

He was reaching for her hand when she straightened.

"I am Prince Roland DeSaunters, and it is my immense pleasure to meet you."

No, Landry thought as she let him take her hand in his and they began to walk down the hallway, the pleasure was definitely hers.

The table could easily seat somewhere around fifty or so people. It was huge and a glossed cherrywood. A pristine white runner stretched its entire length; gold candelabras held tall white candles with golden flames at their tips. Ornate brass chandeliers hung from the high ceilings while several matching sideboards filled the great space. Beneath the table was a plush rug decorated in deep reds, greens and of course gold. But the definite eye-catcher to this room was the enormous arched window situated perfectly behind the head seat of the table. The window had automatic shades that Landry suspected were room darkening as well as provided privacy when needed. The shades were raised tonight so that the last intense colors of sunset over the glistening water were visible.

As if this room and its awe-inspiring view weren't enough, the rest of the royal family was seated at the table and now staring expectantly at her.

Landry already felt a bit lightheaded by the gorgeous man walking beside her and the scent of his intoxicating cologne. Prince Roland had talked the entire time they walked, commenting on the very statues she'd perused not long before. He laughed a lot which made her smile. He walked with a seasoned swagger that said he knew he was not only good-looking, but rich and powerful and none of that meant a thing. She liked him instantly.

As for how she felt about the rest of the family, well, nervous or not, she was about to find out.

"Heads up," Roland said as he continued to guide her down the length of that table to where the others were seated. "Gang's all here!"

As they approached, Prince Kristian stood and so did his father. Seated next to Kristian was Malayka who looked at Landry with her brow raised in question once more. She was most likely wondering why Landry was arriving with Prince Roland. Landry was wondering that herself. The princess sat opposite of Malayka, her expression more amused than questioning.

"Ms. Norris," Prince Rafferty said as he stepped away from the table to stand in front of her as she approached. "It is a pleasure to meet you. Kristian has told me all about you."

Landry did another curtsy—she was getting really good at them now. The prince took her hand, kissing the back of it in a gallant and romantic gesture that stole her breath and made her smile.

"The pleasure is all mine, Your Highness. Thank you for having me in your home. It is a beautiful palace," she said then snapped her lips shut for fear of babbling.

"You are welcome here for as long as Malayka requires your assistance."

His response was more formal than the slight lifting of his mouth as if he were contemplating a smile.

"And this is my sister, the Princess Samantha DeSaunters," Roland announced after turning her once again toward the table.

His hand was lightly touching her shoulder. Landry looked at the princess. In Landry's line of work, she was used to seeing beautiful people—whether it be natural or assisted via surgery, hair extensions, makeup, designer clothes, whatever it took. This woman was actually very pretty, the light makeup and lovely ivory-colored gown she wore only adding to her allure.

Her complexion was a little lighter than her father's, her dark hair curling to her shoulders. Her eyes were intelligent and assessing and the smile she gave Landry was, thankfully, genuine. So Landry mirrored it.

"It's a pleasure to meet you, Your Highness."

"Very nice to meet you, Landry. Kris also told me a lot about you."

Well, Landry thought with a tight smile as she gazed across the table to "Kris." He had been talking about her a lot, hadn't he.

"And you've already met my older brother, Kris, next in line to rule this magnificent island," Roland said as he began guiding Landry to the seat between the princess and another empty chair.

Prince Rafferty had already taken his seat and Kristian was now watching her with an obvious frown as she sat in the high-backed cushioned chair Roland had offered.

"There will be a bridal party meeting on Friday. Everyone that I've selected will be flying in on Thursday. I'm thinking that a lovely breakfast on the north terrace would be nice because there's not much sun on that side of the palace that early in the day," Malayka began speaking, once everyone was seated and servers had arrived with plates of a colorful salad.

"The Children's Hospital brunch is Friday at eleven," Samantha announced, her tone just shy of being frosty.

"Oh," Malayka said, her fork poised over the salad she was just about to dig into. "Well, the palace is enormous, I'm sure we can entertain two groups at the same time. Isn't that right, Rafe?"

"The royal family is expected to attend the brunch.

The Children's Hospital performs in a professional manner throughout the year and is the top medical facility for children in the Caribbean. This is our way of thanking them for a job well done."

Kristian spoke with an air of finality. There was no mistaking his authority, not in his tone, nor in the way his shoulders squared. He wore black. His suit jacket had satin lapels, and his shirt had a white silk tie at the neck. It was a decidedly Mafia look to Landry's eye, but it worked exceptionally well with his buttery complexion. His hair was jet-black, just like the rest of the royal family, but cropped closer than Prince Rafferty's and Roland's. Where Roland's low-cut beard gave him a rugged, handsome quality, Kristian's clean-shaven face suited his dour expressions perfectly.

"Well, I've already made the plans. Everyone is preparing to travel. It's not possible to cancel at this late date," Malayka implored.

The look she was giving Prince Rafferty was almost comical, but Landry knew not to laugh. This was, after all, serious business for the soon-to-be princess. Malayka undoubtedly expected her husband-to-be to stand up to his children in front of her, to let them know that she was getting ready to be the one wielding all the control. Landry should have felt uncomfortable being privy to this private duel of sorts, especially considering she was only the staff. Malayka's makeup lady and hair stylist weren't at this dinner, which would explain why Malayka had been surprised that Landry had been invited. Landry wondered about that too, but the salad was delicious, so she really didn't want to wonder too much.

"We will work something out," Prince Rafferty stated in his deep, booming tone. He also gave Kristian a look that said they would definitely *work it out*, later.

Kristian showed no emotion at all. He proceeded to cut through his salad, lifting measured forkfuls to his mouth to be chewed.

Roland picked that moment to chuckle. "Just let me know which event I'm required to attend. I'll be flying out Friday evening."

"Really? I did not see that on the calendar," Prince Rafferty said to his younger son. "When will you return?"

Roland shrugged and forked a bright red tomato into his mouth. "Don't know."

Prince Rafferty wiped his fingers on a napkin then placed the white cotton square down on the table slowly. "The engagement will be officially announced tomorrow. There will no doubt be press arriving on the island within hours of the news circulating around the world. We all need to be on hand for official photos and interviews."

Landry thought about that statement as she chewed the last bite of her salad. She did not recall seeing any interviews of Prince Rafferty in any of the American papers. Of course she hadn't actually searched for any either.

"You're giving interviews?" Samantha asked. "You never give interviews."

Malayka reached a hand out to rub along Prince Rafferty's arm. "This is the age of social media. We—the royal family—should be as transparent as possible at all times," she told them.

Kristian set his fork down slowly and looked directly at his father.

"The exposure the wedding will elicit for the upcoming months will no doubt improve tourism on Grand Serenity. The more tourists that visit the island, the more money the shop owners in the village will earn. The more money they earn, the more jobs they can provide. It is a win-win situation for all of us," Prince Rafferty stated.

He'd looked around to each of his children, an effort to gain their support, Landry supposed. However, she wasn't certain it was going to work. None of them seemed thrilled about this idea.

"Sounds like you two have this all planned out," Samantha replied.

"Not all," Prince Rafferty continued. "The press conference needs to be arranged for tomorrow morning at ten."

"We have a meeting at the bank tomorrow," Kristian interjected. "It's on the calendar."

Rafe nodded as the next course of their meal arrived. It looked like chicken and vegetables in a dark sauce and it smelled fabulous. Landry immediately picked up her knife and fork and began to cut into the boneless breast.

"You handle the bank meeting and I will stand by my bride-to-be at the press conference. Roland, I want you there, dressed in full regalia and a smile on your face. Put that on your calendar and do not be late," Rafferty said sternly.

"Yes, sir," Roland replied with a salute to his father and a nod to Malayka.

"And you, my Sammy," their father continued giving a much softer look and tone to his only daughter. "I don't want you to feel as though you were left out of the loop on this. Malayka and I just talked about this last night. Furthermore, I would think that you, above everyone else, would be happy to see that Malayka is perfectly able to plan with our island's best interests in mind. She's going to make an excellent princess and I have no doubt she will continue to have this palace running like a well-oiled machine, just as you have."

Samantha did not look impressed. However, she did smile and nod to her father and then, to Landry's surprise, to Malayka as well.

"I look forward to the day when I can hand off a good portion of my duties to you, Malayka. I just hope you know what you're getting into," Samantha said as she lifted her glass of wine and did a solo toast toward the couple.

Landry couldn't help herself, she grinned at the sarcasm in that moment. Sure, it was cleverly masked, but there was no doubt in her mind that the princess was anything but happy about having soon-to-be Princess Malayka taking over anything in the palace.

"We are amusing our guest," Prince Rafferty said.

Landry coughed immediately, embarrassment almost choking her.

"Well, we aim to please here at Grand Serenity Island," Roland added and lifted his glass, mirroring what Samantha had just done to Malayka.

As for Kristian, the scowl that had graced his face from the moment Landry had walked into this room was still perfectly in place as his gaze settled on her.

"I apologize," she said when she was certain her words wouldn't come out in a jumble. "I meant no disrespect. It's just that this scene reminds me of my family. I thought I was going to miss them terribly but it was nice to have this little reminder."

It wasn't a total lie, Landry told herself. She did come from a large family. Her parents had lived in the same house for the entire thirty years they'd been together. And as of ten years ago, her paternal grandparents had also lived in that house, along with Landry's four brothers, sister and her two kids. So yes, she was used to hostile family dinners, just not on a royal scale.

"Well, glad we can entertain you. But I suspect your stay here will also be educational as you watch a new leadership take the reins."

The prince was talking about Malayka, which, for

reasons Landry could not actually put her finger on, she thought was hilarious. Malayka Sampson was going to be a princess. Just five short months ago when Landry had first met her, she was introduced simply as an entrepreneur. Seems like Malayka had found her next business venture. Or perhaps she'd actually fallen in love with a real-life prince. How coincidentally wonderful for her.

"Yes, sir. I believe my time here will be interesting," Landry found herself saying instead of what she was really thinking.

"Interesting indeed. I mean, wouldn't you be anxious to get the ball rolling if you were going to run a Caribbean island?" he asked her.

Landry shook her head. "I'm not sure that would be something I'd be interested in doing, Your Highness."

"Really?" he asked as he sat back in his chair, wineglass in hand. "Are you saying you would turn down an invitation to become princess of this island?"

In a heartbeat, Landry thought.

"Yes, sir, I would. I'm not princess material."

Chapter 3

What is she doing here?

Kris asked himself this several times throughout the dinner. She'd walked in with Roland, arm-in-arm, both of them smiling, looking picture-perfect. He'd frowned.

He had felt his forehead wrinkling, his teeth clenching. Beneath the table where his hands had been resting calmly on his thighs, his fingers had slowly curled into fists. Why did they look like they belonged together when they'd only just met? Or had they?

Roland was his younger brother. He wasn't the immediate heir and so he did not have the duties and responsibilities that Kris had, nor did he express any interest in them. Instead, Roland's goal in life was to see just how much fun he could have before he dropped dead—at least that's what he'd always told Kris. Lately, with all the traveling Roland had been doing, combined with all the gambling and sleeping around with the woman of the month, Kris had begun to believe his brother was more than serious about achieving his life's goal.

That only made seeing him with Landry more annoying.

But it shouldn't have. He didn't know this woman, not well enough. Everything he'd read on paper about her schooling, where she lived in America, what she did for a living, had all been superficial. Kris had no idea who she really was on the inside and thus could not accurately pinpoint her motives in coming here. But there was a motive, he was sure. Everyone had a motive or a master plan.

Especially Malayka Sampson.

When the meal was thankfully over and second rounds of Chef Murray's crêpes Suzette had been devoured, Kris stood, eager to excuse himself. His plan was to retreat to his rooms, to the solitary space he craved so much after a long day of doing his job.

The job that hung around his neck like a heavy chain.

"Well, I'm off for the night," Roland announced as he, too, stood after dropping his napkin to the table. "It has, as always, been a pleasure. But duty calls."

Kris didn't bother to hide his displeasure. "Duty?" he asked and looked down at his watch. "It's almost seven thirty. What business do you have at this hour?"

"Don't you mean what date does he have at this hour?" Sam asked with a smirk.

Roland had already moved from his spot and was now leaning over to kiss his sister's offered cheek.

"Ha ha. And they say I'm the funny one," Roland joked.

Sam took the hand that Roland had rested on her shoulder, squeezing it gently before saying, "Be careful."

"Yes," Rafe began after loudly clearing his throat. "As I mentioned there will be members of the press lingering about once our engagement is announced."

Roland and Kris shared a look. Kris stood slowly and Roland gave a stiff bow to his father, his smile still in place.

"I hear you loud and clear, Dad. But the announcement isn't until tomorrow. That gives me plenty of time to get into as much trouble as I possibly can before then." Roland wiggled his brows as he finished and Kris felt compelled to step in before his father lost his patience.

"I'll walk out with you," Kris announced and then looked to Rafe. "You and I can figure out a time to meet tomorrow after your press conference and my meeting at the bank, but before the meeting with Denton. Good night, everyone."

It was easier to be formal, Kris thought to himself as he recalled Roland and Sam's warm exchange. This relieved the tension of knowing that he would never kiss Malayka's cheek or smile warmly at her. Roland didn't care about how that could be construed to the one person at the table who was an outsider. His brother simply acted, consequences would come later, those that Roland would likely ignore. Kris, on the other hand, did not ignore consequences or repercussions. He was duty bound to consider them with everything he did, from the clothes he wore to the way he pronounced a person's name. He was always under the microscope. Always expected to do and say the right thing.

"Let's go," Roland said after smiling and giving another bow to Landry.

Kris nodded curtly in her direction and found her staring at him after she smiled up at Roland. He chose to walk away then because he did not like how looking at her made him feel.

"She's a looker, I know," Roland said the moment they were out of the dining room.

Their dress shoes clicked somberly on the floors as

they walked toward the foyer. Roland was already unfastening the top button of his shirt. It was as close to being dressed for dinner as his brother had ever deigned to become. While Kris and their father wore a suit and tie, as was most usually their attire, and Sam dressed elegantly as always, getting Roland in slacks, a dress shirt and jacket was as good as they could manage.

"She's working for Malayka," Kris reminded his brother. He did not want to think of how she looked.

"Yeah, that's kind of strange, but then I guess not. That woman acts like an American superstar. She's had an entourage with her since the first time she set foot on this island. And Dad lets her have whatever she wants," Roland stated. "What do you think about that?"

Kris shook his head. "I'm trying not to think about it," he lied. "We're about to conduct the yearly audit on the banks. A few of the board members are nervous about one of the accounts. I've been looking into it, but I want to play it close."

Roland chuckled. "Don't want to step on any toes, huh, big brother? You'll tread lightly with the bankers, just like you will proceed with extreme caution where this royal wedding is concerned." He clapped Kris on the back. "I'm so glad you were born first."

Kris stopped walking just as they approached the double staircase in the family wing of the palace.

"You're still a member of this family, Roland. You still have duties and responsibilities to the monarch. The people of our country still depend on you," Kris told him in a serious tone.

"They depend on me to entertain them," Roland said. "I give them relief from our stuffy family filled with traditions and pomp and circumstance. I breathe a breath of fresh air into this stately fortress and stern but compassionate rule of the DeSaunters family. Don't be dismayed, Kris—I know my role in this family and I play it very well."

He did, Kris thought. Roland played his part perfectly and sometimes, for just a few hours out of a month or possibly year, Kris wished he could be as laid-back and carefree as his brother.

"We do not need any bad press right now," Kris said, shifting gears slightly. "Whatever you're up to tonight, keep it discreet."

Roland pulled off his jacket, holding it by a finger as he tossed it over his shoulder. "Don't I always?"

They both shared a knowing look then, before Roland laughed and Kris reluctantly cracked a smile. He loved his brother and his family, he truly did. That's why his job was so important. Everything he did was for them, for their country.

Once Roland was gone, Kris stood looking around at all the gray-streaked white marble, the shining columns and sprawling staircase. He looked up to the domed top of the room that was painted with puffy white clouds and a soft blue background. He had no idea whose concept that was but suspected it was meant to make a person standing there feel better. Though, for him, it didn't. Every day couldn't be a beautiful and picture-perfect day.

"It's beautiful," he heard her say and slowly tore his gaze away from the ceiling.

"The murals and sculptures I've seen in the palace so far are simply stunning. I'm not usually an art buff, but I know what looks good."

She continued to talk as she walked, her high-heeled shoes clicking over the gleaming floors. Her dress was drastically different from the formfitting outfit Malayka wore and was certainly more intriguing. Kris found himself staring at—of all things—her shoulders. They were pretty, her skin tone the perfect shade of brown, and appeared smooth to the touch. To the taste, he thought as he wondered about kissing her there. He would drag his tongue slowly from one shoulder to the next. Would she tremble beneath him? Would his mouth water? It already was.

"I've never seen a place like this before," she said, reaching her arms behind her back and clasping her fingers together.

Her hair was dark and pulled up so that her slender neck was visible. She walked slowly from one part of the room to the other, looking at things that Kris had seen so many times he could describe them each while blindfolded.

"I should probably head back to my rooms, but every time I come out I see something different. Something more beautiful," she said.

"There is nothing…" Kris said impulsively. Nothing more beautiful than her, he thought, but wisely, did not finish his comment.

She turned then, facing him with her head tilted slightly. "Excuse me?"

No, Kris's mind screamed. No, he would not excuse her and as he was already walking toward her, he apparently would not stay away from her either.

"There is nothing here that you cannot look at as long as you like," he told her. "As a matter of fact, I've asked my sister to give you a full tour of the island tomorrow."

"Oh," she said, seemingly surprised. "I'm only here to work. I don't mean to take up any of the royal family's official time. Besides, I'll be with Malayka early tomorrow morning until after the press conference."

He stopped only a few feet away from her. He was so close he could smell the soft scent of whatever fragrance she wore. It wasn't the powerful come-get-me scent that he'd smelled on so many women he'd met. No, this was lighter, with a sweet, musky aroma instead of a heavy floral one. He liked it. A lot. He also liked how she was looking up at his six-foot-two-inch frame now.

"Sam will be attending the press conference as well. The two of you can leave afterward," he stated.

Then Kris did something he rarely ever did while in someone's company. He slipped both hands into his front pant pockets. It was a casual stance, one that did not equate to the role of a leader.

"I wouldn't want to impose," she said.

Her voice had changed. It was subtle and he doubted even she realized it, but Kris did. There was a smoky tinge to her words and just as he made that realization, she licked her lips. His body tensed.

"She's the president of the tourism board—it's her duty to welcome all tourists to the island," Kris told her and instinctively took another step closer.

"Why?" she asked and he paused. "Why did you ask her to show me around? You know I'm not technically a tourist. I'm here to work for Malayka."

"I know why you're here."

"Then why did you insist I come to dinner? You did that, didn't you? The housekeeper—"

"Ingrid," he interrupted.

She nodded. "Ingrid said I was supposed to be ready at six, that I was expected at dinner. She was in the hall waiting when I left your office earlier today, as if she knew I would be coming out. Why didn't you invite Malayka's hair stylist and makeup artist? Why only me?"

Kris did not have the answers to any of her questions. Another first for him. He had instructed Ingrid to tell her about dinner. All he'd known at that time was that he'd wanted to see her again. Just as he hadn't been able to stop looking at her pictures all week, Kris now couldn't keep his eyes off her. While his more official thought had been that he wanted to know everything there was to know about Malayka's staff, it was Landry, in particular, who had awakened something in him.

"You don't care for dinner? Is that why you're questioning me?" he asked.

She smiled then, a slow and deliberate action.

"You don't want to answer my question," she said. "That's fine. Still, I don't want to impose on anyone. I'll do some sightseeing whenever I'm not working, but I don't think I need a guide."

"What do you need?"

The question was quick and impulsive. Her response was even quicker and bold. *Yes*, Kris thought as he sucked in a quick breath when she'd taken that step closing the distance between them, *it was damn bold*.

"Why?" she asked. "What do you need, Prince Kristian?"

He stared at her for much longer than he figured a smooth and charismatic man should. Then again, those had never been traits Kris possessed. He was the mature prince, the serious one who was all business, all the time. But he'd never done business with a woman who looked and smiled like Landry Norris. None of his dealings were filled with the scent she wore, or the sound of Landry Norris's voice. And nobody, not even the women he'd dated over the years, whether for convenience or for political reasons, had ever made him lose track of what he should be doing.

Yet, his response to her was simple and came as naturally as his next breath. Kris touched a finger to her chin, tilting her head up farther. Her lips parted slightly as her hazel eyes stared back at him. He leaned in closer, wanting desperately to see those eyes filled with lust. Wanting, even more hungrily, to touch his lips to hers, to taste the sweetness of her.

He shouldn't.

He couldn't.

He was a breath away. She leaned into him, her arms remaining straight by her side. Her lips were still parted, her tongue beyond them, teasing and tempting him.

He was the crown prince. She worked for the woman who planned to marry his father.

He couldn't.

Kris closed his eyes and leaned in just another inch or so, until her warm breath smelling of the sweet crêpes they'd just had for dessert fanned over his face. He inhaled the aroma, feeling the heat of desire swelling in the pit of his stomach.

What was she doing? Was she completely out of her mind?

Why on earth had she thought the crown prince of this beautiful island would want to kiss *her*? They'd only met hours earlier. It was ridiculous. Presumptuous and possibly career ending if she were to be kicked off the island. Malayka was exactly the type to spread vicious rumors. And since this one would have a great amount of truth to it, Malayka would happily report back to everyone she knew in the United States.

Landry sighed, letting her head lull back against the door to her room, which she'd slammed closed and locked a few minutes after she'd left Prince Kristian and run all the way to her temporary sanctuary.

She was such a screwup.

Impulsive. Headstrong. Opinionated. Mouthy.

All words Landry had heard before in reference to her personality.

"Men don't want women who push too hard, Landry. They want someone agreeable and calm spirited."

Those were Astelle Norris's famous words to her daughter. They were famous because she'd spoken them more times than Landry could count.

"Wives are submissive to their husbands," Astelle would continue as she sat at the kitchen table doing some chore she thought wifely. Like snapping green beans for dinner or sewing socks so that her husband Heinz Norris's toes wouldn't poke through as he stood in the pulpit of the Baptist church where he pastored.

Landry could feel her eyes rolling back in her head as she recalled one of the more popular disagreements she'd had over the years with her mother.

"I'm not doing any man's bidding. He can cook just like I can and he can go out and buy himself a new pair of socks if his have holes in them. I don't have to be subservient to get and keep a man," was Landry's typical response.

Astelle, with her thinning, but still long silver-gray hair, only shook her head. *"It doesn't make you less of a woman, Landry. It makes you a good woman."*

"To who?" Landry had asked. *"If I give a man that much control over me, who am I any good to? My future daughters will only see that their mother is so fragile and clueless that she can't do anything without permission from a man? My future sons will grow up believing they rule the world, not for their brains or intuition, but because they have a penis so it should be so?"*

In a rare display of anger, Astelle had stood quickly, dropping the beans she'd held into a large yellow bowl as she glared at her daughter through tired gray eyes. *"I've never been clueless, Landry Diane Norris. I graduated*

*at the top of my class at Brighton Business School and I
worked in a law office for the first five years of my marriage until my husband finished school and received his
PhD. I came home and started a family where I took care
of my children and the head of my household. Six productive and intelligent people were brought into this world
because of me and all the lessons I've taught them. My
husband is a pillar of this community. He's a teacher and
a confidant and a good provider. I'm just as proud of him
as I am of our children. So don't you stand there after another failed relationship and pretend to know what my life
has been like or what may have been better for me. I won't
stand for your disrespect."*

By the time her mother had finished speaking her hands
were shaking with rage and Landry felt like crap. Astelle
had left her in that kitchen alone, where Landry spent a
few more moments wallowing in guilt and wondering how
long she should wait before apologizing to her mother.
Her father had come in during that time, rubbing his hand
over Landry's head as he used to do when she was a child.

"Put your foot in your mouth again, huh, pumpkin?"
Heinz had asked with the booming melodic voice of a
southern-born minister.

"Yes, sir," had been her quiet response.

*"She's only telling you what she's learned. That's a
mother's job,"* he said as he went into the refrigerator and
grabbed a bottled water.

Landry watched her father's strong hands—the same
ones that, when she was ten years old, had fixed the chain
on her bike—twist the cap off the water before lifting the
bottle to his lips and taking a gulp. She saw the man who
had carried her mother to the car the night she'd awakened
in pain and stayed at the hospital every second Astelle was
there having her emergency hysterectomy. Landry had

only been sixteen then. He was the same man who had placed money in Landry's hand and told her to go to the grocery store and get some things to have cooked before Astelle came home. The man who had written check after check for Landry to attend college when the scholarships she'd received had run out.

"I'm not the type of woman she is," Landry had admitted. *"I could never be like her."*

Heinz shook his head, his short-cropped black hair having long ago made the transition to snowy white. *"She doesn't want you to be like her. She just wants you to be good and true."*

"To bow to some man and say what he wants to make him happy. Kevin Blake cheated on me with a freshman that had big boobs and a fake butt. What could I have done to make him happy if that's the kind of trash he wanted to chase in the first place?"

"Nothing. Because he was a jerk. But not all men are and your mother is simply trying to prepare you for a mature and fulfilling relationship."

"She's trying to make me a Leave It to Beaver *wife in the age of* The Real Housewives.*"*

Heinz chuckled then. *"Now, those women, you should definitely take note of."*

Landry had been surprised by what her father had said in reference to the reality TV series. But more so because as she'd been talking to him, she'd moved to the seat that her mother had vacated and started snapping the green beans and dropping them in that same yellow bowl.

"You're saying I should take advice from the housewives?" she asked because that made more sense than trying to figure out what she was doing with the beans.

"No," Heinz replied with a hearty chuckle. *"Not at all. What your mother and I have built over the course of our*

marriage is something special and sacred. It's also been very rewarding for us. Of course your mother would want you to find the same type of commitment for your life. The thing is, what I think you're missing about the type of marriage that your mother and I have, is that it's rooted in love. Your mother could not do and say the things she did with regard to our marriage if she didn't love me with every fiber of her being. For that I am forever grateful as there is no greater love on this earth. As for me, I can only thank the Lord daily for the blessing of my wife. I love her phenomenally and I cherish her. That's what she wants for you, Landry. That's what we both want for you."

Well, that was never going to happen, Landry thought as she pushed away from the door and stepped out of her heels, kicking them across the Aubusson rug.

She reached behind and unzipped her dress as she walked toward the rack where she'd left the hanger. Landry stood in the middle of the fanciest room she'd ever had the pleasure of staying in and stripped the expensive dress off her body. She hung it on the rack once more, traipsed over to the bed and plopped down onto the shiny cream-colored comforter.

She'd thought for sure Kristian wanted to kiss her. Everything about him said so. The way he'd stepped to her and touched her chin. His eyes had grown darker, his lips parted. Well, hers parted first because not only had she assumed he wanted the kiss, she'd been anxious for it as well.

With a heavy sigh she fell back on the bed, one arm going over her eyes, her hand to her stomach as if she could possibly calm the butterflies that still danced happily there. She wanted to kiss the prince. Not the sexy flirtatious one that probably would have easily taken her into her arms and kissed her senseless. No, she had to want the other one. The one who looked at her like she was no better than the rug he stepped on. She hadn't been here a full twenty-four hours and already she was messing up.

But tomorrow was another day and she needed to get an early start. Malayka was going to be anxious and irritable. Everything would need to be perfect for her first official appearance as Prince Rafferty's fiancée. So with a resignation to keep her mind on things that it should be on, Landry moved over the bed until she could push down the comforter and slip beneath it and the sheets. Lying on a soft pillow she stared up at the ceiling and attempted to think of the dresses she would pull for Malayka tomorrow. The shoes, earrings, necklace, rings. How her hair would be styled. Makeup soft, or bold?

Those thoughts were quickly replaced by the sights of the windows across the room. Large windows, no curtains, giving a clear view out to the night sky. Dark, but with tiny pricks of light. Stars, Landry thought. There were stars out tonight. What would happen if she wished upon a star?

Not a damn thing, she thought with a chuckle. This wasn't a storybook and wishes did not come true. Sure, she was lying in a king-size bed, in a room in a palace. Tomorrow morning she would watch a prince announce that he was about to make a woman a princess. A woman, who for all intents and purposes, came from the same place that Landry had. And yes, tonight she'd dined with said prince, plus two more and a princess who smiled easily but managed to run their household and island in grand style.

There was still reality. The one where Landry was a business owner and Malayka was a client. She would do this job and then she would return to LA, to her family and her condo. To her world. The princes and princesses would all remain here in the land that looked to be fresh out of a childhood storybook, but had no place in Landry's dreams.

Now that was a buzzkill if ever she'd experienced one.

Landry turned on her side, closed her eyes and forced them to remain that way. She thought of dresses again, of colors and materials. She did not think about Kristian, or his lips, or how a kiss from him would have tasted. She refused, and that took way more energy than planning a wardrobe for any client ever had.

Chapter 4

Kris watched the taped version of the press conference for the third time. There was a throbbing between his eyes as he hit the stop button on the remote, ending the recording seconds before turning the television off.

He was in his rooms now, two hours after his meeting at the bank had ended. His second meeting of the day had been cancelled and his father had never contacted him about when they would meet today. Kris sat back in the leather chair in the sitting area that he'd turned into an additional office and stared down at his desk. He did not have time for this.

Press conferences about wedding plans, announcements about parties, and yes, the blatant disrespect Malayka had just shown to the local dressmakers, were all among the things Kris did not want to deal with. There were too many more important things for him to occupy his thoughts with.

The meeting at the bank and the concern that had been gnawing at him for weeks, for instance.

Grand Serenity Island was an independent territory that had been acquired by the Netherlands in the 1600s. The island did not flourish as the early settlers would have liked because of its dry climate and thus the lack of agricultural prospects. That began to change in the late 1800s when the son of a British sailor named Montgomery Chapman decided there had to be more to this place than gorgeous waters and warm air. Montgomery and his group of slaves discovered the Rustatian Gold Mill, which eventually went on to produce three million pounds of gold. In the immediate years following, the island saw more growth in the building of its first oil refinery, which was also owned by the Chapman family.

By the time Kris's grandfather, Josef Marquise DeSaunters, gained control of the island via his leadership role in the rebellion against the then ruling tyrant, Governor Marco Vansig, the gold mills and oil refineries were the island's main sources of income. However, Vansig's greed and vicious rule had burned many bridges in the trade industry, leaving Josef with no other option than to look for additional opportunities for the citizens of the island to continue to thrive. On the advice of his wife, Josef formed the island's first tourism board and by the early 1980s, when the oil industry began to wane, tourism became Grand Serenity's financial savior.

It was Kris's father, Rafe, who came into rule after Josef's death from throat cancer. Rafe vowed to continue his father's vision for the island. Rafe knew the value of forging strong partnerships on and off the island. This led him to venture to the United States where he met with potential developers and owners of the burgeoning cruise lines. This was also where Rafe met his wife, Kris's mother, Vivienne Patterson, whose father was a Texas oilman.

Kris dragged a hand down his face at the thought. His chest clenched and he spent the next few seconds tamping down the well of emotion that always swelled when he thought of his mother, who had died when Kris was ten years old. When Kris was certain he could concentrate on the pressing matter at hand once more, he opened a large file filled with papers he'd brought back with him from the bank and began sorting them into three piles.

As a young man during his father's rule, Rafe had begun to amass more fortune for the DeSaunters family by constructing financial institutions. He'd been successful with soliciting wealthy international clients, as well as celebrities, to invest and bank with Grand Serenity as a way of remaining ungoverned by their country's financial restrictions. This had been the first aspect of governing the island that Rafe had taught Kris. From the time Kris was a young boy, his father had talked of the banks and how they, along with the tourism, would sustain the island's growth, even as the natural resources continued to dwindle.

Thus came his degree in international finance. Kris spent numerous hours a day poring over financial reports and statements from each of the three banks on the island.

Three months ago, Kris had received reports of two new accounts that had been opened with multimillion-dollar deposits. The accounts had continued to see hefty deposits in the following weeks. This alone did not raise any red flags, however it was the signature cards on the account that did.

A. M. Belle Vansig.

The name had immediately struck a chord in Kris's mind, yet when he'd searched deeper into the account, he hadn't found any further identifying information for this person.

"You're not concerned?" he'd asked his father during one of their morning meetings.

"It's just a name, Kris," Rafe had responded as he'd scooped spoonful after spoonful of sugar into his coffee.

The strong and stern ruler of the great Grand Serenity Island had a vicious sweet tooth.

"A name that has meaning in our family's past and the history of this island," was Kris's counter.

Rafe shook his head. "Marco Vansig and his army were conquered by my father and his soldiers. Their bodies were burned at sea. Vansig had no wife, no children, nothing but his precious gold, which was turned over to the island treasury department upon his death. He was a dark spot in this island's history and then he was gone. Now, decades later, you see the name and what? You think Vansig is reaching up from the grave to cause more mayhem?"

Kris had to admit that the idea seemed far-fetched. There were numerous people throughout the world with the same name that had no connection to each other whatsoever. Still, he'd decided to keep an eye on the accounts anyway.

"Nonetheless, I've been thinking we should implement a more thorough background check for new account holders. With the rise in criminal activity connecting to offshore accounts, we want to be sure that we're working on a higher level."

"Our institutions are not founded on the rules and regulations of other financial facilities. This is why we are able to hold such lucrative accounts. We do not overly tax our customers with paperwork and supervision of their own funds," Rafe had immediately rebutted.

"I know that we are not regulated by such organizations as the United States Federal Reserve or the European Commission and other such places throughout the world. Our customers run from Russia to South America and we retain their autonomy and confidence by not working in any fashion with these other regulating entities. But that does not mean we do not have our own regulatory process. We should still know who we are doing business with."

"We do," Rafe insisted. "There is no need to change the protocols we have in place. It has been working for years."

"Things change, Dad," Kris told his father. "You know that as well as I do. I'm just trying to look out for our future. It's my job."

Rafe hadn't disputed that fact. His father had been the one constantly drilling into Kris's head the importance of his job and his duty. Kris would rule this island and continue what his grandfather and father had built before him. He would not fail. He could not fail.

Just as he could not bring himself to kiss the sexy American last night.

There had been no other reason but his duty. She was a very attractive woman, with a personality unlike the many women who had crossed his path. With Landry Norris there were no pretenses. She had not come into his office batting her eyes, or crossing her bare legs for his perusal. Her reason for being here had been perfectly explained by all the paperwork she'd completed and the way she'd sat across from him answering his questions, even though she thought they were over-the-top. Of course, she hadn't said that—which showed that no matter how honest she seemed, she did have respect for his position. Kris could tell by the way she'd watched him carefully after providing each answer. She'd wondered if the answer was good enough for him, while inwardly not caring because she told herself she had no intention of answering any other way. Her subtle boldness and their conversation had been intriguing to Kris.

So much so, that at last night's dinner he'd found himself watching her, listening to her talk and laugh, more focused on her than all the business issues that he still had to deal with. Kris had no idea when something else had taken over his mind before business.

Last night, she hadn't shied away from him. He hadn't really expected her to; he was the crown prince, after all. Not that he was conceited in any way. To the contrary, Kris wished on more days than he could count that he were just a regular guy. If he were, then he could have kissed her last night and maybe there could have been more, like a long evening in bed, a slow start to the morning after waking with her in his arms.

He sighed heavily and then shook his head. Thoughts like that were for other people, in other places. Not him and definitely not here.

"Nice to see you made it back from the bank in one piece."

Kris looked up to see Roland walking into his private office. Kris hadn't bothered to lock the doors since he was expecting Roland. Besides, his brother rarely knocked on any doors in the palace. Roland Simon DeSaunters always had to make a grand entrance. Their mother used to always tell the story of the night of the Ambassador's Ball when she was barely seven months pregnant and her water had broken as soon as she and Rafe made their entrance into the ballroom. Roland had been born one hour after that moment, yelling at the top of his lungs, announcing his arrival as if they hadn't already known he was coming. Vivienne had always smiled when she retold that story. Rafe, on the other hand, would frown. Their father had frowned a lot where Roland was concerned.

"Nice to see you made it to the press conference and on time," Kris replied.

He was finished removing the papers from the folder and set it to the side on his desk.

Roland closed the office door before taking a seat across from Kris's desk.

"I said I would be there," he told Kris.

"You did."

"I always keep my word," Roland continued. "You know that."

Kris nodded as he looked over to his brother who was now dressed in khaki pants and a polo shirt. Kris couldn't remember the last time he'd been able to dress so casually.

"You are trustworthy," Kris said. "Even the billionaires you swindle out of their money can attest to that."

Roland shook his head. "You've got it all wrong, big brother. I do not swindle. I play cards and I play them well. Those with huge bank accounts and even larger egos should never underestimate that."

His brother was smiling. Kris was not. As long as Kris was alive and well, he was next in line to rule. Roland was not. As such, he hadn't been trained and groomed the way Kris had. That was not to say that Rafe hadn't raised both his sons with a strong and firm hand, because he had. There were rules and they were all expected to follow them because Rafe's wrath was nothing to be laughed at. Sam had been handled differently, still, unshakable integrity and dedication to their island was a given for each one of them. Roland was the only one who did not agree to those terms.

"So that's where you're off to tonight. I saw on the schedule that you're leaving town today and will return in time for the brunch on Friday, before taking off again Friday night. You're going to join in another one of those poker games aren't you?" Kris couldn't hide the disappointment in his tone.

Roland only shrugged. "You run the banks and stand by Dad looking all dour and debonair. Sam smiles prettily at the tourist board meetings. She is the face of the island, a beautiful Caribbean goddess is what I've heard her called. Me, I'm the recluse. That little bit of danger that intrigues the world and probably draws in quite a bit of tourists as well. Just like the Americans who flock to Hollywood to see the homes of the stars," he said with a chuckle. "It's what I do and, just like you and Sam, I do it well."

"Regardless of the repercussions?"

"I'm an adult, Kris. I went to school and graduated just like Dad had commanded. He said since I did not care to attend college like you did, that I had to enlist in the military. The Royal Seaside Navy was less than happy to put up with me for four years, but they did and I completed my time there. I've done my part."

"Have you, Roland?" Kris asked as he leaned forward on his desk. "You don't help with any of the business of this island. Sam and I both carry more of a load than you. Hell, you barely show up for dinner or other functions. You know you're not doing your part."

"I'm doing the part that fell on my shoulders. If my big brother weren't so perfect and my younger sister so pretty, maybe there would have been something left for me. Alas, I'm not into complaining. I'm making the best of my situation."

"I'd give you any one of my assignments if you acted halfway interested," Kris admitted.

Roland drummed his fingers on the arms of the chair. "Thankfully, I'm not. And this isn't the real reason you called me. So why don't we skip the rest of this conversation because we already know how it's going to end."

Kris frowned. He hated when Roland was right.

"Were you paying attention at the press conference this morning, or did you just show up to be seen?" he asked after taking a slow, steady breath and releasing it.

"I heard every word, just like everyone on this island and probably a good portion of people across the world did."

Roland lounged back in the chair.

Kris rubbed a finger over his chin. "Sam doesn't care for her."

"And now, neither do the dressmakers on this island. She basically told them she'd attend her own wedding naked before employing one of them," Roland stated.

Kris looked at his brother again. Candor was one of Roland's strong points.

"Sam cleaned it up well at the end, but I don't know if that's going to be enough. We should do something more," Kris stated.

"Like what? Buy a dress from all the local dressmakers? Aren't the house staff uniforms already manufactured locally?"

Kris was surprised that Roland even knew about the house staff uniforms at all. "Last night you were talking to Malayka's stylist. The two of you seemed...friendly," Kris stated, ignoring the tinge of irritation he felt at the thought.

"Yeesss," Roland drew the word out like he was more than satisfied with the memory himself. "Landry Norris. She was interesting."

Kris didn't need his brother to tell him that. Landry was so interesting Kris had spent a good portion of last night thinking about her when he should have been preparing for his meeting.

"Her job is to advise Malayka on what to wear. What if she suggests a local dressmaker, maybe not for the wedding gown but for something else? It would go a long way for community relations."

Another shrug from his brother. "I guess."

"I want you to suggest this to her," Kris told him.

"Me?"

"Yes, you."

"Why me?"

"Because you think she's interesting, remember? And judging by the way you were looking at her last night, I don't believe it a hardship to ask you to speak with her once more."

Kris's hands had fallen to the arms of his chair, fingers gripping the edges, without thought. Roland leaned forward, resting his elbows on his knees as he stared long and hard at Kris for endless seconds.

"Sam said you told her to take Landry on a tour of the island," Roland began.

"That's correct. As you stated, Sam is the face of the island. People expect to see her out and about especially when guests are at the palace."

"Then why not have her suggest the dressmakers to the royal guest?"

"She might. I know that Sam uses a couple of the local dressmakers herself. I'm asking you because I want to make sure the stylist takes the suggestion seriously," Kris stated.

"The stylist," Roland repeated with a nod. "Her name is Landry Norris. I know you never forget a name, yet you haven't said hers once."

Kris's teeth clenched. "I have these mountains of paperwork to go through today, Roland. Then I have to meet with Dad to brief him and attend yet another dinner with him and Malayka. I'm asking you to do one thing for me and this island's economy. Can you please just take a moment out of your busy social schedule to accommodate me?"

Roland chuckled then. He stood, nodded. "Sure thing, big brother. Who wouldn't do the crown prince's bidding?"

The sarcasm wasn't lost on Kris, but he wasn't in the mood to address it. He had other work to do.

"Thank you," Kris said, moving in his chair so that he could turn his attention to the paperwork on his desk.

"No problem. I'll make sure that Landry Norris knows what the crown prince wants from her…"

Kris's head snapped up at Roland's words but his brother was already gone, closing the door with a definite click behind him.

Chapter 5

His body reacted first.

A jolt of lust so quick and potent Kris almost had to cough to keep from choking. The strong scent of chlorine burned his nose as the balmy temperature from the inside pool area warmed his cheeks.

This was where his training in control and temperament came into play. When he was young, Kris had taken riding, fencing and piano lessons. The latter was because his mother was determined to teach her children something other than duty.

A sword could cut deep and painfully if Kris wasn't in complete control of his own weapon, if his mind wasn't totally focused on the matter at hand. That was the lesson his father had wanted him to learn from the eight-week-long fencing class. There was never any real threat of Kris having to decide local policy via a sword fight. He would, however, need the control and steely resolve of a good leader to face any potential opponent.

In all probability, this learned control and decisiveness was not intended to spill over into Kris's personal life or feelings, but it had. Hence the reason he was now clenching his fists so tightly, the blunt tips of his nails attempting to bite into his skin.

The glistening pool water cast her body in a dreamy seductive haze as he watched intently. She swam gracefully in long measured strokes from one end of the pool to the other. Her bathing suit was yellow, like the sun. A swatch of material covering her backside and a strap crossing her back that he presumed held her ample bosom in place. That was all he saw, other than skin.

Back and forth, Kris watched as she swam, stopping only a few seconds at each end of the pool to take in air. She was counting, he realized after a few more moments of watching. Each lap she did counted toward her goal. He wondered briefly what that goal was and then silently commended her for striving for it in the first place. He also thanked her immensely for her choice of swimwear as five laps later, she climbed out of the pool, giving him a full, unfettered view of deliciousness.

She was curvier than he'd presumed. Generous breasts, full waist, glorious hips and thick thighs. His mouth went dry, his erection hard and persistent. Water rolled off her gorgeous brown skin in slow drops that made him thirstier than he'd ever been before.

At his sides, Kris's fingers unclenched, his palms tingling with the urge to touch. He could see his hands on her waist, holding her close to him, close enough so that he could rub his erection against her. Kris blinked at the abrupt eroticism of his thoughts. It was unlike him, and yet it felt as natural as breathing.

She was coming closer, as he stood only a few feet away from the row of chaise lounges along the side of the pool room. Her hair was slicked back from her face, dripping more water onto her body. Kris wanted to catch every drop, with his tongue. She leaned down to pick up a towel and then stood straight once more. He moved quickly, ducking behind the column that thankfully hid his Peeping Tom presence.

For a few still moments Kris did not move. She knew someone was there. She just didn't know who. This may have been the only cowardly act of his life, but regardless, Kris walked quickly away.

It wasn't until he was locked in his rooms that he thought no, this wasn't the first cowardly move he'd made, but it would most certainly be the last.

"I apologize," Samantha DeSaunters stated the moment they were closed in the backseat of the car together. "I meant to meet up with you last week but my schedule changed abruptly. When I had to change the time of the Children's Hospital brunch to accommodate Malayka's bridal party meeting things sort of spiraled out of control. I'm just getting back on track."

Landry sat back against the cool leather seat, resisting the urge to sigh. It was barely noon and already it was extremely warm on the island. Her nightly swims had been extended to early mornings as a way to cool down. She'd just returned from meeting with Malayka to go over her schedule for next week when the princess had knocked on her door.

"No apology necessary, Your Highness. I've been doing a little sightseeing on my own when I can," Landry said just as the car began moving.

"That's right, Kris did mention that Jorge had taken you

out a few times. Jorge is used to driving the palace guests, visiting dignitaries and such," Samantha said. "And we're alone now, so please call me Sam."

Landry smiled over to Sam and gave her a cordial nod. "Okay, but really I don't need a personal tour. I know that you're all very busy with your own jobs. During the time that I'm here and not working with Malayka, I can certainly entertain myself."

"Nonsense," Sam told her. "You get the royal treatment just like any other guest of the palace. Now, Phillipe is my driver and while he might look tall and a bit scary at times, he's a big ole teddy bear. He's going to take us into town, where I have a quick appointment, and then we'll walk the streets for a bit before having lunch at my favorite place. Afterward we'll spend the afternoon at the museums and we'll be back at the palace in time for dinner."

It sounded like a full day, which coincidentally happened to work well for Landry since Malayka was leaving that afternoon for a weekend trip with the prince. Landry had spent a good portion of her morning with Malayka selecting outfits for the trip. The prince had instructed Malayka that none of her staff could join them and Landry had mixed feelings about that declaration. On one hand, she could certainly use a few dinners without the tension that drifted like heat waves between her and Kristian. On the other, Landry could also use some time away from Malayka who had changed from the budding socialite Landry first met in LA to full-fledged princess mode, even though the title was still months away from being solidified.

"Each one of you have your own driver?" Landry asked to distract herself from thoughts of both Malayka and Kristian.

"Yes," Sam replied. "Rex is my father's driver. He's the palace transportation supervisor. There are five other full-time drivers on staff. Dante is Rex's right hand, so he's been taking care of Malayka's car service needs. Kris's driver is Tajeo and Phillipe sticks with me."

"What about Roland?"

Sam shook her head. "Everybody asks that question at some time or another. What about Roland? Why isn't he coming to the Ambassador's Ball? Why doesn't he stay in the palace as much as the rest of the family?" Sam chuckled then. "Roland is his own man, as he likes to tell us. He drives himself, except when my father insists he act like a royal prince should."

"And how often is that?" Landry inquired with a hint of humor. She liked Roland and his easy smile even though she hadn't seen much of him in the last week.

"Not often," was Sam's reply in a tone that said she liked her brother a lot.

Landry could tell. There was definitely love in this family, even if it was rather stilted in presentation. Landry came from a tight-hugging, wet-cheek-kissing, boisterous family where nobody ever doubted they belonged; everyone felt loved. At the palace, she thought, Prince Rafferty was a serious and domineering father and leader. His children respected him and stuck together because it was what they were taught to do. Love was there, but on well-laid-out terms and with the restrictions of the royal crown. It was as sad as it was a privilege.

"He reminds me of my brother Dominic. He's the second oldest of my siblings and acts like he could easily be the youngest. I call him courageous and adventurous, but my dad insists the correct description should be childish and irresponsible," Landry spoke comfortably as she looked out the back tinted window.

They were riding in a Mercedes-Benz C450 AMG 4matic. Landry only knew this because Dominic loved

cars and since she'd always been madly in love with her
older brother, she'd stuck to him like glue when she was a
little girl. Thus, her own interest in cars had bloomed. It
was white with dark tinted windows. She'd seen another
one a couple days ago when Dante had brought her back
to the palace, so Landry assumed the palace had a fleet of
them. She tried not to be awed by that fact.

"Really? How many brothers and sisters do you have?"
Sam asked.

Landry turned to look at her then. She was a lovely
woman with her pecan skin tone and curly shoulder-length
hair. Landry would have to spend at least an hour with the
hot wand if she wanted her hair to have lush curls like that.
Sam's were natural, Landry suspected, just like her thick,
elegantly arched brows were and the exotic tilt of her eyes.

The princess wore a navy blue silk polka-dot dress with
a sweetheart neckline, a bodice with gathers and bows at
the shoulders. It was a vintage-style dress, circa 1940s,
Landry deduced. There was a layer of tulle on the under-
side to give the dress a full-skirt appearance and her white
platform pumps had navy blue polka-dot bows at the tops.
It was both lovely and classic and Sam DeSaunters wore
it well.

As for Landry, she also wore a dress. A strapless black-
and-white-striped one with a cinched waist and fitted
asymmetric skirt. Her sandals had one strap around the
ankle, one across her toes and a four-inch heel. Sam had
a large-brimmed white hat sitting daintily on the seat between them. Landry hadn't thought that far ahead so she'd
probably be scorched by the Caribbean sun today.

"There are six of us, four boys and two girls. I'm next
to the youngest," Landry told her. "We grew up in a big
house that still seemed too small when we were all at home

and getting into each other's way. Makes me wish I'd lived in a palace instead."

Of course she'd been joking. Landry loved the old ranch-style home her parents still owned. Five years ago they'd built an addition so that Landry's maternal grandparents could move in. By that time, Landry had been happy that she'd had a place of her own, but still enjoyed going back frequently to visit.

"Palace life isn't all it seems at first glance," Sam replied.

"Most things aren't," Landry told her.

Sam smiled then and nodded. "I think I'm going to like you, Landry Norris."

"These fabrics are gorgeous," Landry exclaimed as she ran her hands over silks in rich jewel-tone colors and vibrant prints.

"We have it imported here for special orders," the woman who Sam had introduced as Detali told her. "The Ambassador's Ball is soon."

"You're absolutely right, Detali," Sam said as she moved about in the shop that did not look large enough to hold a tea party, let alone produce dresses. "It's in five weeks and I haven't even thought about what I'm going to wear."

Detali, a woman who stood maybe four feet nine inches tall, and had the straightest, blackest hair Landry thought she'd ever seen, nodded at the princess. "It is late for you."

"I know," Sam continued. She picked up a large-brimmed black hat with a huge red bow around the rim. Removing the white one she wore, Sam tried on the black hat and looked as stunningly gorgeous as she did in the first one.

Landry returned her attention to the lovely cream-colored satin with the intricately designed turquoise flowers. "This would look lovely on Malayka. She mentioned the ball and we brought some gowns with us, but yesterday she was talking about something different, bolder."

When she was met with complete silence, Landry looked up to see Detali and Sam exchanging a look. "What? Did I say something wrong?" she asked. "Is there a special dress code for the ball that I'm not aware of?"

Sam had replaced the black hat and was now smoothing down a few of her curls. "No dress code," she said as she crossed the room to stand closer to Landry.

"At the press conference last week, Malayka indicated that she did not believe any of the local dressmakers could master her style," Sam told her in a hushed tone.

Landry knew firsthand how selective Malayka was about designers. Even with Landry lending her expert advice, Malayka often had trivial excuses for not using a particular designer. "She smokes, so I don't want her designing my clothes." "Her nails are too short." "He has a unibrow." On and on until Landry had begun to present the outfits before giving Malayka the name of the designer, in the hopes that she'd like the clothes so much that the other ridiculous reasons or rejecting them would be dismissed. That's why, even though Landry had also been present at the press conference and had heard Malayka's comment, she simply planned to ignore it. "Does that mean I could not commission a dress to be made for her anyway?"

Sam lifted an elegantly arched brow at Landry's question, the corner of her mouth tilting into a smile. "You are her personal stylist."

"I am and I usually know what will look good on a client before a client even decides it's worth trying. These colors will look great with her complexion. If we could get the right design, this gown would be stunning."

Landry had returned her attention to the material, unfolding it and laying it over the table where she'd been standing. She thought about an A-line gown, something simple, yet chic and daring in some way. It would need to be regal as was the mood they'd decided to portray for Malayka. The wedding gown was already being designed by Peta, as a personal favor to Landry, and also as another boost to Peta's already stellar portfolio. But for this event, the one where Malayka would be meeting the ruling parties from other islands and countries, she should be breathtaking as she stands beside her prince.

"If I brought you some sketches do you think you could come up with something in time?" Landry turned to the front desk that looked more like a hunk of a tree trunk with its top smoothed over, dropped down into a corner. Detali had to be sitting on a stool now because she seemed taller as her wide eyes fixed on Landry.

She looked from her to the princess in question, before opening her mouth to respond.

Landry wanted to say that she was the one in charge of Malayka's wardrobe and that if Malayka was too stubborn to wear it, Landry was certain she had another client back in the States that she could pair with the gown. Either way, Detali was sure to receive more exposure if she agreed, and if Landry was successful in not only commissioning the gown, but also having it sold to a celebrity in the States, then it was a win-win for them all.

It took every ounce of control that Landry had to keep her mouth closed and look to the princess for a response.

"I think it would be a fabulous idea for the soon-to-be princess to wear a gown from a local dressmaker to the ball. With your name attached to the press that will undoubtedly spread from the prince of Grand Serenity's first official event with his American fiancée, more Americans may seek one-of-a-kind attire from Grand Serenity. It is good business for the island as well as your client. Don't you agree?"

Landry smiled as she realized Sam had been thinking along the same lines as she had. Part of her wondered if that was the reason for this little trip here today, but Landry was too excited by the prospect to give it too much thought.

He was sick.

What he was doing was ridiculous.

This was his house. His island. He could have any woman he wanted, whenever he wanted her. That was a fact and not just some colossal stroke to his ego. Kris liked to deal with facts and truths; unshakable reality was where he preferred to live and function.

His mother used to tell him stories at night before he fell asleep. Some were fairy tales that always had happy endings. One night, when Kris was five years old, his father had entered his bedroom just as Vivienne was telling Kris the story of the prince who rejoiced after finally finding his perfect princess. Rafe was furious and demanded that Vivienne cease telling "his heir" these types of stories because a head full of fluff was not what was going to lead his island to greatness. The next night when Vivienne came to tuck Kris in—and as he'd waited patiently for her to begin another story about some faraway land where love was able to heal all wounds—he knew immediately that the next story would be different.

The stories Kris received that night and many nights thereafter were ones of wars won by the strongest and the smartest. Sure, there might be a kiss here or there, or even a damsel in distress at some point, but the core of every story had been the same—honor, integrity, loyalty. Until the words were branded in Kris's mind and his soul.

So it was reasonable that he stood there, in the pool

room that was closest to the center courtyard of the palace, watching as he had done in the last five or six nights. It also made sense that he would lose count of how many times he'd stood there or how long he'd spent thinking about seeing her when he was away. It was all totally realistic. Wasn't it?

Kris let the question remain unanswered as he slipped his hands into the front pockets of his tan dress pants. He still wore his suit jacket, but it was pushed back up his arms. The sage-green tie that seemed calming against the bright white of his shirt was hidden from view by the wide column in front of him. There were a dozen columns along the perimeter of the pool room, separating the white-tiled floor leading to the pool and the elevated section covered in a glossy black marble flooring where a row of chaise lounges sat.

He had always stood behind this one because it offered the best view of the entire length of the pool. Her bathing suit tonight was gray with pineapples all over it. That shouldn't have turned him on, but at this moment Kris wanted nothing more than to taste a fresh, sweet pineapple dripping juice on his tongue and slipping softly into his mouth.

"Why don't you come on in and join me this time?"

The sound of her voice halted Kris's salacious thoughts.

When a wet hand touched his, he realized she'd gotten out of that pool and walked right up to him without him even knowing. So much for being an astute leader. If she were an enemy she would have had the knife embedded in his gut by now. His teeth clenched with the displeasing thought.

"Come on. It's late so I'm sure you're finished with work for the day. A swim would be nice and relaxing. That's why I try to squeeze this in at least once a day," she was saying as she'd already started walking.

Kris followed her because he hadn't had a minute to think of what else to do. She was in front of him, seemingly pulling him along. But Kris never followed anyone. He was a leader, had been since birth, that was a fact.

"Since I've been here on the island I've managed two sessions in this fabulous pool per day. And let me tell you it's been heaven. The pool in my building back in LA is nice, but this scenery combined with the lingering scent of the ocean is total bliss," she continued and stepped up to walk them past the chaise lounges.

There were doors along this wall that led to changing rooms and extra swimsuits for guests.

"Now, I haven't had a chance to get down to the beach, but judging by that view from my room, that water is going to be heavenly. Maybe when Malayka goes away this weekend I'll have to trot myself on down there to try it out."

She stopped then, right in front of one of the doors and looked up to him. Her hair was pulled up in a messy, wet bun with straggling pieces dripping down onto her shoulders. Her face, free of all makeup was perfectly round. Long eyelashes and pretty eyes, pert lips, high cheekbones, were like nothing he'd ever imagined. Yet, every night this was the face he saw before he fell asleep and each morning it was the one he wanted to see as soon as he awoke.

His thoughts startled him because up until this point, Kris hadn't dared consider it a fact.

"I'm sure you have swim trunks in your room, but it's closer to just go in there and grab some that'll fit so we can dive in," she said to him. "I'll wait right here."

He continued to stare at her, watching as her lips moved and her eyes smiled back at him. She was genuine; at this very moment she wanted him to take a swim with her, and Kris, well, he wanted something...different.

Reaching around her he opened the door to the room. Then, he wrapped an arm around her waist and began walking forward, forcing her to move backward.

"Wait...what?" she was saying as he maneuvered her into the room and closed the door behind them.

The lock sounded loudly as he clicked it into place and the smile in her eyes disappeared. It was replaced by something that had Kris growing warmer, instantly.

"You wanted me to take off my clothes. Isn't that correct?"

His question was spoken in a deadly serious tone, his heart beating wildly as he moved closer to her. She moved back until she was against the mirrored wall, shaking her head as she continued to stare at him.

"I was only suggesting you get changed into swimming trunks so that you could go for a swim," she told him.

Kris took off his jacket, extending his arm a bit so that when he dropped it, the material landed on one of the two oak benches instead of the floor.

"Right," he told her. "Well, let me just take off my clothes so that I can slip into those swimming trunks."

She swallowed so hard Kris could actually hear the action. He was removing his tie now and her gaze had dropped down to his fingers.

"You're a grown man—you don't need any help changing your clothes," she said before clearing her throat.

After the tie landed on top of his jacket, Kris immediately began unbuttoning his shirt, first at the cuffs and then down the center. She looked up to him then, determined to keep her gaze on his face. That was fine with him. For now.

When he was bare to the waist, Kris stepped closer to her. "I think I have a better idea than the pool."

"The pool was what I offered. Nothing more," she said definitely.

He continued moving until the tips of her breasts covered scarcely by the wet material of her bikini top touched his chest. It was a scorching dollop of pleasure. The thought of her nipples just on the other side of that material, probably hard and aching for his attention, had him aching, as well. Yes, he admitted to himself, he wanted her to want him as ferociously as he needed her right now. It was all that mattered, all that he cared to think about at that second.

Chapter 6

Again, Landry had quite possibly gone a little too far. She'd known Kristian was watching her for the last couple of days. While underwater one evening she'd caught a glimpse of his silhouette, but when she'd surfaced it was gone. Throughout the rest of the swim she'd continued to stare in that same spot, feeling as if he was still there even though she hadn't seen him again. The next night she'd heard him approach and had a giddy kind of pleasure at knowing that he was watching her.

Did he want her?

Could the prince want to get into this pool with her, and maybe, want something more? Like what? She'd thought about that the next night and then the following night. What could Kristian DeSaunters possibly want from her? Okay, well that was a silly question. He was a man and she was a woman. Sex was the common denominator and Landry could accept that. But she wasn't too keen on Kristian's official title and her temporary employment on this island. The two didn't match up as seemingly sensible as the sex part did.

Yet, here she was, in this small room with him so close and his chest so bare. The air seemed thick as she struggled to breathe in and out, slowly, precisely. It was the only way to keep her mind clear, to focus on what she should do... rather than what she so desperately wanted to do.

"Touch me," he said.

No. Landry almost gasped as she realized those words weren't just a statement. They were a command.

Her mouth suddenly went dry as her gaze involuntarily dropped to his bared chest. His very toned and muscled chest. She had to admit, that in his suits, Kristian did not look as buff and chiseled as he apparently was. Her fingers tingled with the urge to do exactly as he'd instructed. Yet, the part of her that she'd been frequently warned about would not go peacefully into bliss.

"How do you know I want to touch you?"

She'd never seen Kristian smile, but the corner of his mouth twitched and she thought she would lose control if his full smile was as potent as the seriously sexy glare he was giving her now.

He lifted a hand to touch a strand of her wet hair. "I know that it is taking every ounce of your restraint to keep from doing so because your fingers are clenching and unclenching. I know that feeling very well. I've felt it each night I stood watching you."

Well, Landry thought, *that clears up the whole spying because he wants me theory.*

"I also know that it makes more sense for us to get this out of the way sooner, rather than later."

While his previous comment had sent pleasure shivers racing down her spine, this later one irritated her.

"Like a task on your agenda?"

"No," he said in a husky whisper as he stepped closer and let the fingers that had been toying with her hair trace a warm path along the line of her neck. "Like a thirst that must be satiated."

Okay, she could relate to that.

Landry swallowed and shook her head slightly.

"I'm not…" She paused and cleared her throat. "We're not in a position to…um, do this. I mean, I don't think it's proper protocol or whatever."

His head had already begun to lower, his lips brushing lightly over her forehead as she spoke, then moved down to touch the tip of her nose.

"I'm the prince. I create the protocol," he whispered softly over her lips.

The kiss was probably meant to be sweet and seductive. Perhaps a prelude to a long, languid evening of lovemaking, if she were so disposed to believe in such things. Instead, it turned into a fiery duel of tongues and tangle of arms as they gripped each other and held tight, as if this were not only a quest to quench a thirst, but an actual fight for survival as well.

His bare chest pressed against her almost naked one and Landry's blunt-tipped nails dug into the skin of Kristian's shoulders. Moments ago she had been cool from stepping out of the water into the air-conditioned room; now her entire body was warm, growing warmer. Kristian was not only a prince, but he was also a master at this kissing thing. His arms had folded around her back, pulling her up so close to him that only her toes remained on the cool tiled floor. Her head had long since tilted as to offer more access for his delicious assault, her breasts rubbing seductively against him.

It was as if he were attempting to devour her and to her own bafflement, she was offering herself up to him like a buffet feast. In fact, when his hand moved down to cup her butt, she took the initiative and lifted her leg until her inner thigh ran slowly over the material of his pants.

He groaned.

Yes, the crown prince of Grand Serenity Island groaned because she'd brought her leg up and was now wrapping it behind his back.

His hands moved quickly. One holding her firmly in his grasp while the other slipped between them as he undid the buckle and zipper of his pants.

This was not happening, she thought, even as she pressed closer to him. Not close enough because the ache that now throbbed between her legs persisted. This could not be happening.

It should not be…

She moaned when her back was flattened against the mirror and he sucked seductively on her tongue. Her arms were wound tightly around his neck, holding him in place because she wanted more. She knew he did too. His hands were finished moving between them; his length was hard as it pressed against the bare skin of her lower abdomen. He pulled slightly away so that they could both catch their breath. It was a momentary separation as the kiss ensued once more. Their wild abandon filling the room with moans and sighs and guttural urgings.

"I want you," he whispered.

"I want you," she echoed him.

Then suddenly, without preamble, they both stopped. She stilled and he did too. There was no more kissing, no more moaning, only breathing and thinking.

Too much thinking.

Kris loosened his hold on her. When her feet were firmly on the floor, he stopped touching her and backed away. All the while avoiding another glimpse of himself in the mirror directly behind her.

It was there that he'd been reminded, once more, of what he could not do.

He turned his back to her and began fixing his clothes. She did not move but Kris would swear he could hear her thinking, wondering, most likely as angry and confused as he was at this moment. He owed her an explanation and an apology. When his pants were once again in right order, Kris reached over to the bench and pulled on his shirt. He buttoned it as rapidly as he could, desire to get this over with as quickly as possible.

Not for his sake. No, he was thoroughly disgusted with himself for what he'd allowed to happen, what he'd instigated. But he was more disappointed with how he'd treated Landry, a guest to the palace and someone who worked for them.

"Why?"

She asked in the middle of Kris's mental recriminations. How did she know? Of all the questions in the world, how could she grab hold of the one he definitely did not want to answer? The answer to his questions did not matter. Kris knew what he had to do.

"I shouldn't have brought you in here," he said after another deep breath.

Then Kris turned to face her, to look her directly in the eye as he spoke, because she deserved that much.

"I'm not in a position to do this. I knew that when I stood there watching you but I could not turn away. When you confronted me, for a moment I thought... I wondered." He paused and cleared his throat.

"Please accept my apologies. It will not happen again."

He gave her a curt nod and turned to leave, all the while ignoring the inquisitive...no, the assessing look in her eyes.

"It will," she said the moment his fingers touched the doorknob. "You won't like it and I'll probably regret it, but I'm betting that it will happen, Your Highness. That's just the way life goes."

Kris walked out. He did not turn back. But he did not forget her words, not that night, nor the nights that followed.

Chapter 7

"The Ambassador's Ball is not far away. How many dresses do I have to choose from?" Malayka asked Landry as she lounged just a few feet away from the pool.

They were at the south side of the palace, outside, where an infinity pool's edge led down a steep cliff and waves from the sea crashed below. The view was stunning—the brilliant blue ocean reminded Landry of watercolors and the crisp clear powder blue of the sky with its cotton-candy-like clouds never failed to take her breath away. Even with the view, Landry preferred the inside pool near the court-yard because she didn't have to battle with the harsh rays of the Caribbean sun there.

Malayka, on the other hand, had the straps to her hot-pink bikini top pulled down as she lay with her caramel-toned skin glistening in the sun. When she was done, the woman would either have a sun-kissed complexion all over, or look like a ripe tomato.

"Peta is sending the last two you requested—they should be here next week. Since we're not able to use samples and in addition to the changes to the design you requested, they were delayed a few days. Right now there's the blue Balenciaga and the white Versace." Landry spoke from where she sat in a chair beneath an umbrella-topped table. She knew better than to add the fact that they couldn't use samples because most designer samples came in a size 4. Malayka was a 6 or an 8. Landry had made the mistake of mentioning sample sizes before and Malayka had rewarded her with a complete meltdown. Another lesson learned for Landry even though she thought the performance had been more dramatic than authentic. In her business Landry recognized the whole body shaming and desire to be as thin as possible debacle. Only, in Landry's mind, she'd always tried to instill in her clients that size did not matter; it was what was on the inside that counted. That particular conversation had fallen on deaf ears where Malayka was concerned. Still, the woman didn't have to work too hard to keep her cute curvy figure and now that she'd snagged herself a prince, Landry wondered if she would even bother at all after the nuptials.

Resisting the urge to shake her head in pity, Landry decided to focus on something else. Her tablet was propped in front of her, a glass of almost-finished mango lemonade beside it. She held her pen and scribbled notes on the pad she always brought to meetings and kept her sunglasses on, more so to keep Malayka from witnessing her rolling her eyes at the uppity tone the woman had adopted over the last couple of weeks.

Landry had already decided that when the dress arrived from Detali she would simply slip it in with the other dresses for consideration. She had no plans of telling Malayka who had designed the dress until the woman expressed how much she loved it. Landry was banking on that reaction, especially after meeting twice with Detali to look at the design. It was a totally original dress, which would immediately appeal to Malayka. A one-of-a-kind was just what the princess should be wearing. Landry was certain that's how Malayka would feel and she'd better be right or she would certainly be losing her job.

"Are you listening to me?"

Landry lifted her head as Malayka raised her voice. She did not appreciate being yelled at. This wasn't something Landry had needed to tell the people she worked with, even though some of her clients were rumored to have a diva complex. Of course, the relationship with her and her clients tended to go a lot smoother when her assistant Kelli was with her, but that wasn't possible for this trip. Malayka insisted on Landry coming alone.

"Yes," Landry replied. "You're thinking that we should have approached Eleni Verenzia about a dress. However, after the last episode where you returned four original pieces from her, she's not inclined to work with us again."

Landry said *us* but really Eleni just did not want any of her original designs worn by Malayka. Landry had warned Malayka against the unreasonable demands she'd required of the designer.

Clearly annoyed now, because she was undoubtedly hoping to chastise Landry for her lack of attention, Malayka waved her left hand, that huge chunk of gem on her ring finger catching the sunlight. Luckily, Landry had her sunglasses on so the glare didn't bother her too much. Still it was a reminder of something she'd been trying desperately to push out of her mind.

"If she wants to hold a grudge over something so trivial then so be it. I have other options," Malayka quipped.

"Yes. You do," Landry said as she exchanged an email

with Detali's daughter because the woman did not like computers herself. The dress would be ready tomorrow. Detali wanted to deliver it to the palace personally, but Landry's response had been that she would come into town to pick it up. Malayka had a spa day scheduled for tomorrow while Rafe attended to all-day meetings, which meant that Landry would have those hours to herself.

"Do you know where Cheryl is? I thought she was coming to this meeting as well. I told them that I changed my mind and now I want them here before I select my outfits. I mean, it makes perfect sense that when we talk about what I'm going to wear that my makeup artist and hair stylist be here as well. The full package has to be on point at all times," Malayka remarked as she used a peach hand towel that matched her bikini to dab at imaginary sweat on her forehead.

"I thought Cheryl and Amari would be here as well. I sent them each a text last night about the time we would be meeting," Landry said because she knew Malayka would want to know if she'd done her part. Another person may have found it hard to deal with the new Malayka, but Landry was thick-skinned in this arena. She knew the worst-case scenario where her clients were concerned and she also knew the line she'd drawn in her mind for work. And there definitely was a line. Malayka, luckily, had not crossed it just yet. So Landry continued to work without letting the woman's complaints and comments worry her.

Besides, it was too beautiful on this island to be stressed about anything or anyone. Even the prince who had gotten her all hot and bothered last week and then left her standing— unfulfilled—in the changing room. That, she definitely did not want to think about while sitting by the pool.

She'd been doing a good job at ignoring both Malayka and thoughts about the prince until a shadow approaching out of the corner of her eye caught Landry's attention. She didn't bother to turn because she knew who it was from the way her body had instantly warmed.

"There was an accident. Igor apparently lost control of the car and ran off the road down a small embankment," Kris said without preamble when both Landry and Malayka had looked up upon his arrival.

Malayka moved first, jumping up quickly, the top of her bikini moving just as fast, exposing her breasts. Kris managed to turn to face Landry just in time.

"Rafe? Oh my God, Rafe? Is he alright?" Malayka asked.

Landry had already skirted around where Kris stood to stand in front of Malayka, attempting to fix her top, he surmised.

"Tell me about Rafe. What's happened to him? You tell me right now!" Malayka demanded.

Landry faced him then, still blocking Malayka.

"Is he alright?" she asked, her eyes wide, voice just a little shaky.

Kris didn't like the way Landry sounded and he didn't know why he'd asked where she was the moment he'd returned to the palace. Ingrid had readily told him as she'd been assigned to keep an eye on Landry for him. So instead of going to his office or calling for his brother and sister, he'd come to find her.

"My father is safe," Kris replied and gritted his teeth so tight his temples throbbed.

"Oh my…oh," Malayka began and dropped down onto the lounge where she'd been seated, a hand clutching her chest. "Thank you, thank you, thank you. He's safe. Okay, so where is he? I know that Igor was driving him today."

"I thought your father's driver was Rex," Landry said.

She hadn't even looked back at Malayka, but continued to stare at him.

"Rex was ill. Some sort of stomach virus, Dr. Beaumont told us late last night. My father had a meeting at the mines this afternoon and since Rex still wasn't feeling better, he assigned Igor to drive him."

"I knew he was with Igor. That big oaf almost killed my Rafe. Where is he, Kris? You tell me right now. I have a right to know!"

She'd stood again and this time had pushed past Landry until she was standing directly in Kris's face. He liked it better when she was a distance away.

"My father and Jose Realto, the mine supervisor, have been friends for a very long time. Two days ago Jose became a grandfather for the first time. He and his wife, Juanita, invited my father to a celebratory dinner. And that's why my father was *not* in the car when Igor drove off the road."

"Then where the hell is he?"

She was much shorter than Kris's tall frame. Her wavy hair had been pulled back from her face and she wore large round-framed sunglasses that looked too big for her small stature. And she was loud. This wasn't the first time he'd witnessed this and Kris knew it wouldn't be the last. Still, this was the woman his father loved, the one that would soon be the princess of this island. He almost flinched at the thought.

"Maybe you should tell her so she can go see him," Landry said, reminding him that she was still there and that he'd much prefer talking to her.

Looking over Malayka's shoulder Kris found surprising relief at seeing Landry staring at him, her sunglasses now removed as she clenched them in one hand.

"He's in the infirmary, on the lower level of the palace

with Dr. Beaumont. Igor is down there being treated. They believe he has a concussion and a broken arm, but other than that he will recover."

"Well, I'm certainly glad he will recover since he's the one who drove off the damn road!" Malayka continued, before pushing past Kris this time and heading toward the house.

Kris rubbed a hand down the back of his head and let out rugged sigh.

"He's okay," he heard Landry say. "That's good that your father was not injured and Igor will recover."

He nodded, words clogging his throat at the moment. He didn't know which words and that was a problem. There should be no problem speaking. He should know exactly what to say to everyone, at all times.

She touched his arm and Kris looked at her and nodded.

"Alright, well that's a good thing," she continued. "He's safe and he's unharmed. So why don't you just take a deep breath and let that sink in."

What was she talking about?

Kris couldn't answer that question either because he was busy doing as she'd suggested.

"The call came just as I was leaving our attorney's office. I drove straight to the scene because the officer told me my father was not in the car. The car is totaled—it's a miracle that Igor is even alive," he told her.

She continued touching his arm, this time moving her hand up and down in a motion that should not be so soothing. Yet, it was.

"They're going to do a complete investigation and keep me abreast of everything." He nodded again. "So that's it. The prince is fine. Igor is fine."

"But you're not," she said quietly.

Kris did not respond for what seemed like endless moments.

"Have you ever had a normal dinner, Your Highness?"

"Stop calling me that," was his immediate reply. It was in the wrong tone, but he was agitated and frustrated, though, none of that was her fault. Still, she quickly moved her hand from his arm.

"My name is Kristian," he told her after forcing himself to calm. "You can call me Kris."

She looked like she might actually argue with him, but instead gave a slight hunch of her shoulders and then continued.

"Have you ever had a fully loaded pizza and a beer for dinner, Kris?" she asked.

Why was she talking about food? Was she asking him on a date?

While he was coming up with more questions instead of answering her, she continued.

"I'm sure you've never been asked on a date," she continued. "But I don't count this as a *real* date. You need to unwind after this emotional jolt. I know, because when my father fell off a ladder as he tried to change some filter in the church basement, I was hysterical. For the twenty minutes that the doctors thought he might need a hip replacement, I was a nervous nutcase. Those were my brother's words, not my own assessment, by the way."

Yellow was her color, Kris thought absently as he continued to watch her talk. The white pants she wore were fitting every curve of her hips and bottom, but it was the off-the-shoulder yellow top that made her eyes seem brighter, her cheeks just a little higher. Yes, he liked her in that color.

"But once the doctors said he was going to be alright without surgery," she continued, as if she had no idea he was assessing every tiny nuance of her. "I was so relieved I returned to my condo and ordered a whole pizza with all the toppings and grabbed a six-pack of beer. I'd never been a beer drinker before but I felt like I needed something extra that night. I only drank one—gave the other five to my brother the next morning—but the pizza, I completely devoured it."

She gave the smallest smile just as she reached out to touch his arm again. Why did her touch alone calm him in a way that no amount of slow breathing or confirmations from Rafe had been able to do?

"I think it can help you too," Landry finished with a tilt of her head as she looked up at him.

"It might," Kris said. "But I'm guessing that having you with me might be the bigger consolation."

He said it. He meant it. And it was done.

After a complete security check of the car and an extra mechanical check by Tajeo, Kristian and Landry were seated in the backseat headed to a trattoria located on the outskirts of the town.

"I've had pepperoni pizza before. Sam likes it with extra cheese. When she was young and had tea parties, she always had pizza to go along with it. Roland and I weren't invited to the parties, but we snuck into the kitchen and stole slices of pizza before Ingrid had a chance to put them on a platter the way Sam had requested."

Kris had no idea why he'd told her that.

No, that was wrong. He knew why he'd told her, just like he knew why he'd sought her out instead of any of the members of his family. He might not like the answer, but he was certain he now knew for sure.

"My sister, Paula, likes pepperoni too. We can get the meat lovers' pizza with extra cheese if you prefer," she offered.

They were only a couple feet apart. Close enough for him to reach out and take her hand, to have something to hold on to for just a moment. He needed that, but he refrained.

"No. This was your idea so I'm going to try everything you suggest. The loaded pizza with a beer," he answered and then looked over to her.

She was nodding, a smile on her face. "You're gonna love it," she told him.

Kris managed to smile in return as he wondered, what if? His thoughts circled back to why he'd sought her out today, why he'd wanted to see her and only her during this emotional time. Could he possibly? No. He wasn't falling for her. He couldn't be.

"You're picking most of the toppings off your pizza," Kris told her, unable to hide the amusement from his tone.

With all the wonderful places to eat with his favored Caribbean cuisine, Kris found himself quite comfortable seated at the center table in the trattoria. Tajeo had gone in ahead of Kris to let the owners know that he was there. After a ten-minute wait while two patrons finished their meal, settled with the waiter and walked out, Kris stepped out of the car. He waved Tajeo off when he reached to open the door for Landry. Kris opened it himself and offered her his hand. She took it, smiling up at him as she climbed out of the backseat.

"So gallant," she said. "A girl can certainly get used to this treatment."

"A woman should always be treated with the utmost care and respect," he told her as he continued to hold her hand in his.

She did not respond to that, which was a surprise since she usually had a response to everything.

Once inside, they were seated, and Landry enthusiastically placed their order. Tajeo had locked the front door himself and stood there while the staff waited on them only.

"I don't really like the sausage," she admitted in reply to his statement about the pizza. "Or the black olives."

Kris finished chewing the last bite of his second slice. "Then why order a pizza with everything on it?"

"Because it sounds bold and decisive. Like, *I dare you to call me a picky eater*," she told him and took a bite of her second slice that now only had pepperoni, ham, red onions and green peppers.

Kris was allergic to mushrooms so they'd requested a pizza without them.

"You didn't like people calling you names?" he asked.

She shook her head and used her napkin to wipe her mouth before she spoke. "I didn't like my brothers doing anything they wanted and assuming that I couldn't. So whatever they did, I did it too. Sometimes I did it better. But I could not eat raw onions on a hot dog with ketchup. The smell was revolting. The one time I tried, I ended up with my face in the toilet. The next time my mother cooked hot dogs, my brother Geoffrey said I couldn't have any because I was a picky eater. They called me that every time we sat down for a meal for the next month."

Kris couldn't help but smile at that story because it reminded him a lot of how Roland used to treat Sam. "You do know that it's a brother's job to taunt his sister. Is Geoffrey older than you?"

"Yes, I know that's a brother's job. I also knew how to get back at them, as a sister. I let the air out of the tires on all of their bikes," she replied triumphantly. "Four brothers older than me and a younger sister. My parents always wanted a big family."

"Sounds like you had some interesting times," Kris said as he reached for another slice.

He liked the pizza. The beer was just okay. He had a better selection back at the palace, but he would not think of offending the owners by not emptying his glass. Kris was very aware of how nervous the owner looked as he directed his staff to wait on him and Landry. It wasn't every day that the crown prince brought a date to this little spot. In fact, this had never happened before.

"Did you have interesting times when you were a kid?" she asked before taking another bite.

Kris picked up his napkin and wiped his fingers before sitting back in his seat. He contemplated the question, wondering just how he should answer. How much should he tell? How much was too much?

"Did you taunt your sister and beat up your little brother?" she continued with a chuckle. "I cannot imagine you doing either, but I could be wrong."

She wasn't wrong. Not entirely.

"Sam hates spiders," Kris began, the memory startlingly fresh in his mind. "One day when my father was away and I had some time to myself, I spent the entire day walking the property, going into the wooded area just beyond the palace walls. I collected a jar full of spiders." He shrugged.

"I'm not sure I was thinking of what I'd do with them at the time, but when I returned to the house Sam was having one of her dinner parties. She was always hosting a party in the palace."

"She had to entertain herself," Landry offered.

"I guess so. For this one party she wanted Roland and I to attend and she asked us to dress up. I was tired of dressing up. I wanted to eat dinner in my shorts and T-shirt and to keep on the tennis shoes I was wearing even if they were covered in dirt.

"Ingrid insisted that I change. *Let's make your sister happy today*, she'd said. I didn't want to make anyone happy that day. I wanted to make myself happy." Kris lifted his glass and took a sip of the second beer the manager had quietly brought to him.

"I knew that my mother would not like it if she found out that I'd disobeyed Ingrid. And my father would totally lose it if he found out that I'd attended a dinner dressed in shorts and a T-shirt. So I changed and I went down to the main dining room, which had been decorated in pink-and-yellow ribbons. Dolls had been set in each of the chairs at the table except the ones left empty for me and Roland. I sat down and I ate the ridiculous pink cake and sipped the lemonade. Then, when Ingrid walked into the kitchen and Sam was up tending to one of her dolls, I took the jar that I'd slipped into the pocket of my suit jacket and set it in Sam's chair. I removed the lid and then I returned to my seat. I'd just finished my lemonade when Sam screamed.

"There was complete chaos then as you can imagine everyone came running to see what was wrong with the princess. I stood stoically then and put each of the spiders back into the jar. I was punished for the duration of the evening," he finished.

She propped her elbows on the table and watched him intently as he spoke, as if she was thoroughly amused.

"What did you do during your punishment?"

"I sat on my bed and stared at that jar of spiders, giggling every few minutes at the look on Sam's face when she saw them. In the morning I felt bad and went to Sam's room before breakfast to apologize to her. She hit me with her pillow and then made me sit through a private tea party with her special dolls."

"But you were okay with that because you got the chance to do something fun," Landry said thoughtfully.

"You didn't have much time for fun growing up, I suspect. Just like you don't now."

He sat up straighter then, feeling as if too many eyes were on him and he wasn't at his best, or rather his guard had been lowered, when it shouldn't have been.

Clearing his throat, Kris looked at her directly. "I have a duty. The rest is secondary."

In the next moments he gave a nod of his head and the staff were moving to clear the table. He'd asked if she wanted the rest of the pizza and when she'd nodded, he instructed the staff to box it and another one to go.

"Are we returning to the palace?" she asked when he'd stood and waited for her to join him.

Kris looked at her then. He recalled the way her cheeks lifted when she smiled and the sound of her voice as she laughed. He'd watched her lick her lips after each bite of her pizza and frown over the bitter taste of the beer. She'd listened to his story with complete attentiveness and had hit the nail squarely on the head with her assessment of why that memory meant so much to him. She was getting to him; he knew it. He didn't like it, but he couldn't deny it.

"No. Not yet," Kris told her.

Landry giggled as she walked barefoot along the shore-line. Night had fallen, only slithers of moonlight bouncing along the water's edge.

She had no idea when was the last time she'd giggled. Probably never. Landry had always been on a mission to prove to her older brothers that she was just as strong as them, just as resilient as anyone else. She was a girl, but she was not a ninny. How many times had she told them that? She'd lost count.

Yet when she'd tripped over her own stupid feet and almost fell into the rolling tide, Kris had easily wrapped an arm around her waist, saving her from inevitable embarrassment. His grip had been strong and her feet had left the ground almost immediately. It wasn't necessary, but he'd swung her around then, so that the cooler evening breeze brushed over her cheeks and lifted the ends of her hair.

He'd wrapped both his arms around her and held her tight to his chest and as she'd let her head fall back and giggled, he'd chuckled too.

She stared at him as he slowly let her slide down until her feet once again touched the sand. He seemed darker out here, they both did, Landry supposed. But there was something else. A shield had been lowered. She could see it in the lift of his lips and the light in his eyes.

"What? Why are you staring at me like that?" he asked, his hands slipping away from her arms.

"You're different," she told him. "Relaxed."

He immediately stopped smiling. "I'm on the beach and it's getting dark," he replied.

"Are you afraid of the dark?" she asked as she stepped closer to him.

She liked being close to him. Liked it way too much. She'd had one beer in comparison to his two, still Landry felt like it must be going to her head.

"I'm not," he replied.

Landry nodded. "You're not afraid of anything, are you, Kristian? Not afraid of anything, can complete any task, handle any catastrophe. You're all that, but still, right here and now, you're still different."

He sighed then and looked away.

"You don't have to say anything. I just mentioned it," she told him. "I know I can be pushy sometimes, but I'm really not trying to be."

When he didn't respond Landry wondered how she was going to get out of this uncomfortable situation she'd just created. Why couldn't she have just kept her mouth shut and continued with the spinning and giggling?

"You don't treat me like everyone else," he said quietly as he took a few steps back from her and then turned to face the ocean.

"You're not like anyone else I've ever met," she admitted, her voice almost as quiet as his.

The waves seemed much louder then; the wind and every little thing around them seemed bigger, more pronounced than just a few seconds ago. She lifted her hands to push her hair back behind her ears while she tried to figure out why.

"Because I'm a prince?"

Landry shook her head. "And because you're much more complicated than I first realized. There's more in there, isn't there? You walk so tall and hold your head so high. You rule and you organize. But do you live?"

She'd had this very same thought since the days that followed their tryst in the changing room. When Kris had left her alone after apologizing and telling her that it—*they*—would not happen again, she'd told him that it would. Later that night she'd thought that perhaps she should not have said that. Kristian appeared to be a decisive man, something Landry thought came with his title and upbringing. Then she'd dreamt of him, of them making love beneath the warm Caribbean sun. He was smiling in that dream, touching her and enjoying her as she had enjoyed him. In the morning she'd tried to forget the dream but that hadn't worked and eventually her thoughts had turned to the man that would forego physical pleasure for the sake of duty.

He stood with his legs spread slightly apart. Before they'd climbed out of the car to enter the restaurant she'd convinced him to remove his suit jacket by saying, *It feels like it's near one hundred degrees out there. You're mak-ing me hot just looking at you all buttoned up in that suit.*

Surprisingly, he'd only given her an amused look before removing his jacket. A part of Landry hadn't been sure whether he would simply direct his driver to take them back to the palace or argue his position with her. The si-lent acquiescence had caused a different type of trepida-tion in her where the prince was concerned.

Now, he'd even slackened the blue-gray tie he wore so that it hung loosely around his open shirt collar. He still looked out to the water, his hands calmly at his sides.

"I live the life I was meant to live," he responded to the question Landry had nearly forgotten as she'd been so caught up in staring at him.

"Me too," she said, looking out to the water as well. "You ever wonder if there's more though?"

Again, Kristian didn't answer right away. That was fine because Landry figured her mouth had once again gotten her into a strained situation. She now found herself think-ing about her job and her life back home and if that was all she was ever going to have.

"My mother always wanted more," Kristian commented after a while. "She was always bursting with energy and enthusiasm. I could look into her eyes every day and see a new plan for some outing or event at the palace. Something she wanted to do with children or to save the environment. Then, just hours later when I was finished with whatever my father had on my schedule for the day, I'd see her and Sam playing in Sam's bedroom. There was so much pink in there, dolls and doll clothes, a huge doll house that had enough furniture for a human family to reside in it. Her voice was animated and Sam loved it. One day when I asked her how she managed to do all those things, she said simply, *I love my life and I have love in my life.*"

Landry nodded because she knew exactly what his mother had been trying to tell him. Not that this was the way she'd wanted this little outing with Kristian to go. She'd only intended to take his mind off the accident. And she definitely did not want to talk about falling in love and all the ties and rules that went with that.

She walked farther into the water, not really caring that the hems of her capri pants were now getting wet. When she decided she was far enough and Kristian had not said another word, she turned and began kicking water in his direction.

"I'll bet your mother loved this water," she said. "I've been swimming in the pool, but yesterday I finally had a chance to get down to the beach and it's fantastic!"

He looked like he had when she'd asked him to take off his suit jacket and Landry figured she'd be the only one riding back to the palace with wet clothes on, until Kristian surprised her yet again. He didn't rush over and dunk her beneath the water, which is exactly what her brothers would have done. Instead, he approached her, his own pants getting just as wet as hers, and cupped her face in his hands.

Needless to say, Landry immediately stopped kicking water. She may have actually stopped breathing as Kristian's face was suddenly very close to hers. So close her lips parted involuntarily in anticipation.

"You're not supposed to be here," he said, his voice strained. "This is not supposed to happen."

Landry didn't know how to respond to that. What should she say? Or should she maybe just leave? Wade her way out of the water and back to the car that was waiting for them on the bank a short distance away. That would not be a very dignified exit, but it might put a stop to the struggle she heard so clearly in his voice.

Of course that's not what she did because that would have been the easiest and most sensible thing to do. For Landry, there really was no choice.

She moved in closer, eliminating that small breath of space between them and touched his lips with hers. She did not go softly either. It was all or nothing at this point, she figured. Hell, she'd told the prince to take off his jacket, why not go all the way and kiss him beneath the moonlight too?

Chapter 8

Kris kicked the door to his private rooms closed and reached back to make sure the lock clicked into place. He still had an arm around Landry's waist because he hadn't been able to stop touching her the entire ride back to the palace.

The kiss in the water had unleashed something inside him, something he was more than tired of holding back. When they'd finally taken a break for air, Kris hadn't hesitated when he scooped Landry up in his arms and carried her back to the car. She ran her fingers along the line of his jaw as he held her, staring up at him as if she knew exactly what he was thinking. He'd thought the same about her question about him really living his life. How could she have known the one question that haunted him every day?

He'd told her this wasn't supposed to happen, that she wasn't supposed to be here, but Kris was beginning to think that was all wrong.

Tajeo had stood stoically with the back door of the car open and Kris had gently set Landry inside. On the ride back, Kris had pulled her close, his arm locked around her shoulder while he stared forward. She laid her head on his shoulder and they rode in silence, consumed by their thoughts.

He wondered if she knew that his thoughts were totally focused on getting her naked and beneath him in the shortest amount of time possible?

At the palace, Kris walked them through the back door and stepped onto an elevator that the staff normally used. He guided her down the lengthy hallway to his rooms and now could only stare down into her eyes.

"If you don't want this I need you to say so right now," he said, the words tight in his throat, need burning in his gut.

He hadn't bothered to turn on any lights, but several windows were free of the blinds he usually activated at night, so the moonlight spilled in, casting a sensual hue throughout the area.

"I want this," was her simple reply.

Why did everything seem that way with her? It had been so easy for him to watch her night after night as she swam and even easier to lead her into that changing room with him. Even tonight, going to have dinner with her— pizza, of all things—had seemed so natural and necessary at the same time.

When her hand flattened on his chest, Kris touched her cheek once more, moving until he could kiss her again. Their tongues twined softly together, mixing in a gentle prequel to what he knew was going to be a long night.

She moaned softly as he kissed the line of her jaw, down to her neck. Her fingers gripped his arms as his tongue touched the smooth skin of her shoulder. Since he'd ap-

proached her at the pool earlier, Kris had been enamored
by the line of her shoulders, now bared with the design of
her blouse. The contrast between her complexion and the
bright tone of the shirt was nothing short of alluring. While
his hand cupped one shoulder, his fingers moving slowly
over her soft skin, his tongue stroked over the other, gentle
kisses turning quickly into suckling, nipping.

"Kristian." She whispered his name as she leaned into
him.

He'd asked her to call him Kris. She hadn't. Not one
time. He groaned and her hands moved until she was cupping the back of his head.

Desperate to see and taste more, Kris pushed the rim of
her shirt until she let her arms fall to her sides and he could
maneuver the blouse until it was bunched at her waist.
She wore a strapless bra that barely contained the heavy
mounds of her breasts. With movements so slow they were
almost painful, Kris unhooked that bra and watched it
fall to the floor. Using the back of his fingers he rubbed
over both nipples until they were hard and enticing. Could
they…or she, be more tempting than he'd already found
her to be? He didn't think so.

"I won't break," she told him, her tone a breathy whisper.

His gaze found hers quickly and he replied, "I'm afraid
I will."

She touched his wrists then, bringing her fingers down
until they were covering his on her chest. She squeezed
his hands, which resulted in him squeezing her breasts.
She gasped; her tongue slipped out to stroke her lips. He
squeezed again on his own accord this time, watching intently as passion filled her eyes.

"More," she encouraged him and Kris felt as if the heat
in this room might suffocate him.

She felt wonderful in his hands, more so than anything Kris had ever touched before. He knew the second his name fell from her lips again that he needed more as well. Bending slightly, he replaced one hand on her breast with his tongue on her nipple. Stroking it slowly, loving the pebble-hard feel of her flesh against his tongue. Opening his mouth he sucked deep, pulling as much of her into his mouth as he could, inhaling and exhaling to keep himself upright and focused. Squeezing and sucking, her hands tight on the back of his head, her voice telling him, "Yes. More. Please, Kristian," crashed through his system like a torrential storm.

Kris picked her up then, cradling her in his arms as he bent down to take her mouth once more. She hugged him close, meeting the quick and hungry licks of his tongue with mounting fervor of her own. When his feet bumped the platform of his bed, he reluctantly pulled his lips away from hers; their breaths quickened as he rested his forehead against hers for a few seconds.

He placed her gently on his bed, bending immediately to remove the sandals from her feet. There was still a bit of sand there, on her toes, even though she'd wiped furiously with the towel Tajeo had provided for them when they'd returned from the beach. Kris brushed away the tiny sparkles, loving the twinkle of the fiery red polish on her toenails. Next, he reached up to undo the snap of her pants. She was watching him, her gaze intent on every movement of his fingers. Kris found that very arousing and continued.

She lifted her hips slightly off the bed so that he could pull her pants down her legs. His fingers brushed over her thighs and when her pants were completely removed and lying on the floor somewhere behind him, he returned his hands there. Kneading the soft skin, loving the feel of pliant limbs beneath his palms. He pressed gently against her inner thighs and sighed with pleasure as she spread her legs farther for him. Again, his fingers moved over her skin, his pulse quickening as he watched his lighter-toned skin against hers. When his thumbs scraped the material of her panties, Kris had to pause. He closed his eyes, moving his fingers over the puffiness of her mound, and sucked in a deep breath. Closer, his mind roared. He had to get closer.

The shirt came next and Kris heard the distinct tear of material as he'd opted to pull that down her legs as well. He'd have to buy her a new one. A dozen more of this same design, in bright, vibrant colors that would make her skin glow and her smile seem magical.

She was naked now…no, she still wore white panties. The ones that came up high on her waist and were made of what felt like a simple cotton. They should have been too demure to be sexy, too plain to be memorable, but Kris knew he'd never forget them. Not the way they both highlighted and hid the part of her that he ached to see most.

When he reached down to remove them, she shocked him by pushing his hands away.

"Let me," she said, her gaze trained on his as she hooked her thumbs beneath the rim of her panties and pushed them down slowly.

Inch by delicious inch she was bared to him and Kris's mouth watered with anticipation. He wanted to taste and touch, to look and explore, to feel and be felt, all at once.

Moving close to the edge of the bed she reached up and worked the buttons on his shirt until she was able to push it free of his arms. His undershirt came next as Kris found himself watching her fingers in the same way that she'd previously watched his. Her hands were much smaller than his, but still they moved deftly over his body leaving his skin to tingle with warmth as she did so.

They were both naked now. Him standing in front of her, looking down at the dark circles of her nipples, and her looking at him. His chest, his waist, his thighs, his arousal. She perused every part of him, making Kris feel not only naked, but vulnerable to her as well. It wasn't a feeling he was used to, not one that he was certain he knew how to handle, but that was okay. Or at least that's what she'd told him.

"Condoms," she whispered.

"Huh?" he asked, his mind still flip-flopping between being so aroused it was near painful and being afraid that even with his title, he may somehow be lacking to her.

She smiled, running a finger along his lower abs. "Where are your condoms?"

Kris smiled in return as reality slapped him soundly in the face. He moved away from her—even though her touch had been doing something else to him, something sinfully delicious—and retrieved a wooden box from his nightstand drawer. He kept it full of condoms even though he'd never brought a woman there. After setting the box on the nightstand and removing one, he walked to her and on impulse gave her the foil packet.

She opened it immediately and reached for him. Kris groaned inwardly as he stepped closer to her, his body tense with need as he watched her fingers close around him. She stroked him once, twice, and the last edges of his control slipped. Kris sighed and closed his eyes.

Again she stroked him, this time touching his sac lightly. It was enough to have him cursing and gritting his teeth as she did it again and again, until he was thrusting in her hand like a horny teenager about to find his release.

"Enough!" Kris finally managed. His heart was pounding so hard he wasn't sure it was healthy.

She slid the condom on him then and moved back on the

bed when she was finished. When he thought she would hold her arms out and welcome him, she did not. Instead she leaned back on her elbows, with her legs partially spread and waited.

"If you don't want this, I need you to say so right now," she said to him, repeating what he'd asked of her not too long ago.

"I want it," he said without preamble. "Damn it all to hell, but I want it."

Relief rippled through Landry like waves at the ocean. She didn't speak, or show it in any way—at least she hoped she hadn't—but her legs trembled as he touched them. She licked her bottom lip and tried to hold his gaze as he moved over her. That was a task since she'd never been more aroused by a man touching her thighs than she was with him. There was just something about his strong, aristocratic fingers clutching her skin. It made her feel sexier than she'd ever imagined, especially since her thighs and her stomach had always been the parts of her body Landry hated most.

No, she wasn't a slim girl by the world's standards, nor was she technically a thick girl. Somewhere in between was where she'd found herself in her senior year of high school, fluctuating between a size twelve and fourteen. She had a butt and thighs and her waist could use a good cincher, or maybe liposuction, even though she'd never seriously considered either. Now, even though she purchased more size twelves and fit them all perfectly, Landry still loved her curves and dressed to fit her confident and vivacious personality, nothing more and nothing less.

Still, every woman had insecurities about their body, she surmised. Even her smallest client who wore a size two hated her breasts because she thought they were too small. It was a never-ending cycle for women and Landry gave it the time it required. No less than seconds each day.

Tonight, she was in heaven as Kris's gaze was nothing but appreciative of every part of her body. He'd held her D cup breasts in his palms as if he were holding something as precious as the finest china. Then he'd suckled them like he was tasting the best wine ever. But it was when he touched her thighs, when his fingers were on the inside, moving close to her center that she'd known she was done. It was over, whatever resistance there might be in her mind, her body was down for this and whatever else was about to come.

Still, she'd needed the verbal acquiescence, just as he had moments ago.

His fingers were past her thighs now, parting her folds to touch the moistness he'd evoked. Landry sucked in a breath, then let it out slowly as he moved a finger up and down, stirring her juices until she wanted to scream with excitement.

"I wanted to go slow," he said, his voice husky and strained. "We should. I mean, it's the first time, so it should be memorable and…"

"Please," Landry said, cutting him off.

She lay back on the bed and spread her legs wider. Her body humming with desire as his finger continued to move over her tender flesh. She lifted her hips in an effort to guide him.

"Now," she finally whispered. "Right. Now."

He did not hesitate, but sank a finger, plus another, inside her. Landry grabbed the smooth, cool comforter beneath her and resisted the urge to call out. He pumped his fingers in and out of her until she was squirming beneath him.

"Now," he whispered. "Right. Now."

He was over her in seconds, the thick tip of his erection replacing his fingers, stretching her in a move that was so wonderful she could do nothing but sigh. He pumped easily, pressing into her in excruciatingly slow movements.

If there was such a thing as perfection Landry thought this was definitely it. He was filling her. It was tight and warm and so good, her arms trembled as she lifted them to wrap around his shoulders when he leaned forward. He came down on his elbows that he'd planted on either side of her head. His face was close to hers, his body deeply embedded inside hers.

Landry opened her eyes to see him staring down at her. The sadness she'd seen earlier when he'd been talking about his mother had been clouded over by desire. He desired her. The Caribbean prince desired the American stylist. She couldn't believe it and yet, instinctively, Landry felt like it meant so much more. He continued to watch her as he moved. When she lifted her legs, locking them behind his back, he leaned in closer to kiss her lips and Landry knew in that instant, that this was definitely more.

It was just before dawn when Landry managed to move unnoticed from beneath Kris's arm and slip out of his bed. Collecting her clothes wasn't easy, but she'd managed without tripping over anything.

Sometime during the night his blinds had closed partially so that the light that came with a burgeoning sunrise now filtered into the space. It was a very large space, and this was just the bedroom portion. She remembered walking into a full-fledged living room last night and entering through the double doors of his massive room. His bed was huge, sitting back against a side wall of the room on a two-foot-high platform. The bed faced a wall of windows that Landry took a couple of seconds to stand closer to.

This view was phenomenal with a breathtaking drop down the cliffs to where the water crashed and rolled against the rocks. She had more of a beach view in her room, but this right here was simply spectacular. Too bad she did not have time to dawdle. She needed to be out of there before anyone in the house awakened to see her leaving this room. And of course, before Kristian awoke.

Tiptoeing out into the living room where she dressed quickly, Landry barely looked around at the leather furniture and plush rugs. There was a huge desk and chair, a television on another wall, a fireplace and bookshelves. That gave her pause as she wondered what type of books a man like Kristian read. She didn't stay to find out, but moved faster until she made it to the door that she knew would take her out into the hallway. The door had been locked even though she had no recollection of Kristian doing so when they'd come in last night. She unlocked it and slipped slowly out into the hallway.

It was a long walk to her room, so Landry decided to run. Yes, she held her shoes in her hand and ran all the way to her room, not stopping until she was safe behind the door. Then she breathed a sigh of relief about two seconds before a sound scared the crap out of her.

Chapter 9

"You wanna tell me what you think you're doing?"

Kris stopped the moment he walked out of his bedroom to see Roland leaning against the wall, arms folded, face frowning.

"I'd like an answer to that question as well," Sam chimed in from where she sat in one of the reclining chairs in the center of his living room.

A unified attack, Kris thought as he straightened his tie and walked past the both of them, heading toward the minibar in the corner. "Good morning to you both," he muttered.

"It almost wasn't a good morning," Roland continued. "When were you going to tell us that you didn't think Igor's running off the road was an accident?"

"I'm still waiting for a call from my brother to tell me that the car my father was supposed to be riding in was in an accident. But not to worry because my father is safe and sound," Sam added.

If he were actively paying attention to them Kris's neck would have been sore from volleying back and forth between his brother and sister. As it stood, he wanted his usual cup of steaming-hot black coffee, before he actually began talking to either of them.

He was wearing a blue suit today, the usual white shirt and a pink-and-blue tie. He had yet to button his jacket, but knew that the creases in his pants were perfect and the light starch order on his shirt had been well done. He looked the part of the ambitious prince ready for the workday, even if, on the inside, he didn't feel like it.

His coffee—which was already in the pot awaiting him as per the automatic setting—was hot and bitter. It had almost spilled down the front of his pristine white shirt when his brother yelled.

"Dammit, Kris! Don't stand there with your stoic expression and just ignore us!" Roland had pushed away from the wall and now stood beside the chair where Sam sat.

"First," Kris spoke as he set his cup on the counter. "It's too early in the morning for yelling. And furthermore, it's not necessary. I hear both of your complaints and I apologize."

He'd looked up at them. "I should have called you yesterday to tell you about Dad. By the time I returned to the palace he was already in the infirmary with Dr. Beaumont. I checked on him and on Igor and then I went straight to the garage to check on the maintenance reports for the cars. The police wanted a copy, but I wanted to read them first."

Roland nodded. "You wanted to see them so you could deal with whatever was on them. Just like you talked to the police and you talked to Dad. What about us, Kris? When were you going to talk to us?"

"When did you get back in town, Roland?" Kris asked as he came to stand a few feet away from his brother.

"Because the last time I checked…oh no, wait a minute, I usually can't check on you because you don't have enough consideration to put all your globe-trotting trips on the joint calendar."

"Don't do that," Roland snapped back. "Don't try to make this about me, when we're talking about you trying to control everything."

"So you want to talk about me doing my job now? Since when did that interest you at all?" Kris countered. He was beginning to become irritated with being questioned by someone who rarely ever wanted to hear any palace business at all.

"That's enough, you two," Sam interjected. "I think what he's trying to say, Kris, is that you should have kept us in the loop."

Kris turned and was about to respond but Sam lifted a hand to stop him.

"You didn't and you have your reasons, but we're a part of this family too. If you think there was some type of sabotage afoot, we have a right to know."

Kris took another sip of his coffee. He knew they were right. He should have told them, but he hadn't. After seeing his father and speaking to the police all Kris had wanted to do was find Landry. When he had, nothing else seemed to matter. His father was safe and he planned to deal with whatever had happened out there on that road at another time. Landry was with him and he'd focused his attention on her, something he'd never done before.

"You're right and I apologize," he said slowly. That too was something he hadn't done much of in the past.

Weary after the last couple of hours and with a headache brewing, Kris took a seat on the black Biltmore Chesterfield leather couch and set his cup on the side table.

"The brakes were tampered with. The car was never

meant to stop. That's what the cops said. Igor's got a bump on his head the size of an egg and says Rex is the only one with keys to the car. The extra set stays in a lockbox in Rex's office. The car is always parked right outside of Rex's room door, not in the garage. Rex corroborated all of this and said he gave Igor the keys yesterday morning when he came to his room."

"Why aren't all the keys kept in the garage with the others?" Sam asked.

"Because Rex likes to be ready whenever Dad calls," Roland answered. "He doesn't like taking the time to get to the garage and risk the car being blocked in by another one. He's the supervisor so he can make that call."

Sam shook her head. "All the cars are the same. What difference does it make which one he uses?"

Kris looked at Roland, unable to hide his surprise that his brother knew that much about their drivers.

"Dad likes his car. He picked it out and then ordered the fleet," Kris told Sam.

"And we all know that whatever Prince Rafferty wants, he gets," Roland continued, the light tone failing so that he still sounded irritated.

His brother let out a breath and shook his head. "So if somebody messed with that car in particular, there's a good chance they knew it was Dad's car."

"You're saying someone snuck onto the palace grounds just to tamper with the brakes on Dad's car?" Sam asked, clearly not believing what she was hearing.

"It seems that way," Kris stated. "But the palace gates are locked tighter than any prison system I know of. It's almost impossible for anyone who doesn't belong here to get in."

"So that means the person that messed with Dad's car

belongs here, or at least she acts as if she does," Roland added.

A hush fell over the room.

"You're saying that Malayka tried to kill Dad?" Sam shook her head again. "I don't believe that."

"And I don't trust her," Roland stated. "She's an opportunist of the highest quality. I did some checking into her background—"

"I already ran a background check on her," Kris interrupted.

"That was a legal check, I'm sure," Roland told them. "I, on the other hand, am not compelled to use the same approved channels as you are for a thorough search into a person's background."

"What did you find?" Sam asked before Kris could question his brother further.

"I found," Roland started then paused to fold his arms over his chest and look directly at Kris, "that there is no record of Malayka Sampson living in Beverly Hills before two years ago."

"Her birth certificate says she was born in Tallahassee, Florida. She graduated from high school there and then moved," Kris stated, recalling what the report he'd had rushed to him on Malayka had said.

Roland nodded. "Moved where? She's thirty-seven years old. Where has she been since she was seventeen? My guy can find anybody, anywhere, at any time. He has access to the United States' top security networks—FBI and CIA. He also has contacts in the division formerly known as the KGB. He knows everything there is to know and then some. So why can't he find anything on her?"

Kris didn't have an answer to that question. He didn't like that realization.

"Dad was satisfied with the records from Florida," Kris told them.

Sam sat back and ran her fingers through her hair. "He told me that she was from Florida and traveled for years after she graduated with a cheerleading squad. He said she ended up living in Paris for some time, modeling and writing a book. She just returned to the States two years ago."

Roland nodded. Kris frowned.

"Does that sound strange to anyone but me?" Roland asked.

"Yes," Kris answered. He'd heard that same story from his father, after he'd shared the private investigator's report with him. Rafe hadn't seemed fazed by Kris's questions, so he'd stopped asking them. He hadn't, however, stopped wondering.

"Can your guy dig deeper?" he asked Roland. "If we can get the exact name of the cheerleading squad and trace where they were over the years, maybe get Malayka to tell us exactly where she lived in Paris, maybe we can get more information."

"That's just it," Roland told them. "He can get information on anyone, providing that person actually exists. I don't think Malayka Sampson does."

"You mean she's using a fake name?" Sam asked.

"Wait a minute," Kris interrupted. "Let's just take a second to be really clear about what we're saying."

He took a deep breath and let it out slowly. "Dad is planning to marry this woman. She's soon to become the princess of this island. She will be the second-highest ruling party in this palace. That's a lot of power."

"A lot of power," Roland conceded.

"She definitely likes power," Sam added.

Kris knew his duty. He knew he was expected to not only lead the citizens on this island, but also everyone in this palace. His mother had always told him to look after Roland and Sam, that she trusted him to do what was necessary for them throughout their lives. Vivienne trusted him. Kris tried hard to feel as if he'd earned that trust, even when he knew deep down that he hadn't. Still, it was on him, this conversation, this moment, and what the three of them did or said from this moment on, was solely on him.

"Nobody will say a word about this new investigation. It's between the three of us. And you tell your man I want this done pronto. No matter how much it costs I want to know who she is, where she's from and why the hell she's on this island."

Roland nodded his approval, his hands falling to his sides as he reached into his pocket for his cell phone.

"Sam, you find out what you can from Malayka herself. I know you don't like her but she's more likely to let something slip to a woman, than to me or Roland. I want to know everything she does. Everything her staff is doing. The hair stylist, the makeup artist, and—" Kris paused and gritted his teeth. "The stylist. I want to know their every move."

Landry breathed a sigh of relief and slapped a hand to her chest as she flattened her back against the door and saw that the sound was her cell phone, vibrating across the coffee table. She'd left it there yesterday when she'd gone to the pool to meet with Malayka. After talking to Kelli for an hour about how business was going back in Los Angeles, it needed to be charged. Her plan had been to return to her room to shower and dress for dinner as soon as the meeting was finished, so Landry hadn't been afraid of missing anything important.

Apparently, since the sun was now peeking through the open blinds in the bedroom casting hazy rays of light into the sitting area where she stood, her plans for last night had changed and now she had missed something.

Heading over to the table, she picked up the phone, removed the charging cord and opened the screen. Her mother had called several times, leaving voice and text messages, the latest one being just a few minutes ago. Landry immediately dialed her mother's number.

"I would say I'm glad I'm not dead, but that might sound too morbid," Astelle said the moment she picked up on her end.

Landry resisted the urge to frown and instead gave a cheery, "Hi, Mama."

"I've been calling you since last night," her mother continued. "Just because you're thousands of miles away, in the middle of some ocean, doesn't mean you cannot answer the phone. Or return a phone call in a timely fashion. I mean, really, Landry, there could have been an emergency."

And from that sentence alone Landry realized that there wasn't and she took a seat on the couch. "The battery in my phone died, so I didn't even see that you'd called until just now."

Her mother was technology challenged, so Landry knew that talking about her phone would get Astelle to take the conversation in another direction.

"Anyway, I wanted to tell you about the Singles' Social at the church," she said.

Landry laid her head back on the chair and dropped an arm over her forehead. Was her mother really calling her about church events when, as Astelle had so sweetly put it, she was thousands of miles away in the middle of some ocean?

Astelle continued, "Your father and I were talking yesterday morning and we thought it would be perfect if you could attend. Now, it's Saturday night and before you say it, I know that's tomorrow. But you should be able to get those fancy royal people to send you home on a plane so that you can attend. Paula said they probably have their own private jet. More than one actually. Anyway, don't worry about what to wear, I called Kelli and she can get you something from your studio."

It was official, her mother had finally completely lost her mind. Landry berated herself for thinking negatively about her mother. Especially since the scare she'd received concerning her parents before she'd left the States had almost been a deal breaker for her taking this job. Her father had been rushed to the hospital the day after Malayka offered Landry this position. The chest pains he'd been having were concerning enough to have him set up with cardiologists and other specialists within the week. Landry decided that night at the hospital that she would stay in LA. Her father had told her she would do no such thing.

Landry shook her head to clear that memory from her mind. Her mother had already said this wasn't an emergency call so there was no need to think back on that horrible time. Besides, Astelle had just gone quiet which meant she was now waiting for Landry's response.

"I cannot attend the event, Mama," Landry said after taking a deep breath and exhaling slowly. "I'm working here on Grand Serenity Island. The job isn't over until mid-December, after the royal wedding."

"Well, you don't work on weekends, do you?" her mother asked.

"Yes, I do."

Astelle huffed. "You shouldn't work yourself so hard, Landry. You're only given one life—you need to take the time to actually live it."

"I am living my life, Mama. I started this business because it was my dream. It's everything to me and I plan to work as hard as I can to make the best of it," she replied.

"There's more to life than work... Like socializing and giving yourself the chance to meet the right man," Astelle said.

Landry sighed inwardly wondering if her mother would ever talk about anything other than her finding a man and settling down.

"My job actually entails a lot of socializing," she rebutted.

"Oh really? Have you been going to fancy parties or exploring that lovely island with anyone in particular?"

She'd walked right into that one.

"The royal family has been very hospitable. The princess gave me a personal tour."

"That's nice. I hope you were respectful."

"I was, Mama."

"And who else? Didn't you say there was a prince?"

Landry rolled her eyes. Her mother couldn't remember how to install an app on her phone, but she wouldn't dare forget any mention of an eligible bachelor.

"There are two princes, Roland and Kristian. I've met both of them and they've been very pleasant as well," Landry informed her mother.

"Any sparks there? Between you and the princes?"

"Really, Mama. In one breath you want me to come home to attend a church social full of bachelors and in the next you ask if I'm flirting with not one, but both princes." Landry had to chuckle at that herself.

Astelle did not think it was funny. "That's not what I said. I simply asked if there were any sparks there, and I didn't mean with both of them. I was asking if there were sparks with either one."

"No," she replied, quickly.

Too quickly.

"Oh?" Astelle immediately perked up.

"Mama, I really have to get going. I'll call you Sunday night when you're back from church," Landry told her, praying she could get off the phone without giving away the fact that there were not only sparks between her and one of the princes, but that she'd actually just come from his bed.

"I see, well that's fine. You go on and get your work done. I suppose the sooner the job is finished the sooner you'll return home. If that's still the plan. So I'll just tell your father you won't be attending the social and we'll talk to you later. Bye now, and you take care of yourself down there," Astelle said.

"You and Daddy take care too," Landry said. "I love you both."

"We love you too, baby. Go on now, don't be late for what you have to get done. And be nice to everyone there, especially him."

Astelle hung up before Landry could ask her mother who "him" was. Landry was left to stare at her cell phone replaying their conversation in her mind.

If that's still the plan, Astelle had said. *Be nice...to him.*

Landry shook her head and fell back against the chair. Now her mother was thinking she had something going on with someone down here. That was just great. No, it wasn't. Her mother was wrong. Or was she?

She was wearing the clothes she'd had on yesterday, including the shirt with its elastic collar stretched out because Kris had decided to push the shirt down her body, instead of pulling it over her head. Her legs were still a little weak from the multiple times they'd made love throughout the night. Her hair was most likely a matted mess and her lips still tingled from the memory of his kisses.

Was there something going on between her and Kristian?

Now probably wasn't the greatest time to ask that question.

Chapter 10

"We'll have extended security for the Ambassador's Ball next weekend," Rafe said in response to Malayka's inquiry.

Kris had heard her question, every one of them since they'd sat down to dinner almost twenty minutes ago. In the last three weeks since the accident, Malayka had been very concerned about Rafe's safety. They all were. The difference was that Kris and his siblings were taking care of matters on their own. They weren't discussing this situation at the family dinner table and acting as if someone were going to break into the palace at any moment and shoot Rafe while he sat at the head of the table.

Glad that his father had answered her question, Kris finished his dessert and signaled to a staff member that he was ready for another glass of wine. Normally, he drank coffee after dinner, reserving the wine or anything stronger for when he was alone in his rooms. Tonight, he needed wine immediately.

It had been a long day, one where he'd tried to convince himself that these past weeks spent with Landry in his bed weren't such a bad idea. Since the first night that they were together Kris would either seek her out at the pool after dinner or send her a message that they were to meet in his rooms. They never spoke of any specifics to their newfound arrangement, nor did they look any further into the future than the next night that they could be in each other's arms.

This was a first for Kris, a clandestine affair, which seemed more like something Roland would do. He wasn't proud of it and yet, there was a big part of him that hated each morning when Landry would wake early and sneak out of his room. It made sense that she leave before the staff began moving around and could possibly witness her departure. Still, he hadn't been able to let go of the emptiness he'd felt each day when she was gone.

Luckily, or perhaps not, his daily schedule remained full, so it had been unusual for him to have the time to think about the situation with Landry throughout the day. Today, however, was different.

He had meetings throughout the day. The bank, the rescheduled meeting with Quirio about the massive resort he planned to build on the opposite side of the island and then the Skype conference call with the security guy Roland recommended. To tell the truth, if it weren't for Quirio's grand plans and the boost in tourism it would afford the island, Kris would say that all of his meetings had been a disaster.

Gerard Yiker was the former CIA agent who had connections all over the world. He seemed to be an astute man with no real allegiance to any country at this point in his life. He knew things and he knew how to barter them to people who required his intel. Kris did not want to bargain with the guy. He, his father and Rafe's father had sworn to never negotiate with terrorists. Now, Yiker might not be a terrorist in the simplest form of the word but the guy was definitely an extortionist. Which had Kris thinking he might just have someone else in mind who could help them.

After touring the site where Quirio wanted to build the resort, Tajeo had driven Kris directly to the bank for his meetings there. Those meetings had run longer than anticipated and instead of returning to the palace for his Skype call, Kris was forced to use his office there. It was just after the call wherein he'd informed Yiker that he would get back to him with a final answer about whether or not they would be using his services, that Kris noticed something wrong.

His office was located in the very back of the two-story building that housed the bank. The building was constructed with reinforced steel beams and triple-thick concrete. The windows were a bulletproof Plexiglas and there was an intricate alarm system on all the doors. That did not include the mechanisms designed to keep the main vault safe, or the secondary underground vault that no one but Kris, Rafe and the bank manager knew about. Every door inside the building required a key card to enter and thermal scanners were activated each time a person entered through the front and only entrance.

After being in his office for over an hour it was only when Kris had stood to leave that he noticed the plant on the floor near the window. Dirt had spilled out but the bright-colored flower was still rooted in the pot. Wondering why the cleaning staff hadn't taken care of this, he'd walked over to inspect the plant himself. As he knelt down he realized he could hear noise from the street. Between the windows and the extra-thick walls, outdoor sounds had never been able to be heard inside the building. Looking up, Kris realized why that wasn't true today. The window was open.

He stood slowly and reached into his back pocket for his cell phone.

"We've got a problem at the bank," he spoke into the phone as soon as he received an answer.

It hadn't taken long to get Salvin Gathersburgh, the chief guard from the palace, and Tajeo there to survey the scene. Kris had been thoroughly surprised to see Roland walk in as well.

"My text stated that everything was fine," Kris had said to his brother the minute he walked into the office.

Roland frowned. *"Your text stated you thought someone had broken into the bank, but that everything was fine. Who says that?"*

His brother was already walking toward the window, looking at the plant on the floor and then up to the open window.

"Was anything missing from in here?" Roland had asked Kris.

Kris shook his head. *"Nothing. I've checked twice. I have a safe over here beneath this portrait. It wasn't disturbed. Contents are still there."*

"We should check for any type of listening devices and get fingerprints," Salvin told them. *"Probably better if we call the police commander over to have a look too."*

"No," Roland and Kris had said simultaneously.

"Let's keep this under wraps for now. The citizens are still reeling from the accident. We don't need to cause any more panic by making them think that something illicit is going on," Kris stated, even though he was already feeling like they had a major problem.

So hours later, by the time he'd entered the dining room, Kris was in a less than festive mood. In fact, he'd really considered not attending the dinner at all, which would not go over well. Besides, the more he'd thought about skipping, the more he wanted to go, just to see Landry.

"I'm not sure it would look good to have too many guards standing out in the crowds. As you know I've contacted some of my press connections in the States. The first official event of the soon-to-be princess is a big deal for them," Malayka was saying.

Kris knew that if he looked over at her she'd have that gleaming smile she wore especially for the reporters.

"We should continue to use the same discretion with the press as we've done in the past," Sam stated. "I think it would be a good idea if we combine our list of media connections and have all of them vetted according to our usual standards."

"So you want me to run everything I do by you first? That doesn't sound correct. The chain of command…"

"The chain of command does not shift until you are married," Kris interrupted Malayka. "Until that time we have protocols in place and we will continue to use them."

When she dropped her fork to her plate and made a hissing sound, Rafe spoke up. "He's right. Now is not the time to change how we operate here. If you anticipate any extra press attending the event you need to provide their names and contact information to Sam. She knows what to do," he told her. "Actually, now would probably be a great time for her to show you everything she does."

Kris watched as his father extended his arm closing the distance between himself and Malayka by touching her hand. Malayka had been frowning—no, actually she'd been scowling at Sam—but as soon as Rafe touched her hand, her facial features softened and she sighed.

"I guess you're right," she replied.

"Maybe we should cancel the ball," Roland spoke up then.

"What? No! Now that is just too much. Tell him, Rafe," Malayka protested.

"In light of the accident and what happened—" Roland started before Kris interrupted.

"We are a united front. We do not flinch," Kris stated evenly.

He did not look at Roland as he spoke, or his father, but instead found himself staring directly at Landry.

She'd been toying with the whipped cream atop the white chocolate raspberry cheesecake they'd been served for dessert. Not eating it, just moving it around in a swirling motion that was turning it into a sopping white glob. She also appeared to be listening and Kris found it interesting that he wanted to know what she thought. Did she hate hearing these private family discussions? Was she as annoyed at Malayka's continuous talk about the princess-to-be as he was? Did she wonder why it all mattered?

Kris did. He wondered and he tried to keep it all in perspective. It was his job, after all.

"I'm not saying that this isn't serious," he continued, shifting his gaze to his brother. "We need to be on guard."

"What? Why?" Malayka asked and drew questioning looks from Sam, Roland and Kris. "Igor didn't check the brakes on the car. That wasn't a malicious attack. Why do we need to up the security and check out everyone we talk to like they're some type of government spy? And the Ambassador's Ball is a tradition. Right? We can't just stop traditions because of a car accident that didn't even kill anybody."

She was right, the car accident hadn't killed anyone. But it was meant to, and Kris wasn't totally certain what the break-in at the bank meant. To him, those were very good reasons to be on guard.

"The precautions are warranted, regardless of how harmless you believe the car accident was," Kris told her.

"Enough!" Rafe intervened. "I want to see the three of you in my office first thing tomorrow morning. Come, Malayka, we're retiring for the night."

Nobody spoke until they were gone, at which time Landry immediately pushed her chair back and stood.

"I should leave," she said.

"I'll walk you to your room," Roland offered.

Kris clenched his teeth and vowed to remain silent.

"No, thank you," she told him and then looked at Roland apologetically. "I mean, I can make it on my own. Besides, I believe there might be a discussion here once I'm gone that you should be part of."

Roland stood beside her then and lifted her hand to his mouth. "Very well, my dear. You win," he said before kissing the back of her hand.

She smiled as she slipped her hand from his, then turned to say good-night with a nod to him and to Sam. When she was gone his brother and sister looked directly to him.

"We're not canceling the ball and we're ramping up security. I'll say the same to Dad in the morning." Having said that Kris pushed his chair back and stood as well. He walked out of the dining room without another word.

It was a nice evening to think, Landry thought as she walked along the palace grounds. In the early days of being on the island she would spend her evenings with a relaxing swim, alone. Until that one night when everything changed. She'd known it the morning she crept out of his room that things were going to be different. But Landry hadn't realized how much so, not until now.

She'd slept with the crown prince. Not once, but over and over again, she'd spent hours in his bed, beneath him, on top of him, in the shower with him. Then, they would fall asleep in each other's arms, as if they were a real couple. Sighing, she pushed her hair back from her face and looked up to the evening sky. Damn stars and tropical-scented air, that's what had gotten her into trouble in the first place.

When she'd suggested that Kristian join her for some pizza it had only been to help him get through the scare of the accident. There'd been no thoughts to seduction or flirtation; she was certain of that fact. All she'd wanted was to make him feel better. Why, she still had no clue.

Why did it matter if Kristian DeSaunters looked happy or not? She shouldn't feel sorry for the somber way in which he lived his life. It was none of her business. Yet, she'd made it her business, at least for the past few weeks she had.

Landry hadn't lied to him, she had related to the fear he'd felt. When her father had fallen off a ladder and then again when he'd been rushed to the hospital with chest pains, she'd been terrified. So she knew what Kristian had been feeling that day. She knew and she'd tried to help.

Then why did she feel like she'd caused more harm? Because she probably had.

Malayka had met with her wedding coordinator today. They were interviewing caterers and entertainment for the reception. So Landry had time to herself. She stayed in her room in order to make calls and handle other business. She reviewed her finances and sent invoices to her accountant. After lunch she took a long nap and when she woke, caught up on some recent fashion articles.

She had not come out of her room all day.

That's why she was there when the delivery came.

"I wasn't expecting any shipments today," she told the staff members that carried the half dozen boxes into her room.

"It is for you," one of them had said before they both left her alone once more.

There was no name on the box and no cards attached to give a clue where or who they were from so she had no choice but to open one of them. Removing the lid and pushing aside the pastel-colored tissue paper Landry was momentarily speechless. It was a black-and-white blouse, an off-the-shoulder striped bell sleeve. After holding it up to survey it, Landry saw that there was another shirt in the box. This one, a very light tone of gray smocked-neck kimono cold-shoulder blouse. After pulling out all the tissue paper she was irritated to find there was still no card.

That meant she had to open another box, because surely if someone thought to send these to her, they'd at the very least want her to know who they were from.

There were two blouses in each box, a range of colors and styles, but all off-the-shoulder. Twelve of them. The room looked like there'd been a pastel explosion as she'd torn through each box looking for a card. She had found none.

As she stood there looking around and wondering what was going on, her cell phone chimed. It was a task finding the phone in the mess she'd created but eventually she did and saw that she had a text message.

I wanted to replace the top I ripped. I apologize. KRD

Landry read the message over again. He hadn't actually ripped her blouse that first night they were together, but the way he'd tried to take it off had stretched it out of shape. She'd never said a word about it, never asked him to buy her another blouse to replace that one.

She read the text a third time and her lips spread into a smile. She hadn't meant to, but there was a lightness in the pit of her stomach. A silly little rippling of pleasure at seeing his note and looking up at all those blouses.

Suddenly it became imperative to fold each blouse and lay them neatly in one of the drawers she was using. She broke the boxes down until they could be flattened and stacked on top of each other and found a bag in the bathroom that she could put all of the tissue paper into. In her travels throughout the palace she hadn't seen any recycle bins, but she was certain the royal family was concerned with protecting the environment. After showering and dressing for dinner she intended to find out where they kept their recycling and then thank Kristian the moment she saw him in the dining room.

She would thank him and then she would tell him that what they were doing was over.

That plan changed later, when she had entered the dining room and felt the tension. Everyone had watched her as she made her way to the table, offering an apology and a smile. Prince Rafe barely looked up at Landry and Malayka shook her head as if that sole action would admonish Landry for all her wrongdoing. The woman had really started to go on a power trip. Sam had smiled at her in return and Roland stood to pull her chair out for her. Kristian had looked at her and then hurriedly turned away.

That wasn't out of the ordinary. Since they'd been sleeping together, Kristian had made a concerted effort not to talk to her too much during dinners. A part of her had wanted to be angry about that fact, actually about the whole arrangement. Only she didn't remember agreeing to an affair with him. All she'd remembered was how her body had instantly heated at his touch, how his kisses wiped all coherent thoughts from her mind. It had been so good these past weeks and at the same time so very wrong.

Well, tonight, that was going to come to an end. After receiving those blouses from him this afternoon, Landry's mind had been made up. The very next time Kristian sent her one of his private messages, she was going to tell him it was over.

Now, after that tension-filled dinner, a lovely fragrance drew her down a stone pathway to where she could see large trees. A garden, she surmised and continued walking in that direction. Plants and flowers weren't really her thing, but the scents were enticing, almost soothing as she moved through the passageways. In daylight she presumed this garden would be gorgeous with the variety of flowers she saw and the neatly trimmed greenery. At this time of night everything was cast in a dull haze, but still, the effect of this seemingly endless path was breathtaking.

In the distance she could hear water, a slow trickle that added to this serene atmosphere. Landry walked toward the sound until she came to a clearing with expertly cut trees jutting high up into the sky and ponds lining the open area. Grass paths separated the ponds into neat squares, lily pads floating in each. It was gorgeous. Landry walked around one before kneeling and touching her fingers to the water.

"You love the water, don't you?"

She looked up to see Kristian standing on the other side of the pond, his hands tucked into his pant pockets, the action pushing his suit jacket back.

Flicking the water off her fingers as she came to stand, Landry shrugged. "It's relaxing."

"I guess," was his somber response.

He looked regal. No matter what he did or said that

royal air which surrounded him like a cloak could not be dismissed. It had Landry standing straighter, keeping eye contact and for once in her life making a valiant attempt to monitor her words. She had something to say to him and she'd rehearsed it in her mind for the past couple of hours. Still, when she spoke something totally different slipped out.

"What do you do to relax, Kristian?"

He stared for a few moments, as if he might not answer her at all. On several occasions when they'd been together she would do most of the talking. He would do most of the contemplating. She realized now that there were usually more questions than answers. That's what he did, she decided. He thought about each response, made sure what he said was exactly what he wanted to say. She'd have to learn that trick one of these days.

"I like to read," he replied finally.

He started to walk along one side of the pond and Landry followed by walking along the other side.

"What do you read?"

"Mythology. Folklore. History," he replied as casually as reciting the alphabet, instead of actually revealing something personal about himself.

"No romance or erotica?" she asked with a chuckle.

He remained quiet and she clasped her hands behind her back. She would definitely need much more practice in thinking about what she said before saying it.

"My mother used to read to me at night. Fairy tales that were filled with romance and sentiment. I learned very fast that the real world was nothing like a fairy tale and that romance and sentiment were not meant for a prince."

His words were cynical and sad. But Landry knew better than to voice those thoughts.

"I'm not a huge fan of fairy tales either," she stated. "But for different reasons than you, I suppose."

His reply came quicker this time. "Tell me your reasons."

They came to a grassy spot and Landry noted that all she had to do was take a few steps to her left and they would be standing side by side. Kristian continued to walk and so did she.

"Snow White was poisoned by an evil jealous queen and remained at death's door, until a prince came along and saved the day. As a result of yet another evil woman and her father's tyrannical ways, Sleeping Beauty also ended up in a death slumber, until, guess what? Another prince came around and saved her too." She shook her head and continued, "Cinderella inherited a castle and land but was forced to work like a slave because of an evil woman and her daughters. Until—"

"A prince came along and saved her as well," Kristian finished. "I see where you're going with this."

He chuckled lightly and Landry smiled.

"I'm just sayin' young girls can do without growing up believing that they need a man to 'save' them," she added. They could also do without almost falling for a man they had no business even thinking about.

"You would probably end up saving the man," he said, more seriously this time.

Landry shrugged again. "More shocking things have happened," she quipped.

"I'm not in a position to be saved."

"You create your own circumstances, control your own destiny. It doesn't have to be prewritten. Unless you want it to be."

Again, she probably should not have said that to him, and yet, a part of her wondered if Kristian was reaching out for someone to save him. What if he did feel trapped by his title, by this gorgeous island and all that came with it? There could be less appealing trappings, she thought.

They came to the end of the path where those same tall trees that lined the sides of the walkway crossed over and formed a wall. In front of that wall were two stone benches. Kristian took long strides until he turned and sat on one. Extending an arm he said quietly, "Come here."

Landry walked to him without thinking of whether or not she should. His legs were parted and when she took his hand, he pulled her down to sit on his lap.

"I thought about you today," he said, his gaze focused ahead, his arm going around her waist.

She swallowed hard, trying to adjust to the quick jolt of heat that soared through her body at their proximity.

"I thought of you while I was in meetings. When I rode along the winding roads in the car. As I dressed for dinner. When you came into the dining room, I tried not to stare at you. The entire time Malayka talked and when the sweetness of the dessert tickled the back of my throat. I cannot seem to stop thinking about you."

His voice was still quiet, the sound of the ocean in the distance, almost louder than his words. Yet, Landry had heard each one and she'd tensed as if she were naked in front of a ballroom full of people. His words were raw and…what really shocked her, honest.

"I thought of you when I sat in my room today. I tried to work but I couldn't forget where I was, whose house this is or the way back to your room. None of those things are what I should be thinking while I'm here."

They were quiet, because Landry did not know what he was going to say next. All she knew was that as his arm tightened around her waist, she leaned in closer to the wall of his chest. It was warm there, comfortable, easy.

"I said before that you weren't supposed to be here. Nowhere in the plan for my life did an American woman appear. Then I opened that folder and your picture stared back at me. You've been here," he said, lifting his free hand to tap a finger against his temple, "ever since that day. Stuck in my mind and then for the past weeks, in my arms. I don't know why, but I like that. I like it a lot."

That hand came down from his face to cup her jaw, turning her so that she was now staring directly into his eyes. "I like it a lot," he repeated.

"I like it too," she whispered as he pulled her in even closer. In her mind she heard her words replay and a part of her wanted to scream. She did not like being his dirty little secret. Her body, on the other hand, loved it.

Their lips touched lightly, slowly, once and then again. The third time his were parted. She knew they would be and she was ready. Their tongues touched lightly, sweetly. They touched again and twirled around in an enticing motion. His hand slipped around her neck to cup the back of her head, tilting it so that she would fall deeper into the kiss. Her hands moved up the lapels of his jacket, feeling the rise and fall of his muscled chest beneath, until she wrapped her arms around his neck. With an arm still around her waist, he pulled her even closer against him, their breathing growing quicker, louder.

Kris kissed her as if his next breath depended on their contact. His fingers tingled as they moved over the curve of her buttocks and the warm skin at the nape of her neck. She smelled like flowers, or was it the air surrounding them? He couldn't tell, all he knew was that he enjoyed it very much.

He'd liked how she had looked when she walked into the dining room. The simple, yet alluring, style of the dress that looked like a white dress shirt, belted at the waist, showing off her knees and legs. Her hair was pulled back from her face, held together by some sort of band. She'd taken his breath away without even trying.

Finding her here in his mother's garden had been a shock and for a moment he'd felt like it was an intrusion. Tonight he'd wanted to be alone, to gather his thoughts on what was going on in his mind. Then he'd watched her touch that water and he'd wanted her hands on him. He needed her on him, right now.

With a groan of resistance, Kris tore his mouth away. He kept his gaze on hers, watching the way the growing passion had filled her eyes and his fervent kisses left her lips plump and delectable. Reaching into his back pocket he pulled out his wallet and retrieved a condom. Her gaze didn't waver but he knew she was certain of what he was doing. Setting his wallet on the bench beside them, he handed her the condom and then planted his hands around her waist and lifted her up into his lap. She moved in conjunction with his every thought. Turning to face him as she ripped the condom package open, setting the paper on the bench beside his wallet as she straddled his lap.

Kris undid his pants and released his erection. She eased the condom down on his length. He cupped her face in his palms, pulling her down so that he could have her lips again. This kiss was hungry, a taking that said all the words neither of them decided to speak. She was moving, pushing at her dress. He continued to kiss her, but let his hands fall down to her legs. He loved the feel of her skin and dragged his hands slowly up her legs, hating to stop the contact. When he felt the hem of her panties he moved farther until his palms were now cupping her bottom. He squeezed both cheeks loving the sexy purring sounds she made in response. When she circled her hips it was Kris's turn to make noise. He groaned with pleasure and before he could stop himself, he grabbed the material of her panties and ripped them off.

His fingers trembled as they moved between her legs to feel the already wet and plump folds.

"Kristian," she whispered when he touched her there.

He sucked her tongue deeper into his mouth as he pressed his fingers slowly inside her. At the feel of her honeyed walls contracting around his fingers, Kris's body went into overdrive. He pulled those fingers quickly from her and held on to her hips, lifting her until she could come down quickly over his length.

It was sexy as hell, the way she slithered down onto him, her tongue still moving erotically in his mouth. Kris held her tighter, gritting his teeth at the pleasure of being fully ensconced in her heat. His thrusts came quickly after that. She tore her mouth away from his, breathing heavily as she arched her back and circled her hips to match his rhythm.

Pleasure came in sharp pricks against his skin, as if a million darts were being thrown at him all at once. He couldn't think, couldn't speak, he could only feel. She'd wrapped her legs completely around his waist, locking her ankles at his back. He sat up straighter to hold her and to keep them both leveraged as he pounded into her. When her fingers dug into his shoulder and his name became a litany of murmurs and sighs on her lips, Kris thought he would lose it immediately.

She was tight around him, her thighs trembling as she made the climb to her release. He leaned in, licking over the part of the material that covered her breasts. Then he nipped there, wanting desperately to feel her turgid nipple in his mouth once more. He didn't want to take his hands off her, loved the feeling of her bare cheeks in his palms as he moved quickly in and out of her. So he continued to suckle her breasts through the dress, until she made a sound that matched the jerking and stilling of her hips.

With her release came a surge of heat in Kris's body that he knew he'd never be able to explain. He felt as if that heat boiled instantly until there was a blast and before he knew what to say or how to react, he was groaning with his release. By now he was squeezing her so tightly, he was certain it must be painful.

He lowered his forehead until it rested on her chest. She was panting. He was panting. He loosened his grip only slightly on her. She flattened her palms on the back of his head, rubbing slowly as he leaned on her trying to catch his breath.

"Thank you."

He heard the words but wasn't totally sure she should be saying them.

"For what?" he asked without daring to look up at her.

If she was thanking him for sex, Kris wasn't going to be happy. As his mind began to clear of the foggy remnants of release, he wasn't actually feeling jubilant at the moment.

"For the blouses," she said. "I meant to thank you at dinner, but you left. And then you were here and before I could say it…well, just thank you."

Kris closed his eyes to her words, but still did not look up at her. She was thanking him for sending her a dozen shirts when he was pretty sure he was on his way to ruining her life.

How was he supposed to respond to that?

Chapter 11

"You're leaving me again," he said.

Landry had just finished smoothing down loose strands of her hair. Moments ago she'd slipped off his lap and adjusted her dress. As for the remnants of her underwear, she'd stuffed them into the front pocket of her dress and was prepared to make the uncomfortable trek to her bedroom commando-style.

She hadn't been facing him but when he spoke, she turned slowly.

"It's become a habit," she replied. "Leaving without being seen so I don't cause any trouble." The words were bitter in her mouth.

He'd adjusted his clothes as well, and he'd picked up his wallet and the condom paper from the bench. She presumed he'd also disposed of the used condom, but didn't want to think about where or how. Actually, Landry decided, she really just wanted to go back to her room.

"You believe that being with me might cause trouble?"

She almost laughed at the way he managed to sound oblivious to what was going on. "Maybe not trouble, but certainly confusion. At least for me."

"Then why do you do it?"

It took a moment for her to see that he was serious. "You mean, why do *we* do it? I don't know," she told him. "Gluttons for punishment, I suppose."

"Hmm, punishment," Kristian continued. "I hadn't actually thought of it that way."

She took a tentative step toward him and then stopped. Her thoughts were much clearer when she wasn't so close to him. Now was as good a time as any to get this conversation over with. So what they'd just had pretty terrific sex; it was always like that with them.

"How are you thinking of this, Kristian? What do you think we're doing?"

She really wanted him to answer this time because she was so not sure what was going on between them. It had happened so quickly, the change from him and her, to them, together, that she hadn't been able to make any sense of it.

"We're adults," he told her.

"You're right, we are."

"And…dammit!" he yelled, turning away from her.

Stunned for a few seconds at the outburst, Landry could only stare at him, until finally she decided to close the space between them.

"I didn't plan this. I only came here to do a job," she said standing behind him. "And I don't really know how or why it started."

"But it can't continue," he said, whirling around to face her again.

They were standing close this time, so close she could see the twitch of a muscle in his jaw.

"Is that what you're about to say? Or no, perhaps it was more along the lines of we should just go with this. Press on and see where it takes us," he was saying.

Landry didn't like his tone or his words. She squared her shoulders and cleared her throat. "No. What I'm saying is that I don't believe in games. We're attracted to each other, okay, we cannot deny that. I'm usually good at handling any type of relationship and rolling with the punches. But I've never been good at games. As for what would happen beyond the nights we keep spending together, I hadn't thought about it much, not until now."

"I have," he replied tersely. "I've thought about you and us and the inevitability of it all. We're too different, yet the attraction is undeniable."

Landry took a step back at that point, nodding her head as she considered her words.

"You're right again, Kristian. You're a prince and I'm just an American entrepreneur. Those differences are huge and yes, they too are undeniable."

He opened his mouth to say something and then shook his head. "That's not how I meant it," he told her.

"It is and that's fine because like I said, it's true."

He tried again. "We have different lives. We're meant to do different things."

"In other words, I'm a commoner and you're royalty."

"I didn't say that," he quickly replied.

Landry waited a beat and then gave a wry smile. "You didn't deny it either."

He sighed heavily. "Look, you just don't understand the situation I'm in. You have no idea the duties resting on my shoulders, the responsibility that I have to this country and to my family. I can't let her down—I just can't."

"You can't let who down?"

That muscle ticked in his jaw again and silence filled the air.

"Nothing," he finally replied. "You're right. It won't look good for either of us to be seen together like this. You leave first and go back to your room. I'll walk out in a few minutes."

"So that's that—we'll have these little hookups and then we scuttle off in our different directions in secret."

When he looked like he would respond, Landry raised a hand to stop him.

"No need for any more explanations. You've tried that already. We're too different and that's fine. I'm not some starry-eyed girl with dreams of marrying a prince and living in a palace. I've never wanted a serious relationship and least of all one where I would have to compromise my lifestyle for that of a title. I'll just head back to my room now, Your Highness. But please, do me a favor, no more text messages, no more gifts and no more nights like this."

Kristian didn't say another word, nor did he try to stop her. The latter, Landry discovered as she walked back to her room, had hurt the most.

"Good evening," Malayka spoke from behind Landry.

Landry turned so fast after entering her bedroom, and bit back a scream. With her back flattened against the door to her rooms, she stared at Malayka who was sitting with her legs crossed in an oatmeal-color tufted armchair.

"Ah, good evening. Did we have a meeting this late?" Landry asked when she finally got herself together enough to move away from the door and walk farther into the room.

"I'll ask the questions, if you don't mind. Where were you last night? I called you and I came to your room.

You're supposed to be at my beck and call, and you weren't here."

Landry moved slowly, still uncomfortable from her lack of underwear and not in the mood for conversation with her client. She took a seat in the chair that was positioned directly across from Malayka.

"I don't think our contract says anything about *beck and call*," Landry stated in a voice as calm as she could muster after walking quickly down a long hallway only to be frightened by an uninvited guest in her room. "And before you go on, yes, I know that you are about to become the princess of this beautiful island. My job is to dress you for all of your functions leading up to that time. We both have a calendar with those important dates listed. I schedule meetings and fittings with you and I'm present for every one of them. I am doing my job."

Malayka opened her mouth to reply, but Landry shook her head and held up a finger to stop her.

"Just one more thing," she told the soon-to-be princess. "I do not appreciate you letting yourself into my room and questioning me like I'm a child. Now, is there something else?"

Again, Astelle Norris's voice echoed in Landry's head. She'd said too much, and she hadn't monitored her tone. She'd been *sassy*, which was one of Astelle's favorite words to describe Landry. Landry didn't care. Malayka was the type of person who needed to be nipped in the bud sooner, rather than later. If Landry answered the woman's questions tonight without telling her that she was stepping over their professional line, then Malayka would feel as if she could treat Landry any way she wanted to. True, Malayka or rather—as evidenced from her latest check—Prince Rafferty was paying Landry's invoices, so she owed them a measure of respect. But no amount of zeroes on a check would ever mean that Landry was going to tolerate disrespect from anyone.

Malayka didn't move a muscle. Her hair was pulled back from her face with a jeweled band, the sage-colored dress she'd worn at dinner falling to her ankles, gold strappy sandals at her feet. It was a lovely outfit, which Malayka had managed to select for herself.

"This is my house," Malayka began, keeping her saccharine-filled smile in place. "I have a right to know all the comings and goings around here. Besides, I'm concerned for you."

Landry wanted to laugh. From the way that Malayka was looking at her to the blatant lie she'd just told, the scenario was more than a little funny. Instead, she decided she could play this game too, for just a moment.

"Really? Why are you concerned about me?" she asked.

"I've noticed how you've been looking at Kristian."

A jolt of surprise speared through her. Still, Landry kept her face and her response as indecipherable as possible.

"How exactly have I been looking at him?" Landry asked.

Malayka uncrossed her legs then and leaned forward keeping her gaze locked on Landry's.

"You want him," Malayka said candidly. "And before you deny it, let me tell you that it's no secret around the palace that you've been attending every dinner in the main dining room, whereas no other staff has ever been invited. Samantha did her normal tour of the island with you. Roland paid a bit of attention to you. So you may be thinking that you have a chance. But let me tell you right here and now, you don't."

It was hard to digest Malayka's words as her body still tingled in every spot that Kristian had just touched. He'd been rougher tonight than last night and the nights before that, but Landry had loved it just the same. Yet, this woman was telling her she couldn't have a man that Landry had already had, on more than one occasion to be exact.

"He's taken," Malayka continued before Landry could figure out what to say and how best to say it. "Her name is Valora Harrington and she's been betrothed to Kristian since they were both children. They're both natives to this island. The citizens know and love them and expect them to be married, as their fathers agreed upon long ago. So, you see, there's no room for an American entrepreneur in this picture."

Landry did not know what to say. She did not know how to feel. What she did know, however, was that there was no way she was giving Malayka the satisfaction of seeing her stumble.

"I hope Prince Rafferty is doing well this evening. I'm sure these past few weeks have been stressful to him." While Malayka looked surprised that Landry had completely changed the subject, Landry continued. "I'm expecting the last few dresses for you to arrive tomorrow. I've already planned a fitting for tomorrow afternoon. If you'd rather reschedule for another time in the next couple of days, I completely understand. You probably want to spend as much time with your fiancé as possible."

"Fine," Malayka said as she stood.

Landry stood as well, keeping the small smile she'd managed to muster.

"We'll keep our appointment," she told Landry. "And you just remember to keep your distance."

"Los Angeles is a good distance away, Malayka. As soon as our contract is up that's where I'll be. So you can save your warnings for the next woman who crosses your path," Landry told her.

"Right," Malayka said with a nod. "Am I trying on the

Peta Romanti dress tomorrow? She did say she was sending an original for the wedding festivities, right?"

Landry gave a quick nod as she followed Malayka to the door. "Yes, she did. It should be in tomorrow's shipment."

"I was under the impression that you had a personal connection to her," Malayka said when she opened the door.

Or else she might not have been hired? That's what Landry figured Malayka was attempting to say. Again, she wanted to laugh. The only reason Peta had agreed to send a dress for Malayka was because of Landry and also because Malayka was engaged to a prince. Otherwise, that picture that Peta had taken with Malayka over a year ago would have been the extent of the designer's contact with the soon-to-be princess.

"I've known Peta for a few years now and she never lets me down," Landry replied. "It's important to keep good professional relationships in this business."

"Exactly," Malayka said as she turned to give Landry one more sweet smile. "See you tomorrow, Landry."

"See you tomorrow, Malayka."

Their exchange had been weird and mostly uncalled for, except that it had added one more strike to the column of Landry's mistakes.

Chapter 12

The room was empty.

Malayka was late for their appointment. Landry found that to be almost laughable especially considering the condescending tone Malayka had last night in her room.

"He knows to follow my instructions. He'll do what he's paid to do or I'll find someone else to do it," was what Landry heard the moment she'd pushed the rack of dresses into Malayka's new dressing room. Landry didn't understand why a second dressing room had been necessary, but she'd known better than to open that door of discussion. All she wanted to focus on today was her job.

Her deliveries had arrived on schedule. After checking each package, she'd placed each dress on the rack and made her way to the far end of the hall past Malayka's rooms.

The voice belonged to a male and wasn't one that Landry was familiar with. That meant nothing considering there were at least fifty staff members moving throughout the palace at one time or another. Falling back on her no eavesdropping rule, Landry continued to move around the space getting things together for Malayka's impending arrival.

The gown from Detali was zipped in a black garment bag. Landry went into the closet where all the new shoes that had been shipped over from the United States were being stored. She walked up and down the narrow path between the shelves looking for just the right shoes to go with the dress.

"You're not the boss! I get my orders directly from him and then they filter down to you. Don't make me sorry I picked you."

It was that guy's voice again.

She figured he was in the room right next to this one but for whatever reason Landry could hear him entirely too clearly. When she came out of the shoe closet and felt a cool breeze she realized why. The doors to the balcony in this room had been left open. Gauzy white curtains were lifted off the floor as another breeze sifted through. Malayka didn't like feeling too stuffy and she swore this room did not receive the same force of air-conditioning that her bedroom did.

The fact that this was a five-hundred-year-old palace probably had something to do with that. While Landry had seen the rectangular-shaped air-conditioning units positioned along the top line of the walls in most of the rooms in the palace, she knew there were some rooms that did not have any air at all. It hadn't surprised or annoyed her, maybe because she had read all about the history of this palace and the island in the time that she'd been there. She was certain Malayka hadn't done that.

As excited as Landry had been this time yesterday

morning about today's fitting, at the moment, she simply wanted to get it over with. The little bombshell—that was actually more like a gigantic monkey wrench—Malayka had dropped on her last night was still rolling around in her mind.

Kristian was engaged to be married.

With a sigh, and because she could still hear that voice that was doing nothing to drown out her thoughts, Landry approached the balcony doors. More of the neighboring conversation played, just in case she did want to listen attentively.

She did not, still she stepped out on the balcony and saw a man with his back turned to her on the connecting balcony. He wore a white shirt and white slacks and a white baseball cap. Landry still wasn't sure who he was or who he was talking to as he looked toward the doors and said, "I'll be done with this call in a second."

"Nine o'clock," he continued saying. "Not a moment before or after. I don't have to tell you what will happen if you mess this up."

Figuring she definitely did not want to know what was going on at nine o'clock, Landry moved back inside and closed the balcony doors. Snapping the lock into place, she walked away telling herself that she shouldn't have been listening to something that wasn't her business. After all, she had no idea who was talking anyway.

Her business was getting this dress approved so that in several more days Malayka could walk into the ballroom wearing a Detali original and stun everyone in the room. Landry knew for a fact there would be press at the Ambassador's Ball. In addition to the local reporters, Malayka had been sure to issue a press release to the international media. She'd invited Hollywood producers and Wall Street giants, US and European politicians and their wives. It was as if this were the actual wedding, Landry thought when she'd watched Malayka working her own press coverage. But the soon-to-be princess was adamant about documenting her rise to the throne on a national level.

So, for Landry, that meant Detali Designs would also go national, and with it, Landry's name. A win-win for all involved, she told herself as she checked her watch. Malayka was now very late.

Landry was annoyed.

She could be doing other things besides waiting in this room for Malayka to show up whenever she felt like it. She could be in her room kicking herself for being an idiot.

How could she have slept with someone who was engaged to be married? Well, that answer was pretty simple. She didn't know Kristian was engaged. Nothing she'd read in the papers had mentioned it and nobody had thought to tell her that important fact. Or rather, it had never occurred to Landry to ask the question. So naive of her to presume that if he were coming on to her that he must be single. She'd thought he was available, just like her. Oh how wrong she'd been.

No wonder he seemed to be struggling with what they were doing; he was cheating. She sighed, so tired of thinking about this over and over again. "I hope those dresses arrived. I'm not going to be a happy camper if they haven't," Malayka said as she breezed into the room.

Cheryl McCoy, her makeup artist and Amari Taylor, the hair stylist, followed. Landry had seen these two before, which meant she'd witnessed their superior brand of ass kissing, on more than one occasion. Yet another thing she was not in the mood for today.

"The dresses are here. We can get started right away," Landry said as she moved to the rack.

"I hope you pick something colorful," Cheryl spoke with too much excitement. "I'd love to do something lavish with your eyes for this event."

"I don't think *lavish* is a word that should be attached to a princess," Landry mumbled.

Or at least she thought she'd mumbled. As it turned out the others had heard her and after she unzipped the first garment bag she looked over her shoulder to see them staring at her critically. With a shrug she continued to take the first dress out of the bag.

"It's black." Cheryl sighed.

"Black is timeless," Amari added.

He came closer to the rack and reached out to touch the fabric.

"Ooohwee, and it's satin. That's going to lie nicely over your body, Layka." Amari looked over Landry's shoulder with a grin on his face.

He was a tall man, slim and willowy. His thick eyebrows were perfectly arched and definitely the envy of women all over the world. His wavy hair was cut short, hairline shaped precisely. He wore two diamond stud earrings and black nail polish on two fingers on each hand.

"Satin is so ordinary," Malayka replied.

Landry was removing the gown when she turned to see that Malayka—thankfully—had stepped behind the screens to the left of the room.

"Let's decide when we see you in this masterpiece," Amari continued.

He attempted to take the dress off the hanger, with every intention of walking it over to Malayka, and quite possibly going behind the screen to help her put it on. But Landry gave him a look. Yes, one cool and no-nonsense look that had the man pursing his lips and taking a step back while folding his arms over his chest. She didn't give his theatrics the glory of a reply, instead she carried the dress over to the screen and handed it to Malayka.

"This is the Dolce & Gabbana. We sent the first two back, so this is the special order," Landry told Malayka.

Ten minutes later, Malayka had come out to stand in front of the mirror, turning this way and that and getting more opinions than Landry thought were necessary. Her client sighed and told her once more, "Send it back."

Three dresses and an hour and a half later, Landry was rewarded with, "This dress is brilliant!"

If Landry were in a better mood she might have jumped for joy at that exclamation. Malayka turned, looking over her shoulder to see her backside reflection in the free-standing mirrors.

"Yes! That dress is fiyah!" Amari declared and began clapping his hands.

Cheryl was nodding as she smiled. "I'm gonna have a great time with your makeup. Cannot wait until that ball. You're going to be the best-looking soon-to-be princess the people of this island have ever seen!"

Landry didn't speak. She couldn't because the dress was perfect. It was gorgeous and glamorous, unique and just like Amari had said…fiyah!

And it was the Detali original.

Malayka Sampson had just made her day.

Skipping dinner was probably cowardly.

And foolish, Landry thought as she took another bite of the granola bar she'd found in the bottom of her purse.

Six more months and she would be leaving this island and all its picturesque beauty. Including the lovely scene ahead of her at the moment. The Cliffs. Landry had read about them in one of the pamphlets she'd picked up when she'd traveled to the City Center in search of a place to mail postcards to her mother. Astelle collected postcards from wherever she went in the world, from tiny towns to big cities. The only postcard her mother had from an actual island was the one Landry had bought her from Saint Bart's when she'd flown there to assist one of her clients on a photo shoot. Landry was excited to share the pretty cards she'd purchased in one of the quaint little gift shops near Grand Serenity's port.

She'd found the courier's office and mailed over a dozen cards home to her mother, imagining the smile on her face when she received them. Then Landry had returned to the palace. Restless, she wasn't ready for bed and couldn't bear being stuck in her rooms another minute. So she'd called the number that Jorge had given her and asked him to meet her at the front entrance.

After weeks of being in the palace she'd noticed that everyone left from the back of the property where the garage was. She'd asked Jorge to pick her up in the front once and prayed that he wouldn't run back and tell Kristian or the others about her strange request. Instead he'd simply done as she'd asked. That had earned him an ice cream cone that Landry had bought from a beautiful shop in town.

If Jorge wondered why she'd called him again so quickly tonight, he hadn't mentioned it. He simply picked her up and asked where she wanted to go. When she'd said The Cliffs he'd nodded and told her she would love the view from there.

He hadn't lied. The view was magnificent. Landry had no idea how high up she was but she was standing on the peak of a cliff. Smooth rock was visible beneath her feet; not too far behind patches of grass and shrubbery grew. Down below, far down below, the water was still bright turquoise and clear. At least it would have been if it were daylight. As darkness had already fallen over the island, the water still had a crystalline quality as it shimmered against the edge of the rocks. In the distance she could see boats, their lights like a beacon in the otherwise darkness.

Wrapping her arms around her chest, Landry stood perfectly still, looking out to sea as she inhaled the sweet island air. She liked it here, she finally admitted. The slow lifestyle and the friendly people. She loved walking down the cobblestone streets in the City Center and looking at the quaint and colorful buildings that crowded the square. When she stood there she only had to tilt her head up slightly to see more colorful dwellings tucked into the mountainside as if nature had put them there. It was majestic and amazing, soothing and invigorating all at the same time.

"Just when you thought you'd made a grand escape."

Landry jumped and turned, taking a hurried step away from the edge of the cliff before she actually tumbled over, and stared into Roland's laughing eyes.

In contrast to his brother, Roland always seemed to be happy. Except last night he'd seemed irritated at dinner and then again at the press conference she'd watched on television that afternoon, then he'd appeared contemplative and serious. The press conference was a follow-up to the accident. The police chief had spoken, but Kristian had stood right beside him, his face a mask of consternation. It was, of course, a handsome face, but Landry had been more drawn to the sadness that always seemed to cloud his eyes.

Roland had stood beside Kristian, both men dominant in their own way.

"Not trying to escape," she told him with a slight smile. "Just needed some air."

"Hey, I get it," he said, moving closer to where she stood. "With over fifteen bedrooms, two gourmet kitchens and three, not one or two, but three, ballrooms, the palace definitely has a shortage of air."

He chuckled and Landry balled the granola bar paper in her hand.

"We also have food in those two gourmet kitchens. Unless you're on some type of granola diet."

Landry laughed this time.

"You're not like the others. I forget that until I'm in your presence," she admitted.

He shrugged.

"Well, you know, I do my best."

He smelled good. A musk fragrance that was stronger than Kristian's cologne. It fit Roland's bold and brash personality. So did the black dress jeans, fitted beige shirt and black denim jacket he wore.

"You do, don't you," she said. "I mean, you try really hard to be the complete opposite of what others believe you are."

"People shouldn't judge based on what they see and hear. I'm under no obligation to appease them in that fashion," he said.

She nodded because she'd taken that same stance in her own life. Landry refused to act the way her parents wanted her to in order to get and keep a man. She had goals and aspirations and had worked her way to checking each of those little boxes off her to-do list without caring who thought it was a good idea or not.

"I agree," she said. "But then again, I'm not a prince. I'm certain the rules are different for you."

"Why? Because I happened to be born into a family of rulers? If you hadn't noticed, we don't get to select our parents," he said.

"That's for sure," she replied.

"What? You don't like your parents?"

"To the contrary, I love them. I'm not sure they love me all the time, but that's a discussion for another day," she quipped, "or night, I guess."

"Well," he said as he came close enough to wrap and arm around her shoulder and pull her close to him. "We should definitely spend some more time together as it appears we may have something in common."

"What? You have a dysfunctional relationship with your family too? I would have never guessed that one."

Roland had begun walking them down the hill. Landry had been ready to leave, but she liked talking to him.

"With my father, my sister and, oh yeah, my brother," he told her.

"Why? Because he's a liar?" Landry stopped immediately, clapping a hand over her mouth. Dammit, she'd done it again!

"Whoa, what did you just say?"

Landry shook her head, unable to trust herself this time.

"Kris lied to you? About what?"

"It's nothing," she said and continued walking. "Besides, I wouldn't call it a lie since I never asked the question. I guess it's more of an omission."

"And what did my perfect big brother omit?"

"It doesn't matter," she insisted.

"Obviously it does," Roland countered.

He touched her elbow, holding her until she stopped moving. Landry sighed.

"I didn't know he was betrothed," she said with exaggeration to that last word. She hated that word.

"Betrothed? Kris?" Roland shook his head, then stopped. "Oh, you're talking about Valora and that crazy deal her father keeps insisting was made."

"He should have told me that he was promised to someone else. Marrying someone else. Or I should have guessed because isn't that what royals do?" There was a tree behind her and Landry decided to use it because she was exhausted from thinking about Kristian all day. She leaned back and scrubbed her hands over her face.

"First, he's not obligated to mention something that doesn't exist. Valora's father is an old drunk who loves to gamble. When he was younger—and still drinking quite heavily—he played a game of poker with my aging and already sick grandfather. My father said that Valora's dad cheated. Of course, Valora's dad says he did not and that my grandfather lost. The payout was a royal union—a DeSaunters son promised to his daughter, whenever they were born."

She stared at him incredulously then. "What? Are you serious?"

Roland nodded. "It's never been true, but Valora's father tells anyone who'll listen that it is. That's why so many islanders believe it to be true, I suppose."

"Why hasn't anyone in your family set the record straight?"

"The people of Grand Serenity are a romantic sort," Roland told her.

He was standing in front of her now, one hand in his front pant pocket, while he rubbed the other hand down the back of his head.

"They look at the palace and the people who live here and believe all the fairy tales they've ever read. Marriages are arranged—good matches are made via good families. Valora's grandfather fought for my grandfather's army so while they aren't of royal status, there is loyalty there."

"Loyalty," Landry said. "But not enough to really have her and your brother getting married."

"Kris would never agree to an arranged marriage. He's too stubborn for something like that. And Valora, she's as headstrong as my sister. No way those two were ever going to be told who to marry and when."

Landry didn't know what to believe. All she knew at this moment was that she had one heck of a headache and she was still hungry.

"I'm sorry. I shouldn't have called him names and I definitely should not have been talking about him to you," she said and pushed away from that tree. "I'll be heading back to the palace now."

"What's your hurry?" Roland said. "I was just heading out for a little fun, ah… I mean, air. I needed to get some air too."

He was grinning and Landry liked his grin. Kristian wasn't engaged to be married, but she still had no business thinking about him or sleeping with him for that matter. What better way to get those thoughts out of her head than to hang out with Roland for a couple of hours.

"Well, I'm sure if anyone knows where the best 'air' is on this island, it would be you."

"You're absolutely right about that," Roland told her. "I know just the spot for us to get that air and to talk more about why you were so irritated by the notion that Kris would be engaged and not tell you."

Landry opened her mouth to rebut that statement but something told her the action would be futile.

Chapter 13

It was Friday night, and Landry felt like a princess.

Never in all her years of loving fashion and dressing people had she ever imagined feeling the way she did tonight.

After the week she'd had, going to the Ambassador's Ball had been far from her mind. Ordinarily, it wasn't always her practice to attend the events she dressed her clients for. However, as she'd discovered in the past week, this wasn't an ordinary assignment.

The last five days had been full of ordering shoes and accessories and praying they would be delivered on time. There had been two more fittings to make sure the Detali dress was a perfect fit for Malayka. She'd skipped a few more dinners in the dining room and avoided Roland's knowing glances and comments. She hadn't, however, been able to avoid Prince Rafe when he'd decided that he wanted to speak to her.

On Tuesday, he'd surprised her by sitting at one of the huge quartz-topped islands in the kitchen when she'd been returning from another recycle run.

"You are very conscientious," he'd said the moment she appeared through the doorway.

Dressed in old jeans and a faded T-shirt, Landry had been shocked and a little embarrassed to be in the prince's company looking disheveled and tired. She didn't have a mirror directly in front of her but the way she'd been feeling that day certainly showed.

"Just trying to do my part," she replied with a small smile. *"Having a snack?"* Holding a conversation hadn't really been her idea, but simply walking away from him wasn't an option either.

"Doctor says I should watch my sugar intake. Eat more fruits and vegetables, he says," Rafe spoke as he looked down at the bowl of fruit in front of him. *"Last time I checked all this fruit had a ton of natural sugar."*

Landry had stepped a little closer to the island and peeped into the bowl. Strawberries, blackberries, kiwi, red grapes and mandarin oranges. The salad looked tasty and refreshing to her, but the prince did not seem impressed.

"I believe that natural sugar is better for you than refined sugars. At least that's what they told my dad the last time he was in the hospital," she said.

"Your father is sick?" Rafe asked. He put his fork down beside the bowl and looked up to her, clearly dismissing that fruit salad.

Landry quickly shook her head because she hated even voicing those words. *"He's doing well now,"* she replied. *"Two months ago, however, he had a health scare. The doctors suggested he change his diet and cutting out refined sugars was one thing on the list. He was grumpy about it, just like you."*

A chuckle had bubbled up from her chest inadvertently and when she would have clapped her mouth shut and tried to make a speedy getaway, Rafe stopped her by laughing with her.

"I guess you could say I'm grumpy about eating a bowl full of fruit," he admitted. *"We don't grow a lot of fruit here on the island because of the climate. It has to be imported, which, along with exporting, is a steadily developing part of our economy."*

Landry nodded, recognizing the way his duties co-mingled with his personal life, just like Kristian's.

"It's important to eat healthy, especially when your health is at risk. Your constituents would be very encouraged by seeing you eat this salad and take control of your health and well-being."

"Are you suggesting I start a healthy eating campaign?"

"Oh no," she said, shaking her head now. *"I was just making an observation. But I know it's none of my business. I tend to talk too much sometimes."*

Most times, she told herself. She'd especially talked too much to Roland who now knew that something had happened between her and Kristian. No, she had not shared any specifics but it had been pointless to deny the obvious the day they'd gone out for drinks and dessert. The Caribbean gingerbread she'd tasted had been marvelous with its strong flavors of molasses and ginger root; it was also sticky and spicy. Later she'd told him that he'd tricked her with plenty of wine and dessert to get her talking, when in reality, she'd been aching to release some of the tension of her situation to someone.

"You have distinct opinions," Rafe had corrected her. *"I would not call that talking too much in the general sense. You also know how to deal with people. I've watched you with Malayka."*

Oh no, Landry thought. If he'd seen her with Malayka lately, he surely thought she talked way too much, in any sense. Things hadn't really been tense between her and Malayka. They had been eye-opening. The stilted client and stylist relationship they'd had prior to Malayka's surprise appearance in her room had been shifted. Now there was a cordial coexistence. Malayka needed a stylist and she was smart enough to also realize that firing Landry would make it hard to find another stylist without answering some difficult questions. Considering she was months away from being a princess, Landry knew she would be able to hire someone in a heartbeat. Only *that someone* might not be as reputable and as well connected as Landry because news in this business spread just as rapidly as any other gossip in the life of the rich and famous. So they were at a point where Landry spoke concisely about what she knew best and Malayka either listened or risked looking half her best as a result and she did not mention Kristian or Landry's personal life again. It was a great compromise, in Landry's mind.

"I'm just trying to do my job," she'd told Rafe.

"I must admit I had never heard of such a job before. It made sense to me that people selected their own clothes, but I'm beginning to see that you do much more than that. You leave impressions on people with your words and thoughts. Your presence here in the palace has been felt," he said.

Landry hadn't known how to respond so she'd simply said, *"Thank you, sir."*

"No," he continued. *"I believe I will eventually be in a position to thank you."*

He had picked up his fork and with resignation scooped more fruit into his mouth. Landry had taken that as the end of their conversation and left the kitchen.

That had been a few days ago and now she was thinking of the prince's words as she took the last few steps leading to the ballroom entrance. It had not been her intention to attend the ball, but when she received an envelope with the royal insignia melted in red wax on the back, she'd known she was in trouble. It was an official invitation to the ball and for just a few minutes as Landry had read it, she'd felt like Cinderella.

She did not have a dress, nothing that was appropriate for a royal ball so as any other stylist worth her salt she'd slipped into a moment of panic. But just like a fairy godmother and her royal accomplice, Detali and Sam had come to the rescue.

It was after dinner last night when Landry had been toying with the idea of giving in and going for a swim that the two women had knocked on her bedroom door.

"What's this?" Sam had asked, pointing to a dress that was hanging on a rack in the sitting area.

That's where Landry had put it once she'd gone through every item of clothing she'd packed to come to the island. Sure, she could have called on one of her designer friends to ship her something quickly, but she really hadn't wanted to make a big deal out of the ball, or the fact that she was actually going to attend. She'd come to the conclusion that for her position there, the floor-length white dress with its bold pink, blue and black floral design down one side and thigh-high split on the right would be fashionable and appropriate enough. Besides, she only planned to make an appearance and then she would leave. She would not disrespect the prince by ignoring his invitation totally, but she really wasn't in the mood to act as if she were part of this world again.

Landry felt like she'd made that mistake each time she'd lain in Kristian's bed.

"I'm wearing that to the ball tomorrow," she had replied to Sam. *"Is there something wrong with Malayka's dress?"*

That question had been directed to Detali who stood quietly near the door holding a garment bag in her short arms.

"What's going on?" Landry asked when no one had answered.

"As pretty as this is, you cannot wear it tomorrow night," Sam answered then. *"Here, go try this on."*

The princess had taken the garment bag from Detali and handed it to Landry.

"What? No. My dress is fine," Landry told them.

Sam, wearing dove-gray slacks, a wide black patent leather belt and white blouse, stood in all her regal glory, giving Landry a slow shake of her head.

"It's your turn to listen when directed about fashion," Sam told her. *"Now, Detali told me she had something perfect for you and when I saw it I knew she was right. So you just go on in there and try it on. The faster you prove we also have excellent taste in gowns, the sooner you'll be able to continue closing yourself up in this room."*

A part of her had wanted to rebut Sam's statement. Not so much the part about her and Detali knowing just as much about fashion as she did, but the part about her shutting herself in this room. The smarter part of her knew that was a mistake. The last thing she wanted to do was have a conversation about her not attending dinners in the last week with Sam, in front of Detali. So with a huff she'd taken the garment bag and moments later found herself admitting that Sam and Detali had not only been right, but they'd hit the ball straight out of the park with the gown.

Royal blue—one of Landry's favorite colors—and strapless, some intricate beadwork around the bodice and cascading down to the fitted waist. It fanned out from there

in a true princess cut, more of the soft blue material that
ended with a sweep over the floor in an ombré style. What
was really intriguing was the last six or so inches of the
dress that boasted another elaborate design of darker blue
over the lighter shade. When she turned, the flouncy material lifted from the floor to reveal layers of ivory material that perfectly complemented the design at the bottom.

It was gorgeous, Landry thought now as she walked
toward the ballroom, the blue Manolo Blahnik Regilla
pumps clicking on the glossed marble floor. The hallway
was at least twenty feet wide, with its soaring ceiling and
gold leaf wallpaper. Knowing that everyone else had most
likely arrived at eight as the invitation had instructed, she
was the lone straggler. This was, of course, due to her
job and the time she'd spent getting Malayka ready. In
Landry's right hand she held a royal blue satin clutch. Her
left hand was clenched as she battled with nerves. When
she approached the large open white-and-gold doors all
the doubts that she'd tried valiantly to keep at bay these
last few hours came soaring to the forefront.

She didn't belong here.

She wasn't royalty.

This was out of her league.

If her sister, Paula, could see her now she'd die with
envy.

Her mother would squeal with delight at the possibility
of marriage candidates in the ballroom.

Landry smiled. She missed her matchmaking mother.

She approached the two men dressed in full regalia.
Thick gold tassels hung from the shoulders of their white
jackets, sheathed swords on the black leather belts at their
waist, black pants, shining black shoes and they had stern
looks on their faces.

Landry hurriedly opened her clutch to look for the invitation, when another officially dressed man stepped from the side to take her arm.

"Allow me to escort you, Ms. Norris," he said.

"Thank you," she replied, impressed and in awe at the formality.

She shouldn't have been, at least not yet, because as Landry walked down the curved champagne-colored marble steps her breath was taken completely away at the room she was entering.

The ballroom was phenomenal. Even higher ceilings than in the hallway, this one was painted with some type of mural, golden-winged angels floating against the palest green backdrop. There was more gold adorning the walls, framing the floor-to-ceiling windows and serving as the baseboards. The floor itself was a light wood, glossed to perfection with tables along the sides leaving the entire center of the floor open.

Landry was speechless as she took the last step and looked out to the more than three hundred people in attendance. The room was full but there was more than enough space for everyone to move around. A band, complete with a harpist and violinist played a very soft melody while staff dressed in crisp white jackets and black pants moved throughout the room carrying trays of food and champagne.

A camera flash jolted Landry out of the fantasy and she looked to her right to see a small circle of photographers. Another flash and Landry looked away from them.

"There you are." She heard Roland's voice before she actually saw him since her eyes were still trying to adjust after all that flashing in her face.

"I was beginning to think you wouldn't show up," he said as he took her other arm and gave a nod to the man who had escorted her in.

When the man left, Landry walked alongside Roland. She'd never seen him this dressed up before so she couldn't help but stare.

"Ah yes, one of the few times you will see me wearing this getup," he told her with a smile. "This is how a commander in Grand Serenity's Royal Seaside Navy should dress at these prestigious events. I, on the other hand, would have loved nothing better than to throw on some jeans and a shirt and be done with it."

Landry laughed at Roland's honesty but had to admit he wore the outfit well. The white jacket with its gold buttons down the front, light blue sash crossing his chest with two gold medals dangling over was what she now recognized as the royal insignia. Another patch she presumed represented the navy's insignia.

"You look great," she told him.

"No," Roland said as he lifted her free hand to his lips to softly kiss its back. "You look fabulous."

Landry couldn't help but smile, or blush, or whatever. It felt good to be complimented and even better to be whisked so effortlessly onto the dance floor with Roland. They moved to a much slower rhythm than the music playing but Landry didn't care. Roland commented on everyone that they passed on the dance floor. From the prime minister of a neighboring island and his abysmally young, but exceptionally well-mannered new girlfriend, to the oldest member of Grand Serenity's ruling cabinet and his ongoing struggle with going bald—all his words, of course.

Landry laughed and danced and felt at ease, so much so she wouldn't have noticed anyone staring at her, not even Kristian.

She was stunning.

That was Kris's first thought as he saw her coming

down the steps. She'd looked as regal and royal as any of the wives of dignitaries who had previously walked down those same stairs. Her elbow was linked with one of the palace guard's, her head held high, a gracious smile on her face. It was as if she were meant to be here, just like everyone else.

He'd sipped slowly from the glass of champagne he'd snagged from a tray and stood close to one of the windows. It was almost an hour into the event so everyone he needed to greet had already entered. At first, Kris hadn't thought Landry was coming, because he hadn't thought to invite her.

"I'm sending the stylist an invitation," Rafe had told him on Wednesday, after the tense meeting Rafe had called where he scolded his children.

"I must say I'm shocked you hadn't already taken care of that task," his father had continued while Kris stood staring out the window of Rafe's office.

"I've had a lot to do these past few days," was Kris's eventual reply.

"I take that to mean you've met privately with your brother and sister to discuss how the three of you plan to show more respect to Malayka and our upcoming marriage," Rafe stated.

Kris had wanted to sigh. He'd still been irritated with his father's tone and directives in that regard, but once again, he hadn't argued with Rafe. While Roland had been the most vocal in the meeting, expressing his many doubts about the background story Malayka had provided, Kris had eventually calmed his brother and swore to his father that they would do better.

"We're committed to this family and our role in the royal court. We will act accordingly," he'd stiffly replied.

"She's not as bad as you believe," Rafe continued as

he reached into the dark cherry-finished humidor on his desk to retrieve a cigar.

"I'm only inclined to believe the facts," Kris had told him. *"As you've stated, that is what she's already told us about herself. So that's the end of it."*

Kris heard the flick of a lighter and even though he did not turn to look at him, he knew his father was leaning back in his leather desk chair, taking the first big puffs of his favored Cohiba Behike cigar.

"I'm not referring to Malayka," Rafe said slowly.

Kris did turn then. He remained by the window but looked directly at his father. *"I don't understand."*

Rafe took another puff and nodded. He wore a black pin-striped suit today, the jacket tossed over the back of a guest chair across the room, his white shirt crisp, and the canary-yellow tie bright. On his wrist was a gold watch that competed with the black-and-gold cuff links for spectacular gleam. On the ring finger of his right hand was the monarch ring, a thick gold band with the DeSaunters insignia on top. Kris and Roland each had one, but they only wore them on special occasions. Rafe, as the reigning prince, wore his every day.

"Do you think you're the only one who keeps tabs on things around here?" Rafe asked him. *"I know that you will someday be prince of this island, but for now, it's my job to know everything that goes on."*

"Meaning?" Kris had asked, a sense of dread growing stronger in the pit of his stomach.

"Meaning, I know that you've been spending time with that young woman."

Kris could only nod; denial would be pointless and disrespectful.

"We're both adults," was his short reply.

"You're good-looking adults. She's a spirited one. I had

the chance to speak with her alone for a bit yesterday and she was smart and polite and most of all honest. I like that about her. I suspect you did too, hence the reason you invited her to dinner with us in the first place."

Kris still didn't have a logical reason for why he'd wanted Landry at their family dinners. And he wasn't certain that he wanted to continue this conversation with his father.

"So she'll be at the ball—that's fine with me. Now, if you'll excuse me I have some calls to make," he'd said and headed toward the door.

Rafe's booming voice stopped him.

"I didn't marry royalty the first time around. I married the woman I fell madly in love with. Vivienne was intelligent and beautiful and smarter than any of the well-to-do women I'd met in my years. She was an American too, as you may recall."

Kris had inhaled deeply, exhaled slowly and turned to face his father once more.

"I know who and what my mother was," he spoke quietly.

Rafe took another drag from his cigar before setting it in the ashtray. Puffs of smoke haloed around him and when the smoke cleared Kris could see his father staring directly at him.

"Then I'm sure you also know how she felt about building a life around love. Vivienne would never let the title, this palace or anything else come between herself and love. She expected nothing less of her children."

Kris clenched his teeth, but did not let out the sigh he wished to. *"I don't know what you're trying to say, Dad."*

"Yes, you do, son. You're just trying to deny it. You're trying to convince yourself that you're doing the noble thing by staying strong and keeping up the pretense. What you don't realize is that it's not what you say or what you

*even acknowledge publicly, Kris. Your feelings are in the
way you look at her, the tension that immediately bubbles
inside of you when someone else speaks of her. You went
to eat pizza with her and frolicked in the water with her.
You haven't eaten pizza since your sister was young.*"

"*It was just pizza.*"

Rafe chuckled then, a deep, full-bodied laughter that
filled the entire room.

"*It was the beginning,*" Rafe told him finally. "*And the
ending will be what you make it. Remember that, Kris.*"

Kris had forgotten the conversation with his father almost immediately as he'd returned to his office to see a
message from someone he needed desperately to speak
to. He handled the call, made private travel arrangements
and then thought about what his father had said. He was
responsible for the ending. Landry had said something
similar that night in the garden.

"*You create your own circumstances, control your own
destiny. It doesn't have to be prewritten. Unless you want
it to be,*" she'd said. The way she'd looked at him had been
brutally honest because she believed every word of it.

She and his father obviously believed more than he did.

Kris wondered if they were both right. Landry had
walked away from him that night in the garden. She'd
asked him not to contact her again and he'd done as she'd
requested because he understood why she needed it to stop.
The real truth was he hadn't thought he had the strength to
stop their affair himself; his need for her seemed so urgent
and unceasing. Yet, she'd done it. She'd said the words and
she'd meant them. He admired her for that.

He admired her and he hated seeing her in Roland's
arms, all at the same time.

They were dancing close together, Roland's hand was
around her waist, the other holding her hand. He'd even

bent forward and kissed her forehead. Kris's fingers tightened on the stem of the champagne glass.

"Looks like Roland is stealing your woman," Sam said as she came to stand beside him.

Once again, he was prepared to deny the way he felt, but he had been staring at Landry and thinking about her, and dammit, his father must have been right.

"I've seen the way you look at her and I saw the pictures of you and her at the museum in the paper. While the island is speculating, I know firsthand how different you've been behaving since she's been here."

Kris finished off the champagne and immediately looked for a place to dispose of the glass. Catching the eye of one of the staff members, he waited until the man came over and took the glass from him, before replying to his sister.

It was a stall tactic, but one Kris desperately needed. He'd seen the papers as well so he knew what was being said after he'd taken Landry to the opening ceremony of the new exhibit at the museum two weeks ago. It had been an impromptu invitation. He'd fully intended to go alone, as usual. But then he'd thought about her and before he could stop himself he'd gone to her room and made the request. She'd looked hopeful and he knew it. The moment he'd asked her to accompany him, she'd thought it was a date. It wasn't; it was business and he'd been sure to make that known. After explaining that to her, he hadn't touched her or stood too close to her at all during the ceremony and when it was done, he hadn't even offered her dinner, instead telling Tajeo to bring them straight home.

It wasn't a date. He wasn't courting her.

They were just…just…

"Just how do you think I've been behaving? I haven't done anything out of the ordinary," he replied to Sam, even though he knew deep down how big of a lie his words actually were.

"For one, you took her to the museum unveiling and that was after you insisted that she be at the family dinners. You're also keeping tabs of her comings and goings with Jorge."

"As you well know, I'm concerned about everyone riding in our cars now, so that doesn't count."

"You let Jorge pick her up from the front of the palace when everyone else leaves from the back. I know you know about this and you must have approved it or Jorge would not be doing it."

"I'm just concerned for her safety, like everyone else here."

"Yeah right, Kris, tell that to the reporters—they might believe you. But I certainly don't. You've been staring at her since she walked into this room and now that Roland's got his arms—very tightly I might add—around her, you're about to explode with jealousy."

Kris forced himself to look away from where Landry and Roland were; just as Sam said, they were dancing very closely together. He wished for another glass of champagne but knew that it wouldn't look good for him to be seen drinking too many. "I'm not jealous."

Sam was nodding when he looked in her direction. "No, you're not stupid," she told him, "which is what I would have to call you if you stood here like a silly oaf instead of going over there and interrupting their dance. If you want something in life, Kris, you've just got to go out there and grab hold of it with both hands."

He frowned at her then. "Mom used to say that."

"She sure did," Sam admitted. "And it's never been truer than it is now. So get yourself out there and grab what you want."

Kris wasn't taking advice from his younger sister. Nor was he heeding his father's words. He was simply going to ask her to dance with him. It was polite and it would also keep him from having to dance with anyone else, at least for the moment. So he walked out onto the dance floor, excusing himself through the crowd as others danced around him.

Just as he was close enough to them to tap Roland on the back, another woman appeared with a smile.

"Good evening, Your Highness," she said before falling into a deep curtsy, her gaze going from him to Roland and back to him.

Roland had stopped dancing but still held Landry in his arms.

"Well, look what we have here," Roland said with his signature grin in place. "A situation."

Landry looked up to Kris and let her hands fall slowly from Roland's shoulders.

"I believe introductions are necessary," Kris said.

"Yes, they certainly are. Please, let me, big brother," Roland added with a wink.

Kris resisted the urge to frown.

"Landry Norris, this is Valora Harrington," Roland began with a flourish of his arm between the two ladies. "Valora, this is Landry. She's a guest to the palace and is assisting Malayka in preparations for the wedding."

Valora nodded, her short dark hair an intriguing contrast to her buttery skin tone.

"It's a pleasure to meet you," Valora said. "I read in the paper how you've been visiting the local dressmakers. They have wonderful things to say about you."

Landry accepted the hand that Valora extended and smiled in return. "Thanks. I'm happy to meet you as well. As for the dressmakers, there's an amazing amount of talent on this island. I just hope to be able to share it with those in my country soon."

"Of course you will," Roland quipped. "Especially since the gowns you and Malayka are both wearing tonight are made by Detali."

Kris had no idea how his brother knew that, since he obviously had no clue, but he found that he was pleased by the knowledge.

"Your gown is beautiful," Landry said to Valora.

Valora smiled and accepted the compliment but Kris was certain something else was going on there. He could feel the edges of tension and wondered for a moment if it were solely due to his presence.

"Well, Valora. Why don't we take a spin on this grand dance floor," Roland offered. "Kris, you dance with Landry."

Before he could say a word—even though he fully planned to agree with Roland's suggestion—Roland had taken Valora's hand and they were walking away. Kris didn't wait for Landry to respond, he simply stepped in front of her and took her hand. He held her just as Roland had, except their bodies were not nearly as close. They moved slowly, almost mechanically in the same spot.

After a few quiet moments, she sighed.

"You don't have to do this," she told him. "I understand if you wanted to dance with Valora. I mean, I know that you two aren't actually engaged. Roland told me. But still, I get if you'd rather be seen with a native, instead of with me."

"What's that supposed to mean? And how did you find out about me and Valora?" Kris asked as they continued to move.

She looked away, then back to him like she was really considering walking away and leaving him alone on the dance floor. He was thankful when she let out a sigh but looked as if she'd stay.

"Malayka told me you were engaged," she admitted.

"When did she tell you that? Is that why you ended things between us?"

"What?" she asked, surprise clearly on her face. "No. She didn't tell me until after I'd done that. I said we could no longer do what we were doing because it was wrong, for both of us."

"You cannot speak for me," he said. He was getting really tired of people telling him what he felt, and how he should react to what he felt.

"No, but I can speak for what I was involved in. We both knew it was pointless from the start," she said and still would not look directly at him.

She blinked when a camera flashed close to them. On the other side, another flash went off and this time Kris was the one blinking.

"Great," she said with a sigh. "Now they're going to print in the paper that you were dancing with the American stylist. Perhaps they'll say you took pity on me or some other nonsense."

"They've already snapped pictures of us and I would demand a retraction if they dared to insult you in any way," he told her as he looked over her head for one of the guards.

When he saw a familiar face and they exchanged a look, Kris relaxed a bit. But that was short-lived.

"There you are," Malayka said tightly as she came behind Landry to take hold of her arm. "I've been looking everywhere for you. It seems I'm having a wardrobe malfunction."

"Oh no, really? Did something happen to the dress?"

"Something happened alright. A reporter just asked me about my Detali original. I wasn't aware that I was wearing a Detali original, or who the hell Detali is for that matter," Malayka argued.

Kris was just about to say something when Landry shook her head at him. "I can handle this on my own. Let's go," she told Malayka and they walked away.

The cameramen had just taken a flurry of new shots and Kris could imagine what the headline would read.

Soon-to-Be Princess Argues with Crown Prince's Mistress.

He clenched his fists at the thought.

"Hey, we can go over those reports first thing tomorrow. I think I've found something interesting," Gary said after he and another guard had moved the photographers along.

"Sure," Kris said as he looked around the ballroom to see if he could catch a glimpse of the direction Malayka and Landry had headed.

He wasn't comfortable with Malayka's tone and felt like he needed to be close just in case.

Then suddenly noise became deafening. The floor and the walls shook, smoke filled the air instantly and screaming immediately followed.

Chapter 14

Pandemonium quickly ensued as smoke and flames filled the back portion of the ballroom.

Garrison "Gary" Montgomery, Kris's college friend who also happened to be a former captain in the United States Army, had just come to stand by Kris and immediately pushed him to the floor, using his body to cover Kris as the explosion rocked the room.

"You okay?" he'd asked almost immediately.

Kris nodded. "I'm good. Find my father!"

By that point he was getting to his feet and then he was looking around. People were still screaming and running around, falling over each other. Kris instantly began moving. He did not run, but walked quickly, touching people as he went so that he could move by them without knocking them down. When he saw a guard he grabbed the man's arm.

"Get all guards down here. Call the police and the paramedics and find my sister and brother, now!"

The guard took off in another direction and Kris continued to move. Until he stopped to help an elderly woman who had either fallen or had simply sat on the steps, one hand clutching her chest, the other one shaking as she tried to hold on to the railing.

"Ma'am, it's best if we get you out of here," he told her and slipped his arms beneath her to hoist her up off the floor.

She was shaking her head, tears streaming down her face as she said, "My Carl, my husband. I don't know where he is."

Kris nodded. "We'll find him. But he would want you to get to safety. I'm going to help you get out of here."

After another wail she wrapped her arms tightly around Kris's neck leaned into him as he led them around the stairs to another door.

This was the staff hallway, which they used to get to and from the kitchen quickly. Kris walked her through the passageway where there were still people, but a smaller amount since nobody really knew about that area but the staff. When he came to a back door that led out to the side of the palace, he used his foot to kick it open and then hurried through with the woman.

They both inhaled the fresh evening air, sucking in gulps and coughing a little from the smoke that had already began to fill their lungs. Uniformed guards were coming from around the front of the house and Kris waved one of them down.

"Get her out of here," he told the guard. "And find her husband, Carl."

When Kris turned to go back inside, the guard protested.

"Your Highness, you should come this way. We're clearing everyone from the palace," he told Kris.

Kris only nodded. "That's good. Get everyone out. Get them all out and hurry!"

He then walked past the guard, through the door and ran down the hallway. In seconds he was in the ballroom once again. Lifting his jacket to cover his mouth and nose Kris proceeded through the crowd, yelling at them to keep moving to the exits as fast as they could. At the same time he came to another door, the one that he knew was a back stairwell leading up to the second floor. This was where he'd seen Malayka and Landry go only seconds before the explosion.

Kris took the steps two at a time, stopping only when he came to another door which he yanked open. Running down that hallway he let his jacket fall from his face because there was no visible smoke there. This side of the floor housed conference rooms and the room Kris knew that Malayka was now using as a dressing room. That's where they had to be.

He wasn't certain they'd had enough time to actually reach the room but Kris ran in that direction anyway, until he saw her lying on the floor. With fear threatening to choke him, Kris ran faster until his feet were skidding across the floor as he tried to stop. Dropping to his knees he lifted her head and let it rest on his arm as he called her name.

"Landry! Landry! Talk to me!"

He wanted to smack her face to wake her but was too afraid of further hurting her. Instead he grabbed her cheeks between his fingers, shaking her as gingerly as his trembling hands could manage.

"Landry!"

Her eyes fluttered after a few seconds then opened again slowly, her lips parting.

"What did you hit me with?" she asked groggily.

"Not me, baby. Never. I would never hurt you. Ever."

But somebody had.

Somebody had hit Landry and set off an explosive in his house.

"Everybody is accounted for," Roland said as he entered the room about half an hour after the explosion. "Malayka is in her room resting, per your orders. And I stopped by Sam's room before coming back here. She's more pissed off than afraid, but there are four guards with her."

Kris watched as his brother gave a nod to their father and then crossed the carpeted floor, stopping at the end of a leather couch to sit on its wide arm. His jacket was gone, the white T-shirt he'd worn beneath it smudged with dark marks. Rafe sat in a wide, cushioned chair, an unlit cigar between his fingers.

The moment a guard had found him to tell him where his family was Kris had stood, knowing he needed to go to them. He'd taken Landry to her room by then and she'd sat on the sofa, her still-shaking hands holding a glass of water. Another guard had seen Kris bring her in there and immediately offered his assistance. Kris instructed the guard to stay with Landry and had given her one long last look, as she sat huddled beneath his black commander's jacket, which he'd wrapped around her shoulders.

She was alive.

He breathed a sigh of relief and went to make sure the rest of his family were fine as well. They were all accounted for, and all pissed off.

"Brakes have been tampered with, someone broke into the bank and now this," Roland said, the tension in his voice filtering throughout the room. "An explosion at the palace. Who the hell is behind this?"

Roland had shouted the question, displaying the fury

that was no doubt going through each of them. They were in his father's private rooms. Kris stood close to the bar but hadn't allowed himself to fix a drink. They could all probably use one, but he refrained because he wanted his mind to be perfectly clear when the police arrived.

As if he'd silently summoned them, there was a soft knock on the door. Roland stood and walked the length of the floor to answer it. They came in, Salvin leading the way, followed by Captain Vincent Briggins, head of the Grand Serenity Police Force, and Garrison Montgomery. As Roland closed the door and followed the men, Kris walked over to stand near them.

"Let me introduce Garrison Montgomery—he's a retired captain in the United States Army and a personal friend of mine," Kris told them.

"Should he be here right now?" Roland asked.

Kris nodded to his brother. "He's the security expert I hired after our conversation."

The look he was giving Roland was pointed and meant to convey the rest of the statement Kris did not want his father to hear. Instead of paying the exorbitant amount of money and giving in to the ridiculous demands of Roland's associate Yiker, Kris had decided to go another route. Roland nodded his understanding but Kris was certain they'd have a more in-depth conversation about it later.

"What have you found? Who did this?" Rafe asked by way of dismissing whatever else Kris and Roland may have wanted to say.

"It was a small device, very amateurish and working on a remote detonator that was left on the balcony. That's why the major impact was in the back of the ballroom," Salvin began.

"What about injuries? Fatalities?" Kris asked.

Captain Briggins shook his head. "There were two fatalities, Your Highness. They were standing closest to the doors. Other guests were either on the dance floor or seated at their table—this put them at a farther distance from the impact. There are injuries and the last time I checked in, ambulances were circling back from the hospital to transport them all. If it had been a better-built bomb, using more reliable explosives, the fatalities and damages would no doubt be far worse."

Grand Serenity had a population of just over one hundred thousand citizens. There were two hospitals, one on each side of the island, and approximately twelve ambulances. Kris had presumed there would be a large number of injuries, but he hadn't wanted to accept fatalities. He frowned.

"I want to know what is going on here!" Rafe roared.

"If I may be permitted to speak," Gary interjected.

Kris nodded. "Please. This is a closed conversation— what you say here will go no further than this room."

Gary nodded. "First, everyone, please call me Gary. I've been on the island for just a few days, but from what I can tell this is a beautiful place." He cleared his throat. "Except for the circumstances that brought me here."

"Kris called you so I'm assuming there's a need for an outside security expert," Rafe said in response to Gary.

"Yes, I've been looking into each of the incidents that have happened. My investigation is nowhere near complete but as I told Kris before the explosion, I may have found something interesting."

"What is it?" Roland asked.

Gary looked to Kris and then folded his arms over his chest as he began again. "One of the first things I noticed was that these incidents all began after a certain time. Prince Rafferty, you've been seeing Malayka Sampson since late February."

Rafe straightened. "That is correct," he said in a voice that told everyone in the room that he wasn't going to take kindly to anything said against Malayka.

Gary kept talking. Whether or not he was moved to omit anything because of Rafe's tone was something Kris would find out later.

"She first visited the palace in March," Gary continued. "You traveled for three weeks in April and then you returned to the palace alone."

"Yes," Rafe said, coming to his feet now. "She went back to the States to pack her things. I moved her into the palace the first of May, after I proposed to her."

Gary nodded.

"She moved in and then she returned to the States briefly."

"To attend some function she was already committed to," Rafe replied.

"Yes," Gary said. "The Met Gala. Then the second week of May she returned, this time someone came with her."

Kris tensed as he said tightly, "Landry."

Another nod from Gary, this time in Kris's direction.

"The car accident happened in late May, the break-in at the bank—"

"The one nobody thought was important enough to tell me about," Rafe interrupted.

Kris picked up with the story then, the words raspy to his ears. "The break-in occurred in late June."

Almost one month after he'd begun sleeping with Landry.

"I invited her to the ball," Rafe whispered and then shook his head. "Wait a minute—you're not seriously suggesting what I think you are? Landry Norris, the stylist? You really think she's involved in this."

"She's a common denominator," Gary offered.

"She has nothing to gain," Roland added.

"How do we know this?" Rafe asked. "Who is she connected to? Wasn't she thoroughly investigated like anyone else staying at the palace?"

"Yes," Kris answered emphatically. "I did an extensive background check before she came to the island and then I interviewed her when she arrived."

He remembered how pretty she'd looked in that fitted skirt and how nervous he'd thought she was even though she seemed calm. He also recalled the seconds that had ticked by as he'd contemplated kissing her before Sam had interrupted them.

"I don't believe it," Roland said instantly. "She wouldn't do this. She cares about the people here. She went against Malayka in order to bring Detali's talents to the forefront. She wouldn't have done that if she had something against us, our country. There has to be another scenario."

"Where was she when the explosion occurred?" Gary asked.

All eyes fell to Kris.

"We were dancing and then…" He didn't get a chance to finish his statement before the door opened and in a blur of blue material, Landry came bustling in.

"Oh my God! I heard them planning this! I heard them the other day!" she said as she came to a stop in front of him. "I heard it all!"

Landry had been sitting in that room with her head throbbing, trying her best to remember what had happened.

One minute she was dancing with Roland, laughing and joking with him the same way she used to with her brothers back home. The next, she was with Kristian, hating that it felt so good to be in his arms again, when she knew that it wouldn't last. Then, Malayka wanted to speak to her.

From that point on, her memory was foggy, until he was there again, and she was in his arms…again.

Damn, she loved how he smelled. It was unlike any cologne she'd ever known. He'd looked dashing and desirable, in his dark jacket lined with more medals than Roland's, but the same light blue sash crossing his chest. His pants were black too, which gave him an even more debonair appearance. His jaw was strong and tense, as usual, his dark eyes shooting fiery pinpricks in her direction.

Then there was pain and he was carrying her and she was wearing his jacket. He'd left her alone but his scent had remained.

"Saturday," Landry said when she realized Kristian was looking at her as if she'd lost her mind.

Her hair was probably a mess. She'd had an ice pack smashed against the side of it for who knew how long.

"When I walked into the room…um, Malayka's new fitting room. He was in the room next door, or the balcony, I mean," she continued.

"Who was?" Roland asked.

Landry turned and the room also picked that moment to do this spinning thing and she instantly felt nauseous. Kristian was quick. His strong arm wrapping around her waist as he held her up.

"She needs to see a doctor," Kristian shouted. "She's hurt."

"Call for the paramedics to come up here."

She heard another voice say, but Landry couldn't figure out who it belonged to. She was on another couch, Kristian right beside her now. Her head felt as if someone were pounding it with their fists and she wasn't sure how much longer she'd be able to resist the nausea.

"Who did you hear speaking?"

The question came from Prince Rafe; she knew his voice. Turning much slower this time, Landry looked at him.

"I don't know who he is, but he was on the phone telling someone to follow his orders. He kept saying nine o'clock," Landry told them.

"The explosion was at nine-oh-one."

This statement came from another man who was dressed in an official law officer uniform. Two other men that she did not know were also present. The one dressed in a simple gray suit was looking from her to Kristian as if he wanted to say something.

"He was in the house," Roland said. "Someone that works for us planned this."

"I want a list of all the staff on my desk within the hour. Check the palace once more and then lock her down tight. Nobody goes in or out without me knowing," Prince Rafe directed.

The other official-looking guy nodded and hurried out of the room.

"Who else overheard this conversation?"

This question came from the guy in the gray suit. Landry did not know who he was but if he were in this room with Kristian and the rest of the royal family, he must have been important and privy to this discussion.

"Nobody," she answered. "Malayka was late for the meeting. I was there on time and when I entered the room, there was no one else in there. The balcony doors were open and I could hear the voices. I stepped outside for just a second and that's when I saw him on the phone. He was also talking to someone in the room, but I couldn't see that person."

"So you heard this conversation and you never thought to say anything to anyone about it?" Gray-Suit-Guy asked her.

Landry wasn't sure but his question sounded a bit accusatory. But maybe she had a concussion and was confusing things.

"I didn't think to tell anyone. I don't normally eavesdrop and then tell what I've heard," she replied.

"You didn't think that you should share that someone was going to plant a bomb at the ball?" the remaining official-looking guy asked. "And then you were mysteriously not in the ballroom when the bomb went off."

"What?" she asked and pressed her hand to her stomach in an effort to cease the rolling sensation. "Malayka needed something…she wanted to…her dress." Landry took a slow breath and released it. "Wait, you think I… that I knew?"

"We would like to question you further," the official guy said.

"Me?" Landry asked.

She looked around the room to see that all eyes were on her. Then she turned to him. Kristian was staring at her as well. He wasn't saying a word. He wasn't defending her.

The battle was lost.

She jumped up off the couch and ran to the first door she saw and went inside. Luckily it was a bathroom and fortunately she'd made it in time.

Chapter 15

The room was dark and cool. After lying still for a few moments Landry realized that a steady breeze was coming through the windows. No, she thought when she chanced moving slowly to lie on her side, it was coming from the balcony.

She'd opened her eyes and blinked a few times to clear her vision. She still felt drowsy as she once again tried to recall where she was and how she'd come to be there. After noticing that she must've kicked the blankets off while she slept and that she was just a little chilly, she also realized that this wasn't her room.

Landry took her time sitting up. It was slow going because her body felt ten times heavier than usual to move. However, fortunately, she was not experiencing any pain. There had been pain before, she recalled. Intense pain… she lifted a hand to gingerly touch the bandage on her head. It was wrapped all the way around, her hair matted to the sides. Dropping her hands down with a sigh she looked around at her surroundings. A dresser, a picture, anything that would tell her where she was. But she picked up on nothing but the scent.

She was in Kristian's room.

Her location immediately alarmed her because the memory of their last conversation came flooding back.

The DeSaunters family thought she'd planted a bomb in their house. She'd never messed up this big before. Even though she hadn't planted a bomb, so technically this wasn't her mess-up. The sooner she made that point clear, the better she would feel about the rest, which she definitely did not feel like thinking about right now.

Landry took her time climbing out of the bed, stepping down from the bed's platform with careful movements. She was wearing a nightgown that did not belong to her, yet it fit her perfectly. On bare feet she relied on her memory of the space to guide her to the balcony where she figured he had to be because of the persistent breeze from the doors being open. She paused when she stepped outside to find him standing at the railing.

His balcony was much bigger than the one attached to her room, wrapping around to meet the living-room side of his private space. There were chairs and two tables in the area she could see. The air was tinged with the tropical surroundings, a scent she'd come to love in the almost two months that she'd been there. And the man, well, his broad back and opposing silhouette fit perfectly against the backdrop of endless sky and dark, ominous sea.

"You should be asleep," he said without turning around.

Landry didn't want to be comfortable. She wanted to say what she needed to say and then attempt to go back to her room. She wasn't certain what time it was, but she knew she did not want to wake up in Kristian's room come sunrise. But she needed to make sure he knew she was innocent before going back to her rooms, and possibly back home.

"I get the feeling I've slept for long enough," she replied. "How long has it been?"

"About five hours," he responded, still keeping his back to her.

That didn't bother Landry, or she convinced herself that it didn't. She wasn't sure how she would feel if he looked her in the eye and admitted he thought she could do something like this to his family. Not to mention all the innocent people that had been in that ballroom.

"I told you the truth," she began. "As soon as I realized what I'd heard meant something, I came to tell you. The guard hadn't wanted me to move because the paramedics hadn't come to see me yet. He was even more nervous about helping me find your father's private rooms, but I sort of threatened to scream throughout the entire palace if he didn't assist."

Kristian shook his head. "We need better-trained guards."

Landry took in a shaky breath and released it slowly.

"I didn't think about what I'd heard until last night as I was trying to figure out what happened. If for one moment I'd thought that it meant something before, I would have certainly told you," she continued.

"Even though you've made yourself scarce this past week?" he asked.

She sighed and folded her arms over her chest.

"It's been a busy week trying to ensure Malayka was ready for the ball."

"You had dinner in your room or you went out visiting several restaurants in town," he said.

"You know where I went?"

"Each time you left the palace, I knew. The press did as well. After seeing us together at the museum, they've taken an interest in you." His hands gripped the railing and he leaned over it slightly.

He was wearing sweatpants and a T-shirt. His appearance shocked her momentarily because she'd only ever seen Kristian in dress clothes.

"I can't believe you were keeping tabs on me," she said, baffled. "You never trusted me, did you?"

He was quiet a few seconds. "It's my job to know everything that goes on here."

"Was it your job to sleep with me too? If so, you did a good job of it. For four weeks, it was a phenomenal experience," Landry stated, her throat a little dry with the words.

No response came from him.

"Well, I only wanted to tell you that I did not... I would have never planned to set off a bomb in your home. I don't know who that man was or who he was speaking to on the phone or in the other room. I'm not even sure how I received this gash on my head. What I do know is that I'm a professional. I'm good at my job and that's why I was asked to come here. Everything else, what happened between us, I mean, well, that wasn't planned."

She could hear the sound of the sea below and a chill ran through her body. She rubbed her arms.

"So that's all. I'll go back to my room now and I'll speak with Malayka in the morning about finding her another stylist."

Kris remained silent and Landry turned to walk back into the room. She presumed he would let her go, just as he had that night in the garden. He would not talk about this, or anything, for that matter, beyond the few words he'd decided were enough. She'd come to expect nothing more from him. The Crown Prince Kristian DeSaunters was a man of few words, very minimal explanations and no regrets. He was stern in his beliefs, loyal to a fault and the only man to ever have Landry doubt herself. For that, she hated him.

"I made her a promise," he said, his voice so low she almost didn't hear him.

Landry stopped, but this time, she was the one with her back facing him.

"*Promise me you'll be good, Kris.* That's what she'd said. I stood at the side of her bed in that hospital room and she reached her hand out to me. I didn't want to touch it because there was a needle taped down on the back of it. The room smelled funny, sterile and medicinal. *Promise me you'll make your father and me proud*, she'd continued. I took her hand, twining my fingers with hers the way we used to do when I was younger and we went for walks along the beach. I told her I would be good and that I would rule this island the way she and my father expected me to. I promised her."

Landry shivered once more, but this time it wasn't because she was cold. His words were seeping inside of her, creeping into that door she'd vowed to keep closed off to him after the night in the garden.

"After that she told me she loved me. No matter what title I held or how beautiful this palace was, she loved me because I was her son," he said and Landry heard his voice crack on his last word.

There was a quick pause and he continued, "I was her son and I killed her."

Landry turned then, almost too fast as her legs threatened to buckle. Extending an arm, she grabbed hold of the back of a chair that was thankfully close.

"You did what?" she asked.

Kristian turned then as well. He leaned against the railing in a move that looked so casual and so enticing. At another time it might have drawn her closer to him; tonight, it kept her still.

"She loved to ride horses," he began. "We have a stable…we *used* to have a stable down farther to the west side of the palace. She would ride in the hills and then take her horse, Trolly, down to the beach to cool down. I didn't like to ride. Sam did. She loved it as much as my mother. They loved to do a lot of things together."

He looked off to the side, then back to her.

"Sam was her little girl and Roland was her sunshine. I was her constant. She used to say that she knew what I would do and say before I did because I was constantly trying to be an adult. She was right. Instead of riding with her, I watched her ride and when she was finished I took care of the horse and locked up the stable. I was ten years old and one day, that day, I'd been reading a book instead of watching her ride.

"I knew she was out there and I'd come to sit on the cliff to watch her, but I brought a book with me. One my father would have flipped if he saw me with."

"Which book?" Landry asked even though she was sure that wasn't the most important part of this story.

"Romeo and Juliet," he said with a shrug. "I found it in my mother's library. She'd had a bookmark in it so I knew she'd read it. That enticed me to read it too."

"I read it for the first time when I was in the tenth grade," Landry admitted. "I've read it at least a dozen times since then."

"I was so into the book that I almost missed the fact that she'd finished her ride and was coming back to the stables. I had to run to get there in time. She was already wiping the horse down and feeding him carrots. She smiled when she saw me and said it was okay that I hadn't been here, that she could take care of it. I didn't like seeing her doing my job." He sighed. "So I put the book down and I insisted on finishing up for her. There was a storm coming and she said we needed to batten everything down tightly. I agreed. And I thought I'd done that."

He dragged his hands down his face and shook his head. "The storm hit later that evening. We had just finished dinner and one of the staff came in to say that they were being called down to the stables. My mother insisted on going down. My father stood to go with her but I told him I would go instead."

"Because that was your job," Landry said. "You weren't old enough to rule the island yet, but you still had responsibilities."

He nodded. "I went out with her and two of the staff. When we got there the stable doors were swinging in the gusty wind. My mother instantly ran toward the stable. I ran behind her but I tripped over something. I still don't know what, but in the few seconds it took for me to get up and start forward again, Trolly had gotten loose from his stall. He'd barreled through, knocking my mother down. She hit her head on the stall door and only regained consciousness for a half hour before she died."

Landry's hands shook as tears filled her eyes. The sorrow in his tone was heart-wrenching; the rush of realizations and unspoken explanations bombarded her with sadness.

"It wasn't your fault," she said immediately.

"I must've failed to lock the stall doors."

"What if the wind was simply so strong it blew them open?" she insisted.

"I should have bolted them. We knew the storm was coming and it was my responsibility. I was next in line to be leader. How could I lead effectively if I forgot something so simple?"

"Oh, Kristian," she sighed.

He shook his head again as if the act was meant to shake away any pity she might have felt for him. To make his point clearer, he stood straight and took a step toward her.

"I am the next in line to rule. Everything that happens here is ultimately my responsibility. If you were a threat to us, I should have known. But how could I if I were so busy falling…falling into bed with you like some lust-filled schoolboy," he said.

The words stung and Landry struggled to remain standing.

"I should have remained focused. I should have brought Gary in sooner to look things over. That's my job!" he yelled.

Landry jumped at the spike in his voice.

"You couldn't control our attraction any more than I could," she told him. "So no, you can't add that to your list of failures. You and I both decided to sleep together. And don't think you're the only one who had doubts about that because I did too."

A renewed energy surged through her. Maybe it was the anger she'd begun to feel when he spoke like he finally regretted something else in his life, which was sleeping with her.

"Do you think I wanted to come here and get so caught up in a guy, not to mention a prince of all people in this world? I've fought tooth and nail with my parents over submitting to a man, over giving parts of myself to someone, parts that I cherished. After that first night all you had to do was send me a text and I came running. The day you invited me to the museum with you I was elated because I thought it was a real date. We weren't only sleeping together, we were dating. For a moment, one brief second in time, I entertained the idea of us becoming a real couple.

"Do you know what that meant to me? No, you don't. But you probably figure I'm like Malayka and it meant some type of power trip, or possibly that I was enamored by your riches and this island and all that went with the title of being princess. But you would be so very wrong. I never wanted marriage and a happy-ever-after and I certainly never wanted that with a prince!"

Her entire body was shaking with rage now. She wanted to cry and to scream. A part of her ached for him, for that ten-year-old boy who had lost his mother and covered himself in blame for an accident that should not have been his responsibility to control. And another part wanted to punch him in the face for being so callous with her and what they'd shared.

"But you know what, Your Highness? I'm a big enough person that I can admit my faults and accept when I've made a mistake. I came to you willingly. I should have known better. I did actually, but I ignored the warnings. I did what I always do and took a leap. Now I'll deal with the fact that I was wrong about you. I thought you were strong and admirable, but I should have known you were just another conceited jerk believing in your own self-importance more than you actually believed in yourself."

Her heart was thumping, her arms were chilled as she stood there squaring off with him. He looked like he was ready to explode, as if he had so much more he could but of course would not say to her. Landry realized at that point that she didn't give a damn. Whatever else Kristian wanted to say to her, she just didn't care. Not anymore.

"I'm going back to my room now and I'm going to pack my things. I'll be out of here by tomorrow morning. Investigate me some more if you still think I slept with you just so I could plant a bomb in the palace and possibly kill you and your family. Do whatever you have to do."

Landry prayed she wouldn't pass out as he moved. The perfect ending to this scene was her walking out with her head held high. She managed it, on bare feet and wearing a silky nightgown. When she finally arrived at her room she slammed the door shut and slid to the floor where she sat. She cried and then finally, she picked herself up and began to pack, determined to move forward, just as she always had.

In the morning Kris had received word that Landry was gone; he was still sitting on the balcony when Sam came in.

"I heard about what happened while I was safely tucked in my room last night. I won't tell you how big of a jerk you are because you're my brother and I love you," she said as she sat on one of the lounge chairs beside him. "But wow, you are a jerk!"

Kris leaned forward, resting his elbows on his knees.

"I don't need you to tell me what I already know," he said.

How many times had he had that very thought in the hours that he'd been out here?

"She didn't do this," Sam said.

"I know."

"She's gone."

He tried not to react too much to those words.

"I know."

"You're in love with her," Sam continued.

"I'm no good for her," he replied.

Sam chuckled. "That's such a sorry cop-out. And you're too smart to say things like that."

Kris agreed. He was smart. He'd always performed well in school and had done even better in college. He was ambitious and tenacious. He'd been trained to be a pillar of strength in the midst of any adversity. He could negotiate with the best businessmen but always kept his eye on his bottom line. He was not a lover and had never dealt with any relationship issues, ever. So yeah, he guessed that gave him a pass to say some things that weren't so smart, at least once in his life.

"I wasn't smart enough to handle the situation better," he admitted.

"Well, inexperience has to count for something," Sam said.

Trust his younger sister to be the one dishing out words of wisdom. Whenever he and Roland used to argue Sam would come along with one of her many dolls in tow and mediate with such calm maturity Kris had often wondered if she were really meant to be the oldest.

"It doesn't matter," he told her. "I have to deal with whoever is trying to kill us, or Dad, or whatever is going on here." Dragging his hands over his face he came to stand. "I've got to shower and meet with Dad and the guards. We have to get to the bottom of this."

Sam waved a hand. "Dad and Roland have been in a closed-door meeting with the guards and the police chief for the past hour."

"Why didn't they call me? I've been up. If there was going to be a meeting I should have been there," he argued.

"From what Roland told me, you carried Landry down to the health suite. Then you insisted on bringing her up to your room after the doctor had examined her and given her pain medication. He presumed you would not want to be disturbed this morning. I, on the other hand, went to check on Landry in her rooms where I thought she would be. Imagine my surprise to see her packing."

He dismissed the image of Landry packing to leave

from his mind. "This is my house, my job!" Kris insisted. He cursed and headed for the door.

"That's not all there is to your life, Kris," Sam said.

She'd stood as well and now had her hands perched on her hips. The stance and her words reminded him instantly of their mother and Kris swallowed hard to keep the grief at bay.

"Nobody doubts that you're a good leader, you've been tossing that in mine and Roland's faces all our lives. You're Dad's right hand. You know more about the banks than he does. And your birth rank overrules any argument about who will rule next. But, Kris, you've got to live too. Go bike riding, jet skiing, try sky diving, something! Get out of this palace and live a little. The title and all that goes with it will still be here and it'll still be yours."

He sighed heavily and walked to her then. He didn't do this often and he knew he probably should, but Kris pulled Sam in close for a hug. He kissed the top of her head and whispered, "I don't know if I should be leading this country if my baby sister is so much smarter than I am."

She'd wrapped her arms around his waist and laughed. "I won't tell if you don't."

Chapter 16

Two Weeks Later

Astelle took the long fork she had been using to hold the ham in place while she sliced it to poke Heinz lightly on the arm. He was trying to steal a slice and she had to remind him in a gentle tone, "The ham is not for you. There's a pan of baked chicken right there."

With a frown Heinz pulled his arm back. He then reached over to the pan of baked chicken and used his fork to pick up a thigh.

"You'll love it, Dad," Landry said, leaning over to whisper in her father's ear. "I had some of the spices I picked up in Grand Serenity shipped here and when Mom wasn't looking I sprinkled a bit on the thighs and legs because I know they're your favorite."

Heinz smiled at his daughter. "That's my girl."

"I thought I was your girl, PopPop," Giselle, Landry's

sister Paula's four-year-old, said after taking a bite of her corn on the cob.

Her niece's plump cheeks now displayed bits of corn as she chewed earnestly. Landry smiled and picked up a napkin to wipe her face.

"You're my special baby girl," Heinz told her and promptly leaned down to plant a kiss on her newly cleaned cheek.

"Spoiled rotten," Astelle said after slicing the last bit of ham and taking a seat. "Every girl child in this household has been spoiled to the point of no return."

"Tell me about it," Heinz Jr. remarked.

"That is so not true," Landry added. "How many times did the boys get out of chores while Paula and I had to clean this house from top to bottom?"

"Boys shouldn't do girl work," Gramps added.

Landry could only shake her head at her grandfather's comment. She should have expected it because she'd heard similar sentiments from him before. It still never ceased to amaze her.

"It's a different generation now, Gramps," Paula chimed in.

"Yeah, one where women are bringing home just as much money as the men. So if they can share in paying bills, they should be able to share doing chores too," Landry declared.

"Oh boy, she's definitely back," Dominic quipped. "Get out the soapbox."

Her brothers laughed but Landry wasn't surprised; the Norris boys always stuck together.

"Well if somebody has to say it, I guess it has to be me," Landry continued. "Women are always tasked with being independent and resourceful, while men get to work whichever jobs they want and then come home and sit on their butts."

Heinz Sr. shook his head and continued to eat his baked chicken as if he knew where this conversation was going. Astelle tended to her grandchildren and took small bites of the food on her plate.

"That's right. I take care of both my children and I work two jobs. Does that mean their father should be allowed to work his part-time fast-food shifts and then come home and lie on the couch for the remainder of the time?" Paula asked.

Geoffrey shook his head. "Nobody's saying all that."

"Good!" Paula exclaimed. "Because that's some bull and it's precisely why I sent him back home to his mama. I can do bad by myself."

"Takes some people longer to come to their true calling in life than others," Astelle finally spoke. "We should never be so quick or harsh to judge others."

"Oh goodness, she's going to the Bible," Paula whispered.

Astelle and Heinz Sr. heard her and sent warning glares her way, but Paula continued to eat, unbothered.

"So glad I'm in my own place and doing my own thing. I don't have to worry about the balance between men and women in relationships," Landry said.

"Hard work never hurt anybody," Astelle started. "Relationships are hard work, but they're worth it. Ain't that right, Heinz?"

Landry watched as her father nodded. "Absolutely right, my love," he said when he finished chewing.

Landry resisted the urge to frown. She'd had another try at the relationship thing, even if what she and Kristian were doing was a little on the strange side. Still, since coming home, she'd decided she could forego the entire game of love for the duration of her life if need be.

After a few hours had passed, first and second helpings of the meal were done and Gramps was already calling for his dessert. Regardless of their prior conversation Landry and Paula stood to help Astelle gather the dinner dishes and take them into the kitchen. Paula had taken the chocolate cake out to the dining room and Landry followed her with cake plates in one hand, a gallon of vanilla ice cream tucked uncomfortably under her arm and spoons in the other hand.

She'd just made it to the table when Paula started to yell. "Oh my! Oh my! Oh my!"

"What is that child yelling about now?" Gramps asked.

Giselle had gotten out of her chair to go to her mother's side, looking at her with curiosity as she continued to yell. Paula's oldest child was Charles Jr.; he was nine and not impressed by much of anything the adults in this family did or said. So he remained in his seat playing the handheld video game Landry had given him for his last birthday.

In seconds everybody, except Gramps, was up from the table, joining Paula where she was standing in front of the bay window. Heinz Jr. pulled the curtains all the way back and almost knocked over one of their mother's plants.

"Dayum!" Geoffrey crowed as he peered out the window and then bent down to scoop Giselle up in his arms. "Look at that limo."

"Who is that? Y'all invite somebody else to dinner?" Dominic asked.

"No," Astelle said, coming out of the kitchen. "I didn't invite anybody."

Landry hadn't moved. After putting the ice cream onto the cherrywood table covered in her mother's old lace tablecloth, she'd set the plates down slowly. The spoons were still in her hand when she chanced a look out the window. That's the precise moment her heart stammered in her chest.

It couldn't be.

No, she told herself. It wasn't.

He was thousands of miles away, running his island without her there to distract him. Kristian had let her walk out of his room and subsequently out of his life. She'd only spoken briefly to Malayka who didn't seem at all fazed by Landry's announcement that she was resigning and would send her a list of recommended stylists to choose from. Her flight had left the island later that morning and since then she had not heard from or seen anyone from the DeSaunters family.

"Somebody's gettin' out!" Giselle yelled.

"Oh my, he sure is," Paula stated. "He certainly…is."

Landry had already looked away from the window. Her heart was pounding in her chest and she chastised herself for being foolish. The fact was that her body was beginning to warm in a way it hadn't done since she'd been in Grand Serenity. She shook her head and was just about to walk back into the kitchen when Paula's next words stopped her.

"He's fine and he's walking up to our door like he owns this house and everyone in it. Oh my, let me get myself together," her sister said.

Landry knew.

Seconds after the doorbell rang and before she could wrap her mind around what was happening, he spoke.

"My name is Kristian DeSaunters and I'm looking for Landry Norris."

His words trickled through her like a good alcoholic beverage, warm, slow and potent as hell.

"How did you know to come to my parents' house? How did you even know who they were and where they lived?" Landry asked him an hour later, when he walked into her condo behind her.

"I did extensive research on you before you came to the island," he told her. "I thought we went over that already."

"You have people investigated, follow them when they are on your island and then hunt them down when they're not?"

He wouldn't say he'd hunted her down. Not exactly.

Yesterday afternoon, after a meeting with his father and having endured yet another sleepless night, Kris decided to make the trip to the United States. He'd waited long enough. Too long, as his brother and sister not-so-kindly put it.

"I needed to speak to you," was his reply.

Her tone was edgy and he was afraid there would be an argument instead of the calm, mature discussion he'd planned.

"You could have just called," she told him after she'd dropped her purse onto one of two white couches that faced each other.

There was a lot of white in there, the furniture, the huge crystal chandelier hanging from the white ceiling, the large piece of art on one side of the wall and the cheerful looking flowers in the crystal vases sitting on the iron-and-glass coffee table. He'd assumed she would have a brighter decor with colors that represented her vibrant personality. He'd been wrong about her yet again.

"I wanted to see you," he admitted.

Kris was here for one purpose and he was not going to be deterred, especially not by his own foolishness this time.

She stood near a wall with a silver mirror and a pale gray painted table, which held another vase with a burst of deep purple flowers. She liked fresh flowers, he deduced.

"I don't understand why," she replied honestly.

He could always expect that from Landry. Honest candor that he was certain didn't come easy to every person he'd meet in this world.

"I mean, when I left the island I was suspected of setting off a bomb in the palace," she continued, folding her arms behind her back as she leaned against the wall.

She wore blue slacks and a white blouse. One of the ones he'd bought for her as he recalled personally selecting this one with the navy blue stripes and swinging sleeves. There were thick bangles on her arms and a silver choker at her neck. She was still beautiful; that hadn't changed at all.

"Gary and Salvin found the man you heard talking on the phone," he began. He'd hoped to talk to her about all the drama that had ensued on the island after she'd left, later, but if she wanted to hear it now, he would definitely oblige.

"His name was Harry Copeland and he was posing as one of the construction crew that had been hired to work on some structural issues throughout the palace." Kris walked farther into the living area, but he did not take a seat on either of the couches.

She continued to stare at him. Kris was no stranger to people looking at him. That came with the title. Whether he was on a stage giving a speech, riding in a car or simply walking down the street, people looked. But none of them had any clue. Except for Landry. She'd seen through him from the very start.

"He knew about the ball and who would be there because he was working with Amari Taylor, Malayka's hairstylist. It had only taken an hour after reviewing the surveillance tapes and seeing Harry enter and exit that room next to Malayka's dressing room, for the guards to find him. He'd actually come back to the palace to resume working two days after the ball," Kris said with a shake of his head.

He and Gary had figured the guy was going to try again since none of the royal family had been injured in the explosion and they were almost certain that the DeSaunters family were the actual targets.

"Amari?" she asked. "He's such a...a colorful character."

Kris nodded. He thought something similar when he'd first met the man as well.

"Amari's not as talkative as Harry, but we've had them both in custody for over a week now. Malayka was livid when she found out. She explained that you and she had been going to the dressing room to discuss her gown the night of the ball, when she realized she'd lost one of her earrings. She went to her room to get another pair and you said you would meet her in the dressing room. Before you could get there Amari showed up. He's the one who hit you, but he's not saying why."

She appeared surprised and then irritated.

"Let me guess—your cameras picked that up too. Wow, I guess me leaving your room every morning wasn't as much of a secret as I thought it was. Someone was watching all along," she said with a shake of her head.

"Security is important," he told her. "As you can tell, even with all that we already had in place, we still need to step it up. Until we find out what's really going on between Amari and this Harry guy who we think is just a middleman, we're still being targeted."

"Why?"

He shook his head. "I'm not sure. It may be something related to the bank, hence the break-in there, but we're still trying to work that out."

She nodded then. "So why are you here if there's still

more to find out? I know you didn't come this far to tell me about Amari and his cohorts."

He hadn't; she was absolutely right about that. However, Kris wasn't sure how what he actually wanted to say was going to go over with her at this moment.

"No. I didn't," he finally said.

"Then what?"

It sounded like a dare. She'd stepped away from the wall and now had her arms by her sides. Her hair was pulled back into a messy ponytail; huge hoop earrings swung at her ears. She looked casual and classy all at the same time. Kris clenched his hands. He'd never been this nervous about anything in his life before. That's how he knew it was important.

It was very important.

That's why he decided to take a page from her book and just say it.

"I missed you," he told her. "I've never missed anyone in my life like this besides my mother. Every day, every hour of every day I missed you."

She did not move and did not speak.

"I ate pizza. You've been gone for fourteen nights and five of them I had pizza for dinner. I drank beer. In my room, of course, but so much beer. I'd hoped it would make me sleep better, but it didn't."

He took a breath and continued. This was uncomfortable and odd yet he knew it was the most important thing he'd ever do in his life.

"I heard every word you said that morning on my balcony and the many times before that. I didn't give us a chance. I never planned to entertain the idea of an 'us.' It's only a small consolation to know that you didn't either. But I should have. I should have known from the first time I looked at your pictures. You were different—I just wasn't prepared for how different."

Her arms fell to her sides.

"If I were a god with power over the entire universe I wouldn't deserve you. But I want you, Landry. I want the girl who was born in Northern Seton Hospital Center on February tenth, weighing eight pounds and three ounces. I want the girl who kicked the winning goal on her high school soccer team, and the young lady who aced all her classes for the first two years at California State Polytechnic University. And I want the woman who had *Harper's Bazaar* call her back for a second internship and then offer her a full-time job. I know that she's independent and headstrong and can be a little stubborn. But I want her. I love her."

For once in her life, Landry didn't know what to say.

She'd been listening to Kristian talk and watching him at the same time. He looked fabulous in his navy blue suit and light blue shirt. His tie was pink and blue and made his eyes look brighter. His shoes were shined, his hair cut close and shaped up precisely. He was every bit as handsome as she'd thought he was the first time she'd seen him.

And every bit as intimidating.

Why had he really come here? What did he want from her?

He said he loved her. Wasn't that something a woman usually wanted to hear?

Not her. Not now.

She was shaking her head as she started walking toward the door.

"Thank you for telling me that my name has been cleared and that your family no longer considers me a threat. I appreciate you coming all this way for that, but it wasn't necessary. I would have been fine with an email."

She was reaching for the doorknob when his hand covered hers. Landry looked up into his face; she saw a muscle twitch in his jaw, smelled the rich scent of his cologne.

"I couldn't do this in an email," he told her about two seconds before he grabbed her by the waist and pulled her close to him.

The kiss was fast, potent, pure fire.

Her arms wrapped around his neck as if they were always meant to be there and damn if she didn't give totally in to the kiss. She could have sworn she didn't want to, that this was against everything that she'd so fervently believed for so long. She was independent and successful; she did not need to be with a prince, of all people. She did not need the duties and responsibilities that would no doubt come with loving him. He wasn't like any other man and she knew that wasn't just because of the title. She knew and that fact had her pressing her body into his.

He turned them and her back was now against the door. His hands were moving up and down her sides as his tongue dueled dangerously and deliciously with hers. She was drowning; she could feel herself going slowly, but most definitely, under. When he cupped her bottom and lifted her off the floor, Landry sighed, her legs instantly going around his waist.

"Bedroom," he said between nipping little bites on her lower lip.

"Down the hall and to your right," she answered, her palms flattening on the back of his head as he walked.

He moved quickly which was a good and bad thing, because when he entered the room and dropped her onto the bed, Landry wanted to get up and run. Then she wanted to strip and beg.

"I don't know what's happening," she admitted, when he pulled his jacket off and tossed it on the floor.

"I didn't know either but now I'm convinced it's a good thing," he told her and worked on his tie and the first buttons of his shirt.

Landry lifted her blouse up and over her head, tossing it onto the floor the same way he'd done his jacket. She toed off her slip-on flats and then went to the buttons of her pants.

"How is this happening? How will it work?" she asked and then pushed her pants down her legs, letting them fall to the floor as well. "You live on an island and I live here. I have a business and clients and you have thousands of citizens to care for."

He'd removed his shirt and the undershirt he wore beneath it. He was unbuckling his pants when he looked up at her.

"I have a private jet. There's no reason you can't fly to where you need to be, when you need to be there. Detali has been fielding numerous calls from a diverse group of people interested in her designs. That's all thanks to you. Even Sam said she wished there were someone stationed on Grand Serenity who could bring more fashion icons to the attention of our residents."

Landry opened her mouth to say something and then she closed it again, because once more, she wasn't sure what to say.

"I don't… I mean, I can't," she stuttered.

He removed his shoes, his pants and then his boxers. After taking a few seconds to slip on a condom he had in his back pocket, he came closer to the bed; he planted a knee on the mattress between her legs and cupped her face in his hands. "You can do anything you want, from wherever you want, as long as you're with me. As long as I know that at night I can lie down beside you. That I can look into your eyes and tell you how much I love you. How much I need you in my life. Say you'll marry me."

The next kiss was shorter, yet it still took her breath away. He moved quickly to rid her of her bra and panties and then he was over her, sinking deep inside her before she could think of another question or argument.

Epilogue

Two weeks later
The First Royal Wedding

"I love you," Landry said as she stood across from Kristian beneath a trellis full of red begonias.

A few seconds ago her father had handed her off to Kristian, the smile on Heinz Sr.'s face so big Landry feared it might be permanently stuck that way. Her parents had been elated when two days after Kristian had appeared at their house, he was there once again to ask for Landry's hand in marriage.

Sure, it seemed fast. She'd known Kristian for three and a half months, but there wasn't a doubt in her mind that he was the man she wanted to marry.

Of course, Heinz Jr., her niece and nephew, her grandparents and the rest of her brothers were much more excited about getting an all-expenses-paid trip to Grand Serenity

Island. Paula was very interested in meeting Roland, in the hopes that the other prince didn't mind a ready-made family.

Planning a wedding in two weeks was not an easy feat but Sam had jumped right in and worked tirelessly to make this day everything Heinz and Astelle Norris had dreamed of for their oldest daughter. It was all so beautiful, Landry had to admit.

They'd chosen a spot outside the palace, close to the water and the path that led down to the abandoned stables. She'd known that would be important to Kristian as he'd admitted to only feeling close to his mother when he was there.

White chairs lined the lawn and accommodated the one hundred close family and friends that they'd decided to invite on such short notice. There were tall crystal vases at the end of each row of chairs filled to the point of bursting with blue jacaranda, bottlebrush and alpinia. Landry had selected the flowers herself, going for color and excitement as she, Paula and Sam wore all-white dresses.

Landry's dress had, of course, been made by Detali, her new favorite designer. While Peta insisted on making the bridesmaids gowns as soon as Landry told her about the wedding.

Prince Rafferty and Roland were in full regalia, their medals shined to perfection as each of them stood tall at the altar with Kristian.

As for her husband-to-be, Landry could only smile. He was temptingly gorgeous in his black jacket, the gold tassels at his shoulders and the sword at his hip giving him that dashing royal look without anyone even knowing his title. But it didn't matter what he was wearing to Landry. It only mattered what he said.

"I love you. Just you, for who and what you are," he whispered before the minister began the ceremony.

The rest of the day proceeded with all the pomp and circumstance of a royal wedding as Landry eagerly awaited the next morning when she would awake as Princess Landry Norris DeSaunters, owner and managing editor of the new magazine aptly titled *Tropical Fashions*. She was going to have her own magazine where she could focus on all things fashionable throughout the world. She and Sam were also working on a charity fashion show, which they hoped to make an annual event on the island.

Her parents had been right, Landry thought as she and Kristian took to the dance floor in the smaller ballroom inside the palace. She could have it all. She'd compromised by agreeing to move to Grand Serenity. But she didn't feel as if she'd sacrificed who and what she was to be with a man, not even to be with a prince.

* * * * *

HIS ACCIDENTAL HEIR

JOANNE ROCK

For Barbara Jean Thomas, an early mentor and role model of hard work. Thank you, Barbara, for teaching me the value of keeping my chin up and having faith in myself. During my teens, you were so much more than a boss... You were a friend, a cheerleader and a sometimes mom on those weekend trips with the crew. I'll never forget my visit to New York to see Oprah, courtesy of you! Much love to you, always.

One

"Rafe, I need you in the Antilles Suite today." Maresa Delphine handed her younger brother a gallon jug of bubble bath. "I have a guest checking in who needs a hot bath on arrival, but he isn't sure what time he'll get here."

Her twenty-one-year-old sibling—who'd recently suffered a traumatic brain injury in a car accident—didn't reach to take the jug. Instead, his hazel eyes tracked the movements of a friendly barmaid currently serving a guest a Blackbeard's Revenge specialty drink on the patio just outside the lobby. The Carib Grand Hotel's floor-to-ceiling windows allowed for views of the tiki bar on Barefoot Beach and the glittering Caribbean Sea beyond. Inside the hotel, the afternoon activity had picked up since Maresa's mad dash to the island's sundries shop for the bath products. All of her runners had been busy fulfilling other duties for guests, so she'd made the trip herself. She had no idea what her newest runner—her recovering brother who still needed to work in a monitored environment—had been doing at that hour. He hadn't answered his radio and he needed to get with the program if he wanted to remain employed. Not to mention, Maria might be blamed for his slipups. She was supporting her family, and couldn't afford to lose her job as concierge for this exclusive hotel on a private island off Saint Thomas.

And she really, really needed him to remain employed where she could watch over him. Where he was eligible for better insurance benefits that could give him the long-term follow-up care he would need for years. She knew she held Rafe to a higher standard so that no one on staff could view his employment as a conflict of interest. Sure, the hotel director had approved his application, but she had promised to carefully supervise her brother during his three-month trial period.

"Rafe." She gently nudged her sibling with the heavy container of rose-scented bubbles, remembering his counselor's advice about helping him stay on task when he got distracted. "I have some croissants from the bakery to share with you on your next break. But for now, I really need help. Can you please take this to the Antilles Suite? I'd like you to turn on the hot water and add this for a bubble bath as soon as I text you."

Their demanding guest could stride through the lobby doors any moment. Mr. Holmes had phoned this morning, unsure of his arrival time, but insistent on having a hot bath waiting for him. That was just the first item on a long list of requests.

She checked her slim watch, a gift from her last employer, the Parisian hotel where she'd had the job of her dreams. As much as Maresa loved her former position, she couldn't keep it after her mother's car accident that had caused Rafe's head injury almost a year ago. Going forward, her place was here in Charlotte Amalie to help with her brother.

She refused to let him fail at the Carib Grand Hotel. Her mother's poor health meant she couldn't supervise him at home, for one thing. So having him work close to Maresa all day was ideal.

"I'll go to the Antilles Suite." Rafe tucked the bubble bath under one arm and continued to study the barmaid, a sweet girl named Nancy who'd been really kind to him when Maresa introduced them. "You will call me on the phone when I need to turn on the water."

Maresa touched Rafe's cheek to capture his full attention, her fingers grazing the jagged scar that wrapped beneath his left ear. Her mother had suffered an MS flare-up behind the wheel one night last year, sending her car into a telephone pole during a moment of temporary paralysis. Rafe had gone through the windshield since his seatbelt was unbuckled; he'd been trying to retrieve his phone that had slid into the backseat. Afterward, Maresa had been deeply involved in his recovery and care since their mother had been battling her own health issues. Their father had always been useless, a deadbeat American businessman who worked in the cruise industry and used to visit often, wooing Maresa's mother with promises about coming to live with him in Wisconsin when he saved up enough money to bring them. That had never happened, and he'd checked out on them by the time Maresa was ten, moving to Europe for his job. Yet then, as now, Maresa didn't mind adapting her life to help Rafe. Her brother's injuries could have been fatal that day. Instead, he was a happy part of her world. Yes, he would forever cope with bouts of confusion, memory loss and irritability along with the learning disabilities the accident had brought with it. Throughout it all, though, Rafe was always… Rafe. The brother she adored. He'd been her biggest supporter after her former fiancé broke things off with her a week before their wedding two years ago, encouraging her to go to Paris and "be my superstar."

He was there for her then, after that humiliating experience. She would be there for him now.

"Rafe? Go to the Antilles Suite and I'll text you when it's time to turn on the hot water." She repeated the instructions for him now, knowing it would be kinder to transfer him to the maintenance team or landscaping staff where he could do the same kinds of things every day. But who would watch out for him there? "Be sure to add the bubbles. Okay?"

Drawing in a breath, she took comfort from the soothing scent of white tuberoses and orchids in the arrangement on her granite podium.

"A bubble bath." Rafe grinned, his eyes clearing. "Can do." He ambled off toward the elevator, whistling.

Her relief lasted only a moment because just then a limousine pulled up in front of the hotel. She had a clear view out the windows overlooking the horseshoe driveway flanked by fountains and thick banks of birds-of-paradise. The doormen moved as a coordinated team toward the vehicle, prepared to open doors and handle baggage.

She straightened the orchid pinned on her pale blue linen jacket. If this was Mr. Holmes, she needed to stall him to give Rafe time to run that bath. The guest had been curt to the point of rudeness on the phone, requiring a suite with real grass—and it had to be ryegrass only—for his Maltese to relieve himself. The guest had also ordered a dog walker with three years' worth of references and a groomer on-site, fresh lilacs in the room daily and specialty pies flown in from a shop in rural upstate New York for his bedtime snack each evening.

And that was just for starters. She couldn't wait to see what he needed once he settled in for his two-week stay. These were the kinds of guests that could make or break a career. The vocal kind with many precise needs. All of which she would fulfill. It was the job she'd chosen because she took pride in her organizational skills, continually reordering her world throughout a chaotic childhood with an absentee father and a chronically ill mother. She took comfort in structuring what she could. And since there were only so many jobs on the island that could afford to pay her the kind of money she needed to support both her mother and her brother, Maresa had to succeed at the Carib Grand.

She calmed herself by squaring the single sheet of paper on her podium, lining up her pen beside it. She tapped open her list of restaurant phone numbers on her call screen so she could dial reservations at a moment's notice. The small, routine movements helped her to feel in control, reminding her she could do this job well. When she looked up again—

Wow.

The sight of the tall, chiseled male unfolding himself from the limousine was enough to take her breath away. His strong, striking features practically called for a feminine hand to caress them. Fraternizing with guests was, of course, strictly against the rules and Maresa had never been tempted. But if ever she had an inkling to stray from that philosophy, the powerful shoulders encased in expensive designer silk were exactly the sort of attribute that would intrigue her. The man towered over everyone in the courtyard entrance, including Big Bill, the head doorman. Dressed in a charcoal suit tailored to his long, athletic frame, the dark-haired guest buttoned his jacket, hiding too much of the hard, muscled chest that she'd glimpsed as he'd stepped out of the vehicle. Straightening his tie, he peered through the window, his ice-blue gaze somehow landing on her.

Direct hit.

She felt the jolt of awareness right through the glass. This supremely masculine specimen couldn't possibly be Mr. Holmes. Her brain didn't reconcile the image of a man with that square jaw and sharp blade of a nose ordering lilacs for himself. Daily.

Relaxing a fraction, Maresa blew out a breath as the newcomer turned back toward the vehicle. Until a silky white Maltese dog stepped regally from the limousine into the man's waiting arms.

In theory, Cameron McNeill liked dogs.

Big, slobbery working canines that thrived outdoors and could keep up with him on a distance run. The long-haired Maltese in his arms, on the other hand, was a prize-winning show animal with too many travel accessories to count. The retired purebred was on loan to Cam for his undercover assessment of a recently acquired McNeill Resorts property, however, and he needed Poppy's cooperation for his stint as a demanding hotel guest. If he walked into the financially floundering Carib Grand Hotel as himself—an owner and vice president of McNeill Resorts—he would receive the most attentive service imaginable and learn absolutely nothing about the establishment's underlying problems. But as Mr. Holmes, first-class pain in the ass, Cam would put the staff on their toes and see how they reacted.

After reviewing the Carib Grand's performance reports for the past two months, Cameron knew something was off in the day-to-day operations. And since he'd personally recommended that the company buy the property in the first place, he wasn't willing to wait for an over-priced operations review by an outside agency. Not that McNeill Resorts couldn't afford it. It simply chafed his pride that he'd missed something in his initial research. Besides, his family had just learned of a long-hidden branch of relations living on a nearby island—his father's sons by a secret mistress. Cam would use his time here to check out the other McNeills personally.

But for now? Business first.

"Welcome to the Carib Grand," an aging doorman greeted him with a deferential nod and a friendly smile.

Cam forced a frown onto his face to keep from smiling back. That wasn't as hard as he thought given the way Poppy's foolishly long fur was plastering itself to his jacket when he walked too fast, her topknot and tail bobbing with his stride and tickling his chin. It wouldn't come naturally to Cam to be the hard-to-please guest this week. He was a people-person to begin with, and appreciated those who worked for McNeill Resorts especially. But this was the fastest way he knew to find out what was going on at the hotel firsthand. He'd be damned if anyone on the board questioned his business acumen during a time when his aging grandfather was testing all his heirs for their commitment to his legacy.

The Carib Grand lobby was welcoming, as he recalled from his tour six months ago when the property had been briefly shut down. The two wings of the hotel flanked the reception area to either side with restaurants stacked overhead. But the lobby itself drew visitors in with floor-to-ceiling windows so the sparkling Caribbean beckoned at all times. Huge hanging baskets of exotic flowers framed the view without impeding it.

The scent of bougainvillea drifted in through the door

behind him. Poppy tilted her nose in the air and took a seat on his forearm, a queen on her throne.

The front desk attendant—only one—was busy with another guest. Cameron's bellhop, a young guy with a long ponytail of dreadlocks, must have noticed the front desk was busy at the same time as him, because he gestured to the concierge's tall granite counter where a stunning brunette smiled.

"Ms. Delphine can help you check in, sir," the bellhop informed him while whisking his luggage onto a waiting cart. "Would you like me to walk the dog while you get settled?"

Nothing would please him more than to off-load Poppy and the miles of snow-white pet hair threading around his suit buttons. Cameron was pretty sure there was a cloud of fur floating just beneath his nose.

"Her name is Poppy," Cameron snapped at the helpful soul, unable to take his eyes off the very appealing concierge, who'd snagged his attention through the window the second he'd stepped out of the limo. "And I've requested a dog walker with references."

The bellhop gave a nod and backed away, no doubt glad to leave a surly guest in the hands of the bronze-skinned beauty sidling out from her counter to welcome Cameron. She seemed to have that mix of ethnicities common in the Caribbean. The burnished tint of her skin set off wide, tawny gold eyes. A natural curl and kink in her dusky brown hair ended in sun-blond tips. Perfect posture and a well-fitted linen suit made her look every inch a professional, yet her long legs drew his eye even though her skirt hit just above her knees. Even if he'd been visiting the property as her boss, he wouldn't have acted on the flash of attraction, of course. But it was a damn shame that he'd be at odds with this enticing female for the next two weeks. The concierge position was the linchpin in the hotel staff, though, and his mission to rattle cages began with her.

"Welcome, Mr. Holmes." He was impressed that she'd greeted him by name. "I'm Maresa. We're so glad to see you and Poppy, too."

He'd spoken to a Maresa Delphine on the phone earlier, purposely issuing a string of demands on short notice to see how she'd fare. She didn't look nervous. Yet. He'd need to challenge her, to prod at all facets of the management and staff to pinpoint the weak links. The hotel wasn't necessarily losing money, but it was only a matter of time before earnings followed the decline in performance reviews.

"Poppy will be glad to meet her walker." He came straight to the point, ignoring the eager bob of the dog's head as Maresa offered admiring words to the pooch. Cameron could imagine what the wag of the tail was doing to the back of his jacket. "Do you have the references ready?"

"Of course." Maresa straightened with a sunny smile. She had a hint of an accent he couldn't place. "They're right here at my desk."

Cameron's gaze dipped to her slim hips as she turned. He'd taken a hiatus from dating for fun over the last few months, thinking he ought to find himself a wife to fulfill his grandfather's dictate that McNeill Resorts would only go to the grandsons who were stable and wed. But he'd botched that, too, impulsively issuing a marriage proposal to the first woman his matchmaker suggested in order to have the business settled.

Now? Apparently the months without sex were conspiring against him. He ground his teeth against a surge of ill-timed desire.

"Here you go." The concierge turned with a sheet of paper in hand and passed it to him, her honey-colored gaze as potent as any caress. "I took the liberty of checking all the references myself, but I've included the numbers in case you'd like to talk to any of them directly."

"That's why I asked," he replied tightly, tugging the paper harder than necessary.

He could have sworn Poppy slanted him a dirty look over one fluffy white shoulder. Her nails definitely flexed into his forearm right through the sleeve of his suit before she fixed her coal-black eyes on Maresa Delphine.

Not that he blamed Poppy. He'd rather be staring at Maresa than scowling over dog walker references. Being the boss wasn't always a rocking-good time. Yet he'd rather ruffle feathers today and fix the core problems than have the staff jump though the hoops of an extended performance review.

Cameron slid the paper into his jacket pocket. "I'll check these after I have the chance to clean up. If you can have someone show us to our room."

He hurried her on purpose, curious if the room extras were ready to go. The bath wasn't a tough request, but the flowers had most likely needed to be flown in. If he hadn't been specifically looking for it, he might have missed the smallest hesitation on her part.

"Certainly." She lifted a tablet from the granite countertop where she worked. "If you can just sign here to approve the information you provided over the phone, I'll escort you myself."

That wasn't protocol. Did Ms. Delphine expect additional tips this way? Cam remembered reading that the concierge had been with the company since the reopening under McNeill ownership two months ago.

Signing his fake name on the electronic screen, he fished for information. "Are you understaffed?"

She ran a pair of keycards through the machine and slid them into a small welcome folder.

"Definitely not. We'll have Rudolfo bring your bags. I just want to personally ensure the suite is to your liking." She handed him the packet with the keys while giving a nod to the bell captain. "Can I make a dinner reservation for you this evening, Mr. Holmes?"

Cameron juggled the restless dog, who was no doubt more travel-weary than him. They'd taken a private jet, but even with the shorter air time, there'd been limo rides to and from airports, plus a boat crossing from Charlotte Amalie to the Carib Grand since the hotel occupied a small, private island just outside the harbor area in Saint Thomas. He'd walked the dog when they hit the ground at the airfield, but Poppy's owner had cautioned him to give the animal a certain amount of rest and play each day. So far on Cam's watch, Poppy had clocked zero time spent on both counts. For a pampered show dog, she was proving a trouper.

As soon as he banished the hotel staff including Maresa Delphine, he'd find a quiet spot on the beach where he and his borrowed pet could recharge.

"I've heard a retired chef from Paris opened a new restaurant in Martinique." He would be spending some time on that island where his half brothers were living. "I'd like a standing reservation for the rest of the week." He had no idea if he'd be able to get over there, but it was the kind of thing a good concierge could accommodate.

"I've heard La Belle Palm is fantastic." Maresa punched a button on the guest elevator while Rudolfo disappeared down another hall with the luggage. "I haven't visited yet, but I enjoyed Chef Pierre's La Luce on the Left Bank."

Her words brought to mind her résumé that he'd reviewed briefly before making the trip. She'd worked at a Paris hotel prior to accepting her current position.

"You've spent time in Paris, Ms. Delphine?" He set Poppy on the floor, unfurling the pink jeweled leash that had matched the carrying case Mrs. Trager had given him. He'd kept all the accessories except for that one—the huge pink pet carrier made Cam look like he was travelling with Barbie's Dreamhouse under his arm.

"She's so cute." Maresa kept her eyes on the dog and not on him. "And yes, I lived in Paris for a year before returning to Saint Thomas."

"You're from the area originally?" He almost regretted setting the dog down since it removed a barrier between them. Something about Maresa Delphine drew him in.

His gaze settled on the bare arch of her neck just above her jacket collar. Her thick brown hair had been clipped at the nape, ending in a silky tail that curled along one shoulder. A single pearl drop earring rolled along the tender expanse of skin, a pale contrast to her rich brown complexion.

"I grew up in Charlotte Amalie and worked in a local hotel until a foreign exchange program run by the corporate owner afforded me the chance to work overseas." She glanced up at him. Caught him staring.

The jolt of awareness flared, hot and unmistakable. He could tell she felt it, too. Her pupils dilated a fraction, dark pools with golden rims. His heartbeat slugged heavier. Harder.

He forced his gaze away as the elevator chimed to announce their arrival on his floor. "After you."

He held the door as she stepped out into the short hall.

They passed a uniformed attendant with a gallon-sized jug stuffed under his arm, a pair of earbuds half-in and half-out of his ears. After a quick glance at Maresa, the young man pulled the buds off and jammed them in his pocket, then shoved open a door to the stairwell.

"Here we are." Maresa stepped aside so Cam stood directly in front of the entrance to the Antilles Suite.

Poppy took a seat and stared at the door expectantly.

Cameron used the keycard to unlock the suite, not sure what to expect. Was Maresa Delphine worthy of what the company compensated her? Or had she returned to her hometown in order to bilk guests out of extra tips and take advantage of her employer? But she didn't appear to be looking for a bonus gratuity as her gaze darted around the suite interior and then landed on him.

Poppy spotted the patch of natural grass just outside the bathroom door. The sod rested inside a pallet on carpeted wheels, the cart painted in blues and tans to match the room's decorating scheme. The dog made a break for it and Cam let her go, the leash dangling behind her.

Lilacs flanked the crystal decanters on the minibar. Through the open door to the bathroom, Cameron could see the bubbles nearing the edge of the tub, the hot water still running as steam wafted upward.

So far, Maresa had proven a worthy concierge. That was good for the hotel, but less favorable for him, perhaps, since her high standards surely precluded acting on a fleeting elevator attraction.

"If everything is to your satisfaction, Mr. Holmes, I'll leave you undisturbed while I go make your dinner reservations for the week." She hadn't even allowed the door to close behind them, a wise practice, of course, for a female hotel employee.

Rudolfo was already in the hall with the luggage cart.

Cameron could hear Maresa giving the bellhop instructions for his bags. And Poppy's.

"Thank you." Cameron turned his back on her to stare out at the view of the hotel's private beach and the brilliant turquoise Caribbean Sea. "For now, I'm satisfied."

The room, of course, was fine. Ms. Delphine had passed his first test. But was he satisfied? No. He wouldn't rest until he knew why the guest reviews of the Carib Grand were lower than anticipated. And satisfaction was the last thing he was feeling when the most enticing woman he'd met in a long time was off-limits.

That attraction would be difficult to ignore when it was imperative he uncover all her secrets.

Two

As much as Maresa cursed her alarm clock chirping at her before dawn, she never regretted waking up early once she was on the Carib Grand's private beach before sunrise. Her mother's house was perched on a street high above Saint Thomas Harbor, which meant Maresa took a bike to the ferry each morning to get to the hotel property early for these two precious hours of alone time before work. Her brother was comfortable walking down to the dock later for his shift, a task that was overseen by a neighbor and fellow employee who also took the ferry over each day.

Now, rolling out her yoga mat on the damp sand, she made herself comfortable in child's pose, letting the magic of the sea and the surf do their work on her muscles tight with stress.

One. Two. Three. Breathe.

Smoothing her hands over the soft cotton of her bright

pink crop top, she felt her diaphragm lift and expand. She rarely saw anyone else on the beach at this hour, and the few runners or walkers who passed by were too busy soaking up the same quiet moments as she to pay her any mind.

Maresa counted through the inhales and exhales, trying her damnedest to let go of her worries. Too bad Cameron Holmes's ice-blue eyes and sculpted features kept appearing in her mind, distracting her with memories of that electric current she'd experienced just looking at him.

It made no sense, she lectured herself as she swapped positions for her sun salutations. The guest was demanding and borderline rude—something that shouldn't attract her in the slightest. She hated to think his raw masculinity was sliding under her radar despite what her brain knew about him.

At least she'd made it through the first day of his stay without incident. But while that was something to celebrate, she didn't want her brother crossing paths with the surly guest again. She'd held her breath yesterday when the two passed one another in the corridor outside the Antilles Suite, knowing how much Rafe loved dogs. Thankfully, her brother had been engrossed in his music and hadn't noticed the Maltese.

She'd keep Rafe safely away from Mr. Holmes for the next two weeks. Tilting her face to the soft glow of first light, she arched her back in the upward salute before sweeping down into a forward bend. Breathing out the challenges—living in tight quarters with her family, battling local agencies to get her brother into support programs he needed for his recovery, avoiding her former fiancé who'd texted her twice in the last twenty-four hours asking to see her— Maresa took comfort in this moment every day.

Shifting into her lunge as the sun peeked above the horizon, Maresa heard a dog bark before a small white ball of fluff careened past her toward the water. Startled by the sudden brush of fur against her arm, she had to reposition her hands to maintain her balance.

"Poppy." A man's voice sounded from somewhere in the woods behind the beach.

Cameron Holmes.

Maresa recognized the deep baritone, not by sound so much as by the effect it had on her. A slow, warm wave through the pit of her belly. What was the matter with her? She scrambled to her feet, realizing the pampered pet of her most difficult guest was charging into the Caribbean, happily chasing a tern.

"Poppy!" she called after the dog just as Cameron Holmes stepped onto the beach.

Shirtless.

She had to swallow hard before she lifted her fingers to her lips and whistled. The little Maltese stopped in the surf, peering back in search of the noise while the tern flew away up the shore. The ends of Poppy's glossy coat floated on the surface of the incoming tide.

The man charged toward his pet, his bare feet leaving wet footprints in the sand. Maresa was grateful for the moment to indulge her curiosity about him without his seeing her. A pair of bright board shorts rode low on his hips. The fiery glow of sunrise burnished his skin to a deeper tan, his square shoulders rolling with an easy grace as he scooped the animal out of the water and into his arms. He spoke softly to her even as the strands of long, wet fur clung to his side. Whatever he said earned him a heartfelt lick on the cheek from the pooch, its white tail wagging slowly.

Maresa's heart melted a little. Especially when she

caught a glimpse of Cameron Holmes's smile as he turned back toward her. For a moment, he looked like another man entirely.

Then, catching sight of her standing beside her yoga mat, his expression grew shuttered.

"Sorry to interrupt your morning." He gave a brief nod. Curt. Dismissive. "I thought the beach would be empty at this hour or I wouldn't have let her off the leash." He clipped a length of pink leather to the collar around Poppy's neck.

"Most days, I'm the only one down here at this time." She forced a politeness she didn't feel, especially when she wasn't on duty yet. "Would you like a towel for her?"

The animal wasn't shivering, but Maresa couldn't imagine it would be easy to groom the dog if she walked home with wet fur dragging on the ground.

"I didn't think to bring one with me." He frowned, glancing around the deserted beach as if one might appear. "I assumed towels would be provided."

She tried not to grind her teeth at the air of entitlement. It became far easier to ignore the appeal of his shirtless chest once he started speaking in that superior air.

"Towels are available when the beach cabana opens at eight." Bending to retrieve the duffel on the corner of her mat, she tugged out hers and handed it to him. "Poppy can have mine."

He hesitated.

She fought the urge to cram the terry cloth back in her bag and stomp off. But, of course, she couldn't do that. She reached toward the pup's neck and scratched her there instead. Poppy's heart-shaped collar jangled softly against Maresa's hand. She noticed the "If Found" name on the back.

Olivia Trager?

Maybe the animal belonged to a girlfriend.

"Thank you." He took the hand towel and tucked it around the dog. Poppy stared out of her wrap as if used to being swaddled. "I really didn't mean to interrupt you."

He sounded more sincere this time. Maresa glanced up at him, only to realize how close they were standing. His gaze roamed over her as if he had been taking advantage of an unseen moment, the same way she had ogled him earlier. Becoming aware of her skimpy yoga crop top and the heat of awareness warming her skin, she stepped back awkwardly.

"Ms. Trager must really trust you with her dog." She hadn't meant to say it aloud. Then again, maybe hearing about his girlfriend would stop these wayward thoughts about him. "That is, no wonder you want to take such good care of her."

Awkward much? Maresa cursed herself for sticking her nose in his personal business.

His expression remained inscrutable for a moment. He studied her as if weighing how much to share. "My mother wouldn't trust anyone but me with her dog," he said finally.

She considered his words, still half wishing the mystery Ms. Trager was a girlfriend on her way to the resort today. Then Maresa would have to take a giant mental step backward from the confusing hotel guest. As it stood, she had no one to save her from the attraction but herself. With that in mind, she raked up her yoga mat and started rolling it.

"Well, I hope the dog walker and groomer meet your criteria." She stuffed the mat in her duffel, wondering why he hadn't let the walker take the animal out in the first place. "I'm happy to find someone else if—"

"The walker is fine. You're doing an excellent job, Maresa."

The unexpected praise caught her off guard. She nearly dropped her bag, mostly because he fixed her with his clear blue gaze. Heat rushed through her again, and it didn't have anything to do with the sun bathing them in the morning light now that it was fully risen.

"Thank you." Her throat went dry. She backed up a step. Retreating. "I'm going to let you enjoy the beach."

Maresa turned toward the path through the thick undergrowth that led back to the hotel and nearly ran right into Jaden Torries, her ex-fiancé.

"Whoa!" Jaden's one hand reached to steady her, his other curved protectively around a pink bundle he carried. Tall and rangy, her artist ex-boyfriend was thin where Cameron was well-muscled. The round glasses Jaden wore for affectation and not because he needed them were jammed into the thick curls that reached his shoulders. "Maresa. I've been trying to contact you."

He released her, juggling his hold on the small pink parcel he carried. A parcel that wriggled?

"I've been busy." She wanted to pivot away from the man who'd told the whole island he was dumping her before informing her of the fact. But that shifting pink blanket captured her full attention.

A tiny wrinkled hand reached up from the lightweight cotton, the movement followed by the softest sigh imaginable.

Her ex-fiancé was carrying a baby.

"But this is important, Maresa. It's about Isla." He lowered his arm cradling the infant so Maresa could see her better.

Indigo eyes blinked up at her. Short dark hair complimented the baby's medium skin tone. A white cotton headband decorated with rosettes rested above barely there eyebrows. Perfectly formed tiny features were molded into a silent yawn, the tiny hands reaching heavenward as the baby shifted against Jaden.

Something shifted inside Maresa at the same time. A maternal urge she hadn't known she possessed seized her insides and squeezed tight. Once upon a time she had dreamed about having this man's babies. She'd imagined what they would look like. Now, he had sought her out to…taunt her with the life she'd missed out on?

The maternal urge hardened into resentment, but she'd be damned if she'd let him see it.

"Congratulations. Your daughter is lovely, Jaden." She straightened as the large shadow of Cameron Holmes covered them both.

"Is there a problem, Ms. Delphine?" His tone was cool and impersonal, yet in that awkward moment he felt like an ally.

She appreciated his strong presence beside her when she felt that old surge of betrayal. She let Jaden answer since she didn't feel any need to defend the ex who'd called off their wedding via a text message.

"There's no problem. I'm an old friend of Maresa's. Jaden Torries." He extended his free hand to introduce himself.

Mr. Holmes ignored it. Poppy barked at Jaden.

"Then I'm sure you'll respect Maresa's wish to be on her way." Her unlikely rescuer tucked his hand under one arm as easily as he'd plucked his pet from the water earlier.

The warmth of his skin made her want to curl into him just like Poppy had, too.

"Right." Jaden dropped his hand. "Except Rafe's old girlfriend, Trina, left town last night, Maresa. And since

Trina's my cousin, she stuck me with the job of delivering Rafe's daughter into your care."

Maresa's feet froze to the spot. She had a vague sense of Cameron leaning closer to her, his hand suddenly at her back. Which was helpful, because she thought for a minute there was a very real chance she was going to faint. Her knees wobbled beneath her.

"Sorry to spring it on you like this," Jaden continued. "I tried telling Trina she owed it to your family to tell you in person, and I thought I had her talked into it, but—"

"Rafe?" Maresa turned around slowly, needing to see with her own eyes if there was any chance Jaden was telling the truth. "Trina broke up with him almost a year ago. Right after the accident."

Jaden stepped closer. "Right. And Trina didn't even find out she was pregnant until a couple of weeks afterward, while Rafe was still in critical condition. Trina decided to go through with the pregnancy on her own. Isla was born the end of January."

Maresa was too shaken to even do the math, but she did know that Trina and Rafe had been hot and heavy for the last month or two they were together. They'd been a constant fixture on Maresa's social media feed for those weeks. Which had made it all the more upsetting when Trina bailed on him right after the accident, bursting into tears every time she got close to his bedside before giving up altogether. Had she been even more emotional because she'd been in the early stages of pregnancy?

"Why wouldn't she have called me or my mother?" Her knees wobbled again as her gaze fell on the tiny infant. Isla? She had Rafe's hairline—the curve of dark hair encroaching on the temples. But plenty of babies had that, didn't they? "I would have helped her. I could have been there when the baby was born."

"Who is Rafe?" Cameron asked.

She'd forgotten all about him.

Maresa gulped a breath. "My brother." The very real possibility that Jaden was telling the truth threatened to level her. Rafe was in no position to be a father with the assorted symptoms he still battled. And financially? She was barely getting by supporting her family and paying some of Rafe's staggering medical bills since he hadn't been fully insured at the time.

"Look." Jaden set a bright pink diaper bag down on the beach. Cartoon cats cartwheeled across the front. "My apartment is no place for a baby. You know that, right? I just took her because Trina showed up last night, begging me for help. I told her no, but told her she could spend the night. She took off while I was sleeping. But she left a note for you." He looked as though he wanted to sort through the diaper bag to find it, but before he leaned down he held the baby out to Maresa. "Here. Take her."

Maresa wasn't even sure she'd made up her mind to do so when Jaden thrust the warm, precious weight into her arms. He was still talking about Trina seeming "unstable" ever since giving birth, but Maresa couldn't follow his words with an infant in her arms. She felt stiff and awkward, but she was careful to support the squirming bundle, cradling the baby against her chest while Isla gurgled and kicked.

Maresa's heart turned over. Melted.

Here, the junglelike landscaping blocked out the sun where the tree branches arced over the dirt path. The scent of green and growing things mingled with the sea breeze and a hint of baby shampoo.

"She's a beauty," Cameron observed over her shoulder. He had set Poppy on the ground so he could get closer to Isla and Maresa. "Are you okay holding her?"

"Fine," she said automatically, not wanting to give her up. "Just...um...overwhelmed."

Glancing up at him, she caught her breath at the expression on his face as he looked down at the child in her arms. She had thought he seemed different—kinder—toward Poppy. But that unguarded smile she'd seen for the Maltese was nothing compared to the warmth in his expression as he peered down at the baby.

If she didn't know better—if she hadn't seen him be rude and abrupt with perfectly nice hotel staffers—she would have guessed she caught him making silly faces at Isla. The little girl appeared thoroughly captivated.

"Here it is." Jaden straightened, a piece of paper in his hand. "She left this for you along with some notes about the kid's schedule." He passed the papers to Cameron. "I've got to get going if I'm going to catch that ferry, Maresa. I only came out here because Trina gave me no choice, but I've got to get to work—"

"Seriously?" She had to work, too. But even as she was about to say as much, another voice in her head piped up. If Isla was really Rafe's child, would she honestly want Jaden Torries in charge of the baby for another minute? The answer was a crystal clear *absolutely not*.

"Drop her off at social services if you don't believe me." Jaden shrugged. "I've got a rich old lady client paying a whole hell of a lot for me to paint her portrait at eight." He checked his watch. "I'm outta here."

And with that, her ex-fiancé walked away, his sandy-gold curls bouncing. Poppy barked again, clearly unimpressed.

Social services? Really?

"If only I had Poppy around three years ago when I got engaged to him," she muttered darkly, hugging the baby tighter.

Cameron's hand briefly found the small of her back as he watched the other man leave. He clutched the letter from Rafe's former girlfriend—Isla's mother.

"And yet you didn't go through with the wedding. So you did just fine on your own." Cameron glanced down at her, his hand lingering on her back for one heart-stopping moment before it drifted away again. "Want me to read the letter? Or would you like me to take Isla so you can do the honors?"

He held the paper out for her to decide.

She liked him better here—outside the hotel. He was less intimidating, for one thing.

For another? He was appealing to her in all the ways a man could. A dangerous feeling for her when she needed to be on her guard around him. He was a guest, for crying out loud. But she was out of her depth with this precious little girl in her arms and she didn't know what she'd do if Cameron Holmes walked away from her right now. Having him there made her feel—if only for a moment—that she wasn't totally alone.

"Actually, I'd be really grateful if you would read it." She shook her head, tightening her hold on Isla. "I'm too nervous."

Katrina—Trina—Blanchett had been Rafe's girlfriend for about six months before the car accident. Maresa had never seen them together except for photos on social media of the two of them out playing on the beach or at the clubs. They'd seemed happy enough, but Rafe had told her on the phone it wasn't serious. The night of the accident, in fact, the couple had gotten into an argument at a bar and Trina had stranded him there. Rafe had called their mother for a ride, something she'd been only too happy to provide even though it was late. She'd never had an MS attack while driving before.

Less than ten days after seeing Rafe in the hospital, Trina had told Maresa through tears that she couldn't stand seeing him that way and it would be better for her to leave. At the time, Maresa had been too focused on Rafe's prognosis to worry about his flighty girlfriend. If she'd taken more time to talk to the girl, might she have confided the pregnancy news that followed the breakup?

"Would you like to have a seat?" Cameron pointed toward a bench near the outdoor faucet where guests could rinse off their feet. "You look too pale."

She nodded, certain she was pale. What was her mother going to say when she found out Rafe had a daughter? If he had a daughter. And Rafe? She couldn't imagine how frustrated he would feel to have been left out of the whole experience. Then again, how frustrated would he feel knowing that he couldn't care for his daughter the way he could have at one time?

Struggling to get her spinning thoughts under control, she allowed Cameron to guide her to the bench. Carefully, she lowered herself to sit with Isla, the baby blanket covering her lap since the kicking little girl had mostly freed herself of the swaddling. While she settled the baby, she noticed Cameron lift Poppy and towel her off a bit more before setting her down again. He double-checked the leash clip on her collar then took the seat beside Maresa.

"I'm ready," she announced, needing to hear whatever Isla's mother had to say.

Cameron unfolded the paper and read aloud. "'Isla is Rafe's daughter. I wasn't with anyone else while we were together. I was afraid to tell him about her after the doctor said he'd be...'" Cameron hesitated for only a moment "'...brain damaged. I know Rafe can't take care of her, but his mother will love her, right? I can't do this. I'm going to see my dad in Florida for a few weeks, but I'll sign papers to give you custody. I'm sorry."

Maresa listened to the silence following the words, her brain uncomprehending. How could the woman just take off and leave her baby—Rafe's baby—with Jaden Torries while she traveled to Florida? Who did that? Trina wasn't a kid—she was twenty-one when she'd dated Rafe. But she'd never had much family support, according to Rafe. Her mother was an alcoholic and her father had raised her, but he'd never paid her much attention.

A fierce surge of protectiveness swelled inside of Maresa. It was so strong she didn't know where to put it all. But she knew for damn sure that she would protect little Isla—her niece—far better than the child's mother had. And she would call a lawyer and find out how to file for full custody.

"You could order DNA testing," Cameron observed, his impressive abs rippling as he leaned forward on the bench. "If you are concerned she's not a biological relative."

Maresa closed her eyes for a moment to banish all thoughts of male abs, no matter how much she welcomed the distraction from the monumental life shift taking place for her this morning.

"I'll ask an attorney about it when I call to find out how I can secure legal custody." She wrapped Isla's foot back in a corner of the blanket. "For right now, I need to find suitable care for Isla before my shift at the Carib begins for the day." Throat burning, Maresa realized she was near tears just thinking about the unfairness of it all. Not to *her*, of course, because she would make it work no matter what life threw at her.

But how unfair to *Rafe*, who wouldn't be able to parent his child without massive amounts of help. Perhaps he wouldn't be interested in parenting at all. Would he be angry? Would Trina's surprise be the kind of thing that unsettled his confused mind and set back his recovery?

She would call his counselor before saying anything to him. That call would be right after she spoke to a lawyer. She wasn't even ready to tell her mother yet. Analise Delphine's health was fragile and stress could aggravate it. Maresa wanted to be sure she was calm before she spoke to her mother. They'd all been in the dark for months about Trina's pregnancy. A few more hours wouldn't matter one way or another.

"I noticed on the dog walker's résumé that she has experience working in a day care." Cameron folded the paper from Trina and inserted it into an exterior pocket of the diaper bag. "And as it happens, I already walked the dog. Would you like me to text her and ask her to meet you somewhere in the hotel to give you a hand?"

Maresa couldn't imagine what that would cost. But what were her options since she didn't want to upset her mother? She didn't have time to return home and give the baby to her mother even if she was sure her mother could handle the shocking news.

"That would be a great help, thank you. The caregiver can meet me in the women's locker room by the pool in twenty minutes." Shooting to her feet, Maresa realized she'd imposed on Cameron Holmes's kindness for far too long. "And with that, I'll let you and Poppy get back to your morning walk."

"I'll go with you. I can carry the baby gear." He reached for the pink diaper bag, but she beat him to it.

"I'm fine. I insist." She pasted on her best concierge smile and tried not to think about how comforting it had felt to have him by her side this morning. Now more than ever, she needed job security, which meant she couldn't let an important guest think she made a habit of bringing her personal life to work. "Enjoy your day, Mr. Holmes."

Enjoying his day proved impossible with visions of Maresa Delphine's pale face circling around Cameron's head the rest of the morning. He worked at his laptop on the private terrace off his room, distracted as hell thinking about the beautiful, efficient concierge caught off guard by a surprise that would have damn near leveled anyone else.

She'd inherited her brother's baby. A brother who, from the sounds of it, was not in any condition to care for his child himself.

Sunlight glinted off the sea and the sounds from the beach floated up to his balcony. The noises had grown throughout the morning from a few circling gulls to the handful of vacationing families that now populated the beach. The scent of coconut sunscreen and dense floral vegetation swirled on the breeze. But the temptation of a tropical paradise didn't distract Cam from his work nearly as much as memories of his morning with Maresa.

Shocking encounter with the baby aside, he would still have been distracted just remembering her limber arched back, her beautiful curves outlined by the light of the rising sun when he'd first broken through the dense undergrowth to find her on the private beach. Her skimpy workout gear had skimmed her hips and breasts, still tantalizing the hell out of him when he was supposed to be researching the operations hierarchy of the Carib Grand on his laptop.

But then, all that misplaced attraction got funneled into protectiveness when he'd met her sketchy former fiancé. He'd met the type before—charming enough, but completely self-serving. The guy couldn't have come up with a kinder way to inform her of her niece's existence?

On the plus side, Cameron had located some search results about her brother. Rafe Delphine had worked at the hotel for one month in a hire that some might view as unethical given his relationship to Maresa. But his application—though light on work history—had been approved by the hotel director on-site, so the young man must be fit for the job despite his injury in a car wreck the year before. That, too, had been an easy internet search, with local news articles reporting the crash and a couple of updates on Rafe's condition afterward. The trauma the guy had suffered must have been harrowing for his whole family. Clearly the girlfriend had found it too much to handle.

Now, as a runner for the concierge, Rafe would be directly under Maresa's supervision. That concerned Cameron since Maresa would have every reason in the world to keep him employed. As much as Cam empathized with her situation—all the more now that she'd discovered her brother had an heir—he couldn't afford to ignore good business practices. He'd have to speak to the hotel director about the situation and see if they should make a change.

The ex-fiancé was next on his list of searches. Not that he wanted to pry into Maresa's private life. Cameron was more interested in seeing how the guy connected to the Carib Grand that he'd come all the way to the hotel's private island to pass over the baby. That seemed like an unnecessary trip unless he was staying here or worked here. Why not just give the baby to Maresa at her home in Charlotte Amalie? Why come to her place of work when it was so far out of the way?

Cam had skimmed halfway through the short search results on Jaden Torries's portraits of people and pets before his phone buzzed with an incoming call. Poppy, snoozing in the shade of the chair under his propped feet, didn't even stir at the sound. The dog was definitely making up for lost rest from the day before.

Glimpsing his oldest brother's private number, Cam hit the button to connect the call. "Talk to me."

"Hello to you, too." Quinn's voice came through along with the sounds of Manhattan in the background—horns honking, brakes squealing, a shrill whistle and a few shouts above the hum of humanity indicating he must be on the street. "I wanted to give you a heads-up I just bought a sea plane."

"Nice, bro, But there's no way you'll get clearance to land in the Hudson with that thing." Cameron scrolled to a gallery of Torries's work and was decidedly unimpressed.

Not that he was an expert. But as a supporter of the arts in Manhattan for all his adult life, he felt reasonably sure Maresa's ex was a poser. Then again, maybe he just didn't like a guy who'd once commanded the concierge's attention.

"The aircraft isn't for me," Quinn informed him. "It's for you. I figured it would be easier than a chopper to get from one island to another while you're investigating the Carib Grand and checking out the relatives."

Cam shoved aside his laptop and straightened. "Seriously? You bought a seaplane for my two-week stay?"

As a McNeill, he'd grown up with wealth, yes. He'd even expanded his holdings with the success of the gaming development company he'd started in college. But damn. He limited himself to spending within reason.

"The Carib Grand is the start of our Caribbean expansion, and if it goes well, we'll be spending a lot of time and effort developing the McNeill brand in the islands and South America. We have a plane available in the Mediterranean. Why not keep something accessible on this side of the Atlantic?"

"Right." Cam's jaw flexed at the thought of how much was riding on smoothing things out at the Carib Grand. A poor bottom line wasn't going to help the expansion program. "Good thinking."

"Besides, I have the feeling we'll be seeing our half brothers in Martinique a whole lot more now that Gramps is determined to bring them into the fold." Quinn sounded as grim about that prospect as Cameron felt. "So the plane might be useful for all of us as we try to…contain the situation."

Quinn wanted to keep their half siblings out of Manhattan and out of the family business as much as Cameron did. They'd worked too hard to hand over their company to people who'd never lifted a finger to grow McNeill Resorts.

"Ah." Cam stood to stretch his legs, surprised to realize it was almost noon according to the slim dive watch he'd worn for his morning laps. "But since I'm on the front line meeting them, I'm going to leave it up to you or Ian to be the diplomatic peacemakers."

Quinn only half smothered a laugh. "No one expected you of all people to be the diplomat. Dad's still recovering from the punch you gave him last week when he dropped the I-have-another-family bombshell on us."

Definitely not one of his finer moments. "It seemed like he could have broached the topic with some more tact."

"No kidding. I kept waiting for Sofia to break the engagement after the latest family soap opera." The background noise on Quinn's call faded. "Look, Cam, I just arrived at Lincoln Center to take her out to lunch. I'll text you the contact details for a local pilot."

Cam grinned at the thought of his stodgy older brother

so head over heels for his ballerina fiancée. The same ballerina fiancée Cam had impulsively proposed to last winter when a matchmaker set them up. But even if Cam and Sofia hadn't worked out, the meeting had been a stroke of luck for Quinn, who'd promptly stepped in to woo the dancer.

"Thanks. And give our girl a kiss from me, okay?" It was too fun to resist needling Quinn. Especially since Cameron was two thousand miles away from a retaliatory beat-down.

A string of curses peppered his ear before Quinn growled, "It's not too late to take the plane back."

"Sorry." Cameron wasn't sorry. He was genuinely happy for his brother. "I'll let you know if the faux McNeills are every bit as awful as we imagine."

Disconnecting the call, Cameron texted a message to the dog groomer to give Poppy some primp time. He'd use that window of freedom to follow up on a few leads around the Carib Grand. He wanted to find out what the hotel director thought about Rafe Delphine, for one thing. The director was the only person on-site who knew Cameron's true identity and mission at the hotel. Aldo Ricci had been successful at McNeill properties in the Mediterranean and Malcolm McNeill had personally appointed the guy to make the expansion program a success.

With the McNeill patriarch's health so uncertain, Cameron wanted to respect his grandfather's choices. All the more so since he still hadn't married the way his granddad wanted.

Cameron would start by speaking to his grandfather's personally chosen manager. Cam had a lot of questions about the day-to-day operations and a few key personnel. Most especially the hotel's new concierge, who kept too many secrets behind her beautiful and efficient facade.

Three

Seated in the hotel director's office shortly after noon, Cameron listened to Aldo Ricci discuss his plans for making the Carib Grand more profitable over the next two quarters. Unlike Cameron, the celebrated hotel director with a crammed résumé of successes did not seem concerned about the dip in the Carib Grand's performance.

"All perfectly normal," the impeccably dressed director insisted, prowling around his lavish office on the ground floor of the property. A collector of investment-grade wines, Aldo incorporated a few rare vintages into his office decor. A Bordeaux from Moulin de La Lagune rested casually on a shelf beside some antique corkscrews and a framed invitation from a private tasting at Château Grand Corbin. "We are only beginning to notice the minute fluctuations now that our capacity for data is greater than ever. But those irregularities will not even be noticeable by the time we hit our performance and profit goals for the end of the year."

The heavyset man tugged on his perfectly straight suit cuffs. The fanciness of the dark silk jacket he wore reminded Cameron how many times the guy had taken a property out of the red and into the ranks of the most prestigious places in the world. To have enticed him to McNeill Resorts had been a coup, according to Cameron's grandfather.

"Nevertheless, I'd like to know more about Maresa Delphine." Cameron didn't reveal his reasons. He could see her now through the blinds in the director's office. She strode along the pool patio outside, hurrying past the patrons in her creamy linen blazer with an orchid at the lapel. Her sun-splashed brown hair gleamed in the bright light, but something about her posture conveyed her tension. Worry.

Was she thinking about Isla?

He made a mental note to check on the sitter and be sure she was doing a good job with the baby. Little Isla had tugged at his heartstrings this morning with her tiny, restless hands and her expressive face. That feeling—the warmth for the baby—shocked him. Not that he was an ogre or anything, but he'd decided long ago not to have kids of his own.

He was too much like his father—impulsive, fun-loving, easily distracted—to be a parent. After all, Liam McNeill had turfed out responsibility for his sons at the first possible opportunity, letting the boys' grandfather raise them the moment Liam's Brazilian wife got tired of his globe-trotting, daredevil antics. Cameron had always known his father had shirked the biggest responsibility of his life and that, coupled with his own tendency to follow his own drummer, had been enough to convince Cam that kids weren't for him. And that had been before discovering his dad had fathered a whole other set of kids with someone else.

Before an accident that had compromised Cameron's ability to have a family anyhow.

"Maresa Delphine is a wonderful asset to the hotel," the director assured him, coming around to the front of his desk to sit beside Cameron in the leather club chairs facing the windows. "If you seek answers about the hotel workings, I urge you to reveal your identity to her. I know you want to remain incognito, but I assure you, Ms. Delphine is as discreet and professional as they come."

"Yet you've only known her for…what? Two months?"

"Far longer than that. She worked at another property in Saint Thomas where I supervised her three years ago. I personally recommended her to a five-star property in Paris because I was impressed with her work and she was eager to…escape her hometown for a while. I had no reservations about helping her win the spot. She makes her service her top priority." The director crossed one leg over the other and pointed to a crystal decanter on the low game table between them. "Are you sure I can't offer you anything to drink?"

"No. Thank you." He wanted a clear head for deciding his next move with Maresa. Revealing himself to her was tempting considering the attraction simmering just beneath the surface. But he couldn't forget about the gut instinct that told him she was hiding something. "What can you tell me about her brother?"

"Rafe is a fine young man. I would have gladly hired him even without Maresa's assurances she would watch over him."

"Why would she need to?" He was genuinely curious

about the extent of Rafe's condition. Not only because she seemed protective of him, but also because Maresa hadn't argued Trina's depiction of her brother as "brain damaged."

"Rafe has a traumatic brain injury. He's the reason Maresa gave up the job in Paris. She rushed home to take care of her family. The young man is much better now. Although he can become agitated or confused easily, he has good character, and we haven't put him in a position where he will have much contact with guests." Aldo smiled as he smoothed his tie. "Maresa feels a strong sense of responsibility for him. But I've seen no reason to regret hiring her sibling. She knows, however, that Rafe's employment is on a trial basis."

Aldo Ricci seemed like the kind of man to trust his gut, which might be fine for someone who'd been in the business for as long as he had, but Cameron still wondered if he was overlooking things.

Maybe he should confide in Maresa if only to discover her take on the staff at the Carib Grand. Specifically, he wondered, what was her impression of Aldo Ricci? Cameron found himself wanting to know a lot more about the operations of the hotel.

"Perhaps I will speak to Ms. Delphine." Cameron wanted to find her now, in fact. His need to see her has been growing ever since she'd walked away from him early that morning. "I'd like some concrete answers about those performance reviews, even if they do seem like minute fluctuations."

He rose from his seat, liking the new plan more than he should. *Damn it.* Spending more time with Maresa didn't mean anything was going to happen between them. As her boss, of course, he had a responsibility to ensure it didn't.

And, without question, she had a great deal on her

mind today of all days. But maybe that was all the more reason to give her a break from the concierge stand. Perhaps she'd welcome a few hours away from the demands of the guests.

"Certainly." The hotel director followed him to the door. "There's no one more well-versed in the hotel except for me." His grin revealed a mouth full of shiny white veneers. "Stick close to her."

Cameron planned to do just that.

"Have you seen Rafe?" Maresa asked Nancy, the waitress who worked in the lobby bar shortly after noon. "I wanted to eat lunch with him."

Standing beside Nancy, a tall blonde goddess of a woman who probably made more in tips each week than Maresa made in a month, she peered out over the smattering of guests enjoying cocktails and the view. Her brother was nowhere in sight.

She had checked on Isla a few moments ago, assuring herself the baby was fine. She'd shared Trina's notes about the baby's schedule with the caregiver, discovering Isla's birth certificate with the father's name left blank and a birth date of ten weeks prior. And after placing a call to Trina's mother, Maresa had obtained contact information for the girl's father in Florida, who'd been able to give her a number for Trina herself. The girl had tearfully confirmed everything she said in her note—promising to give custody of the child to Rafe's family since she wasn't ready to be a mother and she didn't trust her own mother to be a good guardian.

The young woman had been so distraught, Maresa had felt sorry for her. All the more so because Trina had tried to handle motherhood alone when she'd been so conflicted about having a baby in the first place.

Now, Maresa wanted to see Rafe for herself to make sure he was okay. What if Jaden had mentioned Isla to him? Or even just mentioned Trina leaving town? Rafe hadn't asked about his girlfriend since regaining consciousness. She suspected Rafe would have been walking onto the ferry that morning the same time as Jaden was walking off.

Earlier that day, she'd left him a to-do list when she'd had an appointment to keep with the on-site restaurant's chef. She'd given Rafe only two chores, and they were both jobs he'd done before so she didn't think he'd have any trouble. He had to pick up some supplies at the gift shop and deliver flowers to one of the guests' rooms.

"I saw him about an hour ago." Nancy rang out a customer's check. "He brought me this." She pointed to the tiny purple wildflowers stuffed behind the engraved silver pin with her name on it. "He really is the sweetest."

"Thank you for being so kind to him." Maresa had witnessed enough people be impatient and rude to him that he'd become her barometer for her measure of a person. People who were nice to Rafe earned her respect.

"Kind to *him*?" Nancy tossed her head back and laughed, her long ponytail swishing. "That boy should earn half my tips since it's Rafe who makes me smile when I feel like strangling some of my more demanding customers—like that Mr. Holmes." She straightened the purple blooms with one hand and shoved the cash drawer closed with her hip. "These flowers from your brother are the nicest flowers any man has ever given me."

Reassured for the moment, Maresa felt her heart squeeze at the words. Her brother had the capacity for great love despite the frustrations of his injury. Maybe he'd come to accept his daughter as part of his life down the road.

Until then, she needed to keep them both safely employed and earning benefits to take care of their family.

"It makes me happy to hear you say that." Maresa turned on her heel, leaving Nancy to her job. "If you see him, will you let him know I'm having lunch down by the croquet field?"

"Sure thing." Nancy lifted a tray full of drinks to take to another table. "Sometimes he hangs out in the break room if the Yankees are on the radio, you know. You might check if they play today."

"Okay. Thanks." She knew her brother liked listening to games on the radio. Being able to listen on his earbuds was always soothing for him.

Maresa hitched her knapsack with the insulated cooler onto her shoulder to carry out to the croquet area. The field didn't officially open again until late afternoon when it cooled down, so no one minded if employees sat under the palm trees there for lunch. There were a handful of places like that on the private island—spots where guests didn't venture that workers could enjoy. She needed a few minutes to collect herself. Come up with a plan for what she was going to do with a ten-week-old infant after work. And what she would tell Rafe about the baby since his counselor hadn't yet returned her phone call.

Her phone vibrated just then as her sandals slapped along the smooth stone path dotted with exotic plantings on both sides. Her mother's number filled the screen.

"Mom?" she answered quietly while passing behind the huge pool and cabanas that surrounded it. The area was busy with couples enjoying outdoor meals or having cocktails at the swim-up bar and families playing in the nearby surf. Seeing a mother share a bite of fresh pineapple with her little girl made Maresa's breath catch.

She'd once dreamed of being a mother to Jaden's children until he betrayed her.

Now, she might be a single mother to her brother's baby if Trina truly relinquished custody.

She scuttled deeper into the shade of some palms for her phone conversation, knowing she couldn't blurt out Isla's existence to her mom on the phone even though, in the days before her mother's health had taken a downhill spiral, she might have been tempted to do just that.

"No need to worry." Her mother's breathing sounded labored. From stress? Or exertion? She tired so easily over the past few months. "I just wanted to let you know your brother came home."

Maresa's steps faltered. Stopped.

"Rafe is there? With you?" Panic tightened her shoulders and clenched her gut. She peered around the path to the croquet field, half hoping her brother would come strolling toward her anyhow, juggling some pilfered deck cushions for her to sit on for an impromptu picnic the way he did sometimes.

"He showed up about ten minutes ago. I would have called sooner, but he was upset and I had to calm him down. I guess the florist gave him a pager—"

"Oh no." Already, Maresa could guess what had happened. "Those are really loud." The devices vibrated and blinked, setting off obnoxious alarms that would startle anyone, let alone someone with nervous tendencies. The floral delivery must not have been prepared when Rafe arrived to pick it up, so they gave him the pager to let him know when it was ready.

"He got scared and dropped it, but I'm not sure where—" Her mother stopped speaking, and in the background, Maresa heard Rafe shouting "I don't know, I don't know, I don't know" in a frightened chorus.

Her gut knotted. How could she bring a ten-week-old into their home tonight, knowing how loud noises upset her brother?

"Tell him everything's fine. I'll find the pager." Turning on her heel, she headed back toward the hotel. She thought the device turned itself off after a few minutes anyhow, but just in case it was still beeping, she'd rather find it before anyone else on staff. "I can probably retrace his steps since I sent him on those errands. I'll deliver the flowers myself."

"Honey, you're taking on too much having him there with you. You don't want to risk your job."

And the alternative? They didn't have one. Especially now with little Isla's care to consider.

"My job will be fine," she reassured her mother as she tugged open a door marked Employees Only that led to the staff room and corporate offices. She needed to sign Rafe out for the day before she did anything else.

Blinking against the loss of sunlight, Maresa felt the blast of air conditioning hit her skin, which had gone clammy with nervous sweat. She picked at the neckline of her thin silk camisole beneath her linen jacket.

"Ms. Delphine?" a familiar masculine voice called to her from the other end of the corridor.

Even before she turned, she knew who she would see. The tingling that tripped over her skin was an unsettling mix of anticipation and dread.

"Mom, I'll call you back." Disconnecting quickly, she dropped the phone in her purse and turned to see Cameron Holmes striding out of the hotel director's office, her boss at his side.

"Mr. Holmes." She forced a smile for both men, wondering why life was conspiring so hard against her today. What on earth would a guest be doing in the hotel director's office if not to complain? Unless maybe he had something extremely valuable he wanted to place in the hotel safe personally.

Highly unorthodox, but that's the only other reason she could think of to explain his presence here.

"Maresa." Her hotel director nodded briefly at her before shaking hands with Cameron Holmes. "And sir, I appreciate you coming to me directly. I certainly understand the need for discretion."

Aldo Ricci turned and re-entered his office, leaving Maresa with a racing heart in the presence of Cameron Holmes, who looked far more intimidating in a custom navy silk suit and a linen shirt open at the throat than he had in his board shorts this morning.

The level of appeal, however, seemed equal on both counts. She couldn't forget his unexpected kindness on the beach no matter how demanding he'd been as a hotel guest.

"Just the woman I was hoping to see." His even white teeth made a quick appearance in what passed for a smile. "Would you join me for a moment in the conference room?"

No.

Her brain filled in the answer even as her feet wisely followed where he led. She didn't want to be alone with him anywhere. Not when she entertained completely inappropriate thoughts about him. She couldn't let her attraction to a guest show.

Furthermore? She needed to sign her brother out of work, locate the pager he'd lost and deliver those flowers before the florist got annoyed and reported Rafe for not doing his job. Now was not the time for fantasizing about a wealthy guest who could afford to shape the world to his liking, even if he had the body of a professional surfer underneath that expensive suit.

As she crossed the threshold into the Carib Grand's private conference room full of tall leather chairs around an antique table, Maresa realized she couldn't do this. Not now.

"Actually, Mr. Holmes," she said, spinning around to face him and misjudging how close he followed behind her.

Suddenly, she stood nose-to-nose with him, her thigh grazing his, her breast brushing his strong arm. She stepped back fast, heat flooding her cheeks. The contact was so brief, she could almost tell herself it hadn't happened, except that her body hummed with awareness where they'd touched.

And then, there was the fact that he gripped her elbow when she wobbled.

"Sorry," she blurted, tugging away from him completely as the door to the conference room closed automatically behind them.

Sealing them in privacy.

Sunlight spilled in behind her, the Caribbean sun the only illumination in the room that hadn't been in use yet today. The quiet was deep here, the carpet muffling his step as he shifted closer.

"Are you all right?" His forehead creased with concern. "Are you comfortable with the caregiver for Isla?"

She glanced up at him, surprised at the thoughtful question. He really had been supportive this morning, giving her courage during an impossible situation. Right now, however, it was difficult to focus on his kind side when the man was simply far too handsome. She wished fervently he had that adorable little dog with him so she could pet Poppy instead of thinking about how hot Mr. Holmes could be when he wasn't scowling.

"I'm fine. I have everything under control." *Um, if*

only. Clearly, she needed to date more often so she didn't turn into a babbling idiot around handsome men during work hours. "It's just that you caught me on my lunch hour, so I'm not technically working."

"Unfortunately, Maresa, I am." He folded his arms across his chest before he paced halfway across the room.

Confused, she watched him. He was not an easy man to look away from.

"I don't understand." She wondered how it happened that being around him made her feel like there wasn't enough air in the room. Like she couldn't possibly catch her breath.

"I'm doing some work for the hotel," he explained, pacing back toward her. "Secretly."

Confusion filled her as she tried to sort through his words that didn't make a bit of sense.

"So you're not actually on vacation at all? What kind of work?" She could think better now that he was on the opposite side of the room. "Is that why you were in the hotel director's office?"

"Yes. My real name is Cameron McNeill and I'm investigating why guest satisfaction has been declining over the last two months." He kept coming toward her, his blue eyes zeroing in on her. "And now I'm beginning to think you're the only person who can help me figure out why."

Cameron could feel her nervousness as clearly as if it was his own.

She stood, alert and ready to flee, her tawny eyes wide. She bit her full lower lip.

"McNeill? As in McNeill Resorts?" She blinked slowly.

"The same."

"Why do you think I can help you?" She smoothed the

cuff of her ivory-colored linen jacket and then swiped elegant fingers along her forehead as if perspiring in spite of the fact she looked cool. So incredibly smooth and cool.

He hated doing this to her today of all days. The woman had just found out her brother had a child who would—he suspected—become her financial and familial dependent. What he'd gathered about Rafe Delphine's health suggested the man wouldn't be in any position to care for a newborn, and Aldo Ricci had made it clear Maresa put her family before herself.

"Preliminary data indicates the Carib is floundering in performance reviews and customer satisfaction." That was true enough. "You have a unique perspective on the hotel and everyone who works here. I'd like to know your views on why that might be?"

"And my boss told you I would talk to you about those issues?" Her gaze flitted to the door behind him and then back to him as if she would rather be anywhere else than right here.

Truth be told, he was a little uncomfortable being alone with her under these circumstances himself. She was far too tempting to question in the privacy of an empty conference room when the attraction was like a live wire sending sparks in all directions.

How could he ignore that?

"Your hotel director assured me you would be discreet."

She'd garnered the respect of her peers. The praise of superiors. All of which only made Cameron more curious about her. He stopped in front of her. At a respectable distance. He held her gaze, not allowing his eyes to wander.

"Of course, Mr. McNeill." She fidgeted with a bracelet—a shiny silver star charm—partially hidden by the sleeve of her jacket. "But what exactly did he hope I could share with you?"

"Call me Cam. And I hope you will share any insights about the staff and even some of the guests." He knew the data could be skewed by one or two unhappy visitors, particularly if they were vocal about their displeasure with the hotel.

"A difficult line to walk considering how much a concierge needs to keep her guests happy. It doesn't serve me—or McNeill Resorts—to betray confidences of valued clients."

Cameron couldn't help the voice in his head that piped up just then, wanting to know what she might have done to keep *him* happy as her guest.

Focus, damn it.

"And yet, you'll want to please the management as well," he reminded her. "Correct?"

"Of course." She nodded, letting go of the silver star so the bracelet slipped lower on her wrist.

"So how about if I buy you lunch and we'll begin our work together? I'll speak to Mr. Ricci about giving you the afternoon off." He needed to take her somewhere else. A place where the temptation to touch her wouldn't get the better of him. "We can bring Isla."

Nothing stifled attraction like an infant, right?

"Thank you, Mr. Mc—er, Cam." Maresa's face lit up with a glow that damn near took his breath away; her relief and eagerness to be reunited with the little girl were all too obvious. "That would be really wonderful."

Her pleasure affected him far more than it should, making him wonder how he could make that smile return to her face again and again. Had he really thought a baby would dull his desire for Maresa?

Not a chance.

Four

"You rented a villa here," Maresa observed as she held the ends of her hair in one hand to keep it from flying away in the open-top Jeep Cameron McNeill used for tooling around the private island. "In addition to the hotel suite."

The Jeep bounced down a long road through the lush foliage to a remote part of the island. In theory, she knew about the private villas that the Carib Grand oversaw on the extensive property, but the guests who took those units had their own staff so she didn't see them often and she'd never toured them. She turned in her seat to peer back at Isla, in the car seat she'd procured from the hotel. The baby faced backward with a sunshade tilted over the seat, but Maresa could see the little girl was still snoozing contentedly.

The caregiver had fed and changed her, and before Maresa could compensate her, Cameron had taken care of

the bill, insisting that he make the day as easy as possible
for Maresa to make up for the inconvenience of working
with him. Spending the day in a private villa with yet another caregiver—this one a licensed nurse from the hospital in Saint Thomas who would meet them there—was
hardly an inconvenience. Truth be told, she was grateful
to escape the hotel for the day after the stress of discovering Isla and finding out that Rafe had left work without
authorization. Luckily, she'd signed him out due to illness
and found the pager he dropped on her way to pick up
Isla from the caregiver. Maresa had assigned the flower
delivery to another runner before leaving.

Now, all she had to do was get through an afternoon
with her billionaire boss who'd only been impersonating
a pain-in-the-butt client. But what if Cameron McNeill
turned out to be even more problematic than his prede-
cessor, Mr. Holmes?

"The villas are managed by a slightly different branch
of the company," Cameron informed her, using a remote
to open a heavy wrought-iron gate that straddled the road
ahead. "My privacy is protected here. I'll return to the
hotel suite later tonight to continue my investigation work
under Mr. Holmes's name. Unless, of course, you and I
can figure out the reason behind the declining reviews
before then."

The ocean breeze whipped another strand of Maresa's hair free from where she'd been holding it, the wavy
lock tickling against her cheek and teasing along her
lips. What was it about Cameron's physical presence that
made her so very aware of her own? She'd never felt so on
edge around Jaden even when they'd been wildly in love.
Cameron's nearness made her feel…anxious. Expectant.

"From my vantage point, everything has been running smoothly at the Carib." Maresa didn't need a poor performance review. What if Cameron McNeill thought that the real reason for the declining ratings was her? A concierge could make or break a customer's experience of any hotel. Maybe this meeting with the boss wasn't to interview her so much as to interrogate her.

But damn it, she knew her performance had been exemplary.

"We'll figure it out, one way or another," Cameron assured her as the Jeep climbed a small hill and broke through a cluster of trees.

The most breathtaking view imaginable spread out before her. She gasped aloud.

"Oh wow." She shook her head at the sparkling expanse of water lapping against White Shoulders Beach below them. On the left, the villa sat at the cliff's edge, positioned so that the windows, balconies and infinity pool all faced the stunning view. "I grew up here, and still—you never grow immune to this."

"I can see why." He pulled the Jeep into a sheltered parking bay beside a simple silver Ford sedan. "It looks like the sitter has already arrived. We can get Isla settled inside with some air conditioning and then get to work."

Unfastening her gaze from the view of Saint John's in the distance, and a smattering of little islands closer by, Maresa turned to take in the villa. The Aerie was billed as the premiere private residence on the island; she thought she recalled the literature saying it was almost twenty thousand square feet. It was a palatial home decorated in the Mediterranean style. The white-sashed stucco and deep bronze roof tiles were an understated color combination, especially when accented with weathered gray doors. The landscaping dominated the home from the outside, but there were balconies everywhere to take advantage of the views.

Sliding out of the Jeep, she smoothed a hand over her windblown hair to try to prepare herself for what was no doubt the most important business meeting of her life. She couldn't allow her guard to slip, not even when Cameron McNeill spared a kind smile for Baby Isla as he carefully unbuckled her from the car seat straps.

"Need any help?" she asked, stepping closer to the Jeep again.

"I've got it." He frowned slightly, reaching beneath the baby to palm her head in his big hand. He supported her back with his forearm, cradling her carefully until he had her tucked against his chest. "There." He grinned over at Maresa. "Just like carrying a football. You take the fall yourself before you fumble."

"Ideally, there's no falling involved for anyone." She knew he was teasing, but she wondered if she should have offered to carry Isla just the same.

She couldn't deny she was a bit overwhelmed, though. She didn't know much about babies, and now she would be lobbying for primary custody of Rafe's little girl, even if Trina changed her mind. Maresa knew Rafe would have wanted to exercise his parental rights, and she would do that in his place. Still, it was almost too much to get her brain around in just a few hours, and she had no one she could share the news with outside of Rafe's counselor. Oddly, having Cameron McNeill beside her today had anchored her when she felt most unsteady, even as she knew she had to keep her guard up around him.

Half an hour later, Maresa finally managed to walk out of the makeshift nursery—a huge suite of rooms adapted for the purpose with the portable crib the hospital nurse had brought with her. The woman had packed a bag full of other baby supplies for Maresa including formula, diapers, fresh clothes and linens, a gift funded by Cameron McNeill, she'd discovered. And while Maresa understood that the man could easily afford such generosity, she couldn't afford to accept any more after this day.

Today, she told herself, was an adjustment period. Tomorrow, she would have a plan.

Clutching the baby monitor the caregiver had provided, Maresa followed the scent of grilled meat toward the patio beside the pool. A woman in a white tuxedo shirt and crisp black pants bustled through the kitchen, her blond ponytail bobbing with her step. She nodded toward the French doors leading outside.

"Mr. McNeill said to tell you he has drinks ready right out here, unless you'd like to swim first, in which case there are suits in the bathhouse." She pointed to the left where a small cabana sat beside a gazebo.

"Thank you." Maresa's gaze flicked over the food the woman was assembling on the kitchen island—tiny appetizers with flaked fish balanced on thin slices of mango and endive, bright red crabmeat prepped for what looked like a shellfish soup and chopped vegetables for a conch salad. "It all looks delicious."

Her stomach growled with a reminder of how long it had been since her usual lunch hour had come and gone. Now, stepping outside onto the covered deck, Maresa spotted Cameron seated at a table beneath the gazebo, a bottled water in hand as he stared down at his laptop screen. Tropical foliage in colorful clay pots dotted the deck. The weathered teak furniture topped by thick cream-colored cushions was understated enough to let the view shine more than the decor. The call of birds and the distant roll of waves on the beach provided the kind of soundtrack other people piped in using a digital play-list in order to relax.

Seeing her, Cameron stood. The practice wasn't un-common in formal business meetings, and happened more often when she'd worked in Europe. But the ges-ture here, in this private place, felt more intimate since it was for her alone.

Or maybe she was simply too preoccupied with her boss.

"Did you find everything you needed?" he asked, tug-ging off the aviators he'd been wearing to set them on the graying teak table.

It was cool in the shade of the pergola threaded with bright pink bougainvillea, yet just being close to him made her skin warm. Her gaze climbed his tall height, stalling on his well-muscled shoulders before reaching his face. She took in the sculpted jaw and ice-blue eyes before shifting her focus to his lips. She hadn't kissed a man since her broken engagement.

A fact she hadn't thought about even once until right this moment.

"I'm fine," she blurted awkwardly, remembering she was there to work and not to catalog the finer masculine traits of the man whose family owned the company she worked for. "Ready to work."

Beneath the table, a dog yapped happily.

Maresa glanced down to see Poppy standing on a bright magenta dog bed. Beside the bed, a desk fan os-cillated back and forth, blowing through the dog's long white fur at regular intervals.

"Hello, Poppy." She leaned down to greet the fluffy pooch. "That's quite a setup you have there." She let the dog sniff her hand for a moment before she scratched behind the ears, not sure if Poppy would remember her.

"I had the dog walker pick up a few things to be sure she was comfortable. Plus, with a baby in the house, I thought she might be…you know. Jealous."

She looked up in time to see him shrug as if it was the most natural thought in the world to consider if his dog would be envious of an infant guest.

"That's adorable." She knew then that the Cameron Holmes character she'd met the day before had been all for show. Cameron McNeill was another man entirely. Although his jaw tightened at the "adorable" remark. She hurried to explain. "I mean, the dog bed and all of Poppy's matching accessories. Your mom found a lot of great things to coordinate the wardrobe."

Maresa rose to her feet, knowing she couldn't use the pup as a barrier all day.

"Actually, I borrowed Poppy from my brother's administrative assistant." He gestured to the seat beside him and turned the laptop to give her a better view. "I figured a fussy white show dog was a good way to test the patience and demeanor of the hotel staff. But I'll admit, she isn't nearly as uptight as I imagined." He patted the animal's head; the Maltese was rubbing affectionately against his ankles while he talked about her. "She's pretty great."

Coming around to his side of the table, Maresa took the seat he indicated. Right beside him. He'd changed into more casual clothes since she'd last seen him, his white cotton T-shirt only slightly dressed up by a pair of khakis and dark loafers. He wore some kind of brightly colored socks—aqua and purple—at odds with the rest of his outfit.

"The Carib is pet friendly, but I understand why you thought there might be pushback on demands like natural grass for the room." She glanced down at the laptop to see he'd left open a series of graphs with performance rankings for the Carib.

The downturn in the past two months was small, but noticeable.

"Ryegrass only," he reminded her. "I don't enjoy being tough on the staff, but I figured that playing undercover boss for a week or two would still be quicker and less painful for them than if I hire an independent agency to do a thorough review of operations."

"Of course." She gestured to the laptop controls. "May I look through this?"

At his nod, Maresa clicked on links and scrolled through the files related to the hotel's performance. Clearly, Cameron had been doing his homework, making margin notes throughout the document about the operations. Her name made frequent appearances, including a reference to an incident of misplaced money by a guest the week before.

"I remember this." Maresa's finger paused on the comment from a post-visit electronic survey issued to the guest. "An older couple reported that their travelers' checks had gone missing during a trip to the beach." She glanced up to see Cameron bent over the screen to read the notes, his face unexpectedly close to hers.

"The guy left the money in his jacket on the beach. It was gone when he returned." Cameron nodded, his jaw tense. "Definitely a vacation-ruiner."

She bristled. "But not the staff's fault. Our beach employees are tasked with making sure there are pool chairs and towels. We serve drinks and even bring food down to the cabanas. But we can't police everyone's possessions."

"On a private island where everyone should either be a guest or a staff member?" he asked with a hint of censure in his voice.

"That amounts to quite a few people," she pointed out, without hesitation. "And don't forget, many of our guests feel comfortable indulging in extra cocktails while vacationing."

"A few drinks won't make you think you had a thousand dollars in your pocket when you only had ten."

"Maybe not." She thrummed her fingernails on the teak table, remembering some of the antics she'd seen on the beach. Even before her work at the Carib, she'd seen plenty of visitors to Saint Thomas behave like spring-breakers simply because they were far from home. Her father included. "However, a few drinks could make you think you put your money in your jacket when you actually had it in the pocket of the shorts you wore into the water, where you lost it while you tried to impress your trophy wife by doing backflips off a Jet Ski."

"And is that what happened in this case?" He glanced over at her, the woodsy scent of his aftershave teasing her senses.

"No." She shook her head, regretting the candid speech as much as the memory of her father's easy transition of affection from Maresa's mother to a wealthy female colleague. Today had rattled her. Her mind kept drifting back to Isla and what she would do tonight to keep her comfortable. "I'm sure it wasn't. I only meant to point out that the staff can't guard against some of the questionable decisions that guests make while vacationing."

Cam regarded her curiously. "I don't suppose your ex-fiancé has a trophy wife?"

"Jaden is still happily single from what I hear." She couldn't afford to share any more personal confidences with this man—her boss—who already knew far too much about her. To redirect their conversation, she tapped a few keys on his laptop. "These other incidents that guests wrote about on their comment forms—slow bar service, a disappointing gallery tour off-site—I assume you've looked into them?"

Both were news to her.

"The bar service, yes. The gallery tour, no. I don't suppose you know which tour they're referencing?"

"No one has asked me to arrange anything like this." She might not remember every hotel recommendation, but she certainly recalled specialty requests. "I can speak to some of the other staff members. Some guests like to ask the doormen or the waiters for their input on local sites."

"Good." He cleared a space in front of them on the table as a server came onto the patio with covered trays. "That's one of the drawbacks of maintaining a presence as a demanding guest—I can't very well quiz the staff for answers about things that happened last month."

Maresa watched as the server quickly set the table, filled their water glasses and left two platters behind along with a wine bottle in a clay pot to maintain the wine's temperature. The final thing the woman did was set out a fresh bowl of water for Poppy before she left them to their late lunch.

"I'm happy to help," Maresa told him honestly, relieved to know that the downturn in performance at the Carib was nothing tied to her work. Or her brother's. Their jobs were more important than ever with a baby to support.

"For that matter, I can't reveal the positive feedback we've received about the staff members either." Cameron lifted the wine bottle from the cooling container and inspected the label before pouring a pale white wine into her glass. "But I can tell you that Rafe received some glowing praise from a guest who referenced him by name."

"Really?" Pleased, Maresa helped herself to some of

the appetizers she'd seen inside, arranging a few extra pieces of mango beside the conch salad. "Did the guest say what he did?"

Cameron loaded his plate with ahi tuna and warm plantain chips with some kind of spicy-looking dipping sauce.

"Something about providing a 'happy escort' to the beach one day and lifting the guest's spirits by pointing out some native birds."

Rafe? Escorting a guest somewhere?

Maresa realized she'd been quiet a beat too long.

"Rafe loves birds," she replied truthfully, hating that she needed to mask her true thoughts with Cameron after he'd trusted her to give him honest feedback on the staff. "He does know a lot about the local plants and animals, too," she rushed to add. "That's one area of knowledge that his accident left untouched."

"Does it surprise you that he was escorting a guest to the beach?" Cameron studied her over his glass as he tasted the wine.

His blue eyes missed nothing.

Clearly, he would know Rafe's job description—something he'd have easy access to in his research of the performance reviews. There was no sense trying to deny it. Still, she hated feeling that she needed to defend her brother for doing a good job.

"A little," she admitted, her shoulders tense. Wary.

Before she could explain, however, a wail came through the baby monitor.

Cam hung back, unsure how to help while Maresa and the nurse caregiver discussed the baby's fretful state. Maresa held the baby close, shifting positions against her shoulder as the baby arched and squirmed.

Over half an hour after the infant's initial outburst, the

little girl still hadn't settled down. Her face was mottled and red, her hands flexing and straining, as if she fought unseen ghosts. Cam hated hearing the cries, but didn't have a clue what to offer. The woman he'd hired for the day was a nurse, after all. She would know if there was anything they needed to worry about, wouldn't she?

Still. He didn't blame Maresa for questioning her. Cameron had done some internet searches himself, one of the few things he knew to contribute.

A moment later, Maresa stepped out of the nursery and shut the door behind her, leaving Isla with Wendy. The cries continued. Poppy paced nervously outside the door.

"I should leave." Worry etched her features. She scraped back her sun-lightened curls behind one ear. "You've been so kind to help me manage my first day of caring for an infant, finding Wendy and the baby supplies, but I really can't impose any longer—"

"You are not anywhere close to an imposition." He didn't want her to leave. "I'm trying to help with Isla because I want to."

Maresa's hands fisted at her side, her whole body rigid. "She's my responsibility."

Her stubborn refusal reminded him of his oldest brother. Quinn never wanted anyone to help him either— a trait Cam respected, even when Quinn became too damn overbearing.

"You've know about her for less than twenty-four hours. Most families get nine months to prepare." He settled a hand on Maresa's shoulder, wanting to ease some of the weight she insisted on putting there.

"That doesn't make her any less my obligation." She folded her arms across her chest in a gesture that hovered between a defensive posture and an effort to hold herself together.

Another shriek from the nursery sent an answering spike of tension through Maresa; he could feel it under his fingertips. He'd have to be some kind of cretin not to respond to that. Still, he dropped his hand before he did something foolish like thread his fingers through her brown hair and soothe away the tension in her neck. Her back.

"Maybe not, but it gives you a damn good reason to accept some help until you get the legalities sorted out and come up with a game plan going forward." He extended his arms to gesture to the villa he'd taken for two weeks. "This place is going to be empty all evening once I head back to the hotel to put the Carib staffers through their paces. Stay put with Isla and the nurse. Have something to eat. Follow up with your lawyer. Poppy and I can sleep at the hotel tonight."

She shook her head. "I can't possibly accept such an offer. Even if you didn't own the company I work for, I couldn't allow you to do that."

"Ethics shouldn't rule out human kindness." Cameron wasn't going to rescind the offer because of some vague notion about what was right or proper. She needed help, damn it.

He drew her into a study down the hallway where indoor palm trees grew in a sunny corner under a series of skylights. Poppy trailed behind them, her collar jingling. Even here, the view of the water and the beach below was breathtaking. It made him want to cliff dive or wind surf. Or kiteboard.

He ground his teeth together on the last one. He hadn't been kiteboarding since the accident that ensured he'd never have children of his own. As if the universe had conspired to make sure he didn't repeat his father's mistakes.

"Is that what this is?" She stared up at him with questioning eyes. Worried. "Kindness? Because to be quite honest, this day has felt like a bit more than that, starting down at the beach this morning."

Starting yesterday for him, actually.

So he couldn't pretend not to know what she meant.

"There may be an underlying dynamic at work, yes. But that doesn't mean I can't offer to do something kind for you on an impossibly hard day." He had that ability, damn it. He wasn't totally self-absorbed. "And it's not just for you. It's for your brother, who might need more time to deal with this. And for Isla, who is clearly unhappy. Why not make their day easier, too?"

Maresa was quiet a long moment.

"What underlying dynamic?" she asked finally.

"It's not obvious?" He turned on his heel, needing a minute to weigh how much he wanted to spell things out. Go on the record. But he did, damn it. He liked this woman. He liked her fearless strength for her family, taking on their problems with more fierceness than she exercised for herself. Who took care of her? "I'm attracted to you."

He wasn't sure what kind of reaction he expected. But if he had to guess, he wouldn't have anticipated an argument.

"No." Her expression didn't change, the unflappable concierge facade in full play. "That's not possible."

There was a flash of fire in her tawny eyes, though. He'd bank on that.

"For all of my shortcomings, I'm pretty damn sure I know what attraction feels like."

"I didn't mean that. It's just—" She closed her eyes for a moment, as if she needed that time in the dark to collect her thoughts. When she opened them again, she took a deep breath. "I don't think I have the mental and emotional wherewithal to figure out what that means right now and what the appropriate response should be." She tipped two fingers to the bridge of her nose and pressed. "I can't afford to make a decision I'll regret. This job is…everything to me. And now I need it more than ever if I'm going to take proper care of Isla and my brother."

"I understand." Now that he'd admitted the attraction, he realized how strong it was, and that rattled him more than a little. He was here for business, not pleasure. "And I'm not acting on those feelings because I don't want to add to the list of things you need to worry about."

"Okay." She eyed him warily. "Thank you."

"So here's what I propose. I'm going to need your help on this project. It's important to me." He couldn't afford trouble at the Carib with so much riding on the Caribbean expansion program. The McNeills had their hands full with their grandfather's failing health and three more heirs on the horizon to vie for the family legacy. "Take a couple of days off from the hotel. Stay here with Isla and get acquainted with her while you prepare your family and plan your next steps. I'll stay at the hotel with Poppy."

"Cam—"

"No arguments." He really needed to leave her be so she could settle in and connect with the baby. He understood the crying and the newness of the situation would upset anyone, especially a woman accustomed to running things smoothly. "You can review those files I showed you earlier in more detail. I'd like your assessment of a variety of hotel personnel."

Finally, she nodded. It felt like a major victory. And no matter what he'd said about ignoring the attraction, he couldn't help but imagine what it would be like to have her agree to other things he wanted from her. Having dinner with him, for instance. Letting him taste her full lips. Feeling her soft curves beneath his palms.

"Isla and I can't thank you enough." She backed away from him and reached for the door. "I should really go check on her."

"Don't wear yourself out," he warned. "Share the duties with the nurse."

"I will." She smiled, her hand pausing on the doorknob, some of the tension sliding off her shoulders.

"And that Jeep we used to get here actually goes with the property. I'll leave the keys on the kitchen counter and have a plate sent up from the kitchen for you." He wasn't going out of his way, he told himself. It was easy enough to do that for her.

Or was he deluding himself? He wanted Maresa—pure and simple. But he knew it was more than that. Something about her drew him. Made him want to help her. He could do this much, at least, with a clear conscience. It benefitted McNeill Resorts to have her review those reports. He was simply giving her the time and space to do the job.

"But how will you get back to the hotel?"

"Poppy is ready for a walk." He could use a long trek to cool off. Remind himself why he had no business acting on what he was feeling for Maresa. "We'll take the scenic route along the beach." He held up his phone. "I'll leave my number with the keys downstairs. Call if you need anything."

"Okay." She nodded, then tipped her head to one side, her whole body going still. "Oh wow. Do you hear that?"

"What?" He listened.

"She stopped crying." Maresa looked relieved. Happy. So it was a total surprise that she burst into tears.

Five

If Maresa hadn't needed her job so badly, she would have seriously considered resigning.

Never in her life had she done anything so embarrassing as losing control in front of an employer. But the day had been too much, from start to finish. After the intense stress of listening to Isla cry for forty minutes, she'd been so relieved to hear silence reign in the nursery. The sudden shift of strong emotions had tipped something inside her.

Now, much to her extreme mortification, Cameron McNeill's arms were around her as he drew her onto a cushioned gray settee close to the door. Even more embarrassing? How much she wanted to sink into those arms and wail her heart out on his strong chest. She cried harder.

"It's okay," he assured her, his voice beside her ear and his woodsy aftershave stirring a hunger for closeness she could not afford.

"No, it's really not." She shook her head against his shoulder, telling herself to get it together.

"As your boss, I order you to stop arguing with me."

She couldn't stop a watery laugh. "I don't know what's the matter with me."

"Anyone would be overwhelmed right now." His arms tightened, drawing her closer in a way that was undeniably more comfortable. "Don't fight so damn hard. Let it out."

And for a moment, she did just that. She didn't let herself think about how deeply she'd screwed up by sobbing in his arms. She just let the emotions run through her, the whole great big unwieldy mess that her life had become. She hadn't cried like this when the doctor told her Rafe might not live. Day after day, she'd sat in that hospital and willed him to hang on and fight. Then, by the time he finally opened his eyes again, she couldn't afford to break down. She needed to be strong for him. To show him that she was fighting, too.

She'd helped him relearn to walk. Had that really been just six months ago? He'd come so far, so fast. But she knew there were limits to what he could do.

Limits to how much he could do because she willed it. She knew, in her heart, he would not be able to handle a crying baby even if she could make him understand that Isla was his. It wouldn't be right to thrust this baby into his life right now. Or fair.

She didn't need the counselor to tell her that, even though the woman had finally returned her call and left a message to come by the office in the morning. Maresa knew that the woman was trying to find a way to tell her the hard truth—this baby could upset him so much he could have a setback.

And she cried for that. For him. Because there had

been a time in Rafe's life when the birth of his daughter would have been a cause for celebration. It broke her heart that his life had to be so different now.

With one last shuddering sigh, she felt the storm inside her pass. As it eased away, leaving her drained but more at peace, Maresa became aware of the man holding her. Aware of the hard plane of his chest where her forehead rested. Of the warm skin beneath the soft cotton T-shirt that she'd soaked with her tears. Amidst all the other embarrassments of the day she was at least grateful that her mascara had been waterproof. It would have been one indignity too many to leave her makeup on his clothes.

His arm was around her shoulders, his hand on her upper arm where he rubbed gentle circles that had soothed her a moment before. Now? That touch teased a growing awareness that spread over her skin to make her senses sing. With more than a little regret, she levered herself up, straightening.

"Cameron." Her voice raspy from the crying, his name sounded far too intimate when she said it that way.

Then again, maybe it seemed more intimate since she was suddenly nose-to-nose with him, his arm still holding her close. She forgot to think. Forgot to breathe. She was pretty sure her heart paused, too, as she stared up at him.

A sexy, incredibly appealing man.

Without her permission, her fingers moved to his face. She traced the line of his lightly shadowed jaw, surprised at the rough bristle against her fingertips. His blue eyes hypnotized her. There was simply no other explanation for what was happening to her right now. Her brain told her to extricate herself. Walk away.

Her hands had other ideas. She twined them around his neck, her heart full of a tenderness she shouldn't feel. But he'd been so good to her. So thoughtful. And she wanted to kiss him more than she wanted anything.

"Maresa." Her name on his lips was a warning. A chance to change her mind.

She understood that she was pushing a boundary. Recognized that he'd just drawn a line in the sand.

"I didn't mind giving up my dream job in Paris to care for Rafe and help my mother recover," she confided, giving him absolutely no context for her comment and hoping he understood what she was saying. "And I will gladly give eighteen years to raise my niece as my own daughter." She'd known it without question the moment Jaden handed her Isla. "But I'm not sure I can sacrifice the chance to have this kiss."

She'd crossed the boundary. Straight into "certifiable" territory. She must have cried out all her good sense.

His blue eyes simmered with more heat than a Saint Thomas summer. He cupped her chin, cradling her face like she was something precious.

"If I thought you wouldn't regret it tomorrow, I'd give you all the kisses you could handle." The stroke of his thumb along her cheek didn't begin to soothe the rejection.

Her eyes burned again, reminding her just how jumbled her emotions were right now. Knowing he had a point did nothing to salvage her pride.

"You told me you were attracted to me." She unwound her hands from his neck.

"Too much," he admitted. "That's why I'm trying to be smart about this. I'm willing to wait to be with you until a time when you won't have any regrets about it."

"You say that like it's a foregone conclusion." She straightened, her cheeks heating.

"Or maybe it's using the power of positive thinking." His lips kicked up in a half smile, but she needed air. Space.

"You should go." She wanted time to clear her head.

Tipping her head toward him, he kissed her forehead with a gentle tenderness that made her ache for all she couldn't have.

"I'll see you in the morning," he told her, shoving to his feet.

"I thought I was taking time off?" She tucked her disheveled hair behind one ear, eager to call her mother and figure out what to do about Isla.

"From the hotel. Not from me." He shoved his hands in his pockets, and something about the gesture made her think he'd done it to keep from touching her.

She knew because she felt the same need to touch him.

"When will I see you?"

"Text me when you and Isla are ready in the morning and I'll come get you. I'm traveling to Martinique tomorrow and I'd like you with me."

She arched an eyebrow. "You need a tour guide with an infant in tow?"

"We could talk through some of the data in those reports a bit more. You could help give me a bigger picture of what's going on here." He opened the door into the quiet hallway of the expansive vacation villa. "Besides, I want to be close by if you decide you want to share kisses you won't regret down the road."

He strode away, whistling softly for Poppy as he headed toward the main staircase. He left Maresa alone in the extravagant house with a baby, a nurse and all kinds of confused feelings for him. One thing was certain, though.

A man like Cameron McNeill might tempt her sorely. But he was a fantasy. A temporary escape from the reality of a life full of obligations she would never walk away from. So until her heart understood how thoroughly off-limits he was, Maresa needed to put all thoughts of kisses out of her head.

An hour later, Maresa had her mother in the Jeep with her as she pulled up to the gated vacation villa. She'd calmly explained the Isla situation on a phone call on the way over to her house, arranging for their retired neighbor to visit with Rafe for a couple of hours while Maresa brought her mom to meet her grandchild.

After hearing back from Rafe's counselor that a mention of his daughter could trigger too much frustration and a possible memory block, Maresa had simply told her brother she wanted to bring their mother to meet a girlfriend's new baby.

She'd kept the story simple and straightforward, and Rafe didn't mind the visit time with Mr. Leopold, who was happy to play one of Rafe's video games with him and keep an eye on him. The paperwork requesting temporary legal custody of the baby would be filed in the morning by her attorney, so she'd taken care of that, too.

Now, driving through the gates, Maresa enjoyed her mother's startled gasp at the breathtaking view of the Caribbean.

"I had the same reaction earlier," she admitted, halting the Jeep in the space beside the nurse's sedan. "But this isn't half as beautiful as Isla."

"I cannot wait to meet her." Analise Delphine opened the car door slowly, the neuropathy in her hands one of many nerve conditions caused by her MS. "But I'm still so angry at Trina for not telling us sooner. Can you imagine what happiness it would have given us in those dark hours with your brother if we had only known about his daughter?"

Maresa hurried around the car to help her mother out since it did no good to tell her to wait. Analise had struggled more with her disease ever since the car crash that injured Rafe. Maresa worried about her since her mother seemed to blame herself—and her MS—for the injury to her beloved son, and some days it appeared as if she wanted to suffer because of her guilt. For months, Maresa had encouraged her mother to get into some more family counseling, but Analise would only go to sessions that were free through a local clinic, not wanting to "be a burden."

Maresa had tread lightly around the topic until now, but if they were going to be responsible for this baby, she needed her mother to be strong emotionally even if her physical health was declining.

"Trina is young," Maresa reminded her as she helped her up the white stone walkway to the main entrance of the villa. "She must have been scared and confused between finding out she was pregnant and then learning Rafe wasn't going to make a full recovery."

Analise breathed heavily as she leaned on Maresa's arm. Analise had always been the most beautiful girl on the block, according to their neighbor Mr. Leopold. She'd worked as a dancer in clubs and in street performances for tourists, earning a good living for years before the MS hit her hard. Her limber dancer's body had thickened with her inability to move freely, but her careful makeup and her eye for clothing meant she always looked stage-ready.

"She is old enough to make better choices." Her mother stopped abruptly, squinting into the sunlight as she peered up at the vacation home. "Speaking of which, Maresa, I hope you are making wise choices by staying here. You said your boss is allowing you to do this?"

"Yes, Mom." She tugged gently at her mother's arm, drawing her up the wide stone steps. "He was there when Jaden handed me Isla, so he knew I had a lot to contend with today."

She wasn't sure about the rest of his motives. She was still separating Cameron McNeill from surly Mr. Holmes, trying to understand him. He'd walked out on her today when she would have gladly lost herself in the attraction. Some of her wounded pride had been comforted by his assurance that he wanted her.

So where did that leave them for tomorrow when he expected her to accompany him to a neighboring island?

"Most men don't share their expensive villas without expectations, Maresa. Be smarter than that," her mother chastised her while Maresa unlocked the front door with the key Cameron had left behind. "You need to come home."

Before she could argue, Wendy appeared in the foyer, a pink bundle in her arms. Her mother oohed and aahed, mesmerized by her new grandchild as she happily cataloged all the sleeping baby's features. Maresa paid scant attention, however, as Analise declared the hairline was Rafe's and the mouth inherited was from Analise herself.

Maresa still smarted from her mother's insistence that she wasn't "being smart" to stay in the villa with Isla tonight. Perhaps it stung all the more because that had been Maresa's first instinct, as well. But damn it, Cameron had a point about the practicality of it. The Carib did indeed comp rooms to special guests who provided services. Why couldn't she enjoy the privilege while she helped Cameron McNeill investigate the operations of his luxury hotel?

Putting aside her frustration, she tried to enjoy her mother's pleasure in the baby even as Maresa worried about the future. It was easy for her mom to tell her that she should simply bring Isla home, but it would be Maresa who had to make arrangements for caregiving and Maresa who would wake up every few hours to look after the child. All of their lives were going to change dramatically under the roof of her mother's tiny house.

Maybe she needed to look for a larger home for all of them. She'd thought she couldn't afford it before, but now she wondered how she could afford *not* to buy something bigger. She would speak to her mother about it, but first, it occurred to her she could speak to Cameron. He was a businessman. His brother—she'd once read online—was a hedge fund manager. Surely a McNeill could give sound financial advice.

Besides, talking about the Caribbean housing market would be a welcome distraction in case the conversation ever turned personal tomorrow. If ever she was tempted to kiss him again, she'd just think about interest rates. That ought to cool her jets in a hurry.

"Look, Maresa!" Her mother turned the baby on her lap to show her Isla's face as they sat on the loveseat of a sprawling white family room decorated with dark leather furnishings and heavy Mexican wood. The little girl's eyes were open now, blinking owlishly. "She has your father's eyes! We need to call him and tell him. He won't believe it."

"Mom. No." She reached for the baby while Analise dug in her boho bag sewn out of brightly colored fabric scraps and pulled out a cell phone. "Dad never likes hearing from us."

She'd been devastated by her father's furious reaction to her phone call the night of Rafe's accident.

I've moved on, Maresa. Help your mother get that through her head.

"Nonsense." Analise grinned as she pressed the screen. "He'll want to hear this. Isla is his first grand-child, too, you know."

In Maresa's arms, the infant kicked and squirmed, her back arching as if she were preparing for a big cry. Maresa resisted the urge to call to Wendy, needing the experience of soothing the little girl. So she patted her back and spoke comforting words, shooting to her feet to walk around the room while her mother left a mes-sage on her father's voice mail. No surprise he hadn't picked up the call.

"I bet he'll book a flight down here as soon as he can," Analise assured her. "I should be getting home so I can make the house ready for company. And a baby, too!"

She levered slowly out of her chair to her feet, her new energy and excitement making her wince less even though the hurt had to be just the same as it was an hour ago.

"I don't think Dad will come down here," Maresa warned her quietly, not wanting her mom's hopes raised to impossible levels.

Jack Janson hadn't returned once since moving over-seas. He hadn't even visited Maresa in Paris; she'd briefly hoped that since he lived in the UK, he might make the effort to see her. But no.

"Could you let me be excited about just this one thing? We have enough to worry us, Maresa. Let's look for things to be hopeful about." She put her hand on Mare-sa's shoulders, a touch that didn't comfort her in the least.

If anything, Maresa remembered why she needed to be all the more careful with Cameron McNeill. Like her father, he was only here on business. Like her father, he might think it was fun to indulge himself with a local woman while he was far from his home and his real life.

But once he left Saint Thomas and solved the problems at the Carib Grand, Maresa knew all too well that he wasn't ever coming back.

Cameron had new respect for the running abilities of Maltese show dogs.

He sprinted through the undergrowth on the beach the next morning, about an hour after sunrise, trying to keep up with the little pooch.

"Poppy!" he called to her, cursing himself for giving her a moment off the leash. He'd scoped the beach and knew they were alone on the Carib Grand's private stretch of shore, so he'd figured it was okay.

He could keep up with the little dog on her short legs after all. But Poppy was small and shifty, darting and zigzagging through the brush where Cam couldn't fit. The groomer was going to think he'd gotten the pup's fur tangled on purpose, but damn it, he was just trying to let her have some fun. She seemed so happy chasing those terns.

If only it was as easy to tell what would make Maresa Delphine happy. He'd spent most of the day with her and still wasn't sure how to make her smile again. The concierge had the weight of the world on her straight shoulders.

Catching sight of muddy white fur, Cameron swooped low to scoop up the dog in midstride.

"Gotcha." He held on to the wriggling, overexcited bundle of wet canine while she tried her best to lick his face.

He'd have to shower again before his day in Martinique with Maresa since he was now covered with beach sand and dog fur, but it was tough to stay perturbed with the overjoyed animal. Chiding her gently while he attached the leash, Cam turned to go back up the path to the hotel.

Only to spot Rafe Delphine walking toward the beach beside a well-dressed, much older woman.

Surprised that Rafe had come in to work with Maresa taking the day off, Cameron watched the pair from a hidden vantage point in the bushes.

"Do you know this painter I'm meeting, young man?" the woman asked, her accent sounding Nordic, maybe. Or Finnish.

The woman was probably in her late sixties or early seventies. She had a sleek blond bob and expensive-looking bag. Even the beach sandals she wore had the emblem of an exclusive designer Cam recognized because a long-ago girlfriend had dragged him to a private runway show.

"Jaden paints." Rafe nodded his acknowledgement of the question but his eye was on the ground where a bird flapped its damp wings. "Look. A tern."

Poppy wriggled excitedly. The movement attracted the older woman's attention, giving up Cam's hiding place She smiled at him.

"What a precious little princess!" she exclaimed, eyes on Poppy. "She looks like she's been having fun today."

Rafe's tawny eyes—so like his sister's—turned his way. He gave Cam a nod of recognition, or maybe it was just politeness. Effectively called out of his spot in the woods, Cameron stepped into the sunlight and let the woman meet Poppy, who was—as always—appropriately gracious for the attention.

After a brief exchange with the dog, Cameron continued toward the hotel. He'd known that Jaden Torries was probably trolling for work at the Carib, so it shouldn't be a huge surprise that one of the hotel guests was meeting him at the beach. But why was Rafe bringing her to meet him?

Given how much Maresa disliked her ex-fiancé, it seemed unlikely she would be the one facilitating Jaden doing any kind of work with hotel patrons. Especially since she wasn't even working today. Then again, what if she had found a way to make a little extra income by helping Jaden find patrons? Would she set aside her distaste for him if it made things easier for her?

Deep in thought, Cam arrived at the pool deck. He didn't want to think his attraction to Maresa would influence his handling of the situation, but his first instinct was to speak to her directly. He would ask her about it when he picked her up at the villa, he decided.

Except then he spotted her circulating among the guests by the pool. She'd been here all along?

Suspicion mounted. Grinding his teeth, he charged toward her, more than ready for some answers.

Six

Morning sun beating down on her head, Maresa noticed Cameron McNeill heading her way and she braced herself for the resurrection of Mr. Holmes. She knew he needed to be undercover to learn more about the hotel operations, but did he have to be quite so convincing in his "difficult guest" role? The hard set of his jaw and brooding glare were seriously intimidating even knowing how kind he could be.

She straightened from a conversation with one of her seasonal guests from Quebec who rented a suite for half the year. Pasting on a professionally polite smile to greet Cameron, she told herself she should be grateful to see this side of him so she wouldn't be tempted to throw herself at him again.

Even if his bare chest and low-slung board shorts drew every female eye.

"Good morning, Mr. Holmes." She reached to smooth

her jacket sleeves, only to remember she'd worn a sun-dress today for the trip into Martinique. *Oh, my.* Her skin had goose bumps of awareness just from standing this close to him.

"May I speak to you privately?" He handed off Poppy to the dog groomer who scurried over from where he'd been waiting by the tiki bar.

Cameron certainly couldn't have any complaints about the service he was receiving, could he? People seemed to hurry to offer him assistance.

"Of course." She excused herself from the other guests, following him toward the door marked Employ-ees Only.

He didn't slow his step until they were in the same conference room where they'd spoken yesterday. The cool blast of air almost matched the ice chips in his blue eyes. He shoved the door shut behind them before he turned to face her.

"I thought you were taking the day off from the hotel." His jaw flexed and he crossed his arms over his bare chest, the board shorts riding low on his hips.

She tried not to stare, distracting herself by focusing on the hint of confrontation in his tone.

"I am." She gestured to her informal clothing. "I only stopped by this morning to see my brother and make sure he felt comfortable about his workday."

"And is he comfortable escorting guests to the beach?" Cameron's arctic glare might have made another woman shiver. Maresa straightened her spine.

"I never give him jobs like that. Why do you ask?" Defensiveness for her brother roared through her.

"Because I just saw him walking one of our overseas guests to the shore to meet Jaden Torries."

Surprised, she quickly guessed he must be mistaken.

He had to be. Still a hint of tension tickled her gut. "Rafe doesn't even arrive until the next ferry." She checked her watch just to be sure the day hadn't slipped away from her. "He should be walking in the employee locker rooms any minute to punch his time card."

"He's already here." Cameron pulled out one of the high-backed leather chairs for her, all sorts of muscles flexing as he moved, distracting her when she needed to be focused. "I saw him myself at the beach with one of the hotel guests just a few minutes ago."

"I don't understand." Ignoring the seat, she paced away from all that tempting male muscle to peer out the windows overlooking the croquet lawn near the pool, hoping to get a view of the path to the beach. How could she relax, wondering if her brother might be doing jobs around the Carib without her knowing? She was supposed to watch over him during his first few months of employment. She'd promised the hotel director as much. "I got here early so I wouldn't miss him when he came to work. I want everything to go smoothly for him if I'm not here to supervise him myself."

Cameron joined her at the window, his body warm beside hers as he peered out onto the mostly empty side lawns. A butterfly garden near the window attracted a handful of brightly colored insects. His shoulder brushed hers, setting off butterflies inside, too. She hated feeling this way—torn between the physical attraction and the mental frustration.

"Did you know Jaden was soliciting business from hotel guests?" Cameron's question was quiet. Dispassionate.

And it offended her mightily. How dare he question her integrity? Her work record was impeccable and he should know as much if he was even halfway doing *his* job.

Anger burned through her as she whirled to face him, her skirt brushing his leg he stood so close to her. She took a step back.

"Absolutely not. Until yesterday, I hadn't seen Jaden since I left for Paris two years ago." She frowned, not understanding why Cameron would think she'd do such a thing. "And while I don't wish him ill, my relationship with him is absolutely over. I certainly don't have any desire to risk my job to help a man I dislike profit off our guests."

"I see." Cameron nodded slowly, as if weighing whether or not to believe her.

Worry balled in her stomach and she reined in her anger. She couldn't afford to be offended. She needed him to believe her.

"Why would you think I'd do such a thing?" She didn't want to be here. She wanted to find her brother and ask him what was going on.

Did Rafe even understand what he was doing by helping Jaden meet potential clients for his artwork? Was Jaden asking him for that kind of help?

"That type of business is probably lucrative for him—"

Understanding dawned. Indignation flared, hot and fast. "And you thought I would be a part of some sordid scheme with my ex-fiancé for the sake of extra cash? Even twisting my brother's arm into setting up meetings when I do everything in my power to protect him?"

If it had been anyone else, she would have stormed out of the meeting room. But she needed this job too much and, at the end of the day, Cameron McNeill was still an owner of the Carib.

He held all the cards.

"I don't know what to think. That's why I wanted to speak to you privately." He picked up a gray T-shirt from the back of a chair in the conference room and pulled it over his head.

She watched in spite of herself, realizing he must have been doing work in the conference room earlier that morning since a laptop and phone sat on the table.

"I won't have any answers until I speak to my brother." She was worried about him. For him. For the baby. Oh God, when had life gotten so complicated?

What had her brother gotten into?

"You realize this isn't the first time he's done it." Cameron's voice softened as he headed toward her again. "That customer review that I shared with you yesterday was from someone who said he provided a 'happy escort' to the beach." Cameron's blue eyes probed hers, searching for answers she didn't have.

As much as she longed to share her fears with him, she couldn't do that. Not when he was in charge of her fate at the hotel, and Rafe's, too.

"I remember." She itched to leave, needing to see Rafe for herself. "And now that you've put that comment in context, I'm happy to speak to my brother and clear this up."

She turned toward the door, desperate to put the complicated knot of feelings her boss inspired behind her.

"Wait." Cameron reached for her hand and held it, his touch warm and firm. "I realize you want to protect him, Maresa, but we need to find out what's going on."

"And we will," she insisted, wishing he didn't make her heart beat faster. "Just as soon as I speak to him."

Cameron studied her for a long moment with searching eyes, then quietly asked, "What if he doesn't have a clear answer?"

Some of the urgency eased from her. She couldn't deny that was a possibility.

"I can only do my best to figure out what's going on." She couldn't imagine who else would be giving him extra chores to do around the hotel. Rafe had never particularly liked Jaden. Then again, her brother was a different man since the accident.

"I know that. And what if we learn more by observing him for a few days? Maybe it would be better to simply keep a closer eye on him now that we know he's carrying out duties for the hotel—or someone else—that you haven't authorized." His tone wasn't accusing. "Maybe you shouldn't upset him unnecessarily."

She wanted to tell him she already spent hours supervising her brother. More than others on her staff. But she bit her lip, refusing to reveal a piece of information that could get Rafe terminated from his position.

"I don't want him getting hurt," she argued, worried about letting her brother's behavior continue unchecked. "And I don't know who he's speaking to that would advise him to take risks like this with his job."

The day had started out so promising, with Isla sleeping for five hours straight and waking up with a drooly baby smile, only to take this radical nosedive. Anxiety spiked. Rafe was going to lose this job, damn it. She would never be able to afford a caregiver for Isla and a companion to supervise Rafe, too. Especially not once they lost Rafe's income. Heaven only knew how much he would recover from the brain injury. What kind of future he would have? How much he could provide for himself, much less a child? All the fears of the unknown jumped up inside her.

Cameron hissed a low, frustrated breath between his teeth. "What if we compromise? You confront him now, but if you don't get a direct answer or if you sense there's more to his answer than what he shares, you back off.

Then, we can keep a closer eye on him for the next week and see who is setting up these meetings."

She didn't like the idea of waiting. She knew there was a good chance Rafe wouldn't give her a direct answer. But what choice did she really have? She wouldn't be able to push him anyhow, since his health and potential recovery were more important than getting answers to any mystery going on at the Carib.

"Fine." She turned to the door, eager to see her brother, but she paused when Cameron followed her. "I'd prefer to speak to him alone."

He followed her so closely that she needed to tilt her head to peer up at him.

"Of course." He stood near enough that she could see the shades of blue in his eyes, as varied as the Caribbean. "I'm going to change for our trip. I'll have a car meet you out front in fifteen minutes."

She wondered if it was wise to risk being seen leaving the hotel with surly Mr. Holmes. But then, that wasn't her problem so much as his. She had enough to worry about waiting for the DNA tests to come back so she could finally tell Rafe about Isla. Her lawyer and his psychologist had advised her and her mother to wait until then.

Hurrying away from all that distracting masculine appeal, Maresa rushed into the employee lounge to look for her brother. She'd already called in a favor from Big Bill, the head doorman, to help keep an eye on Rafe for the next few days. Bill was a friend of her mother's from their old neighborhood and he'd been kind enough to agree, but Maresa knew the man could only do so much.

Inside the lounge, the scent of morning coffee mingled with someone's too-strong perfume. A few people from the maintenance staff gossiped around the kitchen table where a box of pastries sat open. Moving past the kitchen,

Maresa peered into the locker area between the men's and women's private lounges. Rafe sat in the middle row of lockers, carefully braiding the stems of yellow buttercups into a chain. Flowers spilled over the polished bench as he straddled it, his focus completely absorbed in the task.

Any frustration she felt with him melted away. How could Cameron think for a moment that her brother would knowingly do anything unethical at work? It was only because Cameron didn't know Rafe. If he did, he'd never think something like that for a moment.

"Hey, Rafe." She took a seat on the bench nearby, wishing with all her heart he could be in a work program designed for people with his kinds of abilities. He had so much to offer with his love of nature and talent with green and growing things. Even now, his affinity for plants was evident, the same as before the accident when he'd had his own landscaping business. "What are you making?"

He glanced up at her, his eyes so like the ones she saw in the mirror every day.

"Maresa." He smiled briefly before returning his attention to the flowers. "I'm making you a bracelet."

"Me?" She had worried he was heaping more gifts on Nancy. And while she liked the server, she didn't want Rafe to have any kind of romantic hopes about the woman. Hearing the flowers were for her was a relief.

"I felt bad I left work." He lifted the flower chain and laid it on her wrist, his shirt cuffs brushing her skin as he carefully knotted the stems together. "I'm sorry."

Her heart knotted up like the flowers.

"Thank you. I love it." She kissed him on the cheek, smiling at the way his simple offering looked beside the silver star bracelet he'd given her two years ago before she left for Paris.

He was as thoughtful as ever, and his way of showing it hadn't changed all that much.

"Rafe?" She drew a deep breath, hating to ruin a happy moment with questions about Jaden. But this was important. The sooner she helped Cameron McNeill figure out what was going on at the Carib Grand, the sooner their jobs would be secure and they could focus on a new life with Isla—if Isla was in fact his child. And even though their lives would be less complicated without the child, Maresa couldn't deny that the thought of Isla leaving made her stomach clench. "Why did you go to the beach this morning?"

She kept the question simple. Direct.

"Mr. Ricci asked." Rafe rose to his feet, dusting flower petals off his faded olive cargoes. "Time to go to work. Mom said I don't work with you today."

She blinked at the fast change of topic. "Mr. Ricci asked you to bring a guest to the beach?"

"It's eight thirty." Rafe pointed to his watch. "Mom said I don't work with you today."

Damn it. Damn it. She didn't want to throw his whole workday off for the sake of a conversation that might lead nowhere. Maybe Cameron was right and they were better off keeping an eye on the situation.

"Right. I have to work off-site today. You'll be helping Glenna at the concierge stand, but Big Bill is on duty today. If you need help with anything, ask Bill, okay?"

"Ask Big Bill." Rafe gave her a thumbs-up before he stalked out of the locker room and into the hotel to start work.

Watching him leave, Maresa's fingers went to the bracelet he'd made her. He was thoughtful and kind. Surely he would have so much to give Isla. She needed to speak to his counselor in more detail so they could brainstorm ideas for the right way to introduce them. It seemed wrong to deprive the little girl of a father when her mother had already given up on her.

For now, however, she needed to tell Cameron that Rafe was escorting guests to the beach because the hotel director told him to. Would Cameron believe her? Or would he demand to speak to her brother himself?

Cameron's seductive promise floated back to her. *If I thought you wouldn't regret it tomorrow, I'd give you all the kisses you could handle.* She'd replayed those words again and again since he'd said them.

She walked a tightrope with her compelling boss—needing him to allow Rafe to stay in his job, but needing her own secured even more. Which meant she had to help him in his investigation.

Most of all, to keep those objectives perfectly clear, she had to ignore her growing attraction to him. His kindness with Isla might have slid past her defenses, but in order to protect the baby's future, Maresa would have to set aside her desire to find out what "all the kisses she could handle" would feel like.

The flight to Martinique was fast and efficient. They took off from the private dock near the Carib Grand's beach and touched down in the Atlantic near Le Francois on the east coast of Martinique. The pilot landed the new seaplane smoothly, barely jostling Baby Isla's carrier where she sat beside Maresa in the seats facing Cameron.

Cameron tried to focus on the baby to keep his mind off the exotically gorgeous woman across from him. The task had been damn near impossible for the hour of flight time between islands. Maresa's bright sundress was so different from the linen suits he'd seen her in for work. He liked the full skirt and vibrant poppy print, and he admired that she wore the simple floral bracelet around one wrist. With her hair loose and sun-tipped around her face, she looked impossibly beautiful. Her movements with Isla were easier today and her fascination with the little girl was obvious every time she glanced Isla's way.

Before she unbuckled the baby's carrier, she pressed a kiss to the infant's smooth forehead. A new pink dress with a yellow bunny on the front had been a gift from Maresa's mother, apparently. They'd spoken about that much on that flight. Maresa had given him an update on the custody paperwork with the lawyer, the paternity test she'd ordered using Rafe's hair and a cheek swab of Isla's, and she'd told him about her mother's reaction to her granddaughter. They'd only discussed Rafe briefly, agreeing not to confront him any further about bringing guests to meet Jaden Torries. They would watch Rafe more carefully when they returned to Saint Thomas. Until then, Bill the doorman knew to keep a close eye on him.

Cameron hadn't pushed her to discuss her theory about what might be going on, knowing that she was already worried about her brother's activities at the hotel. But at some point today, they would have to discuss where to go next with Rafe, and Jaden, too. For now, Cameron simply wanted to put her at ease for a few hours while he gathered some information about this secret branch of his family. The Martinique McNeills had a home in Le Francois, an isolated compound that was the equivalent of Grandfather Malcolm's home in Manhattan—a centrally located hub with each of the brothers' names on the deed. The family had other property holdings, but their mother had lived here before her death and the next generation all spent time there.

Cameron had done his homework and was ready to

check out this group today. Later, after Maresa had time to relax and catch her breath from the events of the last few days, he would talk to her about a plan for the future. For her and for Isla, too. The little girl in the pink dress tugged at his heart.

"So you have family here?" Maresa passed the baby carrier to him while the pilot opened the plane door.

Fresh air blew in, toying lightly with Maresa's hair.

"In theory. Yes." He wasn't happy about the existence of the other McNeills. "That is—they don't know we're related yet. My father kept his other sons and mistress a secret. When his lover tired of being hidden, she sold the house he'd bought her and left without a forwarding address. He didn't fight her legally because of the scandal that would create." As he said it aloud, however, he realized that didn't sound like his father. "Actually, he was probably just too disinterested to try and find them. He never paid us much attention either."

Liam McNeill had been a sorry excuse for a father. Cameron refused to follow in those footsteps.

Cam lifted the baby carrier above the seats, following Maresa to the exit. They'd parked at a private dock for the Cap Est Lagoon, a resort hotel in Le Francois close to the McNeill estate.

"But at least he's still a part of your life, isn't he?" Maresa held her full skirt with one hand as she descended the steps of the plane. A gusty breeze wreaked havoc with the hem.

The view of her legs was a welcome distraction during a conversation about his dad.

"He is part of the business, so I see him at company meetings. But it's not like he shows up for holidays to hang out. He's never been that kind of father." Even Cameron's grandfather hadn't quite known what to do to create a sense of family. Sure, he'd taken in Quinn, Ian and Cameron often enough as teens. But they were more apt to travel with him on business, learning the ropes from the head of the company, than have fun.

Luckily, Cam had had his brothers.

And, later, his own reckless sense of fun.

Maresa held her hair with one hand as they walked down the dock together, the baby between them in her seat. Behind them, the hotel staff unloaded their bags from the seaplane. Not that they'd travelled with much, but Cam had taken a suite here so Maresa would have a place to retreat with Isla. The Cap Est spread out on the shore ahead of them, the red-roofed buildings ringing the turquoise lagoon. Birds called and circled overhead. A few white sailing boats dotted the blue water.

"A disinterested father is a unique kind of hurt," Maresa observed empathetically—so much so it gave him pause for a moment. But then he was distracted by a hint of her perfume on the breeze as she followed him to the villa where their suite awaited. A greeter from the hotel had texted him instructions on the location so they could proceed directly there. "Do you think your half brothers will be glad to see him again? Has it been a long time that they've been apart?"

"Fifteen years. The youngest hasn't seen his father— my father—since the kid was ten." Cameron hadn't thought about that much. He'd been worried about what the other McNeills might ask from them in terms of the family resort business. But there was a chance they'd be too bitter to claim anything.

Or so bitter that they'd want revenge.

Cameron wouldn't let them hurt his grandfather. Or the legacy his granddad had worked his whole life to build.

"Wow, fifteen? That's not much older than I was the last time I saw my dad." Maresa's words caught him by surprise as they reached the villa where a greeter admitted them.

Cameron didn't ask her about it until the hotel representative had shown them around the two-floor suite with a private deck overlooking the lagoon. When the woman left and Maresa was lifting Isla from the carrier, however, Cameron raised the question.

"Where's your father now?" He watched her coo and comfort the baby, rubbing the little girl's back through her pink dress, the bowlegs bare above tiny white ankle socks.

The vacation villa was smaller than the one near the Carib Grand, but more luxuriously appointed, with floor-to-ceiling windows draped in white silk that fluttered in the constant breeze off the water. Exotic Turkish rugs in bright colors covered alternating sections of dark bamboo floors. Paintings of the market at Marigot and historic houses in Fort-de-France, the capital of Martinique, hung around the living area, providing all the color of an otherwise quietly decorated room. Deep couches with white cushions and teak legs and arms were positioned for the best views of the water. There was even a nursery with a crib brought in especially for their visit.

"He lives outside London with his new wife. I spoke to him briefly after Rafe's accident, but his only response was a plea that I tell my mother he's *moved on* and not to bother him again." She stressed the words in a way that suggested she would never forget the tone of voice in which they'd been spoken. Shaking her head, she walked Isla over to the window and stared out at the shimmering blue expanse. "I won't be contacting him anymore."

Cameron sifted through a half dozen responses before he came up with one that didn't involve curses.

"I don't blame you. The man can't be bothered to come to his critically injured son's bedside? He doesn't deserve his kids." Cameron knew without a doubt that he'd suck as a father, but even he would never turn his back like that on a kid.

Maresa's burden in caring for her whole family became clearer, however. Her mother wasn't working because of her battle with MS, her father was out of the picture and her brother needed careful supervision. Maresa was supporting a lot of people on her salary.

And now, an infant, too. That was one helluva load for a person to carry on her own. Admiration for her grew. She wasn't like his dad, who disengaged from responsibilities and the people counting on him.

"What will you do if your half brothers don't want to see your father?" she asked him now, drifting closer to him as she rubbed her cheek against the top of Isla's downy head.

Cameron was seized with the need to wrap his arms around both of them, a protective urge so strong he had to fight to keep his hands off Maresa. He jammed his fists in the pocket of his khakis to stop himself. Still, he walked closer, wanting to breathe in her scent. To feel the way her nearness heated over his skin like a touch.

"I'll convince them that my grandfather is worth ten of my father and make sure they understand the importance of meeting him." He lowered his voice while he stood so close to her, unable to move away.

Fascinated, he watched the effect he had on her. The goose bumps down her arm. The fast thrum of a tiny vein at the base of her neck. A quick dart of her tongue over her lips that all but did him in.

He wanted this woman. So much that telling himself to stay away wasn't going to help. So much that the baby in her arms wasn't going to distract him, let alone dissuade him.

"I should change," Maresa said suddenly, clutching Isla tighter. "Into something for the trip to your brothers' house. That is, if you want me to accompany you there? I'm not sure what you want my role to be here."

His gaze roamed over her, even knowing it was damned unprofessional. But they'd passed that point in this relationship the day before when Maresa had wrapped her arms around him. He'd used up all his restraint then. Time for some plain talk.

"Your role? First, tell me honestly what you think would happen between us this week if I wasn't your boss." He couldn't help the hoarse hunger in his voice, and knew that she heard it. He studied her while she struggled to answer, envious of the way Isla's tiny body curved around the soft swell of Maresa's breast.

"What good does it do to wonder what if?" Frustration vibrated through her, her body tensing. "The facts can't be changed. I'd never quit this job. It's more important to me than ever."

Right. He knew that. She'd made that more than clear. So why couldn't he seem to stay away? Stifling a curse at himself, he stepped back. Swallowed.

"I need to visit my brothers' place. You can relax here with Isla and review the files I started to show you yesterday. Make whatever notes you can to help me weed through what's important." He had to get some fresh air in his lungs if he was going to keep his distance from Maresa until the time was right.

"Okay. Thank you." She nodded, relief and regret both etched in her features.

"When I get back, I'll have dinner ordered in. We can eat on the upstairs deck before we fly back tonight, unless of course, you decide you'd like to stay another day."

Her eyes widened, a flush of heat stealing along the skin bared by the open V of her sundress. He couldn't look away.

"I'm sure that won't be necessary." She clung to her professional reserve.

"Nevertheless, I'll keep the option open." He reached for her, stroking the barest of touches along her arm. "Just in case."

Seven

Just in case.

Hours later, Cameron's parting words still circled around in Maresa's brain. She'd been ridiculously productive in spite of the seductive thoughts chasing through her mind, throwing herself into her work with determined intensity. Still, Cameron's suggestion of spending the night together built a fever in her blood, giving her a frenetic energy to make extensive notes on his files, research leads on Carib Grand personnel, and review her and Rafe's performance in depth. She hadn't found any answers about Rafe's additional activities, but at least she'd done the job Cameron asked of her to the best of her ability.

Now, walking away from the white-spindled crib where she'd just laid Isla for a nap with a nursery monitor by the bedside, Maresa was drawn across the hallway into the master bedroom while she waited for Cameron to return.

What would happen between us if I wasn't your boss?

Why had he asked that? Hadn't she already made it painfully clear when she'd confided how much she wanted a kiss in those heated moments in his arms yesterday? She'd relived that exchange a million times already and it had happened just twenty-four hours ago.

Now, lowering herself to a white chaise longue near open French doors, Maresa settled the nursery monitor on the hardwood floor at her feet. She would hear Isla if the baby needed anything. For just a few moments at least, she would enjoy overlooking the terrace and the turquoise lagoon below while she waited for Cameron to return. She would inhale the flower-scented sea air of her home, savor the caress of that same breeze along her skin. When was the last time she'd sat quietly and simply enjoyed this kind of beauty, let herself just soak in sensations? Sure, the beach around the Cap Est hotel in Martinique was more upscale than the Caribbean she'd grown up with—public beaches where you brought your own towels from home. But the islands were gorgeous everywhere. No one told the beach morning glory where to grow. It didn't discriminate against the public beaches any more than the yellow wedelia flowers or the bright poinciana trees.

It felt as if she hadn't taken a deep breath all year, not since she'd returned from Paris. There'd been days on the Left Bank when she'd sat at Café de Flore and simply enjoyed the scenery, indulged in people-watching, but since coming home to Charlotte Amalie? Not so much. And now? She had an infant to care for.

If Trina didn't want her baby back—and given the way she'd abandoned Isla, Maresa vowed to block any effort to regain custody—Maresa would have eighteen years of hard work ahead. Her time to stare out to sea and enjoy a few quiet moments would be greatly limited. Given the responsibilities of her brother, mother and now the baby, she couldn't envision many—if any—men who would want to take on all of that to be with her. This window of time with Cameron McNeill might be the last opportunity she had to savor times like this.

To experience romantic pleasure.

Closing her eyes against the thought, she rested her head on the arm of the chaise, unwilling to let her mind wander down that sensual road. She was just tired, that was all.

She'd nap while Isla napped and when she woke up she'd feel like herself again—ready to be strong in the face of all that McNeill magnetism...

"Maresa?"

She awoke to the sound of her name, a whisper of sound against her ear.

Cameron's voice, so close, made her shiver in the most pleasant way, even as her skin warmed all over. The late afternoon sun slanted through the French doors, burnishing her skin to golden bronze—or so it felt. She refused to open her eyes and end the languid sensation in her limbs. The scent of the sea and Cam's woodsy aftershave was a heady combination, a sexy aphrodisiac that had her tilting her head to one side, exposing her neck in silent invitation.

"Mmm?" She arched her back, wanting to be closer to him, needing to feel his lips against her ear once more.

It'd been so long since she'd known a man's touch. And Cameron McNeill was no ordinary man. She bet he kissed like nobody's business.

"Are you hungry?" he asked, the low timbre of his voice turning an everyday question into a sexual innuendo.

Or was it just her imagination?

"Starving," she admitted, reaching up to touch him. To feel the heat and hard muscle of his chest.

She hooked her fingers along the placket of his button-down, next to the top button, which was already undone. She felt his low hiss of response, his heart pumping faster against the back of her knuckles where she touched him. He lowered his body closer, hovering a hair's breadth away.

Breathing him in, she felt the kick of awareness in every nerve ending, her whole body straining toward his.

"Are you sure?" His husky rasp made her skin flame since he still hadn't touched her.

Her throat was dry and she had to swallow to answer. "So sure. So damn certain—"

His lips captured hers, silencing the rest of her words. His chest grazed her breasts, his body covering hers and setting it aflame. Still she craved more. She'd only known him for days but it felt as though she'd been waiting years for him to touch her. His leg slid between hers, his thigh flexing against where she needed him most. A ragged moan slid free...

"Maresa?" He chanted her name in her ear once more, and she thought she couldn't bear it if she didn't start pulling his clothes off.

And her clothes off. She needed to touch more of him.

"Please," she murmured softly, her eyes still closed. She gripped his heavy shoulders. "Please."

"Maresa?" he said again, more uncertainly this time. "Wake up."

Confused, her brain refused to acknowledge that command. She wanted him naked. She did not want to wake up.

Then again…wasn't she awake?

Her eyes wrenched open.

"Cameron?" His name was on her lips as she slid to a sitting position.

Knocking heads with the man she'd been dreaming about.

"Ow." Blinking into the dim light in the room now that the sun had set, Maresa came fully—painfully—awake, her body still on fire from her dream.

"Sorry to startle you." Cameron reached for her, cradling the spot where his forehead had connected with her temple. "Are you okay?"

No. She wasn't okay. She wanted things to go back to where they'd been in her dream. Simple. Sensual.

"Fine." Her breathing was fast. Shallow. Her heartbeat seemed to thunder louder than the waves on the shore. "Is there a storm out there?" she asked, realizing the wind had picked up since she'd fallen asleep. "Is Isla okay?"

The white silk curtains blew into the room. The end of one teased along her bare foot where she'd slid off her shoes. She spotted the nursery monitor on the floor. Silent. Reassuring.

"I just checked on her. She's fine. But there's some heavy weather on the way. The pilot warned me we might want to consider leaving now or—ideally—extending our stay. This system came out of nowhere."

She appreciated the cooler breeze on her overheated skin, and the light mist of rain blowing in with it. Only now did she realize the strap of her sundress had fallen off one shoulder, the bodice slipping precariously down on one side. Before she could reach for it, however, Cameron slid a finger under the errant strap and lifted it into place.

Her skin hummed with pleasure where he touched her.

"Sorry." He slid his hand away fast. "The bare shoulder was…" He shook his head. "I get distracted around you, Maresa. More than I should when I know you want to keep things professional."

The room was mostly dark, except for a glow from the last light of day combined with a golden halo around a wall sconce near the bathroom. He must have turned that on when he'd entered the master suite and found her sleeping.

Dreaming.

"What about you?" Her voice carried the sultriness of sleep. Or maybe it was the sound of desire from her sexy imaginings. Even now, she could swear she remembered the feel of his strong thigh between hers, his chest pressed to aching breasts. "I can't be the only one who wants to keep some professional objectivity."

She slid her feet to the floor, needing to restore some equilibrium with him. Some distance. They sat on opposite sides of the chaise longue, the gathering storm stirring electricity in the air.

"Honestly?" A flash of lightning illuminated his face in full color for a moment before returning them to black-and-white. "I would rather abdicate my role as boss where you're concerned, Maresa. Let my brother Quinn make any decisions that involve you or Rafe. My professional judgment is already seriously compromised."

She breathed in the salty, charged air. Her hair blew silky caresses along her cheek. The gathering damp sat on her skin and she knew he must feel it, too. She was seized with the urge to lean across the chaise and lick him to find out for sure. If she could choose her spot, she'd pick the place just below his steely jaw.

"I don't understand." She shook her head, not following what he was saying. She was still half in dreamland, her whole body conspiring against logic and reason. Rebelling against all her workplace ethics. "We haven't done anything wrong."

Much. They'd talked about a kiss. But there hadn't been one.

His eyes swept her body with unmistakable want.

"Not yet. But I think you know how much I want to." He didn't touch her. He didn't need to.

Her skin was on fire just thinking about it.

"What would your brother think of me if he knew we…" Images of her body twined together with this incredibly sexy man threatened to steal the last of her defenses. "How could he be impartial?"

Another flash of lightning revealed Cam in all his masculine deliciousness. His shirt was open at the collar, just the way it had been in her dream. Except now, his shirt was damp with raindrops, making the pale cotton cling like a second skin.

Cameron watched her steadily, his intense gaze as stirring as any caress. "You know the way you have faith in your brother's good heart and good intentions? No matter what?"

She nodded. "Without question."

"That's how I feel about Quinn's ability to be fair. He can tick me off sometimes, but he is the most level-headed, just person I know."

She weighed what he was saying. Thought about what it meant. "And you're suggesting that if we acted on this attraction…you'd step out of the picture. Your brother becomes my boss, not you."

"Exactly." Cameron's assurance came along with a roll of ominous thunder that rumbled right through the villa.

Right through her feet where they touched the floor.

Maresa felt as if she were standing at the edge of a giant cliff, deciding whether or not to jump. Making that leap would be terrifying. But turning away from the tantalizing possibilities—the lure of the moment—was no longer an option. Even before she'd fallen asleep, she'd known that her window for selfish pleasures was closing fast if Isla proved to be Rafe's daughter and Maresa's responsibility.

How could she deny herself this night?

"Yes." She hurled herself into the unknown and hoped for the best. "I know that you're leaving soon, and I'm okay with that. But for tonight, if we could be just a man and a woman…" The simple words sent a shiver of longing through her.

Even in the dim light, she could see his blue eyes flare hotter, like the gas fireplace in the Antilles Suite when you turned up the thermostat.

"You have no idea how much I was hoping you'd say that." His words took on a ragged edge as his hands slid around her waist. He drew her closer.

Crushed her lips to his.

On contact, fireworks started behind her eyelids and Maresa gave herself up to the spark.

Cameron was caught between the need to savor this moment and the hunger to have the woman he craved like no other. He'd never felt a sexual need like this one. Not as a teenager losing it for the first time. Not during any of the relationships he'd thought were remotely meaningful in his past.

Maresa Delphine stirred some primal hunger different than anything he'd ever experienced. And she'd said *yes*.

The chains were off. His arms banded around her,

pressing all of those delectable curves against him. He ran his palms up her sides, from the soft swell of her hips to the indent of her waist. Up her ribs to the firm mounds of beautiful breasts. Her sundress had tortured him all damn day and he was too glad to tug down the wide straps, exposing her bare shoulders and fragrant skin.

Any hesitation about moving too fast vanished when she lunged in to lick a path along his jaw, pressing herself into him. A low growl rumbled in his chest and he hoped she mistook it for the thunder outside instead of his raw, animal need.

"Please," she murmured against his heated flesh, just below one ear. "Please."

The words were a repeat of the sensual longing he'd heard in her voice when he had first walked into the room earlier. He'd hoped like hell she'd been dreaming about him.

"Anything," he promised her, levering back to look into her tawny eyes. "Name it."

Her lips were swollen from his kiss; she ran her tongue along the top one. He felt a phantom echo of that caress in his throbbing erection that damn near made him light-headed.

"I want your clothes off." She held up her hands to show him. "But I think I'm shaking too badly to manage it."

He cradled her palms in his and kissed them before rising to stand.

"Don't be nervous." He raked his shirt over his head; it was faster than undoing the rest of the buttons.

"It's not that. It's just been such a long time for me." She stood as well, following him deeper into the room. Closer to the bed. "Everything is so hypersensitive. I feel so uncoordinated."

The French doors were still open, but no one would be able to look in unless they were on a boat far out in the water. And then, it would be too dark in the room for anyone out there to see inside. He liked the feel of the damp air and the cool breeze blowing harder.

"Then I'd better unfasten your dress for you." He couldn't wait to have her naked. "Turn around."

She did as he asked, her bare feet shifting silently on the Turkish rug. Cameron found the tab and lowered it slowly, parting the fabric to reveal more and more skin. The bodice dipped forward, falling to her hips so that only a skimpy black lace bra covered the top half of her.

He released the zipper long enough to grab two fist-fuls of the skirt and draw her backward toward him. Her head tipped back against his shoulder, a beautiful offering of her neck. Her body. Her trust. He wanted to lay her down on the bed right now and lose himself inside her, but she deserved better than that. All the more so since it had been a long time for her.

"Can I ask you a question?" He nipped her ear and kissed his way down her neck to the crook of her shoulder. There, he lingered. Tasting. Licking.

"Anything. As long as you keep taking off some clothes." She arched backward, her rump teasing the hard length of him until he had to grind his teeth to keep from tossing her skirt up and peeling away her panties.

A groan of need rumbled in his chest as the rain picked up intensity outside. He cupped her breasts in both hands, savoring the soft weight while he skimmed aside the lace bra for a better feel.

"What were you dreaming when I first walked in here?" He rolled a taut nipple between his thumb and forefinger, dying to taste her. "The soft sighs you were making were sexy as hell."

Her pupils widened with a sensual hint of her answer before she spoke.

"I was dreaming about this." She spun in his arms, pressed her bare breasts to his chest. Her hips to his. "Exactly this. And how much I wanted to be with you."

Her hands went to work on his belt buckle, her trembling fingers teasing him all the more for their slow, inefficient work. He tipped her head up to kiss her, learning her taste and her needs, finding out what she liked best. He nipped and teased. Licked and sucked. She paid him in kind by stripping off his pants and doing a hip shimmy against his raging erection. Heat blasted through him like a furnace turned all the way up.

Single-minded with new focus, he laid her on the bed and left her there while he sorted through his luggage. He needed a condom. Now.

Right. Freaking. Now.

He ripped open the snap on his leather shaving kit and found what he was looking for. When he turned back to the bed, Maresa was wriggling out of her dress, leaving on nothing but a pair of panties he guessed were black lace. It was tough to tell color in the dim light from the wall sconce near the bathroom. The lightning flashes had slowed as the rain intensified. He stepped out of his boxers and returned to the bed.

And covered her with his body.

Her arms went around him, her lips greeting him with hungry abandon, as though he'd been gone for two days instead of a few seconds. His brain buzzed with the need to have her. Still, he laid the condom to one side of her on the bed, needing to satisfy her first. And thoroughly.

She cupped his jaw, trailing kisses along his cheek. When he reached between them to slip his hand beneath the hem of her panties, her head fell back to the bed, turning to one side. She gave herself over to him and that jacked him up even more. She was impossibly hot. Ready. So ready for him. He'd barely started to tease and tempt her when she convulsed with her release.

The soft whimpers she made were so damn satisfying. He wanted to give that release to her again and again. But she wasn't going to sit still for him any longer. Her long leg wrapped around his, aligning their bodies for what they both craved.

He tried to draw out the pleasure by turning his attention to her breasts, feasting on them all over again. But she felt around the bed for the condom and tore it open with her teeth, gently working it over him until he had to shoo her hand away and take over the task. He was hanging by a thread already, damn it.

She chanted sweet words in his ear, encouraging him to come inside her. To give her everything she wanted. He had no chance of resisting her. He thrust inside her with one stroke, holding himself there for a long moment to steel himself for this new level of pleasure. She wrapped her legs around him and he was lost. His eyes crossed. He probably forgot his own name.

It was just Maresa now. He basked in the feel of her body around his. The scent of her citrusy hair and skin. The damp press of her lips to his chest as she moved her hips, meeting his thrusts with her own.

The rain outside pelted harder, faster, cooling his skin when it caught on the wind blowing into the room. He didn't care. It didn't come close to dousing the fire inside him. Maresa raked her nails up his back, a sweet pain he welcomed to balance the pleasure overwhelming him and...

He lost it. His release pounded through him fast and

hot, paralyzing him for a few seconds. Through it all, Maresa clung to him. Kissed him.

When the inner storm passed, he sagged into her and then down on the bed beside her, listening to the other storm. The one picking up force outside. He lay beside her in the aftermath as their breathing slowed. Their heartbeats steadied.

He should feel some kind of guilt, maybe, for bringing her here. For not being able to leave her alone and give her that professional distance she'd wanted. But he couldn't find it in himself to regret a moment of what had just happened. It felt fated. Inevitable.

And if that sounded like him making excuses, so be it.

"Should I shut those?" he asked, kissing her damp forehead and stroking her soft cheek. "The doors, I mean?"

"Probably. But I'm not sure I can let you move yet." A wicked smile kicked up the corner of her lips.

"What if I promise to come back?" He wanted her again. Already.

That seemed physically impossible. And yet...damn.

"In that case, you can go. I'll check on Isla." She untwined her legs from his and eased toward the edge of the bed.

He wanted to ask her if they were okay. If she was upset about what had happened, or if she regretted it.

Then again, did he really want to know if she was already thinking about ways to back off? Now more than ever, he wanted to help her figure out a plan for her future and for Isla's, too. He could help with that. A pragmatic plan to solve both their problems had been growing in his head all day, but now wasn't the time to talk to her about it.

The morning—and the second-guessing that would come with it—was going to happen soon enough. He didn't have any intention of ruining a moment of this night by thinking about what would happen when the sun came up.

Eight

A loud crack of thunder woke Maresa later that night.

Knifing upright in bed, she saw that the French doors in the master bedroom had been closed. Rain pelted the glass outside while streaks of lightning illuminated the empty spot in the king-size bed beside her. Reaching a hand to touch the indent on the other pillow, she felt the warmth of Cameron McNeill's body. The subtle scent of him lingered on her skin, her body aching pleasantly from sex on the chaise longue before a private catered dinner they'd eaten in bed instead of on the patio. Then, there'd been the heated lovemaking in the shower afterward.

And again in the bed before falling asleep in a tangle just a few hours ago. It was after midnight, she remembered. Close to morning.

Isla.

Her gaze darted to the nursery monitor that she'd placed on the nightstand, but it was missing. Cameron must have it, she thought, and be with the baby. But it bothered her that the little girl hadn't been the first thought in her head when she'd opened her eyes.

Dragging Cam's discarded T-shirt from the side of the bed, she pulled it over her head. The hem fell almost to her knees. She hurried out of the master bedroom across the hall to the second room where the hotel staff had brought in a portable crib. There, in a window seat looking out on the storm, lounged Cameron McNeill, cradling tiny Isla against his bare chest.

The little girl's arms reached up toward his face, her uncoordinated fingers flexing and stretching while her eyes tracked him. He spoke to her softly, his lips moving. No. He was singing, actually.

"Rain, rain, go away," he crooned in a melodic tenor that would curl a woman's toes. "Little Isla wants to play—" He stopped midsong when he spotted Maresa by the door. "Hey there. We tried not to wake you."

Her emotions puddled into a giant, liquid mass of feelings too messy to identify. She knew that her heart was at risk because she'd just given this man her body. Of course, that was part of it. But the incredible night aside, she still would have felt her knees go weak to see this impossibly big, strong man cradling a baby girl in his arms so tenderly.

Not just any baby girl, either. This was Rafe's beautiful daughter, given into Maresa's care. Her heart turned over to hear Cameron singing to her.

"It was the storm that woke me, not you." She dragged in a deep breath, trying to steady herself before venturing closer.

He propped one foot on the window seat bench, his knee bent. The other leg sprawled on the floor while his back rested against the casement.

"I gave her a bottle and burped her. I think I did that part all right." He held up the little girl wrapped in a light cotton blanket so Maresa could see. "Not sure how I did on my swaddle job, though."

Maresa smiled, stepping even nearer to take Isla from him. Her hands brushed his chest and sensual memories swamped her. She'd kissed her way up and down those pecs a few hours ago. She shivered at the memory.

"Isla looks completely content." She admired the job he'd done with the blanket. "Although I'm not sure she'll ever break free of the swaddling." She loosened the wrap just a little.

"I wrapped her like a baby burrito." He rose to his feet, scooping up an empty bottle and setting it on the wet bar. "You may be surprised to know I worked in the back of a taco truck one summer as a teen."

"I would be very surprised." She paced around the room with the baby in her arms, taking comfort from the warm weight. Earlier, Maresa had put Isla to bed in a blue-and-white-striped sleeper. Now, she wore a yellow onesie with cartoon dragons, so Cameron must have changed her. "Did your grandfather make you all take normal jobs to build character?"

"No." Cameron shook his head, his dark hair sticking up on one side, possibly from where she'd dragged her fingers through it earlier. He tugged a blanket off the untouched double bed and pulled it over to the window seat. "Come sit until she falls asleep."

She followed him over to the wide bench seat with thick gray cushions and bright throw pillows. The sides were lined with dark wooden shelves containing a few artfully arranged shells and stacks of books. She sat with her back to one of the shelves so she could look out at the storm. Cameron sat across from her, their knees touching. He pulled the blanket over both of their laps.

"You were drawn to the taco truck for the love of fine cuisine?" she pressed, curious to know more about him. She rocked Isla gently, leaning down to brush a kiss across the top of her downy forehead.

"Best tacos in Venice Beach that summer, I'll have you know." He bent forward to tug Maresa's feet into his lap. He massaged the balls of her feet with his big hands. "I was out there to surf the southern California coast that year and ended up sticking around Venice for a few months. I learned everything I know about rolling burritos from Senor Diaz, the dude who owned the truck."

"A skill that's serving you well as a stand-in caregiver," she teased, allowing herself to enjoy this blessedly uncomplicated banter for now. "You'll have to show me your swaddling technique."

"Will do."

"How did your visit to the McNeill family home go?" she asked, regretting that she hadn't done so earlier. "I was so distracted when you got back." She got tingly just thinking about all the ways he'd distracted her over the past few hours.

"You won't hear any complaints from me about how we spent our time." He slowed his stroking, making each swipe of his hands deliberate. Delectable. "And I didn't really visit anyone today. I just wanted to see the place with my own eyes before we contact my half brothers."

"But you will contact them?" She couldn't help but identify with the "other" McNeills. Her mother had been the forgotten mistress of a wealthy American businessman. She knew how it felt to be overlooked.

"My grandfather is insistent we bring them into the fold. I just want to be sure we can trust them."

She nodded, soothed by the pleasure of the impromptu foot massage. "You're proceeding carefully," she observed. "That's probably wise. I want to do the same with Isla—really think about a good plan for raising her." She wanted to ask him what he thought about buying a house, but she didn't want to detract from their personal conversation with business. "I have a lot to learn about caring for a baby."

"Are you sure you want to go for full custody?" His hands stilled on her ankles, his expression thoughtful while lightning flashed in bright bolts over the lagoon. "There's no grandparent on the mother's side that might fight for Isla?"

"I spoke to both of them briefly while I was trying to track down Trina. Trina's mother is an alcoholic who never acknowledged she has a problem, so she's not an option. And the father told me it was all he could do to raise Trina. He's not ready for a newborn." Maresa hadn't even asked him about Isla, so the man must have known that Trina was looking for a way out of being a parent.

"Rafe doesn't know yet?" he said, with a hint of surprise, and perhaps even censure in his voice. He resumed work on her feet, stroking his long fingers up her ankles and the backs of her calves.

"His counselor said we can tell him once paternity is proven, which should be next week. She said she'd help me break the news, and I think I'll take her up on that offer. I know I was floored when I heard about the baby, so I can't imagine how he might feel." She peered down at Isla, watching the baby's eyelids grow heavy. "I'm not sure that Rafe will participate much in Isla's care, but I'll have my mother's help, for as long as she stays healthy."

"You've got a lot on your plate, Maresa," he observed quietly.

"I'm lucky I still have a brother." She remembered how close they'd been to losing him those first few days. "The doctors performed a miracle saving his life, but it took Rafe a lot of hard work to relearn how to walk. To communicate as well as he does. So whatever obstacles I have to face now, it's nothing compared to what Rafe has already overcome."

She brushed another kiss along Isla's forehead, grateful for the unexpected gift of this baby even if her arrival complicated things.

"Does your mother's house have enough room for all of you?" Cameron pressed. "Have you thought about who will care for Isla during the day while you and Rafe are working? If your mother is having more MS attacks—"

"I'll figure out something." She had to. Fast.

"If it comes to a custody hearing, you might need to show the judge that you can provide for the baby with adequate space and come up with a plan for caregiving."

Maresa swallowed past the sudden lump of fear in her throat. She hadn't thought that far ahead. She'd been granted the temporary custody order easily enough, but she hadn't asked her attorney about the next steps.

A bright flash of lightning cracked through the dark horizon, the thunder sounding almost at the same time.

She slid her feet out of Cameron's lap and stood, pacing over to the crib to draw aside the mosquito netting so she could lay Isla in it.

"I'll have to figure something out," she murmured to herself as much as him. "I can't imagine that a judge would take Isla away when Trina herself wants us to raise her."

"Trina could change her mind," he pointed out. His level voice and pragmatic concern reminded her that his business perspective was never far from the surface. "Or one of her parents could decide to sue for custody."

An idea that rattled Maresa.

She whirled on him, her bare feet sticking on the hardwood.

"Are you trying to frighten me?" Because it was working. She'd had Isla in her care for a little less than forty-eight hours and already she couldn't imagine how devastated she would be to lose her. It was unthinkable.

"No, the last thing I want to do is upset you." He stood from the window seat, the blanket sliding off him. "I'm trying to help you prepare because I can see how much she means to you. How much your whole family means to you."

"They're everything," she told him simply, stepping out of the baby's room with the nursery monitor in hand. When her father left Charlotte Amalie, she had been devastated. But her mother and her brother were always there for her, cheering her on when she yearned to travel, helping her to leave Saint Thomas and take the job in Paris when Jaden dumped her. "I won't let them down."

"And I know you'd fight for them to the end, Maresa, but you might need help this time." Cameron closed the door of the second bedroom partway before following Maresa downstairs into the all-white kitchen.

She was wide-awake now, tense and hungry. She'd been more focused on Cameron than eating during dinner, and she was feeling the toll of an exhausting few days. Arriving in the eat-in kitchen with a fridge full of leftovers from the catered meal that they'd only half eaten, she slid a platter of fruits and cheeses from the middle shelf, then grabbed the bottle of sparkling water.

"What kind of help?" she asked, pouring the water into two glasses he produced from a high cabinet lit from within so that the glow came through the frosted-glass front.

Cameron peeled the plastic covering off the fruit and put the platter down in the breakfast nook.

"I have a proposition I'd like to explain." He found white ceramic plates in another cabinet and held out one of the barstools for her to take a seat. "A way we might be able to help one another."

She tucked her knees under the big T-shirt of his that she'd borrowed.

"I'm doing everything I can to help you figure out why the Carib's performance reviews are declining." She couldn't imagine what other kind of help he would need.

"I realize that." He dropped into the seat beside her and filled his plate with slices of pineapple and mango. He added a few shrimp from another tray. "But I've got a much bigger idea in mind."

She tore a heel of crusty bread from the baguette they hadn't even touched earlier. "I'm listening."

"A few months ago, I proposed to a woman I'd never met."

"Seriously?" She put down the bread, shocked. "Why would anyone do that?"

"It was impulsive of me, I'll admit. I was irritated with my grandfather because he rewrote his will with a dictate that his heirs could only inherit after they'd been married for twelve months."

"Why?" Maresa couldn't imagine why anyone would attach those kinds of terms to a will. Especially a rich corporate magnate like Malcolm McNeill. She knew a bit about him from reading the bio on the McNeill Resorts website.

"We're still scratching our heads about it, believe me. I was mad because he'd told me he'd change the terms over his dead body—which is upsetting to hear from an eighty-year-old man—and then he cackled about it like it was a great joke and I was too much of a kid to understand." Cameron polished off the shrimp and reached for the baguette. "So I worked with a matchmaker and picked a woman off a website—a woman who I thought was a foreigner looking for a green-card marriage. Sounded perfect."

"Um. Only if you're insane." Maresa had a hard time reconciling the man she knew with the story he was sharing. Although, when she thought about it, maybe he had shown her his impulsive side with the way he'd taken on her problems like they were his own—giving her the villa while he stayed in the hotel, paying for the caregiver for Isla while Maresa worked. "That's not the way most people would react to the news that they need a bride."

"Right. My brothers said the same thing." Cameron poured them both more water and flicked on an overhead light now that the storm seemed to be settling down a little. "And anyway, I backed out of the marriage proposal when I realized the woman wasn't looking to get married anyhow. My mistake had unexpected benefits, though, since—surprise—my oldest brother is getting married to the woman I proposed to."

Maresa's fork slid from her grip to jangle on the granite countertop. "You're kidding me. Does he even *want* to marry her, or is this just more McNeill maneuvering for the sake of the will?"

"This is the real deal. Quinn is big-time in love." Cameron grinned and she could see that he was happy for his brother. "And Ian is, too, oddly. It's like my grandfather waved the marriage wand and the two of them fell into line."

As conflicted as Cameron's relationships might be

with his father and grandfather, it was obvious he held his siblings in high regard.

"Which leaves you the odd man out with no bride."

"Right." He shoved aside his plate and swiveled his stool in her direction. "My grandfather had a heart attack last month and we're worried about his health. From a financial standpoint, I don't need any of the McNeill inheritance, but keeping the company in the family means everything to Gramps."

She wondered why he thought so if the older man hadn't made his will more straightforward, but she didn't want to ask. Tension crept through her shoulders.

"So you still hope to honor the terms of the will." Even as she thought it, she ground her teeth together. "You know, I'm surprised you didn't mention you had plans to marry when you wooed me into bed with you. That's not the kind of thing I take lightly."

"Neither do I." He covered her hand with his. "I am not going to march blindly into a marriage with someone I don't know. That was a bad idea." He stroked his thumb over the back of her knuckles. "But I know you."

Her mouth went dry. A buzzing started in her ears.

Surely she wasn't understanding him. But she was too dumbfounded to speak, let alone ask him for clarification.

"Maresa, you need help with Isla and your family. Rafe needs the best neurological care possible, something he could get in New York where they have world-class medical facilities. Likewise, for your mother—she needs good doctors to keep her healthy."

"I don't understand." She shook her head to clear it since she couldn't even begin to frame her thoughts. "What are you saying?"

"I'm saying a legal union between the two of us would be a huge benefit on both sides." He reached below her to turn her seat so that she faced him head-on. His blue eyes locked on hers with utter seriousness. "Marry me, Maresa."

Cameron knew his brothers would accuse him of being impulsive all over again. But this situation had nothing in common with the last time he'd proposed to a woman.

He knew Maresa and genuinely wanted to help her. Hell, he couldn't imagine how she could begin to care for a baby with everything she was already juggling. He could make her life so much easier.

She stared at him now as if he'd gone off the deep end. Her jaw unhinged for a moment. Then, she snapped it shut again.

"Maybe we've both been working too hard," she said smoothly, trotting out her competent, can-do concierge voice. "I think once we've gotten some rest you'll see that a legal bond between us would complicate things immeasurably."

Despite the cool-as-you-please smile she sent his way, her hand trembled as she retrieved her knife and cut a tiny slice of manchego from a brick of cheese. With her sun-tipped hair brushing her cheek as she moved and her feminine curves giving delectable shape to his old T-shirt, Maresa looked like a fantasy brought to life. Her lips were still swollen from his kisses, her gorgeous legs partially tucked beneath her where she sat. Yet seeing her hold Isla and tuck the tiny girl into bed had been...

Touching. He couldn't think of any other way to describe what he'd felt, and it confused the hell out of him since he'd never wanted kids. But Maresa and Isla brought a surprise protectiveness out of him, a kind of caring he wasn't sure he'd possessed. And while he wasn't going to turn into a family man anytime soon, he could certainly imagine himself playing a role to help with Isla for the next year. That was worth something to Maresa, wasn't it? Besides, seeing Maresa's tender side assured him that she wasn't going to marry him just for the sake of a big payout. She had character.

"I appreciate you trying to give me a way out." He smoothed a strand of hair back where it skimmed along her jaw. "But I'm thinking clearly, and I believe this is a good solution to serious problems we're both facing."

"Marriage isn't about solving problems, Cam." She set down the cheese without taking a single bite. "Far from it. Marriage *causes* problems. You saw it in your own family, right?"

She was probably referring to his parents' divorce and how tough that had been for him and his brothers, but he pushed ahead with his own perspective.

"But we're approaching this from a more objective standpoint." It made sense. "You and I like each other, obviously. And we both want to keep our families safe. Why not marry for a year to secure my grandfather's legacy and make sure your brother, mother and niece have the best health benefits money can buy? The best doctors and care? A home with enough room where you're not worried about Rafe being upset by the normal sounds of life with an infant?"

"In New York?" She spread her arms wide, as if that alone proved he was crazy. "My work is here. Rafe's job is here. How could we move to New York for the health care? And even if we wanted to, how would we get back here—and find work again—twelve months from now?"

"By focusing on the wheres and hows, I take it you're at least considering it?" He would have a lot of preparations to make, but he could pull it off—he could relocate all of them to Manhattan next week. He just needed to finish up his investigation into the Carib Grand and then he could return to New York.

With the terms of his grandfather's will fulfilled. It would be a worry off his mind and it would be his pleasure to help her family. It would be even more of a pleasure to have her in his bed every night.

The more he thought about it, the more right it seemed.

"Not even close." She slid off the barstool to stand. "By focusing on the wheres and hows, I'm trying to show you how unrealistic this plan is. I'm more grateful to you than I can say for trying to help me, but I will figure out a way to support my family without imposing on the McNeills for a year."

"What about your brother?" Cam shoved aside his plate. "In New York, Rafe could work in a program where he'd be well supervised by professionals who would respect his personal triggers and know how to challenge him just enough to move his recovery forward."

She folded her arms across her breasts, looking vulnerable in the too-big shirt. "You've been doing your research."

"I read up on his injury to be sure you had him doing work he could handle." Cam wouldn't apologize for looking into Rafe's situation. "You know that's why I came to the Carib in the first place—to make sure everyone was doing their job."

"It hardly seems fair to use my brother's condition to convince me."

"Isn't it less fair to deny him a good program because you wouldn't consider a perfectly legitimate offer? I'm no Jaden Torries. I'm not going to back out on you, Maresa." And she would be safe from the worry of having children with him since he would never have any of his own. That would be a good thing in a temporary marriage, right?

"We'll sign a contract that stipulates what will happen after the twelve months are up—"

"I don't want a contract," she snapped, raising her voice as she cut him off. "I've already got a failed engagement in my past. Do you think I want a failed marriage, too?" Her eyes shone too bright and he realized there were unshed tears there.

She didn't want to hear all the reasons why they would work well together on a temporary basis.

He'd hurt her.

By the time he'd figured that out, however, he was standing in the kitchen by himself. The thunder had stopped, but it seemed the storm in the villa wasn't over.

Nine

Two days later, Maresa sat behind the concierge's desk typing an itinerary for the personal assistant of an aging rock-and-roll star staying at the Carib. The guitar legend was taking his entourage on a vacation to detox after his recent stay in rehab. Maresa's job had been to keep the group occupied and away from drugs and alcohol for two weeks. With her help, they'd be too busy zip-lining, kayaking and Jet Skiing to think about anything else.

The project had been a good diversion for her since she'd returned from her trip to Martinique with Cameron. She still couldn't believe he'd proposed to her for the sake of a mutually beneficial one-year arrangement and not out of any romantic declaration of interest. Great sex aside, a proposal of a marriage of convenience really left her gut in knots.

Leaning back in her desk chair, she blinked into the afternoon sun slanting through the lobby windows and hit the send button on the digital file. She wished she could have stretched out the project a bit longer to help her from thinking about Cam. He'd been kind to her since she'd turned down his proposal, promising her that the marriage offer would remain open until he returned to New York. She shouldn't be surprised that his engagement idea had an expiration date since he wasn't doing it because he'd fallen head over heels for her. It was just business to him. Whereas for her? She had no experience conducting affairs for the sake of expedience. It sounded tawdry and wrong.

Shoving to her feet, she tried not to think about how helpful the arrangement would be for her family. For her, even. He'd dangled incredible enticement in front of her nose by promising the best health care for her brother. Her mom, too. Maresa felt like an ogre for not accepting for those reasons alone. But what was the price to her heart over the long haul? Her self-respect? Maybe it would be different if they hadn't gotten involved romantically. If they'd remained just friends. But he'd waited to spring the idea on her until after she'd kissed him. Peeled off all her clothes with him and made incredible love.

Of course her heart was involved now. How could she risk it again after the way Jaden had shredded her? Things were too murky with Cameron. There were no boundaries with him now that they'd slept together. She could too easily envision herself falling for him and then she would be devastated a year from now when he bought her a first-class ticket back to Saint Thomas. She sagged back in the office chair, the computer screen blurring because of the tears she just barely held back.

Foot traffic in the lobby was picking up as it neared five o'clock. Guests were returning from day trips. New visitors were checking in. A crowd was gathering for happy hour at the bar before the dinner rush. Maresa smiled and nodded, asking a few guests about their day as they passed her. When her phone rang, she saw Cameron's number and her stomach filled with unwanted butterflies. Needing privacy, she stepped behind the concierge stand to take the call. Her heart ached just seeing his number, wishing her brief time with him hadn't imploded so damn fast.

"Hello?" She smoothed a hand over her hair and then caught herself in the middle of the gesture.

"Rafe is on the move with a guest," Cameron spoke quietly. "Meet me on the patio and we'll follow him."

Fear for her brother stabbed through her. What was going on with him? Would this be the end of his job? She might not want to be involved with Cameron personally, but she needed him to support her professionally. She hoped it wouldn't come down to calling in the oldest McNeill brother, Quinn, to decide Rafe's fate, but they'd agreed that Cameron couldn't supervise her after what had happened between them.

"On my way." Her feet were already moving before she disconnected the call. She hurried through the tiki bar where a steel drum band played reggae music for the happy hour crowd. Dodging the waitstaff carrying oversize drinks, Maresa also avoided running into a few soaked kids spilling out onto the pool deck with inflatable rings and toys.

Another time, she would gently intervene to remind the parents they needed to be in the kids' pool. But she wouldn't let Cameron confront Rafe alone. She needed to be there with him.

And then, there he was.

The head of McNeill Resorts waited on the path to the beach for her, his board shorts paired with a T-shirt this time, which was a small favor considering how much the sight of his bare chest could make her forget all her best resolve. He really was spectacularly appealing.

"Where's Rafe?" she asked, gaze skipping past him to the empty path ahead.

"They just turned the corner. Rafe and a young mother who checked in two days ago with her husband for a long weekend."

Maresa wondered how he'd found that out so quickly. She fell into step beside him. "How did you know Rafe was with a guest? I sent him on an errand to the gift shop about twenty minutes ago."

"I hired a PI to keep tabs on things here for a few days."

Her heeled sandal caught on a tree root in the sand. "You're having someone spy on Rafe?"

"I can't assign the task to anyone in the hotel, especially if Aldo Ricci really has anything to do with assigning Rafe the extra duties." Cameron's hand snaked out to hold her back, his attention focused on the beach ahead. "Look."

Maresa peered after her brother and the petite brunette. Her short ponytail swung behind her as she walked. Rafe didn't bring her to the regular beach, but waved her through a clearing to the east. Maresa wanted to charge over there and split them up. Ask Rafe who told him to bring the woman to a deserted beach.

"What's the plan?" she asked, fidgeting with an oversize flower hanging from a tropical bush.

"We see who he's meeting and confront him when he turns back."

"We'll make too much noise tramping through there." She pointed to the overgrown foliage. "I can't believe that woman is following a total stranger into the unknown." Why didn't vacationers have more sense?

"He's a hotel employee at one of the most exclusive resorts in the world," Cameron reminded her, his jaw tensing as he drew her into the dense growth. "She paid a lot of money to feel safe here."

Right. Which meant Rafe was so fired. Panic weighted down her chest. Today, every penny of Rafe's check would go to extra care for Isla—an in-home sitter to help Maresa's mom with the baby. What would they do when they lost that money?

She would have to marry Cameron.

The truth stared her in the face as surely as Rafe waved at Jaden Torries on the beach right now. Her ex-fiancé stood by the water's edge with his easel already set up—a half-baked artist trolling for clients at the Carib and using Rafe to deliver them off-site so he could paint them. Rafe was risking his job for...what? He never made any money from this scheme.

"I'm going to strangle Jaden," she announced, fury making her ready to launch through the bushes to read him the riot act.

"No." Cameron's arm slid around her waist, holding her back. He pressed her tightly to him so he could speak softly in her ear. "Say nothing. Follow me and we'll ask Rafe about it when we're farther away so Jaden can't hear."

She wanted to argue. But Cameron must have guessed as much because he covered her lips with one finger.

"Shh." The sound was far more erotic than it should have been since she was angry.

Her body reacted to his nearness without her permission, a fever crawling over her skin until she wanted to turn in his arms and fall on him. Right here.

Thankfully, he let her go and tugged her back to the hotel's main beach where they could wait for Rafe.

"Someone is using him," she informed Cameron while they waited. "He didn't orchestrate this himself, and he doesn't receive any money. I would know if someone was paying him."

"That woman he just took down to the beach is partners with the investigator I hired," Cameron surprised her by saying. "We'll find out what's going on. But for now, ask him who sent him and see what he says. Do you want me to stay with you or do you want to speak to him alone?"

"Um." She bit her lip, her anger draining away. He was helping Rafe. And her. The PI was a good idea and could prove her brother's innocence. "It might be better if I speak to him privately. And thank you."

Cameron's blue eyes held her gaze. His hand skimmed along her arm, setting off a fresh heat inside her. "We'd make a great team if you'd give us a chance."

Would they? Could she trust him to look out for her and her family if she gave in and helped him to secure his family legacy? Sure, Cameron could help her family in ways she couldn't. He already had. But what would it be like to share a home with him for a year while they fulfilled the terms of the marriage he needed? Still, while she worried about all the ways a legal union would be risky for her, she hadn't really stopped to consider that he was already holding up his end of the promised bargain—helping all the Delphines—while she'd given him nothing in return.

Maybe she already owed him her help for all that he'd done for her. Even if the fallout twelve months from now was going to hurt far more than Jaden's betrayal.

"You're right." She squeezed Cameron's hand briefly,

then let go as she saw her brother step onto the beach. "If you're still serious about that one-year deal, I'll take it."

"Maresa?" Rafe stopped when he spotted her standing underneath a date palm tree.

She was nervous about confronting him, wishing she could talk to him about everything at once. His secret meeting on the beach. His daughter. His future.

But she worried about how he would handle the news of Isla and she wanted his counselor there. The paternity results were in, and the woman had agreed to meet them at the Delphine residence after work today, so at least Maresa would be able to share that with him soon. For now, she just needed to ask who sent him here. Keep it simple. Nonthreatening.

He got confused and agitated so easily. Which was understandable, considering the long-and short-term memory loss that plagued him. She'd be agitated too if she couldn't remember what she was doing.

"Hi, Rafe." Forcing herself to smile, she hurried over to him. Slipped an arm through his. "Gorgeous day, isn't it?"

"Nancy says, 'another day in paradise.' Every day she says that." Rafe grinned at her.

His work uniform—mostly khaki, but the short sleeves of his staff shirt were white—was loose on him, making her worry that Rafe had lost weight without her noticing. She needed to care for him more and worry about his job less. Maybe, assuming Rafe agreed, a move to New York could be a real gift for their family right now. She needed to focus on how much Cameron was trying to help her brother, mother and niece, instead of thinking about how this growing attachment to him was only going to hurt in the end.

Cameron McNeill was a warmhearted, generous man, and he'd been that way before she agreed to help him, so it wasn't as though he was self-serving. She admired the careful way he'd gone about investigating the happenings at the Carib. It showed a decency and respect for his employees that she'd bet most billionaire corporate giants wouldn't feel.

"We're lucky like that." Maresa tipped her head to his shoulder for a moment as they walked together, wanting to feel that connection to him. "What brought you down to the beach?"

Overhead, a heron flew low, casting a shadow across her brother's face before landing nearby.

"A guest wanted her picture painted. Mr. Ricci said so."

Again with the hotel director?

Maresa found that hard to believe. The man had been extremely successful in the industry for years. Why would he undermine his position by promoting solicitation on the Carib's grounds? Why would he allow his guests to think they were receiving some kind of luxury experience through a session with Jaden, whose talents were…negligible.

"Rafe." She paused her step, tugging gently on his arm to stop him, too. She needed to make sure, absolutely sure, he understood what she was asking. "Did Mr. Ricci himself tell you to escort that woman here, or did someone else tell you that Mr. Ricci said so?"

She'd tried to keep the question simple, but as soon as she asked it, she could see the furrow between Rafe's brows. The confusion in his eyes, which were so like Isla's. Ahead on the path, she could hear the music from the tiki bar band, the sound carrying on the breeze as the sun dipped lower in the sky.

"Mr. Ricci said it." A storm brewed in Rafe's blue gaze, turning the shade from sapphire to cold slate. "Why don't you believe me?"

"I do believe you, Rafe."

He shook off her hand where she touched him.

"You don't believe me." He raised his voice. He walked faster up the path, away from her. "Every day you ask me the same things. Two times. Everything. Everyday."

He muttered a litany of disjointed words as he stomped through the brush. She closed her eyes and followed him without speaking, not wanting to upset him more. Maybe she should have asked Cameron to stay with her for this.

She craved Cameron's warm touch. His opinion and outside perspective. He'd become important to her so quickly. Was she crazy to let him draw her even more deeply into his world? All the way to New York?

But as she followed Rafe up the path toward the Carib, watching the way his shoulders tensed with agitation, she knew that his job wouldn't have lasted much longer here anyway. She'd wanted this to be the answer for him— for them—until they caught up on the medical bills and she could get him in a different kind of program to support TBI sufferers. Now, she knew she'd been deceiving herself that she could make it work. In truth, she'd been unfair to her brother, setting him up to fail.

No matter how much she loved Rafe, she needed to face the fact that he would never be the brother she once knew. For his own good, she needed to start protecting him and his daughter, too. Tonight, she'd give her notice to the hotel director.

For her family's sake, she would become Mrs. Cameron McNeill. She just hoped in twelve months' time, she'd be able to resurrect Maresa Delphine from the wreckage.

* * *

Back in the Antilles Suite rented out to his alter-ego, Mr. Holmes, Cameron reread Maresa's text.

Rafe said Mr. Ricci sent him on the errand. Became agitated when I asked a second time but stuck to the same facts.

Turning off the screen on his phone, Cam stroked Poppy's head. The Maltese rested on the desk where he worked. She liked being by his laptop screen when they were indoors, maybe because he tended to pet her more often. He was going to hate returning her to Mrs. Trager when they went back to New York and his stint as an undercover boss was over.

His stint as a temporary groom was up next. He'd been surprised but very, very pleased that Maresa had said yes to his proposal. He needed to make it more official, of course. And more romantic, too, now that he thought about it. Hell, a few months ago, he'd proposed to a woman he'd never met before with flowers and a ring. Maresa, on the other hand, had gotten neither and he intended to change that immediately.

He needed to romance her, not burden her with every nitnoid detail that was going into the marriage contract. She hadn't been interested in thinking about the business details, so he would put them in writing only. It didn't matter that she didn't know about his inability to father children. She was focused on her own family. Her own child. And for his part, Cameron would make sure she didn't regret their arrangement for a moment by making it clear she had twelve incredible months ahead.

He dialed his brother Quinn to give him an update on

the situation at the Carib, wanting to lay some ground-
work for his hasty nuptials.

"Cam?" His brother answered the phone with a wary
voice. "Before you ask, the answer is no. You don't get
to fly the seaplane yourself."

Quinn was messing with him, of course. A brotherly
jab about his piloting skills—which were actually excellent. But the fact that they were the first words out
of his brother's mouth made Cam wonder about the way
the rest of the world perceived him. Reckless. Impulsive.

And his quickie engagement wouldn't do anything
to change that.

"I'm totally qualified, and you know it," he returned,
straightening Poppy's topknot that she'd scratched side-
wise. He'd gotten his sport pilot certification years ago
and he kept it updated.

"Technically, yes," Quinn groused, the sound of classical music playing in the background. "But I know the
first thing you'll do is test the aerial maneuvering or see
how she handles in a barrel roll, so the controls are off-
limits."

Funny, that had never occurred to him. But a few years
ago, it might have. Yeah. It would have. He'd totaled
Ian's titanium racing bike his first time on, seeing how
fast it would go. He'd felt bad about that. Ian replaced it,
but Cameron knew the original had been custom-built
by a friend.

He hated being like his father.

"If I stay out of the cockpit, will you do me a favor?"
He thought about bringing Maresa to New York and in-
troducing her to his family. Would she look at him the
same way when she discovered that he was considered
the family screwup, or would she take the first flight
back to Saint Thomas?

"Possibly." Quinn lowered his voice as the classical music stopped in the background. "Sofia's just finishing up a rehearsal, though. Want me to call you back?"

"No." The less time Quinn had to protest the move, the better. "I'm bringing my new fiancée home as soon as possible," he announced, knowing he had a long night ahead to make all the necessary arrangements.

"Not again." His brother's quick assumption that Cameron was making another mistake grated on Cam's last nerve.

Straightening, he moved away from the desk to stare out the window at the Caribbean Sea below.

"This time it's for real." He trusted Maresa to follow through with the marriage for the agreed-upon time. "Maresa deserves a warm welcome from the whole family and I want your word that she'll receive it."

"Cam, you've been in Saint Thomas for just a few days—"

"Your word," Cam insisted. "And I'll need Ian's cooperation, too."

For a moment, all he heard was Vivaldi's "Spring" starting up in the background of the call. Then, finally, Quinn huffed out a breath.

"Fine. But the plane better damn well be in one piece."

Cameron relaxed his shoulders, realizing now how tense he'd been waiting for an answer. "Done. See you soon, Brother, and I'll give you a full report on the Martinique McNeills plus an update on the Carib."

Disconnecting the call, Cameron went through a mental list of all he needed to do in order to leave for a few days. He had to have the PI take a close look at Aldo Ricci, no matter how stellar the guy's reputation was in the industry. Cameron needed to make arrangements for a ring, flowers and a wedding. He had to find a nanny, narrow down some options for good programs for Rafe and research the best neurosurgeon to have a consultation with Analise Delphine. He could farm out some of those tasks to his staff in New York. But before anything else, he needed to phone his lawyer to draw up the contracts that would protect his interests and Maresa's, too. He felt a sense of accomplishment that he'd be able to help someone he'd come to care about. This was surprisingly easy for him. As long as they both went into this marriage with realistic expectations, it could all work.

Only when that was done would he allow himself to return to Maresa's place and remind her why marrying him was going to be the best decision of her life. He might have his impulsive and reckless side, but he could damn well take good care of her every need for the upcoming year.

With great pleasure for them both.

Ten

I need to see you tonight.

Standing in her mother's living room, Maresa read the text from Cameron, resisting the urge to hug the phone to her chest like an adolescent.

She stared out the front window onto the street, reminding herself he wanted a business arrangement, not a romantic entanglement. If she was going to commit herself to a marriage in name only, she needed to stop spending so much time thinking about him. How kind he'd been to her. How good he could make her feel. How sweet he was with Isla.

Because Cameron McNeill didn't spend his free hours dreaming about her in those romantic ways. He was too busy investigating business practices at the Carib Grand and fulfilling the legal terms of his grandfather's will. Those things were important to him. Not Maresa.

The scent of her mother's cooking lingered in the air—plantains and jerk chicken that she'd shared with Mr. Leopold earlier. Her mom had warmed up a plate for Rafe when they returned from work, but Maresa's stomach was in too many knots to eat. Huffing out a sigh of frustration, Maresa typed out a text in response to Cameron.

The counselor just arrived. Any time after nine is fine.

She shut off her phone as soon as the message went through to stop herself from looking for a reply. If she wasn't careful, she'd be sending heart emojis and making an idiot of herself with him the way she had with Jaden. At least with this marriage, she knew the groom would really go through with it since he wanted to secure his millions. Billions? She had no clue. She only knew that the McNeills lived on a whole other level from the Delphines.

Here, they were a family of four crowded into her mother's two-bedroom apartment. For now, Isla's portable crib was in Analise's bedroom so they could shut the door if she started to cry. They'd told Rafe the little girl was a friend's daughter and that Maresa was babysitting for the night, but he'd barely paid any attention since he was still upset with his sister.

"Mom?" Maresa called as she opened the door for their guest—Tracy Seders, the counselor who would help them tell Rafe about his daughter. "She's here."

Analise Delphine shuffled out of the kitchen, dropping an old-fashioned apron behind a chair on her way out. The house was neat and clean, but their style of housekeeping meant you needed to be careful when opening closets or junk drawers. The mess lurked dangerously below the surface. How would they merge their lifestyle with Cameron's for the next year? Maresa would speak to him in earnest tonight, to make sure he knew what he was getting into by taking on a whole, chaotic family and not just one woman.

"Thank you for coming." Maresa ushered Tracy Seders inside, showing her to a seat in the living area where Maresa had slept since returning from Paris. She'd tucked away the blanket and pillow for the visit.

The three women spent a few minutes talking while Rafe finished his dinner and Isla bounced in a baby seat on the floor, her blue eyes wide and alert. She wore a pastel yellow sleeper with an elephant stitched on the front, one of a half dozen outfits that had arrived from the hotel gift shop that morning, according to Analise. The card read, "Congratulations from McNeill Resorts."

More thoughtfulness from Cameron that made it difficult to be objective about their arrangement.

Now, the counselor turned to Analise. "As I told Maresa on the phone, there's a good chance Rafe doesn't remember his relationship with Trina. He's never once mentioned her to me in our sessions." She smoothed a hand through her windblown auburn hair. The woman favored neat shirtdresses and ponytails most days, and made Maresa think of a kindergarten teacher. Today, the reason for the ponytail was more apparent: her red curls were rioting. "If that's the case, we'll have a difficult time explaining about Isla."

Analise nodded as she frowned, her eyes turned to where Rafe sat alone at the kitchen table, listening to a Yankees game on an old radio and adjusting the antennae.

Maresa repositioned the crochet throw pillow behind her back, fidgeting in her nervousness. "But we don't need to press, right? We can always just end the discussion and reinforce the relationship down the road when he's less resistant."

"Exactly." Tracy Seders tucked her phone in her purse and sat forward on the love seat. "Rafe, would you like to join us for a minute?" she called.

Maresa's stomach knotted tighter. She hadn't told her mother about Cam's proposal yet, but she'd mentioned it to the counselor on the phone in the hopes the woman would help her feel out Rafe about a move to New York. She feared it was too much at once, but the counselor hadn't seemed concerned, calling it a potential diversion from the baby news if Rafe didn't react well to that.

Now her brother ambled toward them. He'd changed out of his work clothes. In his red gym shorts and gray T-shirt, he looked much the same as he had as a teen, only now there were scattered scars in his hair from the surgery that had saved his life. More than the scars though, it was the slow, deliberate movements that gave away his injury. He used to dart and hurry everywhere, a whirling force of nature.

"Ms. Seders. You don't belong here." He grinned as he said it and the counselor didn't take offense.

"You aren't used to me in your living room, are you, Rafe?" She laughed and patted the seat beside her. "I heard your family has exciting news for you."

"What?" He lowered himself beside her, watching her intently.

Maresa held her breath, willing the woman to take the reins. She didn't know how to begin. Especially after she'd hurt his feelings earlier.

"They heard from your old girlfriend, Rafe. Trina?" She waited for any show of recognition.

There was none.

The counselor plowed ahead. "Trina had a baby this

spring, Rafe. Your baby." The woman nodded toward Maresa, gesturing for her to show him Isla.

She bent to lift the little girl from the carrier.

"No." Rafe said, shaking his head. "No. No girlfriend. No baby."

He got to his feet and would have walked away if Tracy hadn't taken his hand.

"Rafe, your sister will watch over Isla for you. But the baby is your daughter. One day, when you feel better—"

"No baby." Rafe looked at Maresa. Was it her imagination, or did his eyes narrow a bit? Was he still angry with her? "No."

He stalked out of the room this time and Analise made a strangled cry. Of disappointment? Maresa couldn't be sure. She'd been so focused on Rafe and trying to read his reaction she hadn't paid attention to her mother. Gently, Maresa returned Isla to the baby carrier, buckling her in to keep her safe.

"Rafe?" the counselor called after him. "I have a friend in New York City I would like you to meet. Another counselor. She lives near where the Yankees play."

Maresa's mother drew a breath as if to interrupt, but Maresa put her hand on her mom's arm to stop her. Analise's eyes went wide while Rafe spun around, his eyes bright.

"The Yankees?" He stepped toward them again, irresistibly drawn. "I could go to New York?" He looked at Maresa, and she realized how much she'd become a parent figure to him in the last months.

"Maresa." Her mother's voice was stern, although she kept her words low enough that Rafe wouldn't hear. "You know that's not possible."

Maresa squeezed her mom's hand, while she kept her

eyes on Rafe. "We could all go if you don't mind seeing a new doctor."

Rafe raised his arm above his head and it took Maresa a moment to realize he was pumping his fist.

"Yankees." He smiled crookedly. "Yankees! Yes."

The counselor shared a smile with Maresa while Rafe went to turn up the radio louder, a happy expression lingering on his face as he sank into a chair at the table.

"Maresa?" Analise asked. "What on earth?"

They both rose to their feet to walk the counselor to the door, and Maresa gave her mother an arm to lean on. Thanking the woman for her help that had gone above and beyond her job description, Maresa waved to her while she walked to her car. Only then did she face her mother, careful to keep Analise balanced on her unsteady feet.

"I'm getting married, Mom." The announcement lacked the squealing joy she'd had when she told her mother about Jaden's proposal. But at least now, with a contract sure to come that would document what she was agreeing to, Maresa knew the marriage would happen as surely as she knew the divorce would, too. "He cares, Mom, and wants to help with Rafe however he can."

Analise bit her lip. "Maresa. Baby." She shook her head. "After everything I went through with your daddy? You ought to know men don't mean half of what they say."

Maresa couldn't have said what surprised her more—that her mother recognized her father had played her false, or that Analise sounded protective on Maresa's behalf.

"I know, Mom." Maresa watched as the counselor sped away from the curb. "But this is different, trust me. I don't have any illusions that he loves me."

"No love?" Her mother grabbed her hand and squeezed—probably as hard as her limited mobility allowed. "There is no other reason to marry, Maresa Delphine, and you know it."

Right. And fairy tales came true.

But Maresa wasn't going to argue that with her mother right now. Instead, she hugged her gently.

"It's going to be okay. And this is going to be good for Rafe. I want us all to move to New York where he can get into a supervised care program that will really help him." She remained on the front step, breathing in the hot air as the moon came out over the Caribbean. Palm trees rustled in the breeze.

"Honey, once you get your heart broke, you can't just unbreak it." Her mother's simple wisdom was a good reminder for her.

She would be like Cameron and look at this objectively. They could be a good team. And just maybe, she could keep her heart intact. But in order to do that, she really shouldn't be sleeping with her charismatic future husband. It was while she was in his arms, kissing him passionately and sharing her body with him, that her emotions got all tangled up.

"I understand," she promised, just as Isla let out a small cry. Her mother insisted on being the one to check on the baby. Before Maresa could follow, a pair of headlights streaked across her as a vehicle turned up her street.

A warm tingle of anticipation tripped over her skin, telling her who it was. What kind of magic let her know when Cameron McNeill was nearby? It was uncanny.

Yet sure enough, on the road below, a dark Jeep slid into the spot that Rafe's counselor had vacated just a short time ago.

Maresa's fiancé had arrived.

* * *

Half an hour later, Cameron had Maresa in the passenger seat of the Jeep. They'd left Isla at her mother's house since the women agreed the baby was out for the night after a final feeding. Or at least until the 3:00 a.m. bottle feeding, which had been her pattern the last few nights.

He'd kept silent in front of Maresa's mom about the fact that he'd been the one to provide that bottle to the baby two nights before. Analise Delphine had been cordial but not warm, unmoved by the bouquets of tropical wildflowers he'd brought for each of them. No doubt Maresa's mother was concerned about the quick engagement, the same way Quinn had been concerned. Both women were worried about Rafe's reaction to his daughter, which had been adamant denial that she belonged to him. Just hearing as much made Cameron's heart ache for the little girl. He knew Maresa would be a good mother figure to her. But how hard must it be for a girl to grow up without a father? Or worse, a father who was a presence but didn't care to acknowledge her?

Of course, one day, she would know that Rafe suffered an injury that changed his personality. But still…he hated that for Isla, who deserved to grow up with every advantage. With a lot of love. Cameron didn't know why he felt so strongly about that. About her. Was it because of the baby's connection to Maresa? Or did he simply have a soft spot for kids that he'd never known about? He'd never questioned his comfort with giving up fatherhood before, but he wondered if he'd always feel as adamant about that.

Now, the breeze whipped through the Jeep since he'd taken the top down. With the speed limit thirty-five everywhere, they were safe enough. Poppy was buckled into her pet carrier in the backseat, her nose pressed to the grates for a better view.

Maresa had shown him how to leave the city and climb the winding road at the center of the island to get to Crown Mountain where he'd rented a place for the night. He hadn't mentioned the destination because they weren't staying there for long, but he didn't want to give her a ring on the doorstep of her mother's home. They might be marrying for mutual benefit, but that didn't mean the union had to be devoid of romance.

She'd had a rough year with her brother's injury and now the surprise baby. And he could tell she'd had a rough evening, the stress of the day apparent in her quietness. The tension in her movements. He wanted to do something nice for her. The first of many things.

"You're very mysterious tonight," she observed as she pointed to another turn he needed to take.

"I don't mean to be." He ignored her directions now that they were close to the cottage he'd rented. He recalled how to get there from here. "But I do have a surprise for you."

She twisted in her seat, her hair whipping across her cheek as she looked backward. "It will be a surprise if we don't get lost since you didn't follow my directions."

"I've got my bearings now." He used the high beams to search for a road marker the owner of the secluded property had mentioned. "There it is." He spotted a bent and rusted road work sign that looked like it had been there for a decade.

Behind the sign lurked a driveway and he turned the Jeep onto the narrow road.

"I'm sure this is private property," Maresa ducked when he slowed for a low tree limb.

"It is." He could see the house now in the distance high up the mountainside. "And I have a key."

"Of course you do." She slouched back in her seat. "I'm sleeping on a couch while you have a seemingly infinite number of places to lay your head at night."

"It helps to own a resort empire." He wouldn't apologize for his family's hard work. "And soon you'll be a part of it. We've got properties all over the globe."

"Including a mountain cottage in Saint Thomas?" She folded her arms, edgy and tense.

"No. I rented this one." He turned a corner and spotted the tropical hideaway that promised amazing views from the terraces. "Come on. I'm anxious to show you your surprise."

"There's more?" She unbuckled her seatbelt as he parked the Jeep in the lighted driveway surrounded by dense landscaping.

Night birds called out a welcome, the scent of fragrant jasmine in the air. The white, Key West-style home was perched on stilts, the dense forest growing up underneath it, although he spotted some kayaks and bikes stored down there. The main floor was lit up from within. Visible through the floor-to-ceiling window, the simple white furnishings and paint contrasted with dark wood floors and ceiling fans.

"Yes and I'm hoping you're more impressed with the next one than you are with the cottage." He stepped down from the Jeep and went around to free Poppy, attaching her leash so she didn't run off after a bird.

"I'm impressed," Maresa acknowledged, briefly brushing against him as she hopped out, unknowingly tantalizing the hell out of him. "I'm just frazzled after the way I upset Rafe down by the beach tonight and then again when we tried to tell him about Isla." She blinked up at Cameron in the moonlight, her shoulders partly bared by the simple navy blue sundress she wore. "It hurts to be the one causing him so much distress after all the months I've tried to take care of him and help his recovery."

The pain in her words was so tangible it all but reached out to sucker punch him. He wanted to kiss her. To offer her the comfort of his arms and his touch, but he didn't want to take anything for granted when the parameters of their relationship had shifted. He settled for brushing a hair from her forehead while Poppy circled their legs.

"They say we often lash out at the people we feel most comfortable with. The people who make us feel safe." His hand found the middle of her back and he palmed it, rubbing gently for a moment. Then he ushered her ahead on the path to the house where he punched in the code he'd been given for the alarm system.

A few minutes later, they'd found enough lights to illuminate the way to the back terrace, which was the main feature he'd brought her here for.

Poppy claimed a chair at the back of the patio and Cam added an extension to the leash to give her lots of freedom to explore. She looked as though she was done for the night, however, settling into the lounger with a soft dog sigh.

"Oh, wow. It's so beautiful here." Maresa paused at the low stone wall that separated them from the brush and trees of the mountainside.

Peering down Crown Mountain, they could see into the harbor and the islands beyond. With a cruise ship docked in the harbor and a hundred other smaller boats in the water nearby, the area looked like a pirate's jewel box, lit up with bright colors.

"Would you like to swim?" He pointed to the pool that overlooked the view, the water lit up to show the natural stone surround and a waterfall feature.

"No, thank you." She wrapped her arms around herself. "It's a beautiful night. I'm happy to just sit and enjoy this." Her tawny eyes flipped up to his. "But I'm curious why you texted me. You said you needed to see me tonight?"

It occurred to him now that part of the reason she'd been tense and edgy on the ride was because she'd been nervous. Or at least, that's how he read her body language now. Wary. Worried.

He wanted to banish every worry from her pretty eyes. And he wanted it with a fierceness that caught him off guard.

"Only because I wanted to make sure we were on the same page about this marriage." He dragged two chairs to the edge of the stone wall so they could put their feet up and look out over the view. "That you felt comfortable about it. That if you had any worries or concerns, I could address them."

Also, he just plain wanted to see her again. Spend time with her when they weren't working. When the whole of the Carib Grand hotel wasn't looking over their shoulders. He didn't want her to feel like he was rushing her into something she wasn't ready for.

"I'm not worried for my sake." She tipped her chin at him as she took her seat and he did the same. "But I'd be lying if I said I wasn't worried about my family. My brother seems excited to go to New York, but my mother thinks it's crazy, of course." She wrapped her arms around herself. "And Isla... I worry that a year is a long time for a baby. How can she help but get attached to you in that time?"

It was a question that had never crossed his mind. But even as he wanted to deny that such a thing would happen, how could he guarantee it? The truth was, he was already growing attached to the little girl and he'd known her less than a week.

"She'll have a nanny," he offered, not sure how else to address the concern. "I've already asked my staff to arrange for candidates for you to interview when we get to New York. And whoever you choose will have the option of returning to Saint Thomas with you if you want to return next year."

"Where else would I go?" She frowned.

"Maybe you'll decide to stay in New York." He couldn't imagine why she'd want to leave. "I've already found a program for Rafe that he's going to love. There's a group of gardeners who work in Central Park under excellent supervision—"

"Don't." She cut him off, shaking her head. Her eyes were over-bright. "We'll never be able to afford to stay there after the year is up and—"

"Maresa." Hadn't he made this clear? The guilt that he might have contributed to her stress by not explaining himself stung. Yes, he'd kept quiet about his inability to father children since they were entering a marriage of convenience, and it wouldn't be a factor anyway. But there were plenty of other things—positive, happy things—he could have shared with her to reassure her about this union. "I'll provide for you afterward. And your whole family. I'm having my attorney work on a fair settlement for you to review, but I assure you that you'll be able to stay in New York if you choose." Maybe the time had come to make things more concrete. He dug in his pocket and found the ring box.

A jingle sounded behind them as Poppy leaped down

from her perch and dragged her leash over to see what was happening. She sat at his feet, expectant. The animal was too smart.

"That's kind of you," Maresa said carefully, not seeing the ring box while she looked down at the harbor. The hem of her navy blue sundress blew loosely around her long legs where she had them propped. "But when you say the marriage will be real, how exactly do you mean that?"

He cracked open the black velvet and leaned closer to show her what was inside.

"I mean this kind of real." He pulled out the two carat pear-shaped diamond surrounded by a halo of smaller diamonds in a platinum band. It was striking without being overdone, just like Maresa. "Will you marry me, Maresa Delphine?"

He heard her breath catch and hoped she liked the surprise, but her eyes remained troubled as she took in the ring.

"I don't understand." Sliding her feet to the stone terrace, she stood. She paced away from him, her blue dress swirling around her calves. "Is it a business arrangement? Or are we playing house and pretending to care about one another as part of some deal?" She spun to face him, her hands fisting on her hips. "Because I don't think I can do both."

Carefully, he tucked the ring back in its box and set it on the seat before he followed her.

"I'm not sure we'll be *playing* at anything," he replied, weighing his words. "My house is real enough. And I care about you or I wouldn't have asked you to do this with me in the first place."

He studied her, looking for a hint of the woman who'd come apart in his arms not once, but three times on that night they'd spent together in Martinique. He'd felt their connection then. She had, too. He'd bet his fortune on it.

"You might think you care about me, but I'm not the efficient and organized concierge that you met when you were pretending to be Mr. Holmes." She folded her arms over her chest. "Maybe I was pretending then, too. I fake that I'm super capable all day to make up for the fact that I keep failing my family every time I turn around. The real me is much messier, Cameron. Much less predictable."

He weighed her rapid-fire words. *O-kay.* She was worried about this. Far more than she'd let on initially. But he was glad to know it now. That's why they were here. To talk about whatever concerned her. To make a plan for tomorrow.

For their future.

"The real you is fascinating as hell." Maybe it was his own impulsive streak responding, but a little straight talk never scared him off. "No need to hide her from me." He reached to touch her, his hands cupping her shoulders, thumbs settling on the delicate collarbone just beneath the straps of her dress.

"Then answer one thing for me, because I can't go into this arrangement without knowing."

"Anything."

"Why me?"

Eleven

It was all too much.

The moonlight ride to this beautiful spot. A fairytale proposal from a man who promised to take care of her struggling family. A man who wasn't scared off by the fact that she'd just inherited a baby.

With her mother's warning still ringing in her ears— that there was no other reason to marry if not for love— Maresa needed some perspective on what was happening between them before she signed a marriage certificate to be Cameron's wife.

"Are you asking me what I find appealing about you?" He lifted a dark eyebrow at her, his gaze simmering as it roamed over her. "I must not have done my job the other night in Martinique."

"Not that." She understood the chemistry. It was hot enough to make her forget all her worries. Hot enough to make her lose herself. "I mean, with all the women in the world who would give their right arm to marry a McNeill, why would you ever choose a bride with a new baby, an ailing mother and a brother who will need supervision for the rest of his adult life? Why go for the woman with the most baggage imaginable?"

As she said the words aloud, they only reinforced how ludicrous the notion seemed. Women like her didn't get the fairytale ending. Women like Maresa just put their heads down and worked harder.

He never stopped touching her, even at her most agitated, his fingers smoothing over her shoulders, brushing aside her hair, rubbing taut muscles she didn't know were so tense. "Let's pretend for a moment that Rafe had never been injured and he was just a regular, twenty-two-year-old brother. How disappointed would you be in him if he chose who to date—who to care about—based on a woman's family life? Based on, as you call it, who had the least baggage?"

Was it Cam's soothing hands that eased some of her tension? Or were his words making a lot of sense? Listening to him made her feel that she'd denigrated her own worth—and damn it, she knew better than that.

"All I'm saying is that you could have made your life a lot simpler by dating someone else." She edged closer to him, drawn by the skillful work of his fingers. He smelled good. And she'd missed him these last two days. "Is that what we're doing, by the way? Dating?"

She wished she didn't need so much assurance. But she'd been jilted before. And she would be making a big leap to follow him to New York, leaving her job behind.

"Married people can date," he assured her, his voice whispering over her ear in a way that made her shiver. "And much more. The two aren't mutually exclusive."

Closing her eyes, she leaned into him, soaking up his

hard male strength. She inhaled the woodsy pine scent of his aftershave, not fighting the chemistry that happened every time he came near her. He tilted her face up to his and she closed her eyes. Waiting.

Wanting.

His thumb traced the outline of her jaw. Brushed her cheek. Trailed delicious shivers in its wake.

When his lips covered hers she almost felt faint. Her knees were liquid and her legs were shaky. She wound her arms around his neck, savoring the brush of five o'clock shadow against her cheek when he kissed her. The gentle abrasion tantalized her, reminding her of the places on her body where she'd found tiny patches of whisker burn after the night they'd spent together.

"You rented this house for the night," she reminded him, her thoughts already retreating to the bedroom indoors.

"I did." He plucked her off her feet, lifting her higher against him so their bodies realigned in new and delicious ways.

"And you haven't even asked me inside." She arched her neck for him to kiss her there, inhaling sharply as he ran his tongue behind her ear.

"I didn't want to be presumptuous." His fingers found the zipper in the back of her dress and tugged the tab down, loosening the soft cotton.

"Gallant." She kissed his jaw. "Chivalrous, even." She kissed his cheek. "But right now, you should start presuming."

He chuckled quietly as he lowered Maresa to her feet again and whistled for Poppy, unhooking the pup's leash where he'd fastened it earlier.

"Let me just grab the chairs." He opened the door for

Maresa and then jogged back to return the furniture to where they'd found it.

Cam was back at her side in no time, hauling her toward the bedroom that he must have scoped out earlier. As if walking on a cloud of hope, she followed him into the large, darkened room where pale blue moonlight streamed through open blinds overlooking the ocean, spotlighting the white duvet of a king-size bed.

It smelled like cypress wood and lemon polish and possibility. Then Cameron's arms were around her again. He slid his hands into her dress, watching with hungry eyes as the fabric slid to the floor and all the possibilities became reality. She hadn't worn much underneath and he made quick work of it now, peeling down the red satin bra and bikini panties that had been her one splurge purchase in Paris. She'd liked the feel of that decadent lace against her skin, but Cameron's hands felt better. Much, much better.

He cupped between her thighs and stroked her with long fingers until she was mindless with want. Need. She felt a deep ache for them to connect in any way possible to help alleviate the nerves in her belly. To ease her reservations about marriage that she desperately didn't want to think about.

Especially not now.

She tugged at his shirt, wanting it gone. But the longer he touched her, the less her limbs cooperated. She couldn't think. She could only feel. Or there was something inherently perfect about only feeling, about abandoning concerns and taking this moment for the two of them, only them, the rest of the world be damned for now.

When the first shudders began, he covered her mouth with a kiss, catching her cries of release. He was so generous. So good to her. He held her while she recovered from the last aftershock. She wanted to return all that generosity with her hands and lips, but he was already lifting her, depositing her where he wanted her on the bed while he stripped off his clothes.

Another time, she would ask him to strip slower so she could savor the ways his muscles worked together on his sculpted body. But right now, she craved the feel of him inside her. Deeply. Sooner rather than later. She waited until he'd found a condom, then sat up on the bed, pulling him down to her.

With unsteady hands, she stroked him, exploring the length and texture of him, wanting to provide the same pleasure he'd given her. He cupped her breasts, molding them in his hands. Teasing the sensitive tips with his tongue. Sensation washed through, threatening to draw her under again. He reached for the condom and passed it to her, letting her roll it into place.

He spanned her thighs with his palms, making room for himself before he thrust into her deeply, fully. She stared up at him and found his gaze on her. He lined up their hands and fit his fingers between each of hers before drawing her arms over her head, holding them there as she took in the moment of them, connected, as one, and a shimmer rippled along her skin.

With the moonlight spilling over their joined bodies, she had to catch her breath against a wave of emotion. Hunger. Want. Tenderness. A whole host of feelings surged and she had to close her eyes against the power of the moment.

He started a rhythm that took her higher. Higher. She lifted her hips, meeting his thrusts, relishing the feel of him as the tension grew taut. Hot.

He still held her hands, her body stretched beneath

his, writhing. He didn't touch her anywhere else. He only leaned close to speak into her ear.

"All mine." The words were a rasp. A breath.

And her total undoing.

Her back arched, every nerve ending tightening for a moment before release came in one wrenching wave after another. She squeezed his hands tight and she felt the answering shock in his body as he went utterly still. His shout mingled with her soft cries while the sensations wrapped around them both.

Replete, Maresa splayed beneath him, waiting to catch her breath. Eventually he rolled to her side but he kissed her shoulder as he went. He brushed her damp hair from her face, smoothing it, pulled the white duvet over her cooling skin and fluffed her pillow. Her body was utterly content. Sated. Pleasurable endorphins frolicked merrily in her blood.

But her heart was already heading back toward wariness. The sex had been powerful. Far more than just chemistry. And she wasn't ready to think about that right now. Not by a long shot.

Yet how long could she delay? Not more than a moment apparently. She didn't have a choice when all too soon she felt Cameron lean over the bed and dig in the pile of clothes. When he came back, he slid something cold along her hand and then onto her left ring finger.

"You should wear this." He left the diamond there and tugged her hand from the covers so they could see the brilliant glint of the stones in the moonlight.

The engagement ring.

She swallowed hard, trying not to think about what it would have been like to have him slide it into place for real, kissing her fingers to seal the moment.

Maresa turned to look at his handsome profile in the

dark, his face so close to hers. He must have felt her stare because he turned toward her, too.

"It's beautiful," she told him honestly, feeling that he deserved some acknowledgement of all his hard work to make this night special for her, even if this marriage might very well break her heart in a million pieces. "Of course I love it. Who wouldn't?"

The words were out of her mouth before she could rethink them. Cameron smiled and kissed her, pleased with her assessment.

But Maresa feared she wasn't just talking about the ring. She was talking about the night and what they'd just shared. Her emotions were too raw and this was all happening way too fast. But somehow, in spite of her better judgment and the mistakes of her past, she was developing deep feelings for him. Very real feelings.

How on earth was she going to hide it from him for the next twelve months? He'd brought her here tonight to discuss their plans for a future. A move to New York. A union that would benefit both of them on paper.

If she had any hope of holding up her end of the agreement to walk away in twelve months, she needed to do a better job of shoring up her defenses.

Starting right now.

Twelve

Two weeks after he first placed a rock on Maresa's finger, Cameron prepared to introduce her to his family. Seated in the third-floor library of his grandfather's house on Manhattan's Upper East Side, Cam sipped the Chivas his brother Ian had just handed him. The three brothers had gathered in the late afternoon to discuss the other McNeill situation before a dinner with their wives, their father and grandfather. He hadn't wanted Maresa to arrive at the house unescorted this evening but she'd been excited to visit Rafe on-site at his new work program during his first full day. It was the first sign of genuine happiness Cameron had seen from her since they'd signed the marriage certificate.

He was trying to give her time to get acclimated to New York before meeting the McNeills, not wanting to make her transition more stressful with the added pressure of a family meeting. He'd even kept the courthouse marriage a secret for the first week—a ceremony conducted by a justice of the peace in Saint Thomas to help keep the McNeill name out of the New York papers. But he could keep things quiet for only so long. Quinn had known a marriage was in the works and finally harassed the truth out of him—that Cam had relocated all the Delphines, including baby Isla, to his place in Brooklyn. Rafe was so excited to see his favorite baseball team play that Cameron had finagled a friend's corporate box for the season, an extravagance Maresa had chided him about, but not for too long after seeing how happy it made Rafe. She didn't know it yet, but Cameron was flying in Bruce Leopold, the Delphines' neighbor in Charlotte Amalie, to attend the team's next home series with Rafe.

Cameron ran a finger over one of the historic Chinese lacquer panels between the windows overlooking the street while he waited for his brothers to finish up a conversation about a hotel Ian had been working on. Cameron felt good about where things stood with all of Maresa's family now. Analise had warmed to him considerably after seeing the in-law suite, thanking him personally for the modifications he'd made so she could get around more easily. It hadn't taken a construction crew long to add handrails to the tub and a teak bench to the shower stall, along with new easier-to-turn doorknobs in all the rooms and an intercom system in case she needed anything.

Isla was sleeping longer stretches at night and Maresa had personally hired a live-in nanny and a weekend caregiver who were settling in well. She seemed pleased with them, and her legal suit for permanent custody of the baby should be settled within the week now that Cameron had gotten his legal team involved to expedite things. Trina wasn't interested in visitation, which made

Maresa sad, but Cameron told her she might change her mind one day. For his part, he enjoyed spending time with a twelve-week-old far more than he ever would have imagined. He liked waving off the nanny at 5:00 a.m. and walking around his house with the baby, showing her the view from the nursery window and discussing his plans for the day. Sometimes, when she stared up at him with her big blue eyes, Cameron would swear she was really listening.

If only his new wife seemed as content. She'd been pulling away from him ever since the night he'd slid the ring onto her finger and he wanted to know why.

"Earth to Cam?" Ian waved his own glass of dark amber Scotch in front of Cameron's nose. "You ready to join us or are you too busy dreaming of the new bride?"

Cam shook his head. "I'm waiting for you to quit talking business so we can figure out our next move with Dad's secret sons."

He wasn't going to talk about Maresa when she wasn't around. He would introduce his brothers to her soon enough and they would be impressed. Hell, they'd be downright envious of him if they hadn't recently scooped up impressive women themselves.

Lowering himself into a leather club chair near one of the built-in bookshelves full of turn-of-the-century encyclopedias that had amused him as a kid, Cameron waited for his brothers to grill him on his fact-finding mission to Martinique.

Quinn took the couch across from Cam and Ian paced. One of them must have hit the button on the entertainment system because an Italian aria played in the background. Quinn must be refining his musical tastes now that he was marrying a ballerina.

"You didn't give us much to go on," Ian noted, pausing

by an antique globe. "You said all three of them—Damon, Gabe and Jager—keep a presence in Martinique?"

Cameron remembered that day of sleuthing well. The only thing that had kept him from feeling resentful as hell about seeing the McNeill doppelgängers had been knowing that Maresa was waiting for him back at the Cap Est Lagoon villa. They'd shared an incredible night together.

"Correct. Jager runs the software empire." They'd all read the report from the PI who'd found the brothers in the first place. "Damon actually founded the company, but he's been noticeably absent over the last six months since his wife disappeared shortly after their wedding." From all accounts, the guy was shredded about the loss, even though he hadn't made the disappearance public. Talking to a few people close to the family about it had made Cameron all the more determined to figure things out with Maresa. "And Gabe, the youngest, runs a small resort property. Ironic coincidence or a deliberate choice to mirror the McNeill business, I can't say."

Frowning, Quinn set down his glass on a heavy stone coaster with a map of Brazil—a gift from their mother. "I thought they were all involved in software? Didn't the PI's report say as much?"

"They are. But they each have outside specialties and interests," Cameron clarified.

Ian took a seat on the arm of the couch at the opposite end from Quinn. He picked up a backgammon piece from a set that remained perpetually out and flipped it in his hand. "Just like us."

Quinn leaned forward. "One obvious way to bring them into the fold is to see if the one who has a resort—Gabe?" He looked to Cam for confirmation before continuing. "We ask him if he's interested in stepping into Aldo Ricci's spot at the Carib now that Cam ousted him.

With good reason, I might add." He lifted his Scotch in a toast.

Ian did the same. "Here, here. Good job figuring that one out, Cam."

Enjoying a rare moment of praise from his brothers, Cam lifted the glass in acknowledgement and took a sip along with them. With the help of another investigator, Cameron had confirmed that Aldo Ricci had been taking kickbacks from low-end artists passing their work off as far more valuable than it was to the guests. With Ricci's worldly demeanor and contacts around the globe, he was someone that guests trusted when he assured them a sitting with a famous artist was difficult to procure.

But for a fee, he could arrange it.

Ricci hadn't just done so with Jaden Torries, but a whole host of artists at the Carib Grand and at properties he worked for before coming to McNeill Resorts. Cameron had released him from his contract and the company lawyers would decide if it was worth a lawsuit. Certainly, there would be public relations damage control. But at least the Carib was free of a man who gladly preyed on employees like Rafe to facilitate meetings—employees who were working on a trial basis and could be terminated easily. Cameron was certain the performance reviews would improve with the manipulative director out of the picture.

Good riddance to Aldo Ricci. The arrogant ass.

"You want to ask Gabe McNeill to take Aldo Ricci's job?" Cameron went on to explain that the youngest McNeill's resort was on a much smaller scale.

"All the more reason to get him accustomed to the way we do business," Quinn insisted. "You know Gramps insists we bring them in—"

A scuffle at the library door alerted them to a newcomer's arrival. Malcolm McNeill pushed his way through the door with his polished mahogany walking stick before Ian could reach him to help.

"I heard my name," the gray-haired, thinning patriarch called without as much bluster as he would have even a few months ago. "Don't think you can conduct family business without me."

Cameron worried to see the toll his grandfather's heart attack had taken on him in the past months. Malcolm had booked a trip to China after initially changing his will, saying he didn't want to discuss the new terms. But having his heart attack while abroad had meant the family couldn't see him for weeks afterward, and they hadn't been able to find out much about treatments or the extent of damage until he was well enough to travel home. It had really scared them.

More than ever, Cam was grateful to Maresa for agreeing to this marriage. Crappy relationship with his father notwithstanding, Cam's family meant everything to him. And even though he'd resented having his grandfather dictate his personal life, it seemed like a small thing compared to the possibility of losing him. For most of Cameron's life, he wouldn't have been able to imagine a world without Malcolm McNeill in it. Now, he sure didn't want to, but he could envision it all too well when he saw how unsteady Gramps was on his feet as Quinn helped him into a favorite recliner.

"We need the women, I think, to really make this a party," Gramps observed once he caught his breath. He peered around the room, piercing blue eyes assessing each the brothers. "Family business needs a woman's touch."

Ian lifted his phone before speaking. "Lydia just texted

me. She and Maresa are waiting for Sofia downstairs before they join us."

Cameron resisted the urge to bolt to his feet, strongly suspecting Maresa would rather meet the other women on her own terms. She was great with people, after all. It was part of what made her so good at her job. Still, it bothered him that he wasn't with her to make the introductions himself.

"Good." Gramps underscored the sentiment by pounding his walking stick on the floor. "In the meantime, Cameron, you can give me the update you already shared with these two." He nodded to Quinn and Ian. "When are the rest of my grandsons coming to New York to meet me?"

Cameron was secretly relieved when Ian stepped in to field the question for him. Maybe, as a recently married man himself, Ian knew that Cam was nervous about tonight. Finishing off the Scotch more quickly than he'd intended, he got to his feet and prowled around the room, looking at antique book spines on the walls without really seeing them.

He was uneasy for a lot of reasons tonight. One reason was that discussion of the other McNeills stirred old anger about his father's faithlessness to the woman he'd married. Cam resented that his father's selfish actions resulted in three other sons and a whole life they'd known nothing about. But, as he now watched his grandfather listen to Ian with obvious interest, Cam had to respect the old man for refusing to limit his idea of family. Gabe, Damon and Jager were all as important to Gramps as Ian, Quinn and Cameron.

It didn't matter that he'd never met them.

For the first time, it occurred to Cam that he had more in common with his grandfather than he'd realized. All his life, Cam had been compared to his reckless, impulsive father. But Cameron would never be the kind of man who cheated on his wife. More importantly, he was the kind of man who could—like his grandfather Malcolm—embrace a wider definition of family.

Because Rafe was Cam's brother now. And Analise's health and safety were as important to him as his own mother's.

As for Isla?

Could he adore that little girl more if he'd fathered her himself? Like Malcolm McNeill, Cameron would never let go of the Delphines. He would use all his resources to protect them. Most of all, he would love them.

The insight hit him with resounding force, as sudden and jarring as the impact of that old kiteboarding crash that had stolen his ability to father children of his own. He didn't need to avoid having a real family for fear of repeating his father's mistakes. He already had a real family and he needed to start treating all of them—especially Maresa—like more than contractual obligations.

Because twelve months weren't ever going to be enough time to spend with her. Twelve years weren't going to cover it, in fact. He needed to make this marriage last and now that he knew as much, he didn't want to wait another second to let her know. Because, yes, he'd always have some of that impulsiveness in his character. Only now he knew he'd never let it hurt the woman—the family—he loved.

"Will you excuse me?" he said suddenly, stalking toward the library door. "I need to see my wife."

"We've been dying to meet you," Sofia Koslov told Maresa in the foyer of the impressive six-story Italianate mansion that Malcolm McNeill called home.

Maresa tried not to be intimidated by the tremendous wealth of her surroundings and the elegance of the beautiful women who had greeted her so warmly. Dark-haired Lydia McNeill, a pale-skinned, delicate nymph of a woman who worked in interior design, was married to Cam's brother Ian. The blonde ballerina Sofia was engaged to Quinn and due to marry within the month.

Both of them appeared completely at home on the French baroque reproduction benches situated underneath paintings Maresa was pretty sure she'd seen in art history books. Cushions of bright blue picked up the color scheme shared by the two huge art pieces. Dark wooden banisters curled around the dual stone staircases leading up to the second floor. A maid had told her the men were on the third floor and they were welcome to take the elevator.

Un-freaking-believable. Maresa had been overwhelmed by Cameron's generosity ever since arriving in New York, but seeing the roots of his family wealth, she began to understand how easy it was for him to re-order the world to his liking. He might have grown his own fortune with his online gaming company, but he'd been raised in a world of privilege unlike anything she'd ever known.

"Thank you." Maresa hoped she was smiling with the same kind of genuine warmth that her sister-in-law and soon-to-be sister-in-law demonstrated. But it was difficult to be so out of her element. Knowing she was going to be a part of this family for only eleven and a half more months hurt, too. "I will confess I've been nervous to meet Cameron's family."

Lydia nodded in obvious empathy. She wore a smartly cut sheath dress in a pink mod floral. "Who wouldn't be nervous? They are the *McNeills*—practically a New York institution." She gestured vaguely to the painting above her head. "This is a Cézanne, for crying out loud. I was a wreck my first time here."

Sofia slanted a glance at Lydia. "With good reason, since we witnessed our first McNeill brawl." She shook her head and tugged an elastic band from her long blond hair, releasing the pretty waves from the ballerina bun. She wore dark leggings with a gray lace top, but her style was definitely understated. No makeup in sight and still incredibly lovely. Sofia turned to Maresa and winked. "Your husband is a man of intense passion, we discovered."

"Cam?" Maresa asked, since she couldn't imagine him getting into a physical fight with anyone, least of all his family. He'd been incredibly good to hers, after all.

Lydia opened her purse and found a roll of breath mints, offering them each one before explaining, "It wasn't really a brawl. But Quinn, Ian and Cameron were devastated to learn that their father had a whole other family he'd kept secret for twenty-plus years. Cam landed a fist on his dad's jaw before they all settled down."

Maresa found it impossible to reconcile her knowledge of Cameron with the image they painted. But then again, he had proposed to Sofia mere months ago in a moment of impulsiveness. Maresa knew he'd gone on to extend the offer of marriage to Maresa because he thought he knew her much better. Because they had a connection. But was she really just another impulsive choice on his part?

Her stomach sank at the thought. No matter how hard she struggled to keep her feelings a secret from him these past two weeks, she feared they'd only gotten deeper. Seeing him walk around Isla's nursery with the little girl in his arms at the crack of dawn the past few mornings chinked away at the defenses she needed around him. How effective were those defenses when just the idea that he'd chosen her in a moment of rashness was enough to rattle her?

Drawing a fortifying breath, she sat up straighter on the bench seat. "He's been incredibly good to me and to my family," she said simply.

From somewhere down the hall she thought she heard the swish of an elevator door opening. Maybe the maid was returning to call them in for dinner?

Sofia flexed her feet and pointed her toes, stretching her legs while she sat. "That doesn't surprise me. We were all glad to hear that he's so taken with your little girl."

Lydia leaned forward to lower her voice. "And for a man who swore he'd never have kids, that's incredible." She reached to squeeze Maresa's hand. "His brothers are relieved you've changed his mind."

Footsteps sounded nearby. But Maresa was too distracted by the revelation to pay much attention. Her world had just shifted. Cameron had never said anything about his stance on children.

"Cam doesn't want kids?" She thought about him singing to Isla in the temporary nursery he'd outfitted for her personally while his construction crew worked to remodel an upstairs suite for her that would be ready the following week.

Had his show of caring been as fake as their marriage?

A male shadow fell over her right as her eyes began to burn. "Maresa."

Cameron stood in the foyer at the foot of the stairs, his face somber. Lydia and Sofia greeted him briefly but he didn't so much as flick a gaze their way before the other women excused themselves.

Maresa stood too quickly, feeling suddenly light-headed at the news that she was being carefully deceived. He'd never wanted children. Did that mean he'd also never wanted a wife? That their marriage was even more of a pure necessity than she'd realized? She felt duped. Betrayed.

And just how many other secrets was her husband keeping from her in order to secure the McNeill legacy?

She cleared her throat. "I don't feel well. If you can make my excuses to your family, I need to be leaving." Picking up her purse, she took a half step toward the massive entryway.

Cameron sidestepped, blocking her path. "We need to talk."

Even at a soft level, their voices echoed off all the marble in the foyer.

"What is there to talk about? Your wish not to have children? Too late. I already heard about it." Hurt tore through her to think she was letting Isla grow attached to him.

"I should have told you sooner—" he began, but she couldn't listen. Couldn't hear him explain how or why he'd decided he didn't enjoy kids.

"Please." She brushed past him. "I spent so many hours interviewing potential nannies and caregivers. I should have devoted more time to interviewing my husband." She couldn't help but remember all the ways he'd stepped into a fatherly role.

All those little betrayals she hadn't seen coming.

"It's not that I don't like children, Maresa." He cupped her shoulders with gentle hands. "I had an accident as a stupid twenty-year-old kid. And as a result—medically speaking—I can't father children."

Thirteen

Cameron was losing her.

He could tell by the way Maresa's face paled at the news. He should have told her about this sooner. He'd disclosed his net worth and offered her a prenup with generous financial terms and special provisions for her family.

Yet it had never crossed his mind to share this part of his past. A part that would have had huge implications for a couple planning a genuine future together. A real marriage. He'd been so focused on making a sound plan for the short-term, he hadn't thought about how much he might crave something more.

Something deeper.

"Please." He shifted his grip on her shoulders when she seemed to waver on her feet. "There's a private sitting room over here. Just have a seat for a minute, and let me get you a glass of water."

She looked at him with such naked hurt in her tawny eyes that it felt like a blow to him, too.

"Isla has to be my highest priority. Now and always." Her words were firm. Stern. But, thankfully, her feet followed him as he led her to the east parlor where they could close a door and speak privately.

"I understand that." He drew her into the deep green room with a marble fireplace and windows looking out onto Seventy-Sixth Street. The blinds were tilted to let in sunlight but blocked any real view. Cameron flicked on the sconces surrounding the fireplace while he guided her to a chair near the fireplace. "I admire that more than I can say."

He wanted to tell her about the realization he'd had upstairs with his grandfather. That he was more like Malcolm McNeill than he'd realized. But that would have to wait and he'd be damn lucky if she even stayed and listened to him for that long. He had the feeling the only reason she'd followed him in here was because she was too shell-shocked to decide what to do next.

He needed to talk fast before that wore off. He made quick work of pouring the contents of a chilled water bottle from a hidden minifridge into a cut-crystal glass he pulled off the tea cart.

"It's not fair to Isla to let her grow attached to you." Maresa closed her eyes as he brought over the cold drink, opening them only when he sat down in the chair next to her. "Even if what you say is true—that you like kids—I should have been thinking about it more before I agreed to this marriage." She accepted the drink and took a sip. "Not that I'm backing out since we signed a binding agreement, but maybe we need to reconsider how much time you spend with her, given that you won't be a part of her life twelve months from now."

The hits just kept coming. And feeling the full brunt of that one made him realize how damned unacceptable he found this temporary arrangement. He needed to help her see that they could have a real chance at something more.

"I hope you will change your mind about that, Maresa, but I understand if you can't." He wanted to touch her. To put his hands on her in any way possible while he made his case to her, but she sat with such brittle posture in the upholstered eighteenth-century chair that he kept his hands to himself. "I never knew how much I would enjoy a baby until I met you and Isla. I never had any experience with kids and told myself it was just as well because my father sucked at fatherhood and everyone has always compared me to him."

She looked down at the glass she balanced on one knee but made no comment. Was she waiting? Listening?

Hell, he sure hoped so.

He plowed ahead. "Liam McNeill is reckless and impulsive, and even my brothers said I was just like him. I've always had a lot of restless energy and I channeled it into the same kind of stuff he did—skydiving and hang gliding. Whitewater rafting and surfing big waves. It was a rush and I loved it. But when a kiteboarding accident nearly killed me I had to rethink what I was doing."

Her gaze flew up to meet his. She had been listening. "How did it happen?"

"Too much arrogance. Not enough sense I wanted to catch big air. I jumped too high and got caught in a crosswind that slammed me into some trees." He'd been lucky he remained conscious afterward or he might have died hanging there. "The harness I was wearing got wrapped around my groin." He pantomimed the constriction. "The pain was excruciating, but I needed to cut myself down to alleviate the pressure threatening to cut off all circulation to my leg."

"Wasn't anyone else there to help?" Her eyes were wide. She set her glass aside, turning toward him as she listened.

"Not even close. That crosswind blew me a good half mile out of the water. My friends had to boat to shore and then drive and search for me. They called 911 and the paramedics found me first." He felt the warmth of her leg close to his. He wanted to touch her but he held back because he had to get this right.

"Thank God. You could have lost a limb." She frowned, shaking her head slowly, empathy in her eyes.

For the moment, anyway, it seemed as though she was too caught up in the tale to think about how much distance she wanted to put between the two of them. Between him and Isla. His chest ached with the need to fix this, because losing his new family was going to hurt worse than if he'd lost that leg. If she chose to stay with him, she needed to make that decision for the right reasons. Because he'd told her everything.

"Right. And that's how I always looked at it." He took a deep breath. "A lifetime of compromised sperm count seemed like I got off easy—at the time. I lost my option of being a father since my own father sucked at it and I was already too much like him. Right down to the daredevil stupidity."

She eased her hand from under his, twisting her fingers together as if restraining herself from touching him again. "Do you do things like that anymore?"

"Hell no." He realized he still clutched the water bottle in his hand. He took a sip from it now, needing to clear his thoughts as much as his mind. "I channeled all that restless energy into building the gaming company.

I designed virtual experiences that were almost as cool as the real thing. But safer. I know life is too precious to waste."

"Then you're not all that much like your father, after all," she surprised him by saying. She set down the cut-crystal glass and stood, walking across the library to the fireplace where she studied a photo on the mantle.

It was an image from one of the summers in Brazil with his brothers and their mother. They all looked tan and happy. He'd had plenty of happy times as a kid and he wanted to make those kinds of memories with Maresa and Isla. Maybe he'd convinced himself he didn't care about having a family because he'd never met Maresa. He'd been holding on to his heart, waiting for the right person.

"That's what I came down from the library to tell you tonight." He crossed to stand beside her, reaching to lay his hand over hers. "It's taken me a lifetime to realize it, but I've got plenty of my grandfather's influence at work in me, too."

"How so?" She turned to face him. Listening. Dialed in.

She was so damned beautiful to him, her warmth and caring apparent in everything she did. In every expression she wore. He wanted to be able to see her face every day, forever. To see how she changed as they grew older. Together.

Cameron prayed he got the words right that would make her understand. He couldn't lose this woman who'd become so important to him in a short span of time. Couldn't afford to lose the little girl that he wanted to raise with as much love as he'd give his own child. In fact, he wanted Isla to be his child.

"Because Gramps would never turn his back on family." He gathered up her hands and held them. "He insists we bring my half brothers to New York and cut them in on the McNeill inheritance, even though he's never met any of them. I was upset about that at first, mostly because I'm still mad at my father for keeping such a hurtful secret from Mom."

"I don't like hurtful secrets." Maresa's eyes still held traces of that pain he'd put there and he needed to fix that.

"I didn't withhold that information about my accident on purpose," he told her honestly. "I didn't give it any thought. And that's still my fault for being too concerned about the physical whys and wherefores of making the move to New York work instead of thinking about the intangibles of sharing...our hearts."

"Our what?" She blinked at him as though she'd misunderstood. Or hadn't heard properly.

"I got too caught up in making this a business arrangement without thinking about how much I would come to care about you and your whole family, Maresa." He tugged her closer, trapped her hands between his and his chest so that her palm rested on his heart. "I'm in love with you. And I don't care about the business arrangement anymore. I want you in my life for good. Forever."

For a long moment, Maresa couldn't hear anything outside of her heart pounding a thunderous answer to Cameron's words. But she wasn't sure she could trust her feelings. She didn't plan to let her guard down long enough for him to shatter her far worse than Jaden could have ever dreamed of doing.

Except, when her heart quieted a tiny bit and she began to hear the traffic sounds out on Seventy-Sixth Street— the shrill whistle of someone hailing a cab and the muted laughter of a crowd passing the windows—Maresa realized that Cameron was still here. Still clutching her hands tight in his. And the last words he'd said to her had been that he wanted her to be a part of his life forever.

That hadn't changed.

And since he'd done everything else imaginable to make her happy these last two weeks, she wondered if maybe she ought to let down her guard long enough to at least check and see if he could be serious about a future together.

Her mind reeled as her heart started that pounding thing all over again.

"Cameron, as tempting as it might be to just believe that—"

"You think I would deceive you about being in love?" He sounded offended. He angled back to get a clear view of her eyes.

"No." She didn't mean to upset him when he'd just said the most beautiful things to her. "But I wonder if you're interpreting the emotions correctly. Maybe you simply enjoy the warmth of a family around you and it doesn't have much to do with me."

"It has everything to do with you." He released her hands to wrap one arm around her waist. He slid the other around her shoulders. "I want every night to be like that last night we spent in Saint Thomas when we made love in the villa at Crown Mountain. Do you remember?"

She remembered all right. That was the night she'd understood she was falling for him and decided she needed to be more careful with her heart. As much as she'd treasured their nights together since then, she'd been holding back a part of herself ever since. Her heart. "I do."

"Even if it was just us, I would want you in my life

forever. But it's a bonus that I get your mom and your brother and your niece." His touch warmed her while his words wound around her heart and squeezed. "Getting to be a part of Isla's life would be an incredible gift for me since I can't have children of my own. But I understand that could be enough reason alone for you to want to walk away. I don't want to deny you the chance to be a biological mother."

She could see the pain in his eyes at the thought. And the love there, too. He wasn't pushing her away, but he loved her enough that he would be willing to give her up so she could have that chance. That level of love—for her—stunned her. And she knew, without question, she didn't need a child of her own to find fulfillment as a mother. She was lucky to have a baby who already shared her family's DNA, something she was reminded of every time she peered down into Isla's sweet face. If they wanted more children, she felt sure they could open their hearts to more through adoption. If Cameron could already love Isla so completely, Maresa knew he could expand his sense of family to other children who needed them.

"I have a lifetime of mothering ahead of me no matter what since Isla isn't going anywhere." She would make sure Rafe's daughter grew up loved and happy, even if Rafe never fully understood his connection to her. He smiled now when he saw Isla, and that counted as beautiful progress. "Isla is going to fill my life and bring me a lot of joy so I'm not thinking about other children down the road. If I was, however, I agree with your grandfather that we can stretch the definition of what makes a family. We could reach out to a child who needs a home."

"We?" His eyes were the darkest shade of blue as

they tracked hers. "Are you considering it then? A real marriage?"

The hope in his voice could never be faked. Any worries she'd had about him deceiving her in order to secure his family legacy melted away. He might act on instinct, but he did so with honest intentions. With integrity. She'd seen the love in his gaze when he'd held Isla. She should have trusted it. He was so different from Jaden, and she'd already let her past rob her of enough happiness. Time to take a chance on this incredible man.

Even when he'd been masquerading as Mr. Holmes, she'd seen the real man beneath the facade. She'd known there was someone worthy and good, someone noble and kind inside.

"Cameron." She pulled in a deep breath to steady herself. "I've been holding back from loving you because I've been terrified of how much it would hurt to let you go a year from now."

He tipped his head back and seemed to see her with new eyes. "That's why you've pulled away. Ever since—"

"That night on Crown Mountain." She nodded, knowing that he'd seen the difference in her since then. The way she'd been holding herself tightly so she didn't fall the rest of the way in love.

She was failing miserably. Magnificently.

"I'm so sorry if I hurt you that night," he began, stroking her face, threading his fingers into her hair tenderly.

"You did nothing wrong." She cupped his beard-stubbled cheeks in both hands. "I just couldn't afford to love a man who didn't love me back. Not again. I went halfway around the world to get over the hurt and humiliation of Jaden, so I couldn't begin to imagine how much a truly incredible guy like you could hurt me."

For her honesty, she was rewarded with a hug that

left her breathless. Cameron's arms wrapped around her tight. Squeezed. He lifted her against him, burying his face in her hair.

"I love you, Maresa Delphine. So damn much the thought of losing you was killing me inside." His heart-felt confession mirrored her own emotions so perfectly she felt her every last defense fall away.

She closed her eyes, swallowed around the lump in her throat. And hugged him back, so tightly, her body tingling with happiness.

"I love you, Cam. And I'm not going anywhere in twelve months." She arched back to see his face, loving the happiness she saw in his eyes. "I'm going to stay right here with you and be as much a part of your family as you already are of mine."

He grinned, setting her on her feet again and sweeping her hair back from her face. "You have to meet them first."

She laughed, her heart bubbling with joy instead of nerves. With this man at her side, the future stretched out beautifully before her. It wouldn't necessarily be perfect or have no bumps along the way, but it was a real-life fairy tale because they would take on life together. "I do."

"And that's not happening today." He kissed her cheek and temple and her closed eyes.

"It isn't?" She wondered how she got so lucky to find a man who loved her the way Cameron did. A man who would do anything to protect his family.

A man who extended that protectiveness to her and everyone important to her.

"No." He cupped her face in his hand and brushed a kiss over her lips, sending a shiver of want through her. "Or at least, it's not happening until the dessert course."

"We can't leave them all waiting and wondering what's happened."

"They'll get hungry. They'll eat." He nipped her bottom lip, driving her a little crazy with the possessive sweep of his tongue over hers. "I have a whole private suite on the fifth floor, you know."

"Of course you do." She wound her arms around him as heat simmered all through her. "Maybe it would be a good time to celebrate this marriage for real."

"The lifetime one," he reminded her, drawing her out of the parlor and toward the elevator. "Not the twelve-month one."

"Or we could wait until we got home tonight," she reminded him. "And we could celebrate it after we tuck Isla in after her last feeding, when we are at home."

"Our home," he reminded her as he stepped inside the elevator cabin. "So you really want to go meet the McNeills?"

"Every last one of them." She didn't feel nervous at all now. She felt like she belonged.

Cameron had given her that, and it was one of many things she would treasure about him.

About their marriage.

"As my wife wishes." He stabbed at the button for the third floor. "But don't be surprised when I announce a public wedding ceremony to the table."

She glanced up at him in surprise. "Even though we're already married?"

"A courthouse wedding isn't nearly enough of a party to kick off the best marriage ever." He lifted their clasped hands and kissed her ring finger right over the diamond set. "We're going to make a great team, Maresa."

He'd told her that once before and she hadn't believed him nearly enough. With his impulsive side tempered by his loving nature, he was going to make this marriage fun every day.

"I know we will." Squeezing his hand, she felt like a newlywed for the first time and knew in her heart that feeling would last a lifetime. "We already are."

* * * * *

MILLS & BOON

MODERN

Power and Passion

Prepare to be swept off your feet by sophisticated, sexy and seductive heroes, in some of the world's most glamourous and romantic locations, where power and passion collide.

LET'S TALK
Romance

For exclusive extracts, competitions
and special offers, find us online:

- facebook.com/millsandboon
- @MillsandBoon
- @MillsandBoonUK

Get in touch on 01413 063232

For all the latest titles coming soon, visit
millsandboon.co.uk/nextmonth

MILLS & BOON

THE HEART OF ROMANCE

A ROMANCE FOR EVERY READER

MODERN

Prepare to be swept off your feet by sophisticated, sexy and seductive heroes, in some of the world's most glamourous and romantic locations, where power and passion collide.

HISTORICAL

Escape with historical heroes from time gone by. Whether your passion is for wicked Regency Rakes, muscled Vikings or rugged Highlanders, awake the romance of the past.

MEDICAL

Set your pulse racing with dedicated, delectable doctors in the high-pressure world of medicine, where emotions run high and passion, comfort and love are the best medicine.

True Love

Celebrate true love with tender stories of heartfelt romance, from the rush of falling in love to the joy a new baby can bring, and a focus on the emotional heart of a relationship.

Desire

Indulge in secrets and scandal, intense drama and plenty of sizzling hot action with powerful and passionate heroes who have it all: wealth, status, good looks…everything but the right woman.

HEROES

Experience all the excitement of a gripping thriller, with an intense romance at its heart. Resourceful, true-to-life women and strong, fearless men face danger and desire - a killer combination!

To see which titles are coming soon, please visit

millsandboon.co.uk/nextmonth